MIRAGE

MIRAGE

BY

J. Robert Janes

DONALD I. FINE, INC.
New York

Library of Congress Cataloging-in-Publication Data

Janes, J. Robert (Joseph Robert), 1935–
Mirage : a novel / by J. Robert Janes.
p.   cm.
ISBN 1-55611-340-4
I. Title.
PR9199.3.J3777M5   1992
813'.54—dc10   92-53084
CIP

Manufactured in the United States of America

10 9 8 7 6 5 4 3 2 1

Nothing is right, but that it seems right.

Author's Note

Mirage is a work of fiction. Though I have used actual places and times, I have treated these as I saw fit, changing some as appropriate. Occasionally the name of a real person is also used for historical authenticity, but all are deceased and I have made of them what the story demands. I do not condone what happened during these times. Indeed, I abhor it. But during the Occupation of France the everyday crimes of murder and arson continued to be committed, and I merely ask, By whom and how were they solved?

To Ed Hill for all his kindness and constant encouragement

1

At a place where the road pitched down through the gorges, the land sloped steadily upwards to the barren branches of the trees.

The fog was everywhere, hugging the road, putting frost on the tall, sear grasses, riming the stones and the spokes of the bicycle. Drenching the body.

Jean-Louis St-Cyr slid his hands into the pockets of his overcoat and waited. At dawn, Fontainebleau Forest gave itself entirely over to the birds, those that had not had the great good fortune to have migrated.

It was eerie and it was silent. It was cold, damp and a lot of other things. Kohler's breath steamed impatiently and once in each breath, the Bavarian's nasal passages would pinch and whistle with barely controlled fury.

A giant of a man with the heart and mind of a small-time hustler, the Gestapo agent stood knee-deep in bracken, looking down at the body. Was he thinking of the Russian Front, of his sons, of death, or merely of his shoes that might, quite possibly, be leaking? Sometimes one never really knew with Hermann – oh for sure, one could guess, but Hermann . . . He'd been a Munich detective before his transfer to Berlin, before his ascendancy to Paris. A good one too. Probably.

The Bavarian nudged the corpse with the toe of his right shoe but didn't look up. 'So, what about it, Louis?'

The accent was harsh, guttural, the French quite passable because Hermann, being Hermann and stubborn, had seen to it that he spoke the language. One found out so much more that way. It facilitated things – all things. Gestapo things. Especially girls.

St-Cyr chose not to answer immediately. A last leaf fell

through the hush to crash into some boulders with its load of frost and scrape its way to patient rest.

Hermann took no interest in the leaf, in the beauty of its death, the curled edges, the ring of encrusting frost, not even the fact that the leaf was from a plane tree and that such trees were a rarity in this part of the Fontainebleau Forest.

Always it was blitzkrieg, blitzkrieg. December 1942, the Occupation. Now the whole of France, as of last month.

'We shall have to see, won't we?' he said at last.

Accustomed to such delays, the Bavarian sucked on a tooth and snorted, 'It's one less Frenchman for us to worry about.'

Must he be so blatant? 'We've no evidence he was involved with the Resistance, Inspector. Perhaps . . .'

'Perhaps *what*? *Mein Gott*, you French. A lonely road like this, death in the small hours? Pedalling like hell to avoid the patrols? He hit a patch of ice and went off the road.' Kohler smashed a meaty fist into a palm. 'That boulder settled him, Louis. That one. That one right there!' He pointed fiercely.

Blood was frozen to the rock that had killed the boy. Blood and dark brown hairs. 'I admit that it appears as you've suggested, Inspector, but the bicycle, my friend, it's undamaged.'

So it was. Irritably Kohler dragged out a cigarette and began thumbing a lighter that just wouldn't co-operate. 'Please, allow me, Hermann.'

'*Ja, ja,* of course. That lousy bed last night, I didn't sleep a wink. So, what do you really make of it?'

St-Cyr found his pipe and began the ritual of packing it. Inwardly Kohler threw up his hands in despair. Sometimes Louis took for ever! As at meals, especially lunch. Two hours if he could get them. Two!

Not a shred of tobacco was lost. Hard up on the rations again. So, that made them equal.

Tobacco was the great leveller these days. It brought out the worst in people, bought friends, information, pretty girls.

Several minutes passed in which neither of them moved from where they'd been standing. Hermann was the taller – bigger in every way. At fifty-five years of age he understood only too well the vagaries of life. He'd cock an eye at something new but beyond that, no surprise, only a stolid acceptance of human frailties. He frowned at his superiors, remaining remote from them. The bulldog jowls, sad, puffy eyelids that bagged and drooped to well-rasped cheeks and shrapnel scars, served only to emphasize the hidden thoughts behind the faded blue and often expressionless eyes. The nose was pugnacious, the lower jaw that of a storm-trooper. Hermann had come up through the ranks, but then, so had he. They were like two streams flowing around their little island of the war to commingle and proceed as one because they had to. That was the way of things these days. One couldn't choose. The Occupation saw to that.

'It's my birthday,' managed St-Cyr, sucking on the fire. 'At seventeen minutes past the hour of 3 a.m. on 3rd December 1890,' he waved the pipe, 'my mother had me in the back of a carriage on the boulevard St Michel. No doubt in exactly the same place my father first had her. They were heading for the Hospital du Val Grâce and he ran over a cat. Naturally, he stopped to see if the creature could be saved, but then . . .'

He gave the Frenchman's fluting look and gestured to the heavens before cramming the pipe-stem back between his teeth.

Mais alors . . . alors . . . always it was, but then . . . then, as if some hidden whim of the Almighty had chosen to break the clouds with a fart! 'I thought all your women had their brats at home?'

'As now,' went on St-Cyr, agreeably ignoring the racial slur. 'But father . . . You had to know him to understand, Inspector. A lover of nature.' He indicated the forest and then the fields that lay below them in the distance, but neglected to elaborate on the fact that the time of birth and that of the death could almost have been the same.

The furnace was going well. At fifty-two years of age, Louis was inclined to be plump, to let the dust settle on things, but to be very careful when blowing it off.

Somewhat shabby, somewhat diffident, he had the broad, bland brow, the brown ox-eyes of the French, a moustache that was thicker and wider than the Führer's and grown long before the war and thus left in defiance of it. The distant air of a muse, the heart of a poet and the hands of a . . . what? stormed Kohler. A fisherman, a gardener, a reader of books in winter. A chief inspector of the Sûreté Nationale, the Criminal Investigation Branch at number 11 rue de Saussaies.

St-Cyr had been all but alone in the building the day the

11

Wehrmacht had marched into Paris and the Gestapo, the SD and the Abwehr into the Sûreté. Kohler knew Louis had been caught in the act of destroying several confidential files.

The dark brown hair was thick and brushed to the right with a careless, indifferent hand. The bushy eyebrows arched. Both men returned their gaze to the victim who lay on his stomach in the grass, arms at his sides, the hands turned outwards as a ballet dancer might if stung by a bee.

'I'll admit he could have been struck on the forehead,' grumbled Kohler dispassionately.

'Then positioned so as to make it look like an accident – although the murderer should not have placed the arms and hands like that,' said St-Cyr, mainly giving back what they both thought.

'Or turned the head so that it rested on a cushion of leaves.'

'A woman?' asked St-Cyr, tossing the question out at random.

'Another of your "crimes of passion", Inspector?' snorted Kohler. The French . . . They'd kill each other over the silliest things. 'Looks about twenty or so. An escaper?' he asked.

St-Cyr shrugged. 'If so, then why kill him?'

'Why not?' demanded the Bavarian with a snort. 'He'd only have been someone's trouble.'

'Ah yes, of course,' replied St-Cyr acidly. 'The decree of this past July regarding acts of sabotage including the aiding of escaped prisoners of war, downed British or American airmen and those running from the labour gangs. Yes, it could well be because of someone's trouble but then, why here, why a meeting in the dead of night – why the cry from the darkness, the beam of a torch perhaps, Hermann? No, my friend, this one wasn't an escaper.' St-Cyr crouched but still didn't touch the body. 'The clothing's too good.'

Kohler acknowledged that it was: grey flannel trousers, a newish brown leather, three-quarter length coat, black beret, grey scarf and black gloves. 'He's not from one of your seminaries, is he?' The youth of France had taken to the priesthood in droves rather than be called up. Cowards, the French. Cowards!

'That is something we must check. There are several possibilities in the area. Anything else, Inspector?'

Damn him! St-Cyr could use the title 'Inspector' like a knife! 'Was he a collaborator or involved in the black market, Louis?'

'Or had he jilted his lover?'

'A nobody then,' muttered Kohler. 'I'm going for a crap in the woods. I'll take a look around up there.'

'Good thinking, Hermann. The grass, eh? It's been beaten down.'

One footprint appeared up on the crest of the slope, next to the edge of the forest. 'I knew you'd notice that,' replied Kohler lamely.

'There's a footprint in the mud on that bank. See what you make of it.'

A small sacrifice to Germanic thoroughness. Unleashed – baited properly – Hermann would now begin to work. St-Cyr ran his eyes over the victim. Height, 1550 centimetres; weight, 68 kilos; hair, dark brown; eyes, dark brown.

The boy had walked right into it. He hadn't suspected a thing. But had he known the murderer? He'd have come over the crest of the hill on his bicycle and would have started down. Then for some reason he had stopped, walked into the grass and had set the bicycle down before taking those last few steps.

The pockets were empty – not a shred of ID. St-Cyr let out a curse. Tracing people was always trouble. These days identity cards and ration cards were in such demand.

'We're going to have to have a photographer,' he called out to the forest above.

'I could have told you so,' came the reply, dark in the woods beyond the top of the slope.

Squatting probably. 'There's one in Barbizon just along from the Kommandantur. Does weddings and picnics.'

'I'll go in a minute. She dropped her purse.'

The bushy eyebrows lifted questioningly. The victim came into view again. 'Her name?' sang out St-Cyr.

'None whatsoever, my friend. Just the empty purse.'

Had it been left deliberately?

St-Cyr turned the body over. Apart from the mess of the forehead, the wide-open eyes and the clothing, the boy looked at peace and hid his identity well. No rings, no sacred medallions or cross on its chain – not even a fountain pen. Just nothing.

Kohler came back and handed him the purse. 'Beaded silk – something a woman would take to a dinner party.'

The Frenchman used the forefinger and thumb of his right hand to hold the purse gingerly. He examined it with the eye of a born connoisseur before bringing it up to his nose for a whiff of the forgotten perfume all such purses were bound to contain.

'Is he Jewish?' asked Kohler, hitting all the possibilities and taking back the purse.

'Want me to have a look?' taunted St-Cyr, 'or can we leave it until he's on ice?'

'Who says we're carting him off to Paris?'

'The purse, Inspector. You're forgetting the purse. That's not something from around here.'

'Perhaps he stole it?'

'Perhaps, but if so, why was it emptied and left for us to find?' This would often happen in the case of a robbery, of course, but . . .

The Bavarian hunched his shoulders. 'I'll go and get the photographer.'

'Better ring the boys in blue while you're there. Paris, Hermann. Take my advice. This one wants to go to the morgue.'

Kohler nodded grimly. St-Cyr watched as the Bavarian drove off in what had once been his car, that great big beautiful black Citroën.

Then he went back to work. The purse could, of course, not have been empty at all but merely dropped in haste.

Hermann always kept a few things to himself.

The woman – for it was the print of a woman's low-heeled shoe – must have been fairly young and agile. After the killing, she had climbed a nearly vertical bank of some three metres by grasping branches and the stems of young trees. At one place, she'd pulled out a birch sapling.

St-Cyr took the time to replant it.

At another place, high up on the slope, she had encountered wild raspberries and had hooked a stocking.

Silk like the purse. Unheard of these days, except if prewar or purchased on the black market. A tragedy if she was of little means.

Eventually he came to the spot where Kohler had dropped his trousers. Sure enough the purse hadn't been empty. Hermann had availed himself of a silk handkerchief before depositing the rest of the contents into a pocket.

14

So, a young man – a boy of eighteen or twenty – and a young girl, perhaps of the same age, perhaps of wealth, but equally perhaps of humble station, a servant, a maid, a governess – something like that.

And a meeting on this lonely road, in the midst of this lonely forest.

Yet she knew the boy would be along. Was she alone in this, or had there been someone with her? The murderer?

Try as he did, St-Cyr could find no evidence of anyone else. But the girl hadn't run blindly into the forest. Ah no, far from it. There was a footpath up there beyond the top of the slope and she'd known of it – known it well enough to have come by it perhaps and to have gone back along it in the dark.

To where? he wondered. The town of Fontainebleau was a good fifteen kilometres to the east-south-east; Barbizon perhaps four kilometres behind him, Chailly-en-Bière a little more, but to the north, and Paris some forty-five kilometres farther.

The path must cut across the road, so she had either had a bicycle there or someone had waited for her in a car.

Then why hadn't that someone come with her?

Again he went carefully over the ground. The victim wasn't all that far from the road – perhaps five metres, the bicycle a little nearer to it. Between the single footprint, the body and the road there wasn't a sign of anything.

Then the girl had killed the boy.

It saddened him to think of such a thing. Automatically he thought of young lovers, of a jealous rage, only to come back to earth at the purse.

Beaded silk. He wished now that he hadn't handed it back to Hermann. Hermann had a way of keeping things like that.

But still there was the memory of it. The pale, sky-blue shimmering silk that was electric and would have been so against a young woman's thigh, the beads that hadn't been cheap and shoddy, but had been strands of seed pearls.

The scent that had been that of a very expensive perfume – he could see the girl lying in her chemise, silk on silk, with dusky eyes so full of tears.

Ah, Mon Dieu, it would be such a sight but so far from the truth!

*

15

As the car shot across the flat farmlands around Barbizon, Kohler gave the Citroën all it had. He was in a foul humour and knew it. The General von Schaumburg, the Kommandant of Greater Paris and the Wehrmacht's big cheese himself, was a personal friend of that arch little file-toothed bastard, the General von Richthausen, the Kommandant of Barbizon. Hence the call at dawn to drag them out of bed. Hence the, 'Two detectives and both of you asleep? Get on your feet, Kohler.'

'*Jawohl, Herr General. Heil Hitler!*' *Ja, ja*, you son-of-a-bitch!

But why the goddamned interest? Why set the Gestapo and the Sûreté on to something that wasn't even in their turf and could just as well have been left to the local flics and the Préfet of Paris whose beat it was? Ah yes.

Why, unless those local flics weren't any good and von Richthausen, being a von like the rest, had got his back up?

A nothing body. A kid, for Christ's sake! Murders like this, who cared? If clean of complications then forget it. No leads to the Resistance or to other tantalizing things meant no further interest in so far as Boemelburg was concerned. *Kaput!*

A few reports of course, but no big deal. Control, control, that's what Louis needed.

'Bury the bastard and let's get home!' he roared, leaning on the horn as he passed a sleepy farmhouse, not realizing its inhabitants were already in the fields.

Barbizon swung into view. One dead-dog street of shops, restaurants and hotels, wires strung across the place, a church, the Lady of Whatever, down at the end and few people about.

As he shot past the Préfecture a flic came out to get on his bicycle. Kohler stomped on the brakes. People ran or froze, depending on their natures. 'The photographer,' he bellowed. '*Vite! Vite!* Hurry up!'

The blue cap fell on the stones. 'There . . . monsieur.'

'Where, for Christ's sake?'

'Three doors past the Kommandantur.'

'*Merci.*' Again the accelerator, but briefly. Then the brakes.

His fist opened the door. The shop sign flew off to skid across the floor as the photographer remained etched in celluloid, pinned there struggling into his shop coat. All bones and shoes and glasses, a narow face, about forty-five years old, a mop of dark brown hair over the brow. 'Get your camera and come with me,' shouted Kohler.

'Hermé, do as he says,' shrilled the wife, running into the shop with a breast bare and the child still suckling.

At once the place was in an uproar. 'I haven't done anything!' cried the photographer. 'I've got a christening at nine!'

'Gestapo!' shouted Kohler, flashing his badge. 'You can piss on the brat's head at nine thirty.'

The photographer threw a terrified glance at his wife. Hard-eyed, brown-haired, about thirty-five years old and not quite over the hill. 'Do as he says, Hermé. Don't be a fool.'

The man bolted. Kohler gave the place the once-over before letting his eyes settle on the woman.

'Will you pay?' she asked defiantly.

'Of course,' he breathed. 'We wouldn't think otherwise.' He began to look about the shop more closely. Against one wall there were several painted backdrops, thousand-year-old scenes in front of which newly married couples could stand or puke: a rose arbour, a lake with mountains in the distance and a cream-coloured sun, a cottage that needed a new foundation . . .

'Nice,' he said. 'Very nice.'

The woman burped the child but didn't cover the breast. 'What's the painting of the Eiffel Tower for?' he asked.

She was too watchful.

'German soldiers on leave. They like to have their pictures taken in front of it so that they can say they've been to Paris.'

Kohler cocked an eye, then used a stumpy forefinger to pull the lower lid down so as to emphasize the fact, 'Interesting,' he said. 'So what's taking the husband so long?'

'He has to cut the film. It's in such short supply . . .'

Kohler nodded and went right past her. He flung the curtain aside, strode down the mangy corridor to the red light, but stopped at bursting in.

'You've got enough film,' he said.

The light went out. The door opened. 'Now let's have a look, my friend,' he said, pushing past the photographer who closed the door and switched on the light.

My God, it was dull in here. How could a guy work in a place like this? Ribbons of newly developed negatives hung above the sink. Kohler thumbed a couple. The woman had a passable

17

figure. Was that lust in her eyes? Did she really enjoy being photographed like that? The Eiffel Tower seemed a little out of place.

'So, okay, my friend, I'll ask you only once. From whom do you get your film?' The canisters were big enough to have belonged to Goebbels himself.

Merde! The Gestapo! They were all the same. 'I buy it on the black market.'

'Like hell you do. Paris is too far. You'd need an *ausweis* – a goddamned *laisser-passer* – six times a week.'

'One of the soldiers gets it for me.' That was closer to the truth. 'He takes things into the city and he brings things back.' That was better. 'The Feldwebel takes a cut.' The Staff Sergeant . . . Better still. 'As does the Lieutenant but you mustn't . . .'

Again he exhaled. 'I won't. Don't worry, I'll keep it in the bank. Now come on. We've a different kind of body for you to work with.'

The frost had all but gone from the rims of the bicycle but still clung to the spokes. The blood on the stone had absorbed the sun's earliest rays but had failed to run. A curious thing.

St-Cyr stood over the corpse, talking to it as was his custom when in private. He no longer asked the routine stuff – Who are you? Where were you heading? Why did she kill you? – he'd been through all that.

Instead, he asked, Why me? Why here? Why now?

There was something, call it what you will, but the corpse of this boy made him feel uneasy.

No matter how hard he tried, this feeling wouldn't leave him. He had the frightened photographer take shots from several angles, including two of the place where the purse had been found and one of Kohler's spoor, just for the record.

When the Bavarian insisted that the two of them be captured on film, he knew he couldn't object. Chummy photographs with the Gestapo were too dangerous, but a sort of counter-blackmail-insurance for that shot of the spoor with its handkerchief.

Damning evidence he'd rather not have around. 'It's bad enough having to work with them, eh?' he said to the photographer. 'You send me the negatives and I'll see that you get paid. No extra prints, you understand?'

The Gestapo pouch at the Kommandantur would be used.

'He won't say anything, will he?' asked Hermé Thibault.

St-Cyr was solicitous. 'Him? Not a whisper. Hey, it's simple with them, my friend. You give them what they want and they go to sleep.'

Like dragons in their dens.

The boys in blue came with their black gasogene van and the corpse was wrapped up. 'You sure you know what you're doing?' asked Kohler as they started off to overtake the van. 'Laying that stiff on ice in Paris makes more of him than he deserves.'

St-Cyr stared out the window. They'd begin to accelerate about now. Yes . . . yes, here it comes . . . 'Why won't you let me see the contents of that purse, Hermann?'

The Bavarian rapped the horn and pushed the accelerator to the floor. Gravel beat the fenders. 'Because I can't, my friend. Look, I'm sorry, eh? It's just the way things are. Let's put him in a pauper's grave and forget it.'

'An accident?'

'Yes, an accident.'

'But it's gone a little too far for that, hasn't it? From Kommandant to Kommandant, I think. Questions, Hermann. Answers will be needed. Von Schaumburg's no fool.'

'Von Schaumburg's an ass! The purse has nothing to do with him.'

'Then with whom does it have an association?'

Kohler lifted a tired hand to signal thanks to the boys in blue as the car shot down the road. 'I'm not sure, Louis. I want a little time to think it over. For now, the matter's private.'

'So, I'll catch a bit of sleep then, if you don't mind, Inspector.'

'Don't get in a huff. You know there are things I can't tell you.'

St-Cyr pulled the fedora down over his eyes but couldn't resist a sigh and then, 'Just don't expect me not to find out.'

Photographs with the Gestapo, silk purses and bodies on ice, where would it all end?

'I don't like it, Hermann. No, me, I can honestly say I don't.'

'Then that makes two of us.'

Idly St-Cyr wondered what racket the photographer had been involved in. 'Dirty pictures of his wife,' snorted Kohler. 'Now catch a few winks while you can.'

19

A reader of minds, eh? 'Remember to get my car serviced. The carburettor needs adjustment.'

'That's only water in the fuel. I'll give it a dose of alcohol. That'll help burn off everything.'

That and the speed.

'It's nice not to have to worry about other cars,' sighed St-Cyr. 'That's one thing the war's done for us. Cleared the roads of unnecessary traffic.'

'There's a convoy ahead. Hang on.'

One of them had to have the last word, so for now he'd let it be but he wished the worry would go away, wished Hermann hadn't insisted on that photograph of the two of them. If that should ever get into the wrong hands . . . Who'd understand that the smile or the grin had been partly out of necessity and partly out of . . . what? Respect? Ah no, not quite – that wasn't the word he'd use though there was respect. There had to be after what the two of them had been through.

Friendship then? Partnership? A certain begrudging loyalty? God forgive him, he didn't know. It was so hard to define. With Hermann it was as if, to survive and live with himself, he had to leave his body, to rise above it all and look down on the two of them only to laugh at some of the Gestapo's antics and laugh at his own predicament. God's curse.

Laugh if you will, my friend, he said, but it's no laughing matter.

Ah no, it certainly wasn't.

The street was narrow and slicked by the rain that had departed. At four o'clock the granite paving bricks were dark, and the shouts of the boys echoed in the distance as the street rose up to their angular shapes which were etched against the hurrying dusk.

Small, square, two- and three-storeyed houses of brick or stucco crowded in but here and there a bit of garden had been left.

There were no cars – how could there have been? All bicycles, and the velo-taxis some used to earn their living, were either still on the streets in the heart of the city, or carefully put away.

Alone, St-Cyr walked towards the boys. Would it be France against Germany today, or the Resistance against the Gestapo?

Being boys, they wouldn't say if asked but would only dart secretive looks at one another as their leader stepped forward to answer, Priests against the Nuns, or some such thing.

Not that they ever really made fun of him. Being a cop did set one apart from all others, no matter how much one wanted to be included.

Belleville was Belleville – the XX Arrondissement and the home of so many little people. All walks of life, several races – immigrants not just from the Auvergne in the early days, but from Russia, Armenia, Hungary, and more recently, in the late 1930s, Jews fleeing from the Nazis in Germany. Algerians too. Even a family of Negroes who now lived in almost total seclusion and terror for their lives as did the few remaining Jews.

The rue Laurence Savart was little different from so many others. Shopkeepers, artisans, bank clerks and brick-layers (if not taken by the Todt Organization to build the defensive works of the Atlantic Wall); tailors, seamstresses, insurance brokers, printers, cooks and doormen. Perhaps that was what he liked most about the place. Its life.

The chestnut tree in Madame Auger's garden had been newly pruned – firewood again! Given another winter like the last one, the woman wouldn't have a stick left.

The Vachons were tidy people; their garden, what he could see of it, had been well put to bed. Leaves had been worked into the soil. Vachon grew such fabulous tomatoes, the jungle of them could only have been fertilized by secret additions of the family's excrement.

The beans had been magnificent too, whereas . . .

The house at number 3 was very pleasantly situated behind a low brick wall and imitation Louis XIV wrought-iron fence. The gateposts were of brick and the iron gate was substantial.

St-Cyr went to open the gate, then thought better of it. Pausing, he swept his eyes over the garden. All the plants had had to be removed – the rose bushes and the magnolias his mother had loved, her irises and hyacinths . . .

Like so many others these days he'd raised what crops he could. But work with Kohler had often taken him away and the wife . . . well, Marianne, she was no lover of the soil.

At a shout, 'Hey . . . oo-oo, Monsieur the Detective,' he

21

turned and saw the ball bouncing towards him down the long slope of the narrow street, dark against the dark.

'A moment, boys,' he shouted, dropping his briefcase to meet the ball and begin to work it up to them. 'Split . . . come on, you – you also, my friend. Hup . . . Hup . . . Go for it!'

He was past the first of them, deftly working the ball from foot to foot before expertly passing it to a forward. For the next ten minutes he forgot himself, forgot the war, the murder, the wife – all of it.

As he walked back to the house, he threw a tired but grateful salute to his friends.

Unseen by him, one of them whispered to the new boy from Alsace, 'He's a specialist in murder but has lost his beautiful car.'

'Does he carry a gun?'

'Ah no, they have taken that from him too.'

'Marianne, I'm home.'

St-Cyr flung the briefcase into a chair and went through to the kitchen. 'Marianne,' he called again.

Five days in the south on a dead end that had seen them camping overnight in Barbizon and on the road at dawn.

'Marianne . . .' The house was cold, the draining board, sink and table empty.

He went back through to the sitting-room to stare at the wireless, then at the couch with its little bits of Chantilly lace, then at his favourite armchair by the fire.

Nothing . . . the books he'd been reading – the volume of Daudet was still spread open on an arm. Everything was just the way he'd left it when Kohler had barged in to take him away.

Parting the curtains, he looked out into the darkness. 'Marianne . . .'

She'd been unhappy, upset – so many things. Being the second wife of a cop hadn't been any better for her than it had been for the first wife of that cop.

Too many late nights, too many murders, and now, why now the war and all that it entailed.

Had she taken their son to see her mother? She'd have needed a special *ausweis* for that, a thing not easy to come by. No, not at all. Quimper, like the rest of the coastal areas, was in the

22

Forbidden Zone. The boy was only four years old and very close to her. Though she would have been worried about him, she could have done it. She was a girl of great determination, a woman with a mind of her own and the body to go with it. Ah yes, the body.

St-Cyr pinched the bridge of his nose and shut his eyes. This war, he said. This lousy war.

Kohler and his Gestapo associates lived at the Hôtel Boccador which the Gestapo had requisitioned for the duration. Hermann could find him a fast answer but would it make any difference?

Heading back through to the kitchen, he collected the brief-case on the way and took from it the three, fist-sized lumps of coal he'd managed to pick up from a railway siding near Lyon. The loaf of bread Kohler had squeezed out of a baker in Beaune had got a little stale and dirty, but the round of cheese the Bavarian had stolen was just as good as ever.

Looking at the cheese, St-Cyr nodded sadly and said to the walls as if to a priest, 'Someone's loss is my gain.'

There was virtually no milk in Paris. The boy had had to have his calcium. Kohler had insisted.

Spread on the table were St-Cyr's bread coupons and the green tickets for the week's ration of meat, wine and potatoes et cetera, should he be able to purchase such things.

As he put through the call, he experienced again the humiliation and sadness the defeat of France had brought. 'Hermann, it's me. My wife's gone.'

As expected, Kohler gave him the name of a whore on the rue Mouffetard but said he'd see what he could do. 'Want me to tell them to bring her back?'

'No. No, just ask them to let her know I was worried.'

The call done, he climbed wearily to the bedrooms. A fallen négligé brought back its memories, a pair of briefs reminded him that older men and younger women don't always mix.

Philippe had taken his favourite toy, a water pistol that had been made in Hamburg before the war. The gift of a German soldier in the street, or so his wife had said.

A German soldier.

*

23

'Steiner, the Hauptmann Erich, age thirty-two, attached to the Ministry of Supply. Wife: Hilda, age twenty-eight; children: Johann, age four, Stephanie, age three, Hans, age two, and young Erich, age one month, two days. The wife and kids are at home in Regensburg.'

'Anything else?' demanded Kohler, pinching the last possible smoke from the butt before carefully grinding it out in the ashtray and saving the remaining tobacco.

'Good-looking. A real ladies' man. Been here since last August, arrived in all that heat – that's when he first met her out walking in the Bois de Boulogne. She had the kid with her. Steiner used the boy as an intro – My son, your son, Frau . . .? Pictures from home and all that shit. She didn't fall for it, not at first, not that one. It took him a month's hard labour.'

'Why wasn't I notified?' grumbled Kohler, more offended by the omission than by the infidelity of his partner's wife. These days no one really knew everything the others knew, not even about oneself.

'You didn't ask,' commented Glotz, of Countersubversion Special Unit X, the Watchers in charge of keeping tabs on the Sûreté Murder Squad, among other things.

'So, okay. What's the address?' asked Kohler, feigning apology and a tiredness that was genuine. Crises, there were always crises these days.

Glotz reached for his coffee. 'Hermann, I'd leave it for now, if I were you.' Overweight and overstuffed, he blew on the mug before taking a sip.

Kohler spread his meaty hands on the counter. He hated shits like Glotz but acknowledged they were necessary. 'My partner needs his wife. If he doesn't get laid it puts him off his feed. Besides, my friend, I think the poor bugger really loves her. The Frogs . . .' He sadly shook his head. 'Come on, be a buddy. Don't be so tight about it.'

'You planning to kick down the door?'

'Perhaps.'

The grin was wolfish. Glotz enoyed baiting Kohler. 'A flat in one of those modern apartment buildings over by the Bois de Boulogne.'

The fashionable West End. 'The address,' breathed Kohler. It was nearly 3 a.m.

Glotz didn't like the look. 'Number 33, avenue Henri-Martin.'

Double the address number of St-Cyr's house and double that of the clock!

The date of the murder also, and of St-Cyr's birthday. Jesus Christ!

Kohler was impressed by the coincidence but didn't believe in omens. 'The apartment number?' he asked quietly.

'Thirteen. It's on the third floor at the back. There's a roof terrace. He likes to sunbathe.'

'In this weather?'

Glotz grinned and shook his head. 'In the heat and in the nude. The woman as well. Last October 11th to be precise.'

'Thanks. I'll be in touch.'

'Don't do anything I wouldn't do. He's a nephew of von Schaumburg.'

'He's *what*?'

'I just thought you ought to know.'

Von Schaumburg's nephew.

'Leave it for a bit, Hermann. He'll soon tire of the woman and she'll have to go home to your buddy.'

'He's not my buddy. He's my partner. That used to mean something to a man like me but you wouldn't know about it.'

'Perhaps not. I'm really a lawyer.'

'I've always hated lawyers. They're always so dishonest.'

'I'd be careful what you say.'

'Is that a threat?'

Glotz reached for his coffee. 'Of course not, Hermann. It's only a warning that the walls have ears.'

'Then let the bastards listen!'

'Louis, it's me. Look, something's come up. Try to get a bit of sleep and I'll see you in the morning.'

'Is she safe?'

'Yes, she's safe.'

'And the boy?'

'With a nursemaid. Look, it's okay. I've checked it all out. Now go to sleep.'

For a long time there was only silence from the other end of the line – a waste of several centimetres of Gestapo listening tape.

'It's that lieutenant, isn't it? Steiner.'

'Yes . . . Yes, his name is Steiner. Louis, I would have told you if I'd known. I would have tried to put a stop to it.'

'Thanks. I'll see you in the morning. Oh, anything on that you know what?'

'No, there's nothing to report on that.'

Still in his street clothes, St-Cyr lay in the dark on their bed, wrapped in three blankets and smoking the last of his tobacco ration. The purse had been of silk, very French, very *femme fatale* – from one of the fashion boutiques. The perfume had been someone's very special concoction. Nothing mass produced. Not that scent. Ah no.

But from a silk purse, without knowing of its contents, and a single whiff of expensive perfume, can a humble French detective sketch not only the figure of the woman but also the rest? Her character, her likes and dislikes. The reasons why, perhaps, she had waited in the car on that lonely forest road while her maid had gone to fetch the purse and had killed the bearer of it?

Steiner was a power to be reckoned with. Only in thinking of the murder was there escape from the hard reality of what had happened.

The photographs were grainy. In an attempt to please, Barbizon's photographer had made them a set of 25×20 blow-ups but these were streaked as if by specks of sand. Old photographic paper? wondered St-Cyr. Damp in any case, at some point in its career. Things were so hard to get these days. One bought on the black market or worked some other fiddle but one never really knew what one was getting.

In spite of the graininess – indeed, because of it – the boy's features were etched more sharply. He looked beatific, saintly. Some mother's son. The face was long and narrow, the mop of dark brown hair curly and careless or carefree. The cheekbones were hard and finely moulded, the mouth somewhat small, as was the chin. The nose was long and typically French, hawkish and of the upper class.

The deep brown eyes had clouded over but their expression was still one of surprise.

A small, brown mole marred the angelic left earlobe. Was twenty years not too young an estimate? In spite of the apparent youthfulness, there was hesitation.

St-Cyr couldn't put his finger on the reason, but now felt the boy might possibly be a little older. Some men are always young – young at fifty even. At fifty-two their wives . . .

I'm not young-looking, he said. I'm shabby, tired and a whole lot of other things, and I mustn't let her leaving interfere with my work.

Quickly he went through the photographs, pausing now only at the shot of him and Kohler grinning into the lens. The Bavarian's arm was draped over his shoulder. The body was at their feet and the thing looked a little too much like they'd been out hunting and had bagged the poor bugger before breakfast.

Kohler should have been in vaudeville. One thick-soled shoe rested on a boulder. The conqueror and the conquered, working side by side. The Gestapo and the French Sûreté.

Setting the prints aside, he went through the negatives, flashing each up before the grimy window.

When he came to the last of them, St-Cyr resisted feeling ill and went back through them again.

There was no negative of him and Kohler. Either the photographer hadn't listened, or Kohler had pocketed it.

Failing these two possibilities, there was a third: that someone else in the Gestapo had taken it; and then a fourth: that the Kommandant of Barbizon had had a look or had asked one of his staff to do so, in which case the negative had been pilfered so as to have a visual record of the two men who were on the case – a possibility, yes. Very much so.

And finally there was a fifth possibility: that somehow the Resistance had got to that pouch or to that photographer.

He dropped the last of the negatives on to the pile. Couldn't something have been easy? Just one little thing?

The office was on the fifth floor of the Sûreté, overlooking the courtyard that led on to the rue Saussaies in the heart of the city. The Citroën wasn't in the courtyard, so either Hermann hadn't been in yet, or he'd been in and had gone out.

Chances were Hermann had the negative.

St-Cyr wondered what sort of squeeze his partner had put on the photographer. Had the Bavarian wanted to share the blame and give the photographer the chummy evidence of this? Had that been the reason for the photograph of the two of them?

Or had it simply been because of the purse and its handkerchief, because of his asking to have the spoor photographed – a kind of mutual blackmail, You don't tell the boss, and I won't show this to you-know-who?

It was one more thing to worry about in a morning of worries but serious. Ah, Mon Dieu, it most certainly was. The Resistance, they were beginning to kill collaborators. They tended to shoot first and listen afterwards to explanations of why one hadn't been a collaborator at all.

They'd never understand, not those boys. Things had already gone too far, and were only worsening. They'd not believe he'd thought of resigning many times, had thought of applying for a transfer south – neither of which would have been allowed.

They'd never believe the lives he'd saved by destroying their dossiers.

They'd only look at that photograph and pull the trigger.

The dog-eared, badly smudged business card gave the name *Hermé Thibault, Photographer with Excellence, Barbizon*, and the telephone number. Beneath the name were the words: *Christenings, weddings and funerals*, as if space was so limited, life demanded no further record.

The bill that had been submitted revealed a firmness not seen in the photographer. He reached for the telephone, said to hell with the Gestapo listeners, and asked the switchboard to get him the number.

A harsh female voice broke like glass over his head. 'Hello! Hello!' as if she'd tear his heart out.

'Madame Thibault?'

Instantly the woman was wary. 'Yes . . . Yes, it's me.'

'Madame, I am Inspector Jean-Louis St-Cyr of the Sûreté Nationale. Your husband took some photographs for us yesterday. He was to include all of the negatives but . . .'

He heard her suck in a breath. There was a longer pause, during which a head was shaken vehemently perhaps.

Then the harshness crept back. 'You'll get the last one when the bill has been paid in full.'

'Madame, I must warn you . . .'

'Warn if you like, Monsieur the Inspector. We're sick of you people not paying your bills.'

The bitch hung up! At once there was that sense of loss, of self-doubt. Of course, a little blackmail of their own, and why not?

But why hadn't he anticipated it? He should have. He would have if Marianne hadn't . . .

Kohler stood in the doorway, grinning from ear to ear. 'Want to take a little drive?' he asked.

'Let me send them the money, eh? Just this once.'

It wasn't easy being a French cop working for the Nazis. Kohler almost felt sorry for him. 'It's just not your day, is it?'

'No, I don't think it is.'

'Von Schaumburg wants to see us in his office at eleven o'clock. The Major's asking for us now, and Boemelburg, being Boemelburg, wants his word as well. *After* the Major.'

'But . . . but we haven't even got started?'

Kohler shrugged. 'I told you we should have let that bastard rot in a pauper's grave. Pretty boys like that are always trouble. Any new thoughts on why our young friend wasn't in a prisoner-of-war camp or in the Reich as a labourer?'

'None . . . None at all at the moment.'

'Well, you'd better have a damned good reason, Louis. Word has it von Schaumburg's out for blood.'

'Then we'll use the possibility of the priesthood for now.'

'I knew you'd see it my way,' roared Kohler. 'Now relax. I'll tell the old fart the boy broke his vows and was in trouble with a married woman.'

'Was he?'

Kohler pulled down a lower eyelid and stared at him but said nothing further. As St-Cyr stepped into the hall, the Bavarian opened their lock-up and took from it the Frenchman's gun in its shoulder holster. Without a word, he thrust the weapon into St-Cyr's hands and motioned him to put it on. After all, it was only a Lebel six-shooter, the old Model 1873.

But a devil's gun in the right hands. Besides, it would impress the French Chief and show the little bastard that the two of them meant business and the Gestapo trusted St-Cyr.

Shooters for the French cops were only issued when on serious operations. Handcuffs always.

Vain, insanely jealous of his position, very political, officious and a real shit, Major Osias Pharand glared at them from behind what had once been his secretary's desk.

'Von Schaumburg,' he hissed. 'Only this moment another call. Beauschamp, the Préfet of Barbizon, wishes to know why he was not notified and why the Sûreté should think to arrogantly bypass the local police. Auger, the Mayor of Barbizon, has also telephoned. So, *what* have you to report, eh? Out ripping off the *tabacs* when you should have been attending to business?'

'As a matter of fact, Monsieur le Director, I'm out of tobacco,' said St-Cyr.

Pharand never spoke directly to the two of them, preferring the French edge of the sword. 'Well, what about it?' he demanded.

With a knuckle he irritably dusted the carefully trimmed black pencil of his moustache before clasping the pudgy hands in impatient expectation.

Kohler stood back while St-Cyr laid out the photographs and went over things with his boss. Pharand hadn't been around the day of the defeat. He'd run just like most of them but had been only too willing to return, even if it had meant giving up his precious office. Violently anti-Semitic, a real Jew-baiter, he hated the Jews even more than the Resistance which he hunted down with rabid enthusiasm.

Their necks or his, and wasn't war wonderful? No inbetweens, thought Kohler.

'Details,' muttered Pharand acidly. 'Von Schaumburg will want details.'

'Once we've identified the victim, the rest should be easy,' said St-Cyr.

'Have Records come up with a blank?' demanded the Major.

'No . . . No, they have not begun the search, Monsieur le Direc . . .'

'Then ask them to do so immediately. Let me know the moment you have anything. Don't breathe a word of it to anyone else.'

He snapped his fingers for the photographs St-Cyr had held

back. 'More shots of the body, Monsieur le Director. Nothing new.'

'Yes, yes . . . Quickly!' A snap again. 'Please allow me to judge.'

When he came to the photograph of Kohler's spoor with its white silk handkerchief he lifted questioning eyes to St-Cyr but went on.

The safari photograph caused but a moment's impatience. At fifty-eight years of age, Osias Pharand knew the ropes.

'The Sturmbannführer Boemelburg can see you now. Dismissed.' He tossed a hand but couldn't resist adding, 'I'm warning you, St-Cyr. If this affair involves the Resistance, please do not attempt to hide things. I know you're soft. It won't be tolerated a moment longer, eh? Do you understand?'

Shit and more shit, and the day had only begun.

'Would you really attempt to hide things?' asked Kohler as they went along the hall.

'Of course not. How could I with you looking over my shoulder?'

'I just thought I'd ask, Louis. Nice of your boss to remind me, though.'

'He's all heart, that one, and often confused.'

'Well, leave this one to me. Boemelburg's got his head screwed on.'

'Word has it that he's becoming forgetful.'

'At least he knows what building he's in.'

More couldn't be said, for Kohler had knocked. 'Enter,' came the summons with just a trace of impatience. 'Both of you this time, Hermann. I want answers.'

The office, though spacious, had none of Pharand's former trappings. Gone were the works of art, the clutter of Chinese porcelains. In their place were street maps of Paris and all the major cities and towns in France, batteries of telephones and teleprinters, and, lost among the pins, the obligatory photograph of the Führer.

No man for the finer sensibilities, Boemelburg hadn't thought the antique limewood desk large enough and so had had the carpenters nail boards over its top. The clash of plain pine with the Louis XIV carvings always moved St-Cyr to whimsy. But then he'd known Boemelburg from before the war, from their

31

work with the IKPK, the International Organization of Police, with its headquarters in Vienna.

An old and much respected policeman, Boemelburg spoke fluent French, having worked for a time in Paris in his younger days as a heating and ventilating engineer.

The Head of SIPO-SD Section IV, the Gestapo in France, was a favourite and much trusted friend of Gestapo Mueller in Berlin.

The handshake was firm. 'Well, Louis, it's good to see you.'

'And yourself, Herr Sturmbannführer.' What else was he to have said? wondered St-Cyr. I am as the rabbit while passing through the lion's cage.

'Hermann, a chair,' thundered Boemelburg, indicating that the two of them were to sit opposite the desk. 'So, gentlemen, a small murder? Perhaps, Hermann, you could fill me in and then, Louis, you could add the more important details your partner will no doubt have forgotten.'

Kohler grimaced at the warning. St-Cyr half-listened as his partner began. Boemelburg was well up in his sixties, the blunt head almost shaved of its bristly iron grey hairs, and the blue Nordic eyes watery but not from sympathy.

A big man, like Kohler, he had the split-minded compartmentalization necessary for the first-class cop. He knew Paris like the palm of his hand and, like all first-class cops, had the inherent suspiciousness of a small boy who has just had his favourite pencil stolen in class.

No bully, he had knocked about, and it showed not so much in the ragged countenance or the tired lift of the eyes, but in his silent analysis of what had really gone on. The truth.

As Head of the Gestapo in France, Boemelburg dealt mainly with counter-terrorism and subversion – the Resistance and the Allied agents who were increasingly being dropped into France – but there were spill-overs into all other departments: the black market, the press, common murder, bank robberies, et cetera.

His liaison with the Sûreté had begun on that fateful day of the defeat and St-Cyr could still remember how Boemelburg had barged in the front door from that empty, empty street only to find him in Records and shake his head before saying, 'Now, Louis, that will be enough of that.'

Fair was fair in Boemelburg's eyes, but now that the order

had changed, he'd expected one hundred per cent co-operation or else.

The choosing of hostages and the signing of their execution orders also fell to him.

As a sideline, he had the distasteful task of overseeing two notorious French units: the Intervention-Referat – hired killers and known criminals who did the Gestapo's work when they wanted to appear dissociated from it, as in kidnapping, extortion, murder or bombing of some nuisance politician or industrialist; and the Bickler Unit whose school trained informers and infiltrators before sending them out to do the Gestapo's bidding.

With Pharand both St-Cyr and Kohler knew they might avoid things, with Boemelburg it would be out of the question.

'This purse, where is it?' asked the Chief.

'In the lock-up,' said Kohler blandly.

'Has Louis had the privilege of seeing its contents?'

'Not yet. I thought it might be better, Herr Sturmbannführer, if we discussed it in private.'

'Why?'

Kohler shrugged. 'There's nothing specific, Herr Boemelburg. Women's things – cosmetics, a small amount of money . . .'

'How much?' rapped the boss.

'A million francs.'

'Idiot! A million . . . *Gott in Himmel*, Hermann, a cop's lockup? Why isn't it in my safe?'

'I was going to suggest that, Herr Sturmbannführer. The money isn't in francs – she'd have had to have a sack for that. It's in diamonds.'

'Diamonds!' stormed Boemelburg. 'The black market, eh? A currency fiddle? Theft – what about it? Were they reported?' All such things had had to be written down and the lists submitted to the authorities. 'This purse, go and get it.'

'Of course, Herr Sturmbannführer.' Kohler even clicked his heels and bowed.

Boemelburg fumed. 'Diamonds . . . Louis, what do you make of it?'

Trust Hermann to keep that little bit of information to himself. St-Cyr affected a dryness that was admirable. 'It's news to me, Walter.'

The head tossed briefly in acknowledgement. 'What's it smell like then?'

'Still a crime of passion.'

'Then why is von Schaumburg so interested?'

'Perhaps because the Kommandant of Barbizon is a personal friend of his.'

'Talk . . . these days there is always talk behind our backs. So, how have you been?'

'Busy.'

Again there was that nod, the intuitive understanding that enough had been said. 'Did Pharand insist on your checking the boy out with Records?'

'He did, but my feeling is, Walter, they won't have anything.'

'Even with the diamonds?'

'Yes, even with them. You see, the boy looks to be of money, isn't that right? The son of an aristocrat, one of our wealthy industrialists perhaps. Records won't have anything because if they once had, the file would have been . . . Well, you know what I mean.'

Pulled. 'It's the same at home, Louis. Some things never change. See that Hermann behaves himself. Drop everything. Satisfy von Schaumburg we're doing a good job. Berlin has asked for this.'

Berlin.

More couldn't be said because Kohler had entered without knocking. The Bavarian strode up to the desk and dropped the purse in front of his boss. With heavy hands Boemelburg shoved aside the day's mountains of paperwork before emptying the purse on to the desk.

A hand spread the contents out, then he stood up to get a bit of distance and have a better look at things.

'A woman of substance,' he said, indicating the crystal perfume vial, the ivory cigarette holder, monogrammed silver cigarette case, lipstick, compact, small, tight roll of ten-thousand-franc notes, condoms in their very own little silk purses, a tiny pencil in its silver tube . . .

'Address book, where is it?' demanded Boemelburg, saving the whereabouts of the diamonds for the last.

Kohler drew himself up. 'Not present, Herr Sturmbannführer.'

Was that pity in Walter's gaze? wondered St-Cyr.

'And the diamonds?' asked Boemelburg quietly.

'Being evaluated, Herr Sturmbannführer.'

Evaluated! Bullshit! 'Where?'

'Fournier's on the rue du Faubourg St-Honoré.'

Boemelburg glanced at his watch before fixing Kohler with a general's eye. 'How are things going for our boys on the Russian Front, Hermann? I ask because I haven't the time to listen to the wireless.'

Kohler swallowed before lamely saying, 'Not too well, I guess, Herr Sturmbannführer.'

'Then you'd best go and get them, eh? Oh, and Hermann, take a velo-taxi. Don't you show up in front of the Kommandantur in that car Louis has been forced to let you drive. We're to be seen as needing an increase in our gasolene allocation. Be late for your meeting with von Schaumburg. Five minutes, so as to emphasize we're overworked. Oh, and leave the guns here. You're not going to impress him with those. You're not members of the Carbone* gang, not yet. And have a strategy,' went on Boemelburg.'The two of you back to the site of the crime for some spadework then on to the seminaries – work on the red herring of the novice priest. Lay it all out for him and listen to what he has to say. Don't mention the purse or the diamonds. Let him tell you about them. Berlin . . . I'm warning you, Hermann. Berlin has asked for this.'

'Berlin?' bleated Kohler as they beat a retreat down the hall.

St-Cyr gave a magnanimous toss of his hands. 'That just shows you what happens when generals talk to generals.'

'And the Wehrmacht has to give in to Himmler's wishes and let the Gestapo look after the policing of France. No doubt that little vegetarian fart has addressed a joint meeting of the Oberkommando der Wehrmacht, the High Command itself!'

Everyone knew that the honeymoon was over. In the first years of the Occupation the Army had been very correct with the people – far more decent with the French than if the shoe had been on the other foot. True, the economy had been and was being plundered, and now the young and not so young were being taken away to enforced labour. And true, in spite of

---

* The most notorious of the Intervention-Referat gangs.

all protestations to the contrary, more than 1,500,000 French soldiers still languished in prisoner-of-war camps within the Reich.

But acts of violence had increased – some of which had been set up on Himmler's orders – and now the Wehrmacht had been forced to relinquish the policing to the Gestapo.

Understandably they weren't happy about it.

'Who is this guy anyway?' demanded Kohler, glaring at one of the photographs.

'A nobody, Hermann. A flea in the elephant's ear.'

'Or up his ass!'

'You should have told me about those diamonds.'

'I couldn't.'

'Any special reason?'

'No . . . No, nothing special. Just a feeling I have.'

'Walter's asked me to keep an eye on you, Hermann. I think I'd better.'

'Want a fag?'

'Yes . . . yes, I would like that very much, and a canister of pipe tobacco if you can find such a thing.'

Kohler knew he'd have to let him have the last word but couldn't resist saying, 'You're learning, Louis. *Gott in Himmel* but you are!'

Turcotte was in charge of Records, lord of his empire. The Sûreté's card index files and dossiers occupied the whole of the sixth floor, the top floor, and the card indexes before the war had been as good if not better than the Gestapo's in Berlin. Even the innocent had cards just in case they should stray from the straight and narrow or be related to someone who did. Apply for a hunting licence, a marriage certificate, passport or visa and automatically one got a card. Age, sex, marital status, number of children, closest relatives et cetera, et cetera . . . It was all here.

Beyond the maze of lead-grey filing cabinets, neglected windows gave back the surrealistic smearings of careless pigeons.

More rain, thought St-Cyr – his mackintosh was leaking. He'd have to find some glue or varnish – waterproofing compound was unheard of with Stalingrad so much in the news and the Russian winter begun.

Idly he wondered what would happen here if the Germans should lose, which they would. He was certain of it. A faint

36

glimmer of hope. It was what kept one going. That and Marianne and the boy, and thoughts of the small farm he'd like to have . . .

Provence and retirement from all the slime, but now . . . why now, there was only Stalingrad.

Turcotte came back into view. 'Well, what is it this time?'

Kohler showed him the worst of the photographs. 'We need an ID on this one. He's very dead.'

The lark's eyes snapped light. 'Do you always carry a purse like that, or is today something special?'

'It's St-Cyr's birthday plus one, so we're going out to celebrate. Now give, eh? The boss has to know.'

'The boss . . . Your boss.'

St-Cyr got ready for the load of wind but it didn't come. Boemelburg must have phoned upstairs.

He shot the green requisition ticket over the counter but didn't receive any thanks.

Turcotte had a staff of seventy detective-clerks in grey smocks but dealt with this request himself, disappearing into the warren to find the photographic section and and the missing persons' bank. 'When was he killed?' came the shout, fast fading.

'Three a.m., 3rd December,' called St-Cyr, not wishing to complicate things. 'A back road from Fontainebleau to Barbizon.'

'No other leads?'

'None, I'm afraid.'

'Thanks. Thanks a lot, my friend. Why don't you guys do your homework *before* you come up here to demand the world?'

He was at the photographic desk now. They could hear him saying, 'Top priority,' but then his voice must have dropped to a whisper.

Kohler pulled down a lower eyelid and made a face. 'Are you really serious about that tobacco?' he asked quietly.

'Yes, of course I am.'

'Won't half a tin do?'

'At a pinch, yes. Yes, of course.' Anything. I'm desperate, St-Cyr wanted to say but didn't.

The Bavarian glanced around before flicking open the counter door and stepping through. He had perhaps ten seconds and he used them all to reach Turcotte's frosted, glassed-in cubicle, wing open the lower desk drawer, find the tobacco and return.

He was beaming when the lark came back and demanded the return of his tobacco. 'Don't you ever let me catch you doing that again!'

'Sorry, Émile. You know how it is. Louis, here, is fresh out. His wife's buggered off and the poor bastard has the humps.'

The lark clucked his tongue. 'Come back this afternoon. We're to do a full search. The Sturmbannführer Boemelburg has demanded it.'

'You could have told us.'

'You're not trustworthy. I had to find out.'

'The diamonds . . .? But, monsieur, they are not here.'

Kohler gripped the edge of the bevelled Victorian glass counter. 'What the hell do you mean, they're not here?'

The manager of Fournier's was a frightened little man who couldn't keep still. 'We had to take them to an expert – one who is very well qualified, you understand?'

'A Jew?' snapped Kohler, rocking the air.

Frantically the manager's eyes flew to his customers who were scattered about the fashionable shop. 'Yes . . . Yes, I'm sorry, monsieur, but . . .' He threw up his hands in despair. 'I can have them back by five o'clock.'

Kohler's fist hit the glass. 'You'll have them back in one hour or else.'

'Hermann, please. Allow me,' soothed St-Cyr with a brief smile. 'Monsieur, you did not let the diamonds leave this shop. To do so would be to lose all credibility and your licence. So . . .' He ran his eyes over the sunken treasure that lay beneath the glass. 'So you will have the diamonds here by five o'clock as you've said, or else.'

'But . . .'

St-Cyr raised a silencing hand. 'No buts, my friend. Your messenger won't be followed. Just see that the stones are ready and have your evaluation clearly recorded on the packet, signed by yourself and witnessed with the date as well, so that we can compare it with our other appraisals.'

'Your other . . .?'

'Yes. It's always best to get three or more appraisals before selling, isn't that so?'

Of course it was.

Out on the rue du Faubourg St-Honoré they climbed back into the velo-taxi and told the girl to take them to the Kommandantur. 'As fast as you can, eh?' said St-Cyr.

Kohler was all shoulders and arms, the twin wicker baby carriages just big enough for one of them. 'Louis, I'm sorry about the diamonds. I really do apologize.'

St-Cyr shrugged. 'Think nothing of it, my friend. What are a few little things like that between partners? But the woman's address book, Hermann . . . That I should most certainly like to see.'

'It's in my room at the Boccador, under the carpet.'

St-Cyr shook his head in wonder. 'And you're supposed to be a Gestapo detective. Care to tell me about it?'

The girl's rump was going from side to side, the jacket creeping up above her slender waist to reveal a pink sweater and blouse. 'Later, perhaps. Look, I still want to think about it, Louis. This thing . . .'

This little murder. 'Yes, I know it's trouble.' Mon Dieu, he wished Hermann wasn't so big across the shoulders!

The wheels of the velo-taxi breathed over the rain-slicked stones, adding their lack of sound to Paris's general hush. Apart from the few German cars, and occasional Wehrmacht lorries, there were no other motorized vehicles in sight. Only bicycles and more and more of them, and the inevitable velo-taxis of course.

It was like riding through creamed soup on a spoon.

The girl signalled a left as she turned on to the rue Royale and the grey light made greyer still and more majestic the splendid Corinthian columns of the Madeleine.

St-Cyr wept for France when he saw the church. Always it was like this. Dry tears and unspoken thoughts, a tightening of the throat.

The girl was wearing trousers of heavy twill and, with a start, he realized they'd been dyed and that they were from among the leftovers at Dunkirk.

British Army fatigues – sometimes half the nation was partly dressed in them. 'She looks quite good in them,' confided Kohler with an appreciative grin. 'Cute, wouldn't you say? *Gott in Himmel*, Louis, I'd like to see those trousers down around her ankles.'

'Don't get any ideas, Hermann. We've work to do.'

The Kommandantur rose out of the near end of the Place de l'Opéra, one of twin buildings on either side of the avenue de l'Opéra. A great big, black-and-white signboard was curved above its entrance to fit the curve of the wall.

No one could have missed it, but German road signs gave the directions anyway.

Every Parisian who wanted to do anything had eventually to turn up here. It was the house of papers and rubber stamps.

The girl pulled into the kerb and swung breathlessly around to smile at them. What the hell, one had to. 'So, one hundred and fifty francs, if you please, messieurs.'

'Your name?' snapped Kohler.

She lost the pretty smile. 'My name . . .?' she began, looking for a fast exit.

'And the address,' announced Kohler, dragging out his notebook.

St-Cyr found two one-hundred-franc bills and said, 'Come on, Hermann, we've better things to do.'

Unfortunately the clock on the wall above the entrance gave the bull's-eye of ten past eleven.

Von Schaumburg wasn't pleased. In fact, he wasn't even there.

'He's gone to the morgue. The general has suggested that if you two gentlemen can spare him the time, he'd be glad to meet you there.'

Out on the Place the girl with the velo-taxi had vanished.

The corpse was only one of many. Three nuns were weeping over the shrouded bier next door, while a priest thumbed his prayer book as if unable to decide which page to use for cigarette paper.

Cold . . . it was so cold, the condensation had frozen on the walls. Great yellowish-grey-green curds hung like snot awaiting a thaw.

Sounds echoed. White-coated, solemn grey men, their pill-shaped white box hats often smeared by bloody thumbprints, moved about the place as if butchers drifting through ether. Some dragged rubber hoses, others pushed brooms or pulled window wipers across the puddled floor. One carried a meat saw, another a clipboard.

There was a cough, and then a cloud of filthy cigarette smoke.

The grizzled moon-face of their attendant turned to them and the fleshy lips parted to betray a set of rotten teeth. 'So, my friends, do you want the shroud removed or merely pulled back?' He indicated the nuns.

Kohler said, 'Remove it.'

'Entirely?' asked the man, with surprise.

'We're detectives,' came the answer.

The nuns turned away in horror. The youngest one stole a further glance. The boy was beautiful – like Christ in alabaster, rigid with rigor and so pale.

'I was right,' breathed Kohler. 'The bugger's been circumcised, Louis. Will you take a look at that.'

'I am. How many times must I tell you that little surgical procedure is as much for hygiene's sake as for religion's? He's no more Jewish than you are. Now cover him up.'

'Frightened by the sight of death, eh?'

St-Cyr shook his head, but as the priest and the nuns had fled, there was no sense in fussing. 'Where's the general?'

'Talking to the Chief,' replied the attendant.

'Then tell him we're here.'

The man departed, leaving them alone with the corpse. The boy was slight, he had an angel's build. Bluish shadows had grown beneath the eyes which were now closed.

The lips looked cold.

'Let's tell the general the boy's Jewish. It'll go a lot easier for us, Louis. Don't be a stick about it.'

'Von Schaumburg's a Prussian of the old school, Hermann.'

'A real Junker's bastard. He hates you French.'

'And you Gestapo, so we're even.'

'Then you handle it, eh?'

'He won't let me.'

'He's a dyed-in-the-wool bachelor, a real shit when it comes to protocol and morals – marital fidelity and all that crap.'

'He won't have heard about Marianne.'

'He probably has. Nothing much gets past him. Look, I'm going to show him the boy's wanger. I've got to.'

'Scars . . . are there any scars?' asked St-Cyr loudly, as the

41

sound of highly polished jackboots broke from across the marble floor.

'One under the left arm, across the upper ribcage. Looks to be about five centimetres long. An old scar. Not stitched. Probably a fall as a child.'

St-Cyr wrote it all down. The steps grew closer. 'Anything else?'

'Right nipple has a small nick below it. Recent, Louis. The wound's not even closed. Now what the he . . . e . . . ll?'

'Attention!'

Kohler crashed his heels together without even thinking. St-Cyr let the hand with its notebook fall to his side. 'General . . .'

Von Schaumburg was taller, bigger than Kohler. The shoulders of the open greatcoat betrayed none of the advanced years, the peak of the military cap shone sharply through the perpetual gloom.

'What is the meaning of this?' he demanded – not quite a shriek.

Rock of Bronze to his staff, Old Shatter Hand to others, von Schaumburg waited. Kohler began.

The general listened. One meaty hand crushed black leather gloves that could be swung. The other hand irritably stuck the monocle over its eye, magnifying the blue intensity. 'You . . . your names?' he demanded. 'Gestapo,' he spat. 'Imbeciles. Who is he, why did he die, and who killed him?'

Kohler began it all again only to be interrupted by, 'His name, damn it?'

'We don't know that yet, General.'

'Why?'

Round and round it would go, sighed St-Cyr inwardly only to have the thought interrupted by, 'The Führer should never have let you people into France. I warned him there'd be trouble. The Army are perfectly capable of looking after things. This could have been settled in an instant.'

'By burying the boy?' asked Kohler. 'He's Jewish, General.'

Kohler reached for the boy's penis.

'Jewish my foot! That's not always the case, you idiot! This matter must be settled and quickly. I want full reports on my desk each morning at 0700 hours until the case is solved.'

'Even if he's Jewish and a nobody, General?' tried Kohler desperately. 7 a.m. was just a bit too early. Jesus!

Kohler . . . Munich . . . One of Mueller's boys.

Von Schaumburg took in the sagging jowls, the shrapnel scars . . . Kohler . . . Artillery . . . Yes, yes, he'd been in charge of a battery of field guns on the Somme. A lieutenant then. No decorations for bravery. Taken prisoner, 17 July 1916.

The face had the look of dissipation. Too much drink and too many women.

Von Schaumburg popped the monocle into the hand which had hung there all this time as if waiting for him to spit it out. 'Behave like the soldier you once were, *Sergeant* Kohler. This,' he indicated the corpse, 'is to be handled with discretion not with the fingers of a clumsy ox. The General von Richthausen, the Kommandant of Barbizon, has asked for my assistance in the matter as have others. Discretion, Kohler. Discretion. Need I say more?'

Old Shatter Hand himself. 'No, General. I think I've got the message.'

'Good. Then I give you exactly two days to clear the matter up. Any suggestions of impropriety from either the corpse or yourselves and I will take the appropriate action. Am I understood?'

Not just down to sergeant, but stripped of all rank. 'Yes, General, you're understood.'

'Now see that the body is treated with respect.'

He fixed them each with a last glance, hesitating but a fraction longer with St-Cyr.

Then he turned and left them.

'Probably going to inspect the brothels,' snorted Kohler. 'That always gets him in an uproar.'

'You didn't say anything about the possibility of the boy being a priest,' offered St-Cyr.

'Did I have a chance? The Jew business was better.'

'Von Schaumburg's no fool, Hermann. He knows far more about this than he's saying.'

'My thoughts exactly.'

St-Cyr ran his eyes over the boy. A name had been called out into the darkness as the sound of the bicycle had approached. Then the brakes had been applied. There'd have been hesitation, the boy searching the roadside before saying softly,——is that really you?

43

Yes . . . Yes, it's me,——.

But you were supposed to meet me at——. Why didn't you?

We were late. Something came up. Did you bring the purse?

Yes . . . Yes, I've got it.

Then the boulder – grasped fiercely in both hands and smashed against that forehead with all the strength of her tender years.

Or did they argue first? Did the boy not demand something in exchange for the purse?

Did he honestly have that look about him? A blackmailer? Ah no, not him.

A priest, a saint, a novice.

Tears . . . terror – the realization of what she'd done. A torn stocking. No time. Must climb. Must run!

Now wait – wait, Louis. The position of the hands, eh? The hands, my friend.

The forest then, and then, at the end of that footpath, scraped and bruised and still in tears, she would have yanked the car door open. Madame . . . Madame, I have lost the purse!

Idiot! Go back and find it. You must!

No . . . No, I can't, madame. I have hit him. He's dead. I know he's dead!

Weeping, the girl collapses on the seat.

End of scene, end of frame. No splicing needed yet. But why madame? wondered St-Cyr, strangely exhausted by the film his imagination had conjured for him.

Why not mademoiselle?

It was an excellent question for which he had no adequate answer, only a feeling that was so hard to explain.

'Louis, I hate to interrupt your thoughts, but have a look at this.'

Kohler came back into focus through the misty eyes of the cinematographer. There were three small bruises in a tight little row on the fair skin of the boy's upper right thigh.

'Were you thinking what I am?' asked the Bavarian. 'If so, von Schaumburg's interest may not be out of place.'

St-Cyr smoothed a thumb over the marks as a wave of sadness engulfed him. 'No . . . No I wasn't, Hermann. My film was quite different and only of the boy's last moments.'

2

Les Halles had once been the belly of Paris, full of shouts, full of produce, but now . . . ah, Mon Dieu, it was such a shame, a mere vestige of its former self.

Pathetic! Yes, that's what it was. And all because of the curfew! And the gasolene and diesel fuel restrictions, of course.

St-Cyr flung the cigarette butt away as he strode beneath the first of the colossal iron-and-glass pavilions that had once contained the heart and pulse of Paris and its environs.

Because of the curfew, the farmers couldn't get their produce to market until two or three in the afternoon when, normally, they would have started the long journey homeward.

Because of the fuel restrictions and the requisition of virtually all motor vehicles, only a paltry number of gasogenes struggled into the city, to here.

Others, of course, had better luck but they unloaded at the best hotels and restaurants, or sold straight off the back and quickly.

As a result, a flourishing black market existed and those without the cash or trade went hungry while in the north, milk was being fed to the pigs and the potatoes were all being shipped to Germany.

'The Boches are fools,' he said to the cavern of that empty place. As in the morgue, his steps echoed and seemed to follow him as a man's conscience should.

Hermann had gone to his hotel to collect the address book. The Bavarian would stop in at the office to pick up the purse and to check with Records. They'd meet later at Fournier's.

He, himself, would try to settle the perfume business.

45

Let's face it, my friend, he said to himself, we're running scared. This whole thing is beginning to smell.

There were no vegetable sellers, no carrots to be had, no cabbages, no apples either. As he passed the Bistro St Ruby-Martin, he recalled the 5 a.m. onion soup, the steaming vapours of a late night's ending over wine as well as coffee and a marc. Sipping and sorting his notes while listening to the background shouts of the market and drinking in the aromas.

Out on the rue St Denis, he headed for his second choice: the Taverne Moderne, cast out of the 1870s, still complete with its gaslights and Belle Époque etched windows.

Subdued lighting and crowded little tables with red chequered cloths. Water and ration tickets and maybe . . . just maybe a bowl of their leek soup with a few croutons to raft about and make the memories come.

'Hello, Henri. Can you look after me, eh?'

'The soup is very good today, monsieur, as is the lamb casserole.' (The two items were scrawled in chalk on the blackboard.)

Lamb, squirrel or cat – was it cat? 'Excellent!' exclaimed St-Cyr with a famished grin. 'My wife and little son have gone to see her mother for a few days, so I must fend for myself.'

Henri couldn't have cared less. Courville, the great talker and former owner of the Taverne, had sensibly sold up on the day before the Defeat and hadn't been seen since.

We're all new to each other, no matter how many years we've known each other, said St-Cyr to himself as he crowded into a shared table with a heavy-set businessman who liked to have the table for his elbows and was forced to move his plate and cutlery into full retreat.

'Monsieur,' acknowledged St-Cyr with a curt nod, while smoothing out the recovered territory.

The man merely grunted and continued breaking bread into his casserole. Not a crumb was wasted.

Water in the lamb. Was it a stew, then? wondered St-Cyr. These days one took what one got.

He spread two bread tickets and one meat coupon on the table only to hear his other half grunt, 'You'll only need the one for bread. Don't tempt the bastard with two. There's no wine, so forget it.'

46

No wine. The blood of France. He thought to ask, just in case, then looked around and thought better of it. To a man, the patrons attended to their lunch with dogged determination.

So what are we to do? he asked himself. That business of the tiny bruises was not healthy, nor was the business of the negative Barbizon's photographer had retained.

He would send a money order off from the post office, then he'd head for the classy shops of the Place Vendôme. But would knowing the perfume lead to the woman, and what if she were found, what then?

The leek soup was perfect. Magnificent! Such an aroma, one could derive sustenance from its vapours alone.

He longed for a little grated cheese.

The man across the table said, 'Use some of your bread. You'll get no croutons from them.'

St-Cyr wished he'd go away.

Two days . . . that's all they had. Perhaps a third if there was significant progress.

He hoped the thing really had nothing to do with the Resistance. Hermann couldn't be expected to tread lightly.

So far they had avoided the inevitable. Each day, however, had brought them closer and closer to that final moment of decision.

To kill or not to kill Hermann. He'd hate to have to fire the shots. The Resistance would hunt him down in any case. They'd never listen. Not to him.

I live on the edge of a chasm, he said to himself. Is it any wonder Marianne could no longer stand it?

Like so many these days, she had had to make up her mind. She wasn't a bad woman, ah no, one mustn't get that idea. Like most Bretons, she was immensely capable, self-reliant and resilient. That business of her not liking the garden was simply because she'd had more than her fair share of farming and had come to Paris to escape it.

Unlike so many, she had resisted the streets even though desperate. She'd been employed as a domestic in a banker's villa near St Raphaël. Murder had intervened and he had faced her across an Aubusson carpet and known.

She had agreed to become his housekeeper – on a trial basis. A virgin at twenty-nine years of age. Can one believe it?

47

That job had led to marriage after a year – a *year* of absolute chastity! Of walking in the parks or along the quais, of sitting shyly in a café when time and work allowed.

All of which had been thrown away in one month with the Lieutenant Steiner.

Von Schaumburg's nephew.

'Don't you like the casserole?'

St-Cyr blinked. 'It's too hot. I was letting it cool.'

In the name of Jesus, he cried out to himself, what the hell has happened to me? It was as if God had not only deserted him but had crooked a finger and told him to climb up into Heaven to have a look down at himself.

If the truth were told, it was the life that she'd hated most but that still didn't explain why he'd been forced to work for the Germans.

That I could have done without, he said, but knew it was no use.

What does one do when one must calm oneself? One walks. One absorbs – takes an interest in one's surroundings. The Paris of 1942 was vastly different from the Paris he had known. Oh for sure, the streets still beckoned but they were often so empty, so silent. As if on the moon perhaps. St-Cyr felt himself reaching out to them, his body being dissolved through extensions of the pores.

He began to think of the film of the murder, to run it back through the projector, stopping at each frame.

From a vendor's steaming charcoal burner outside the National Library he didn't ask, How come the charcoal, my friend? but only for a bag of roasted chestnuts.

From a flower-seller on the Place Vendôme he bought two last white roses and a red carnation.

The chestnuts, half gone by then, were meaty and full of flavour. The roses piqued his nostrils.

The film had stopped again at the positioning of the body, the hands in particular. Had the woman done that and then left no trace of her having done so? Had the girl still been sobbing her heart out in the car?

It was a thought – one certainly couldn't expect a maid, a silly young thing who'd just killed her lover, to . . .?

Ah, her lover? He continued cranking the projector . . . one certainly couldn't expect the girl to have paused after having killed the boy, to have done such a considerate thing as to have laid the arms to the sides and turned the hands outwards, to have turned the head sideways and laid it on a bed of leaves . . .

No, the woman, the driver of that car – and by now he was thinking it must have been a big car, something flashy – the woman must have brought the girl back and done it herself. But then . . . why then, that would indicate the boy must have meant something to her.

And, of course, she did not go after the purse. At least, he didn't think she had.

Again he brought the roses up to his nose, first pinching the left nostril and then the right.

After a decent interval it was the carnation's turn, he filling his lungs slowly while cursing the habit of tobacco which only ruined one's sense of smell.

Then the chestnuts, first the crumpled bag and both nostrils for a whiff, then a single nut broken with the front teeth, the pinching of a single nostril.

The frames of the film were now being seen before the Place Vendôme whose column of stone rose beneath spiralled bronze and Trojan horses to a bust of Napoleon as Caesar.

Unsandbagged by the Germans who thronged the Place with their French girlfriends or who walked stiffly as they always did, among the Parisians who had come, as always, to window-shop if not to buy.

There were a few staff cars, suitably polished, a few generals . . .

If one discounted the uniforms and took in the lingerie, one could almost believe there was no Occupation.

This, too, was a sadness. The fashion industry's ready accept-ance and open doors.

But, he gave a shrug, not to have opened those doors was to have gone against the decree of 20 June 1940, and to have lost the businesses.

From the Opéra to the Étoile, from the Madeleine to the Champs-Élysées, the rue Royale and the Faubourg St-Honoré, business was still booming, though things were, of course, more difficult to obtain.

The lingerie grew closer. Silks, satins and midnight lace, through which the mannequins' figures could not but show, were seen beyond the film, the girl, the boulder, the instant of death, the woman in her car, anxiously smoking a cigarette while waiting for her maid to bring her that purse. Waiting . . .

St-Cyr wiped his shoes on the mat and removed his hat before entering the shop which had, so suitably, been named, Enchantment.

The silver bell rang. The polished oak panelling, glass display cases and marble columns met his eyes. Aphrodite beckoned in life-sized alabaster with splendidly uptilted breasts and the scents of perfume and toilet soaps about her. Diana stood in gold with arrow pointing, and a laundry-basketful of under-garments scattered at her feet.

'A woman must undress to dress, Louis.'

'Chantal, it's magnificent to see you looking so lovely.'

St-Cyr took her hand in his and brought it to his lips – never mind the Nazis browsing in the shop with their French whores, never mind the war, being married and deserted by one's wife and only child, never mind any of it.

'How's Muriel?' he asked. 'Me, I don't see her, Chantal. Has she . . .?'

The tiny bird of a woman smiled – she had such a beautiful smile. Perfectly done. Never too much. 'She's fine. And you, my friend?'

They were both well up in their seventies. 'Me? Ah, fine, of course. Here, I have brought you each one of the last roses I could find.'

She kissed his cheek and embraced him as such women do. Like a feather, like a breath of delicately scented air.

Vivacious, made-up, wearing a dress of the latest cutting – dark blue, very close-fitting, calf-length and matching the high heels – Chantal Grenier had been in the business all her life, as had her partner and associate.

The hair was blonde – never grey – cut short and bobbed in the latest fashion. The rings and bracelets were of silver today, of lapis lazuli. A blue day then – did it have some meaning or was it merely the whim of fashion?

She had a very tiny voice, very clear and bell-like. 'You are suitably impressed, Louis. This pleases me.' She tossed her little head and smiled again before pursing her lips. 'But come . . . come.' She gathered him in by the arm. 'Let me show you the shop. We've changed the décor. Did you not notice more than those?' She indicated the statues with a toss of a hand. 'Mere trifles, Louis. Stone and fake gold. Men need the real thing, eh? Isn't that so?'

At once the energy flowed from her in motion, the eyes, the tossing of the head, the purposeful strut.

Still very beautiful, she made him welcome. After all, he was a cop, and God would not have had it otherwise, eh? Ah no. Not with this one.

'Your wife was in this morning with a certain someone,' she whispered coyly. Cruel . . . it was so cruel of her to do that. Muriel would be sure to scold her. Muriel.

'Jeanette, see to the Captain, would you please, dearest? He's shy, that one, eh? Try to ease his mind. You're so good at it.'

A burly, plod-minded Prussian the size of Kohler. A general with an Iron Cross First-Class with Oak Leaves was gazing benignly on.

To the Eurasian shopgirl, Chantal said, 'Kim, I want the silks brushed. Please, I insist, dear. All of them. You do such a superb job of it. Ah, Mon Dieu, Louis, if all our girls were as good as this one, there'd be no troubles.'

They reached the far end of the shop and passed between rows of headless, legless mannequins whose remaining anatomy was flimsily clad.

'One shouldn't sneeze in the company of such women,' offered St-Cyr drily.

'Nor in the company of these, Louis.' She parted the curtains and said, 'Girls, it's all right. This is only Monsieur Jean-Louis St-Cyr, the famous detective from the Sûreté.'

They were naked and there were three of them. All trying on the latest things while Muriel, grey-haired and dressed in a severe suit of grey pinstripe with broad lapels, smoked one of her endless cigarettes and hardly lifted an eye to him.

'They're a feast, aren't they, Louis?' teased Chantal, squeezing his arm. 'Me, I thought you would like to see them. That one with the dark hair and the splendid breasts is Martine; that one

51

who is very petite like me and so magnificent, is Brigitte, and the last, a favourite for us because she is everything a young girl should be, is Julie. Alas, they are all taken, Louis, but me, I will console you.'

They took tea in the cluttered office. St-Cyr fingered fabrics – silks, taffetas, crushed velvets, satins and laces. He loved to touch them.

In turn, she stroked his hand and let concern well up in her lovely brown eyes that were still so very clear and large, the lashes long. 'Now tell me about it, eh? Why a German, Louis? Oh for sure he's handsome, but he will drop her. We both know this.'

He shrugged. 'That's not why I came,' he said lamely. 'Chantal, I need your help. We're on a murder case – a boy. It doesn't make much sense but there's something about it I don't like.'

She understood but waited patiently. She refilled his cup but followed Muriel's ritual of first pouring the milk and then adding the sugar. Two teaspoonfuls. Louis had once been such a handsome man – they'd both agreed about this. He still could be if only he'd . . .

'First, there is the perfume,' he said, 'and then there is the purse.'

He was lost to her now, the eyes distant as he conjured up the film of the murder. 'The perfume,' he said. 'It has civet as its fixative. That particular tincture has been used to remove certain rough edges, you understand. Me, I think there has been a little too much jasmine – it's a shade heavy, Chantal. This is something very personal – a woman who knows her own mind and is very positive, isn't that so? Lavender is involved – that breath of spring, the essence of constant love. A touch of angelica, some vetiverol and bergamot, I think. Yes, I'm certain of it.'

She looked with admiration at this cop who could be so sensitive. Her tiny heart exploded at those words of his.

While concentrating on the perfume, he continually felt the fabrics as a designer would.

That a woman should ever leave such a man! Ah, Mon Dieu, what was the world coming to?

'The purse,' said St-Cyr distantly. 'The scent was on it. There was a small crystal vial as well – twists of cobalt blue glass – candy stripes of it, Chantal. Very, very nice. Very expensive. Something Victorian, I think.'

'English?' she asked quietly.

'Yes . . . Yes, English. With a silver top in the shape of a crown.'

'A sceptre?' she prodded.

'Yes . . . Yes, the head of a sceptre.'

'And the purse, Louis. It struck you, did it not?'

His eyes were moist and sad – wounded. Ah Mon Dieu! 'Electric, Chantal. Shimmering flashes of bluey-greens – forks of them beneath beads that were pearls.'

At once she was firm. 'The pearls would spoil the look of the silk. The woman should have asked for sequins or cut-glass beads so as to flash the fire of the silk and match the motions of her body as the dress moved with her. Like Northern Lights, Louis. The aurora borealis.'

'Flowing, Chantal – rippling across the heavens as she moved,' mused St-Cyr. 'It is what I have thought myself.'

'Is she German or French, this murderess?'

'Ah! She did not commit the crime, not her. At least, I do not think she did.'

'But is she French, my friend?'

He nodded – longed for a cigarette but realized Kohler had only loaned him one and that he'd carelessly tossed that away, not thinking to have saved the butt. The big shot on a case.

She obliged and told him to take several. 'As many as you think will tide you over. Go on. Ah, don't be shy. The Boches, they bring us plenty.'

The generals, the captains and the lieutenants.

'What did Marianne buy?'

'Some lingerie, what else? He picked it out for her. She was very shy about it, Louis. Muriel made her undress – completely, you understand – while I kept the lieutenant busy with little things.'

Was nothing secret any more? 'So, you can help?' he asked. 'The purse first, I think, and then the scent. The one should lead you to the other, and my feet are tired.'

'How much time do you have?'

'Two days.'

'Two . . .?' She raised her pencilled eyebrows.

'The General von Schaumburg has insisted,' he said, grimacing.

'My poor Louis, it's just not your day. Muriel will know what to do. Try to call back this evening or in the morning, but not before eleven thirty, please.'

'I'll be out of town by then.'

'At the scene of the crime?'

'Yes, at the scene.'

So it was still to be a kind of secret from them. 'You do not trust us?' she said – one would have thought her near to tears. 'It's always the same.'

'Fontainebleau and a back road to Barbizon. Three a.m., and a boulder right between the eyes.'

'A crime of passion?' she asked, delighted with his confidence.

'Yes – me, I think so but I am wondering what sort of passion and this, my dear, dear Chantal, I firmly resist telling you.'

At the door she took his hand in hers and brought it to her lips. 'Take care, my dear detective. Don't worry so much about your wife. A far more brilliant star will come to shine over you and share your bed. Me, I am certain of this.'

Not until he was out of sight of the shop did he stop to look at the vial of perfume he'd pinched.

As a man to the woman of his dreams, he opened the tiny vial and brought it to his nose. First one nostril and then the other – no need for blotting paper samples. None at all.

Muriel had called it Mirage.

Satisfied, he screwed the silver sceptre back down on its candy stripes of cobalt blue glass and ice-clear crystal.

Then he lit up, gratefully filled his lungs, and started out again.

Now he'd find the maker of the dress to which the purse had belonged, and then he'd find the name of its owner.

Kohler gripped the counter. 'What the hell do you mean, your boys lost him?'

Glotz continued mining the bulbous, hairy nose before examining the dross with the eye of a scientist. 'Just *that*, my fine Bavarian friend. He bought a sack of salted chestnuts.'

54

Glotz rolled the dross into a ball.

'So what the fuck have chestnuts to do with things, eh?' demanded Kohler.

The Bavarian was even picking up the French idiom. Been too long on the beat perhaps. Due for a change. Siberia.

Glotz flicked the cannon-ball away. 'Look, it's simple, Hermann. After he left the restaurant on the rue St-Denis, St-Cyr played the man on holiday but paid no attention to the whores. He bought a sack of chestnuts, then went into the National Library to borrow a book. Who knows? He left two of the chestnuts on one of the desks in the central reading room.'

'You schmucks! You call yourselves the Watchers. Christ Almighty, don't your boys know that place has seventeen exits that are clean? Louis had his eyes on you all the time.'

Louis . . . 'So, what's he up to that requires such secrecy?'

Kohler silently cursed himself. 'Nothing. It doesn't matter. Louis had to have a bit of time off.'

Glotz grinned. He ran pudgy fingers over the plain oak desk that was scarred with scratches and initials. 'He didn't go to see his wife,' he said and smirked. Toying with Kohler had its moments.

'Louis wouldn't do that. He has his pride.'

'So, where did he go then?'

One could push shits like Glotz only so far. 'I don't know. Looking up a few friends, I guess. Louis has plenty of them from before. He'll be working on the murder. He'll tell me all about it when I see him. We're heading south again.'

'You taking the Frenchman's shooter with you?'

'Yeah, I'm taking it with me.'

'How long?'

'Overnight – a couple of days – a week. Christ, I don't know.'

'What about von Schaumburg's daily reports?'

Did Glotz have ears everywhere? 'What about them, eh? We'll telephone the old fart and let the world know all about it.'

Implying the Gestapo tapped von Schaumburg's line, which they did.

Glotz fiddled with a pencil. 'This murder, Hermann. From what I hear it's a matter of some concern.'

The diamonds, probably. Jesus Christ! 'It's a nothing case. A nobody. Just some pretty boy who got his head bashed.'

'By a girl.'

'Yes, by a girl.'

Glotz fingered his double chin. 'You're not telling me much, Hermann. It would be better if you did.'

'Fuck off. You creeps don't know your jobs. Me, I thought you were supposed to be really something. Top quality. Right from Himmler's nest.'

Eggs. So, all right, you prick! 'Care to hear a little something, or are your ears still plugged from the Somme?'

'Listen, you . . .'

'Okay, so I'll listen.'

Kohler knew Glotz had him where he wanted him but even so he had to say, 'You should have been with us. We'd have shown you what war was all about.'

'Lawyers don't manhandle field guns.'

'No, I guess they don't. Besides, you'd have been too young, wouldn't you? Still at your mother's breast.'

'I resent that. I was eight years old at the time.'

Kohler nodded. 'You see what I mean. Some men never leave the tit.'

The hand closed over the cigarettes and matches. As he got up, Glotz tugged the heavy suit jacket down over his fleshy rump and paused to button it.

'You're getting fatter,' breathed Kohler. 'Like pork. Paris suiting you, eh?'

Glotz ignored the remark. One word to von Schaumburg from Kohler and there'd only be more trouble. But still there was the matter of the diamonds to consider. Yes, there was that, and something else.

Down in the bowels of the Sûreté, the smells rocketed up at them. They passed several detention cells. There was water on the stone floor in two or three places, blood in another. Weeping from one cell, the sounds of some poor bastard throwing up his guts in another.

Kohler gripped himself. An interrogation already? That maid . . . that little piece of ass with her boulder . . .

They went into the sound room at the far end of the corridor. Green lights, headphones, perpetual dusk and silence, batteries of tape recorders slowly turning. Secrets, . . . secrets . . . Only one of so many such rooms.

Glotz took him to a spare machine and found a spool of tape. 'So, the earphones, Hermann. You put them on, in case you didn't know.'

They both did, and the spool began to turn. At first there was nothing, then some static, the scraping of bedsheets perhaps. Finally, a woman's earthy sigh.

Then the voice of a man, the accent unmistakably German. 'Liebchen . . . higher . . . higher. Yes . . . yes, that's it. Higher still. Now in.'

The woman gave another sigh, a moan – a series of these – and then a savage grunt as she pushed herself back against him.

The bed began to rock, she to moan and twist her head from side to side and suck for air, Steiner to laugh. In and out. In and out. 'Erich . . . Erich . . . more . . . more. Hurry . . . Hurry. I'm coming, chéri. Coming. Ah, Mon Dieu, Mon Dieu . . . Come, Erich. Come!'

She threw her face into the pillows, perhaps biting them, was utterly lost apparently as Steiner slammed home and let her have it with a ragged gasp, a slap of choice rump, and a final, 'Ahh,' that was long and tortured.

The woman cried out too. 'Your knees . . . Your knees, Erich. I must grip them as I . . .'

She must have straightened up – left the pillows or something. Then the purring started, the whimpering. 'Erich . . . Erich, don't ever leave me.'

Kohler dragged off the earphones but found only sadness and defeat.

Glotz watched him closely. The Bavarian's eyes were a pale, insane blue and very hard. No smiles . . . none whatsoever.

'So, what the fuck do you want me to say?'

'Nothing. I just thought you'd like to hear it. We'll try to have some film for you the next time you're in.'

'And Louis?' Kohler swallowed.

Glotz removed the spool of tape and caressed it. 'That depends entirely on yourself, Hermann. A little more co-operation, I think. Yes . . . yes, that and a closer watch on your friend.'

And the diamonds – one mustn't forget them, thought Kohler, sensing even greater trouble but not wishing to think about it.

'Shits like you deserve the Russian Front.'

'Perhaps it is yourself who deserves it, Hermann.'

'What's that supposed to mean?'

The creep slid the spool of tape back into its box. No doubt he'd listened to it several times.

The Bavarian didn't like him, but liking or not liking really had nothing to do with things. He wouldn't look at Kohler yet. No, he'd pause, and then he'd say, 'Full reports on this murder, Hermann. Everything you give von Schaumburg. Everything you give the Sturmbannführer Boemelburg and,' he turned to look up at him, grinned, and continued, 'everything that Frog of yours finds out. Yes, that, Hermann, and everything the two of you hold back. It's a matter of priority. Orders straight from Berlin. Now bugger off and find him. Make the Frog croak or else we'll have him in for a listen.'

Kohler grabbed the jacket and burst the button. 'You shit! You haven't the fuck of an idea what it's like out there, have you?'

The jungle.

Glotz brushed himself down and examined the empty threads. 'Berlin will hear of this, Hermann. Your conduct is under investigation so don't forget it.'

The scissors and the sewing machines were going like crazy in the cutting room of the Salon Chez Nadeau above the shop on the rue de la Paix.

St-Cyr could see his fingers beneath the remnant of silk, it was so sheer. The late afternoon light filtered in. Outside, a bit of snow was falling.

He brought the silk up to his nose. Ah, Mon Dieu, such sensuality. A cheek was brushed.

For an age he sat there, an island in that sea of busy women, a man in touch with an image, a mirage.

His fedora lay on the table to one side.

'Is she tall?' he asked, but the girl had left him to give orders to someone or to carry them out herself. Very capable, a very petite *jeune fille*. Brown hair, brown eyes, still a certain fierce hesitation even yet. That of a cornered rat. Age twenty-four now and still unmarried. Rescued from the streets at the age of fifteen and given a lecture, 300 francs and a job or else.

Saved, some would have said, but not to her face. Too busy

58

now to remember, and anyway, one shouldn't hold that sort of favour over a girl. Ah no, one certainly shouldn't.

He reached for the shears and carefully cut off a wedge of the fabric, sufficient to catch its shimmering iridescence.

Sylviane Valcourt came back with her boss, he tall, suave and extremely handsome – age forty-two, married with three children, a mistress in Auteuil and a summerhouse near Châteaudun.

Julian Nadeau's hand was on the girl's shoulder. The dark grey suit had the look of elegance about it, so did the silvery blue tie and the white shirt with its starched collar.

The dark eyes betrayed a certain inner anxiety. The girl was watchful.

'Sylviane, would you leave us, please?' asked St-Cyr. 'I'm sure you'd sooner get on with something else, eh? Just for a few minutes. I promise I won't keep him too long. It's really nothing.'

Nadeau told her it was okay but brushed a hand over the back of her neck for good measure. 'Louis is an old friend. Please see to the Baroness's things. She wants the dress for this evening. Everything must be perfect.'

'Did you think I didn't know that?' came the acid retort.

She still had the walk, that saucy flick of her hips that had so intrigued the patrons of the rue St-Denis. St-Cyr followed her with his eyes before holding out the wedge of fabric in question and then carefully pocketing it.

The dark eyes settled on him. 'Must I?' asked the designer and part owner – only part owner – of this cushy little business.

'I think so,' said St-Cyr. 'One old favour deserves a new one, eh? Isn't that so?'

'That business was over years ago. Must you . . .'

'Insurance fraud and arson, Julian. Questions are still being asked. It's just too bad, my friend. Me, I've done all I can but you know how the Germans are. Records – ah, Mon Dieu, you should see the records those boys have got their hands on.'

He rolled the remnant bolt over to take up the rest of the fabric and emphasize the point.

'How did you know we'd made the dress?'

St-Cyr shrugged. 'Me, I didn't. You were one of six possibilities. The sixth on my list.'

The little insult couldn't fail to help.

'Who told you it was us? Was it Callot . . .?' Nadeau irritably ran a hand over his beautifully trimmed black hair. 'Lelong . . . it was that Lelong.'

'It was guesswork, Julian. None of your competitors fingered you. Pure legwork, and a simple process of elimination.'

'Look, I can't tell you the woman's name. Some things must be in confidence. There's an absolute principle involved. Absolute!'

Suddenly bored with it all, St-Cyr got off the dressmaker's stool and reached for his hat. 'She's a singer in a nightclub, Julian.' It was just a guess, a shot in the dark.

Nadeau nodded and felt the fatherly patting of his elbow. 'So, okay, let's leave it, eh?' said St-Cyr. 'If not the name of the woman, then that of the club.'

'What's she done? Look, I'm not interested in her, Louis. She's just a customer. Once – only once. A referral and trouble at that.'

The things one learned. 'I didn't say you were interested in her, and so far as I know, she hasn't done a thing.'

Now a gentle squeeze of the forearm just for good measure.

'Then why . . .' began the designer irritably, only to break and give in. 'The Mirage on the rue Delambre. It's a cabaret.'

'It's got a nice name. Me, I'm aware of the place but,' St-Cyr gave another shrug, 'I must confess I did not think to connect the two.'

Before he could be asked what he'd meant, St-Cyr was in among the seamstresses, nodding to one, exclaiming over the dress another was making. A last look down the long length of the cutting room showed Julian and his assistant forlornly staring his way while the women continued to bend to their work.

He waved his hat and left them to it. He thundered down the staircase, clicking his heels to some unheard dance tune.

When he reached the ground floor, he straight-armed the shop door and was soon absorbed in the traffic's hush.

Trust Muriel to have named the perfume after the club but why the pearls instead of glass beads or sequins?

Perhaps Sylviane had run out of them.

Kohler was drowning his sorrows in a small café directly

across the rue du Faubourg St-Honoré from Fournier's. He was writing up the next day's report for von Schaumburg.

'I thought I'd file it early, Louis, so as to get ahead of him. Boemelburg was pleased with the idea. What did you come up with this afternoon?'

'Not a blasted thing. Me, I'm beginning to think all my contacts have deserted me.'

'Well, never mind. Oh, hey, I've got something for you. The last can in Paris, Louis. The very last – even with the original seals.'

Five hundred grams of pure gold, Virginia pipe tobacco.

'The bastard owed me one,' said Kohler. 'I thought you'd be pleased?'

'Me, I am. Certainly,' exclaimed St-Cyr, raising two fingers for more beer.

But not breaking, not giving in, though it hurt.

'I've got the address book,' hazarded Kohler.

The Frenchman waited for the beer to arrive before saying, 'Good. *Salut!*'

'I've got the monogrammed silver cigarette case,' offered Kohler. 'It was in the purse.'

Good again. Another sip. 'Louis, this thing's too hot for us. You know that, don't you?'

The poor guy actually grimaced before saying, 'Yes . . . Yes, I'm beginning to be aware of this.'

The Bavarian reached for his refresher and decided to let him have the last word. A guy needed that now and then.

'What did Records cough up?' asked St-Cyr, not leaving his beer.

'Nothing. A mug-shot's being circulated to all district Gestapo offices and préfectures of police.'

'Good.'

Kohler silently swore. Louis was being tight at a time like this! Reluctantly he slid the address book along the zinc between them and watched as St-Cyr carefully opened it.

The penmanship was very neat, very feminine. It was not an address book, but a record of assignations.

5 *April/42 – the château* Which among the hundreds? he wondered.

21 *April/42 – the Louvre: Sculptures Gallery, 4.10 p.m.* Which

piece of sculpture, eh? So many had been taken to repositories in the south. Things were slowly filtering back, but still the galleries had that empty look.

28 April/42 – evening performance. Main foyer of the Opéra during the first intermission of Puccini's La Bohème Champagne perhaps?

7 May/42 – Fontainebleau: the Palais. Afterwards the Auberge de la Renard d'Or, then a walk in the woods Nice, that was very nice.

18 May/42 – Place de l'Opéra just before noon – 11:53 exactly Did he detect a note of sharpness in the use of the word *exactly*?

19 May/42 – Hotel Ritz, Room 211 at 10.00 a.m. A German officer then. One of von Schaumburg's staff? he wondered. The Army had requisitioned the Ritz.

14 June/42 – Fontainebleau Woods, the Crossing of the Thorn Bushes. About 3.00 p.m. From there to the car-park at the Gorges de Franchard.

St-Cyr had forgotten his beer. Kohler watched him intently before asking, 'What is it, Louis?'

The Frenchman gave a shrug. 'I was just visualizing the map of Fontainebleau Woods. That crossing is to the east of Barbizon some two, maybe three kilometres; that car-park is south from there perhaps four or five kilometres. I will have to check.'

'But it's lonely?'

He knew what Kohler was thinking. 'Not particularly. But then . . .' he tossed an indifferent hand . . . 'the woods are not as well visited as before the Occupation, so yes, my friend, it could quite possibly have been lonely.'

'Anything else?' asked Kohler, only to see him continue with the list.

18 June/42 – the château This assignation had lasted for two days. There then followed a series of places in quick succession, the first three of which had been in the Unoccupied Zone.

27 June/42 – Marseilles
28 June/42 – Lyon
29 June/42 – Nevers
30 June/42 – Orléans
1 July/42 – Tours
2 July/42 – Angers

And then: *7 July/42 – 4.17 p.m., main floor, Galeries Lafayette* (one of Paris's largest department stores.)

8 July – Barbizon, Hôtellerie du Bois Royal . . .

'Do you mind if I keep this overnight?' asked St-Cyr. 'I'd like to give it some thought.'

'Be my guest.' Louis hadn't wet his whistle in ages so what the hell was up?

'And the cigarette case?' asked St-Cyr. 'You might just as well let me have everything, Hermann. It'll make things easier, eh?'

Kohler thrust the thing at him. The Frenchman ran his eyes and a thumb over the Russian silver. Even during the last days of the Tzars, they had produced some outstanding pieces.

The case was of silver-gilt, so a silvery-grey, but with delicate patterns and scrolls in deep, dark blue, pale turquoise, ruby red and golden yellow enamel.

The initials had been inscribed on the inside of the lid: NKM in large letters that used up more than half the available space.

There were twelve cigarettes beneath the clip.

Kohler grinned and said, 'Go on. Try one, Louis. I already have.'

The cigarettes were Russian. If the woman used them then she had to have the lungs of a T-35 tank!

Eyes watering, St-Cyr went to stub the thing out only to have Kohler grab him by the wrist and pluck the cigarette away. 'There's no sense in wasting it, is there?'

He shook his head. 'Now for Fournier's, I think, and a look at those stones you held back.'

Must he be so pious about it? 'I didn't ask Glotz to have you tailed, Louis.'

The moustache was wiped with a knuckle. 'Me, I was certain you hadn't but then . . . ah, what can I say, Hermann? Sometimes you and I, we ought to confide everything in each other, eh?'

Then why the hell don't you? demanded Kohler but didn't bother to say it.

There were eighteen uncut diamonds in the soft brown velvet bag with its drawstring of twisted gold silk thread. Ice blue, emerald green, yellow – a soft, frosted pink, a frosted white – waterworn both of those. Cubes, modified cubes and octahedra with sharp crystal faces and angles.

In weight, the crystals varied from perhaps one to five or six carats. St-Cyr held his breath. It was a stunning collection.

Fournier's manager anxiously pressed the evaluation sheet

down on the glass of the display case. The writing was a scribble, barely legible but beside each stone there was a long dash, then the weight in carats and an estimate of the value as is, and if cut and polished.

'You won't say anything about this?' pleaded the man. 'It would only cause trouble.' He dabbed at his brow.

'Of course not,' soothed Kohler. 'You can depend on us.'

The man was stung. 'Who else could give such an evaluation? The Jews controlled the diamond trade before this . . . this war. He's very good. He can cut them for you, Monsieur the Commissioner. He can . . .'

'Inspector,' answered Kohler. 'He's the Chief Inspector.' He tossed his head towards St-Cyr. 'We work as a team, just the two of us. *All* alone.'

The little man flicked his gaze anxiously from one to the other of them, wondering what the devil was really up. 'If you have them cut and polished, messieurs, the stones will be of much more value and far less difficult to sell.'

St-Cyr fixed him with a look he reserved for the worst of the worst. 'But as is, they are much better than currency and far more portable.'

Russian silver and Russian diamonds? he wondered.

Uncut, their value exceeded 1,500,000 francs. 'An estimate,' offered the man lamely. 'I hope it agrees with the others?'

Kohler gave him a look that spelled the Santé Prison. 'How much is that wrist-watch? That one,' he said, stabbing the glass with a shark's forefinger.

The dark eyes glistened with suppressed rage. 'It's 8,495 francs.'

The Bavarian grimly nodded. 'At least 2,000 more than it's worth, wouldn't you say, Chief?'

St-Cyr trickled the diamonds back into their little bag. 'What he means, monsieur, is that we have forgotten you already, eh? Just as you have forgotten all about this little business.'

He folded the evaluation sheet and, pocketing the diamonds, headed for the door.

Outside on the rue du Faubourg St-Honoré the evening's traffic had begun. There were bicycles and more bicycles. 'Hermann, just what, exactly, would you have done with the diamonds?'

64

Kohler snorted gruffly. 'What the Christ do you think? This war can't last for ever, Louis. We both know it.'

The war in Russia had got to Hermann after all. St-Cyr raised his eyebrows but didn't bother to warn him to be careful what he said.

They crossed the street and headed along towards the rue d'Anjou. 'Others must know of them,' offered St-Cyr.

Again there was that snort. 'Yes, others now know of them.'

'Then the matter's settled and their value can go into your report for Boemelburg and mine for Pharand.'

'But not the one for von Schaumburg, not yet.'

They passed a hat shop, another with leather handbags and gloves. There were fewer items, more spaces between them. 'Louis, why not tell me what you turned up this afternoon? This thing . . .'

'Yes, yes, I know it smells.'

'I can't let you keep the diamonds. Boemelburg will want to put them in his safe.'

Was there a hint of bribery in Hermann's voice? 'Only for this evening, Hermann. Tomorrow morning you can have them locked up. Stall a little.'

'Glotz will try to have you tailed.'

'But of course. It's understood, eh? So don't make so much of it. I'll be in touch if I need you.'

'I'll pick you up in the morning. We're going back to Fontainebleau to have a look around.'

'Let's hope it won't be necessary. There are far too many seminaries and von Schaumburg will insist we visit every one of them.'

'Glotz will use three men this time, Louis. One to hang back and two for you to see and lose.'

'But of course, my friend. I would not have expected less.'

Had Louis been touched by the compliment? 'Then take care. I'll be seeing you. Don't lose the rocks.'

They parted at the boulevard Malesherbes, St-Cyr heading towards the Madeleine and the entrance to the Métro there; Kohler to return to the Sûreté to pick up the car and to file his reports to Boemelburg and to Glotz.

*

High up on the rue Laurence Savart the boys were playing soccer again but stopped when they saw him trudging sadly towards the house.

Guy Vachon was the one to say, 'He's lost his wife. First the revolver, then the car, and now the wife.'

'Next thing you know, there'll be a funeral,' said Hervé Desrochers.

'We'd better let him have the ball,' said someone else. 'He looks unhappy.'

'He's thinking about another murder,' whispered Dédé Labelle. 'He always looks like that when he's contemplating a case. Let's just wave. That'll make him feel better.'

They did so, and St-Cyr waved back only to hesitate at the gate and then to open it.

Marianne, of course, was not at home. Methodically he hung the overcoat up, then plunked the hat on its peg and kicked off his shoes.

Then he went through to the kitchen to put the kettle on and to water the geraniums.

Later he sat by their bed with the light on above him and the diamonds scattered over the lace spread next to the cigarette case, the little notebook, and the vial of perfume.

Hermann was right. The case could only mean trouble for them.

9 July/42 – the Ritz again. Time 9.13 p.m. Stayed until after curfew. Left by the back stairs. Was driven home.

He opened the can of tobacco and began to pack his pipe.

Was driven home . . . Again he felt uneasy. Berlin wanting to know, von Schaumburg, Boemelburg, Pharand – Glotz as well – and of course the Kommandant of Barbizon, its mayor and chief of police.

Is it what I'm beginning to think it is? he wondered.

There was only one person who could really tell him. Not the maid, ah no, not her.

Reflections caught the shimmering iridescence of the fabric in the open lid of the cigarette case.

Would she be tall and willowy – a chanteuse with blue eyes and blonde hair?

Intelligent? he asked. But of course. Daring? That too. Why else the diamonds?

Someone's wife? he asked and thought not. The condoms in their little silk sleeves revealed a woman who not only knew what she wanted but went after it.

'Trouble,' Julian Nadeau had said. A customer of his shop only once, and trouble even then. 'A referral.'

Firefly lights and tiny blue flames broke the ever-present darkness of the streets. Occasionally a Gestapo car roared by or that of some German officer, but even then the black-out regulations called for tape across the headlamps and only thin slices of light.

All too soon the bicycles disappeared and the silhouettes of the pedestrians hastened to the nearest entrance to the Métro as the curfew hour approached.

St-Cyr was conscious of the two sets of footsteps: one ahead of him but across the street; the other behind him but on his side of the street.

Like Eros in the ether, we hunt each other, he said.

He hadn't been able to shake them. Glotz had really done a job this time.

A patrol approached – still some distance from them. Jackboots turned a corner. Their hobnails hammered, hammered at the dank, damp air through which the flakes of falling, melting snow gave but their hush of misery.

Suddenly a figure bolted out of the darkness ahead, and the sound of his shoes clattered on the paving stones. Running . . . running now for his life.

St-Cyr flattened his back against a wall. A whistle blew – shrill and hurting the ears, alarming everyone. A couple began to run – had they been necking in some doorway? The girl cried out, 'Henri, my heels . . .'

Her voice was filled with despair.

The boots hammered, hammered. The patrol broke into chase. Shouts of, 'Halt! Halt or we'll fire!' shattered the night.

Footsteps thundered past. The girl fell sideways into him, only to bounce away and hit the pavement, her boyfriend gone. 'Henri . . . Henri . . . Don't leave me!'

St-Cyr swore and leapt to grab her. 'In here. Quickly. Quickly. Sh!'

Lights were flung across the walls. The butt of a rifle hit the courtyard's wooden wall and burst the door open with a crash.

More lights. More shouts.

Now only this: a German corporal with a torch. He shone it into each nook and cranny. Garbage tins, littered refuse and empty, empty doorways began to appear with excruciating regularity.

Gunfire came from the corner of the street. The girl lunged! St-Cyr clamped his arm more tightly around her waist. She kicked him hard. She bit the hand that stifled her screams. He let her bite him.

'Don't. Please don't,' he hissed into her ear. 'There are Gestapo in the street. Gestapo!'

Her hair was soft and it smothered his face.

The corporal's torch settled on a cat which bolted as the sounds of gunfire came again.

Then there was only silence and the falling, melting snow.

The corporal stepped through to the street, accidentally hitting the courtyard's wooden wall with the butt of his rifle. Cautiously St-Cyr eased his grip on the girl.

When released, she didn't run. 'I've hurt your hand,' she said, still shaking.

'It's nothing,' he sighed, searching for his handkerchief and then wrapping it around his left hand. 'The boy will have got away. He'll be all right. You mustn't worry.'

'I'm not. He's a pig to have left me like that.'

'Have you far to go?'

They were so close. It was so dark. 'The rue Vavin. It's on the other side of the Luxembourg Garden. Number 23. Upstairs. At the top. I live with my sister and her husband. They've two kids, a boy and a girl.'

'Are you a student?' he asked.

'Yes . . . yes, I'm a student. You've no need to worry. I'm not a prostitute. I've no diseases but you must wash the cut and put some antiseptic on it as soon as possible.'

He'd do that of course, and he told her this. 'Let's go together then. The rue Vavin is on my way.'

She seemed relieved.

'You've broken a heel,' he said, cursing his luck.

The girl removed her shoes. 'This way I can run better. Have you a spare pocket? Mine, they are not big enough.'

He shoved the shoes into his overcoat and they started out. Her feet would be freezing. 'You'll catch a cold,' he said.

Once on the street, the steps began again. One set ahead of them, the other behind.

At first the girl tried not to notice them. They darted across the boulevard St Michel, leaving the Sorbonne behind them.

The steps were still there on the rue Racine. She gripped his arm. She said, 'Do you hear them?'

He answered, 'Yes . . . Yes, I hear them. Do you know the statues of the queens of France in the Garden?'

'Who doesn't?' she said tensely.

'Could you become one of them for a little while?' At this rate he'd never get to the Club Mirage. It would be out of the question.

They passed the Odéon, passed several staff cars with their dozing drivers, and headed down the rue de Medicis towards the entrance to the Garden.

The steps ahead quickened; those behind settled back a little. These boys were good, very good. They had anticipated the Garden; they'd even accepted the girl and had figured it all out.

As yet he hadn't seen or heard the third man Kohler had mentioned.

'So, okay, my friends,' hissed St-Cyr to the girl as their steps speeded up. 'In and to your left. Find the statues and let me find you there.'

He was gone for ever and when he came back, he moved so silently it was only by the smell of the stale pipe smoke that had clung to him in the courtyard that she realized he was there.

The girl had used her head and had stood directly behind one of the statues that looked down on the Medicis Fountain, wrapped in its cocoon of winter.

Quietly and calmly he said, 'They're gone. I've lost them, but there is still one other.'

He took her by the hand, and when she stepped down, she stood so close to him she could feel his breath on her face. 'Who are you?' she asked. He was a little taller than she.

'It doesn't matter. Let's just say, a fellow creature of the night.'

Her hand wrapped itself more firmly around his. Walking among the frozen flowerbeds – shivering, it was true – she felt a strange elation. Fear, yes – there was still some distance to go, but with this 'creature of the night' she knew she'd get home safely.

As to his 'other one', there were no steps that she or he could hear, and standing together, searching the darkness over the Garden, nothing but the silhouette of the Palais, the line of the roof tops, and the night sky above.

No bombers tonight. No air-raid sirens. The city was so quiet.

At the entrance to number 23, the girl asked if he'd come up, and he heard himself saying, 'I can't. I've something that has to be done.'

Again he was so close. She let a breath escape and quickly slid her arms about his neck. 'Hey . . . Hey,' began St-Cyr. Ah, Mon Dieu . . .

Her lips found his. His moustache tickled. Clinging to him, she pressed her eager young body to his and when they parted, he felt her breath against his chin and heard her softly saying, 'Thanks . . . Thanks for seeing me home.'

The third man stood alone by a darkened lamppost and when St-Cyr came along the street, Kohler stepped out to join him. 'You should have gone upstairs with her, Louis. That little piece of ass had the hots for you.'

'Me, I don't even know her name.'

'Since when did names have anything to do with it, eh?'

'Since when did you start working for Glotz?'

'I'm not. Boemelburg gave me the order.'

'Where's Glotz's third man then?'

'Lying in a gutter, kissing the pavement. If he asks, I'll say it was you.'

More trouble! 'Well, come along, my friend. Me, I'm too tired to argue.'

Kohler let out a snort. 'Admit it, Louis, I had you nailed.'

'If I'd known it was you, Hermann, I'd have lost you first and then the others.'

'Where to?' asked Kohler blithely.

'The Mirage, on the rue Delambre. I think I've found our woman.'

'Let's hope she spreads her legs. That little girl of yours has given me the humps.'

'She's not my girl but I've still got her shoes.'

Trust Louis! Kohler let out a burst of laughter. 'You don't just take a girl's shoes off, Louis. You take off all her clothes!'

The Club Mirage had done just that to seven beauties and this shut Hermann up.

Mesmerized, and grinning hugely, the Bavarian barged into the crowd until forced by its sheer numbers to stop.

The stage was still a kilometre away across a sea of tables and the postage stamp of a dance floor. There were some ostrich plumes for show perhaps, or to catch the draught of high-stepping legs and jostled breasts whose nipples appeared unnaturally red beneath the lipstick and the toothy smiles. The eyes were heavily made up, the hair dusted with sequins and decorated with plumes. The band played loudly first, and jazz second. The lead sax player, on a brief respite, read his news-paper while the piano player, caught between bars, refilled a glass from the shaky bottle above the keys.

'It's a nice place, Louis,' said Kohler appreciatively. 'Don't get a hard-on,' he added, jabbing him in the ribs. 'I'll talk to the one in the middle. She looks okay, doesn't she?'

A buxom blonde with spreading hips and gams like stumps. 'That isn't her,' said St-Cyr. It can't be!

'I didn't say it was. Will her tits sag in later life from all that bouncing?'

'Probably. Most Frenchwomen have sagging breasts anyway, Hermann. That's why your Army's here to hold them up.'

'Okay . . . Okay, let's circulate, eh?' Enough was enough.

'I'll take the balcony. Perhaps I can find us a table up there.'

'Round the side, on the right at the front, by that general.' Kohler stretched out an arm, the quintessence of discretion.

The general sat alone with a bottle of Krüg. Grey against the grey of the tobacco smoke that filled the air, he appeared solitary and aloof in that sea of ogling men.

He was smoking a cigarette. One black-gloved hand held the ivory holder.

The girls came to the end of their number and raised their

arms high above their heads before bowing to tumultuous applause, whistles and calls of 'How about a lay?' 'Over here, liebchen.' 'Right on the table!'

A gap in the throng on the lower stairs opened, and St-Cyr shot into it.

Before the war, clubs like the Mirage operated from 9 p.m. until dawn and people came and went. Now, because of the curfew at 12 p.m., they might lose a few customers but most simply stayed the night.

Locked in, but for the chosen few who could leave at any time, the clientele were subjected to the constant hustling of drinks, the endless talk, lots and lots of dancing and, interspersed with the sets, the increasingly risqué performances.

There were women in the crowd – French girls with their German boyfriends and lovers, occasionally a pimp and one or two of his girls, a few black market hoods and their molls, the usual riff-raff and lots of uniforms.

As he reached the balcony, the dancing began again. Couples filled the floor, crowded so closely they could hardly move. In defiance of the Reich and of anyone else who cared to object, the band played their version of 'Begin the Beguine'.

Cheek to cheek, fingertips of the men's left hands pressed hard against those of their partners' right hands, the couples rocked and turned. St-Cyr was caught, trapped momentarily by two non-coms who were heading for the washroom.

Forced to face the crowd, he saw the faces of the times transfixed in memory, frame by frame. The distant look of a woman whose German lover might be leaving soon; that of the German soldier who had really come to like and love his girl. Laughter here, whispered little confidences there. Blank stares up at him or at others on the balcony, from a thin man with big ears and very short, slicked-down, wavy light brown hair.

A girl who sat alone, waiting for her escort. Two men who were about to ask her to dance.

What did their faces say? Forget . . . forget . . . Live only for the moment.

Remember . . . remember later when you're old and this war is finished.

The women were not all young – far from it – but most of the men, being of the military, were under the age of fifty and over half of them would have been in their twenties. Even those with the older women who so often looked a little lost.

Their husbands in prisoner-of-war camps in Germany no doubt.

Marianne had liked to go dancing. Involuntarily St-Cyr searched the crowd for her until, finally lifting his eyes, he sought out the empty table Kohler had spotted only to find it taken and the general gone.

When he found a set of stairs behind a curtain, they led down to the kitchens at the back, and to the dressing-rooms. At once there was the din from the kitchens, the shouts, the smells and, behind him, the racket from the band and the crowd.

Quickly he ran his eyes over the doors: four of them and then a lavatory, or was it merely a closet? The place reeked of cheap perfume, toilet water, garlic, onions and sour red wine among other things.

The girls burst from one of the rooms to form a conga line against one wall of the corridor, their bare seats to each other. Mocking laughter in their eyes when they saw him standing there. One even swung her chest his way.

'A singer?' he asked. 'Hasn't this place got its chanteuse?'

Her eyes were big, brown, hard and glistening with mischief. Close up she looked to be over forty. 'I'll sing anything you want, my pretty, just so long as the price is right.'

Talcum powder had been spilled on her knees and all down the front of her.

'A girl in a fabulous dress made of this.' St-Cyr dragged out the remnant.

One by one the girls looked at him. The one with the big eyes and the big chest said, 'Hey, what's she done?'

He managed the self-conscious grin of a Peeping Tom caught in the act. 'Nothing. Me, I just had to see her again.'

'Then see and listen hard, my little bird. She'll be on in ten minutes.'

They crowded along the corridor. Apparently they were to run on to the stage or something.

He walked past the kitchens and found the door to the courtyard at the back. From there, between close walls that shot up to shuttered windows in the darkness, it was perhaps a hundred metres to the street.

73

There was a Daimler parked outside the courtyard door. The general from the balcony was sitting in the back. A lighter flicked, a gloved hand came into view and then the ivory holder and the cigarette. Smoke curled up from the flame. St-Cyr waited, unable to move from the crack in the courtyard door.

Frame by frame his camera turned.

Then the lighter went out and the car returned to darkness.

What was it about the stiffness of that hand? The shattering of a grenade? The concussion of a bomb?

Lost in thought, he eased the door shut and retraced his steps.

Kohler forced his way up to the bar and ordered two doubles from the Corsican with the face of ground meat and the hands to go with it.

'Pastis and beer – German if you have it,' he shouted, elbowing more space and turning to grin at the squirt who'd thought to object.

The swift dark eyes of the Corsican barman saw cop – this was apparent and deliberately so.

'The beer's from Alsace. You can take it or leave it.'

Kohler lit a cigarette. 'Make it three of them then,' he grinned, not batting an eye.

The fist gave the zinc a whisper wipe with the dirty cloth. 'You on business or pleasure, eh?'

Gott in Himmel, the racket was really something! 'Pleasure. I'm interested in the big one.' He tossed his head towards the stage and the thunder of kicks. 'Does she go with the boys, eh?'

'With you?' grinned the Corsican.

The fist with its rag had stopped. Kohler resisted the impulse to grab the bastard and yank him across the bar. 'With me,' he breathed.

'Then ask Rivard. He's her husband.'

Again there was that grin.

Kohler flicked a glance the length of the bar, then said, 'Let's have the drinks and I'll ask him later.'

'Rivard' looked like something out of a zoo. The red plaid workshirt and open leather jerkin revealed the gut of an iron barrel. He had the face of a mountain. All crags and clefts and paralysing cliffs. The wavy, jet black hair of a first-class hood.

It was he who watched the trade, never ceasing to let his eyes sift over the crowd.

'It's a nice place you've got,' acknowledged Kohler, hoisting the first of the beers and returning his gaze to the barman.

The Corsican watched him down it. Would the Gestapo now drink the pastis – without water?

'Those are for my buddy,' said Kohler, not bothering to add that he found the taste of anise and liquorice insipid. 'So now, my friend, while I've got your ear, you'll answer a few things, eh?'

'Fuck off.'

A hand shot across the bar but stopped to pat the chest. 'Just a few little questions. This is too nice a place for us to shut down, so . . . some answers. One: who owns it?'

'We do – my brother and I.' It was nothing secret.

'Rivard?' asked Kohler, not believing a word of it.

'Yes, my brother.' The man turned away to serve more drinks. He never really stopped – all grace and fluid motion. Lovely with the knife, no doubt.

'Drugs?' asked Kohler, smelling them.

'Don't be stupid, my friend. Where would we get them these days?'

'The same place you got the beer and the pastis.'

'No drugs. Search if you like.'

Kohler drew out his whistle and laid it on the bar. 'Are you serious?' he asked, toying with it.

He opened his jacket – still had his overcoat on. He let the Corsican see the Walther P-38 in its shoulder holster.

The man shrugged and turned to shout the length of the bar, 'Hey, Remi, we've got a hot one here. Wants to know if we'll serve him some hashish. Is it the oil you wish, monsieur?' fluted the Corsican.

Kohler's fist closed about the second beer.

'Brother' joined 'brother'. 'Look, all I want is the answer to one simple question.'

They waited. The kicks came to an end – more thunderous applause and all eyes turned towards the stage but three pairs of them.

'Why do you boys call this place the Mirage?'

It was Remi Rivard who grunted, 'Use your eyes, turd. Watch and see for yourself.'

They were both grinning.

Caught, transfixed, St-Cyr stood in the corridor beside the door to the kitchens. The woman who had come out of the second dressing-room was tall and willowy, just as he had imagined. But there all similarity ceased. From the back she had the most stunning figure of any woman he'd ever seen. The shimmering silk beneath the strands of tiny pearls was electric. The back was straight, the shoulders square and very fine, the waist slender, the hips . . . the seat . . . Ah, Mon Dieu, such a gift. Straight from the gods and only for them.

The legs were long and the fabric of the sheath clung to them. Her arms were bare except for bracelets of diamonds. There was a diamond choker round her neck. The soft blonde hair was piled up in waves and curls to reveal delicate lobes and dangling ear-rings of diamonds also.

For one split second their eyes had met and even from a distance of perhaps ten metres, he had known hers were not just blue but a superb shade of violet.

As he watched, she moved gracefully up on to the stage.

The house lights were dimmed. He shut her out of his mind for the moment – Hermann would report at length.

He went along to the dressing-room. The cheering died down. A hush took its place and then he heard her saying quite clearly in beautiful French, 'My dear, dear friends, I have a song that is especially for you.'

St-Cyr opened the door and stepped inside the dressing-room. At once another female voice said, 'Monsieur, what are you doing?'

It was the girl, the maid, the killer of that boy.

'Are you from the police?' she asked, dismayed and badly frightened. Just sitting there on her mistress's chair before the dressing table. Hands poised in her lap, the mending clutched. Reflections of her in the mirror.

He shook his head and managed a fatherly smile. 'The police? Ah no, mademoiselle. My name is Roger Dumont, from the fire marshall's office. I am merely here to see if you have the proper number of extinguishers in this establishment.'

She tossed her head and returned to her mending. 'I think it is in the corner, behind the screen.'

Had there been tears in the dark brown eyes? The girl was about twenty-two, of medium height and delicate build, but with strong touches of the peasant and brisk little movements. Quite petite – lashes that were long and almost black. Lips that were . . .

St-Cyr went behind the dressing screen. Clothes were scattered everywhere. A pair of white silk briefs, complete with lace, was draped carelessly over the top of the ancient fire extinguisher. 'It should be out in plain view, mademoiselle,' he said severely. 'Can you tell me, please, when it was last serviced? There is no tag.'

He had a momentary flash – a frame of the singer's figure in that sheath, buffed down, stripped completely and absolutely, before putting on the dress. Done in a hurry too. Had they been arguing? Surely she'd have had plenty of time?

She'd have raised her slender arms perhaps. Who knows? It was a thought.

He dropped the underpants as the maid came round the other end of the screen. 'You must ask the Rivards, monsieur. Me, I know nothing of such things.'

She was really quite firm about it. 'Would your mistress?'

The head was tossed, the short brown hair bounced. 'No, of course not. Is there anything else, monsieur?'

Her wounded eyes took him in . . . Steady, he said silently. Steady, my pretty thing. 'Has my visit upset you in some way, mademoiselle?'

The girl turned from him as if struck. The shoulders shook. St-Cyr picked his way through the clothing and came to stand behind her. 'You poor thing,' he said gently. 'Me, I have upset you.'

'It's nothing,' she said, bowing her head and hiding her face in a hand. 'Nothing, monsieur.'

The girl burst into tears. On the way out, she snatched up her coat, then fled along the corridor and out into the courtyard.

When he reached the street, St-Cyr found the Daimler gone and the girl standing destitute at the side of the road some thirty metres from him. She was staring down at the tiny blue flame that flickered from its kerosene pot. Was it safe to leave her like that? She'd break to pieces if he touched her. So fragile. Like glass. Like something de Maupassant might have written about.

The pull the girl exerted was almost magnetic. He could not leave her, yet he knew he must. In spite of the tears – in spite of everything – he had to ask himself if she had really killed the boy?

Tearing himself away from the courtyard door, St-Cyr went back to the dressing-room – was moving swiftly when he found the purse with its beads of silk.

What the hell . . . had Hermann . . .?

It was an exact duplicate of the one Kohler had found in the woods.

There was nothing in it. Nothing yet but tissue paper. Her ID and other papers, the keys to her flat, to a car, money, et cetera were in a dark blue alligator handbag behind the screen. The photograph didn't do her justice. The ID gave her name as Gabrielle Arcuri.

The address was Apartment 22, number 45, boulevard Émile Auger. It wasn't very far from the flat where Marianne was staying. In fact, it must be just around the corner.

A small brown purse yielded up the maid's name: Yvette Marie Noel, of the same address.

For a moment he stood there looking at the girl's photograph. The nose was aquiline, the eyes . . . ah, what could he say?

It's my night for young girls who are in trouble, he answered. There were some photographs, small snapshots – the turrets of a château, an osier field, farmhands at work, happier times perhaps. The boy – the photograph badly crumpled and blotched by tears. The Loire – he was certain of it. Flat-bottomed punts lay among distant reeds.

Reluctantly he stuffed the things back into her purse, then retraced his steps to the balcony only to catch sight of the stage and hear himself drawing in a breath. 'The mirage,' he gasped. 'Ah, Mon Dieu, it's magnificent!'

The pearls gave their lustre to the shimmering, sky-blue opalescent silk that was moulded so well to her body, every curve, every feature was at once exposed to view and yet not exposed.

She had the voice of a nightingale – strong and throaty, yet full of warmth and bell-like clarity. Wrapped in it, in the motions of her arms as she gripped the microphone or held them out, the audience was spellbound. Gabrielle Arcuri was at once every man's dream of a lover and the heart's dream of home.

And the song? he asked. Ah, but of course, 'Lilli Marlene'.

3

'Excuse me, Monsieur the Detective, but would you like my mother to take care of your house?'

It was Antoine Courbet from across the street. St-Cyr looked questioningly beyond the boy only to see the lace curtain fall into place.

The serious eyes continued to haunt him. 'We thought, monsieur, since you were on a very difficult case and your wife and son have departed, you might be away. The geraniums in your windows, monsieur, they do not look well. The pipes, they might freeze . . .'

'How much?' asked St-Cyr, resigning himself to the inevitable.

'Fifty francs a day.'

'Thirty-five, Antoine. Sadly, I cannot pay more.'

'Don't detectives make a lot of money?'

'Not this one.'

'But you're a chief inspector . . .?' The Germans had docked his wages too, the poor man. So sad in the eyes and wounded in the heart. It was just as Maman had said to Madame Auger. He'd go to seed and take up with whores or the bottle.

St-Cyr heaved a sigh. The whole street would now know the exact state of his house and goods but what the hell.

'The geraniums are worth saving, Antoine. Tell your mother I will leave a key for her under the mat.'

Kohler had dropped him off at around 3 a.m. He'd probably awakened the whole street with the hole that had mysteriously appeared in the Citroën's muffler. Another classic example of Gestapo care.

St-Cyr shut the door and went through to the kitchen. As he

patted the pockets of his overcoat, he remembered the girl's shoes and drew them out.

One heel hung by a few bent nails.

She'd been a girl of medium height and slender frame, a student. Eager . . . impetuous perhaps – that would explain why she'd been out after curfew. That would be the reason for the sudden embrace.

The kiss, he said, touching his moustache. The dark plays such mysteries with us. She not knowing who he was; he not knowing her.

He'd fix the heel before returning the shoes – some rubber cement if he could find such a thing, and then a few new nails, or perhaps he could simply straighten the others?

A shoemaker, he answered positively. It's a wise man who recognizes his limitations. The girl was far too young. He wasn't getting into that mess again. So many of the young men of France were away in the prisoner-of-war camps, the older men were having a field day.

Not him, of course. Ah no.

Kohler would be by in a few minutes. Being on Berlin time meant that the clock had been shoved ahead and everyone got to work an hour earlier – never mind the late nights. Those were extra.

He couldn't blame Marianne for leaving him. It was no life for a woman to share. Alone and celibate, he could take up fishing again. Ah yes. And the euphonium – he'd played it in the police band before the first wife had objected to his practising an hour or two a week. He'd played it in the interval between her and Marianne, had worked like a fiend and had got his embouchure perfect, the fingering . . .

Of course he'd be rusty now, but a few licks and he'd be in shape.

He didn't say, I'll kill Steiner. He knew it would be senseless to even try.

Others would be shot – hostages – and as for himself, he still had no taste for the guillotine.

The diamonds lay beside the velvet pouch. 1,500,000 francs and he was worrying about thirty-five francs to pay a housekeeper!

The notebook was to one side – more entries still to go

through. The monogrammed cigarette case didn't bear Gabrielle Arcuri's initials.

What, exactly, had happened and why was Berlin taking such an interest in things? Have we a scandal beyond all proportions? he asked himself, feeling sad for that little maid – sympathizing with her. She hadn't looked like a killer but then, ah Mon Dieu, so few of them ever did.

Records still had not come up with the name of the victim. He'd have received a call if they had.

Yet Yvette Noel had known the boy, had had a photograph of him in her purse. By just such things are criminals brought to justice, isn't that so? he reminded himself.

Had the next of kin been too afraid to claim the corpse?

Kohler leaned on the horn. St-Cyr scooped up the Arcuri woman's things and stuffed them into his pockets.

Out on the street, heads had appeared from several windows and doors. Hermann was in a foul mood and hit the gas while St-Cyr was only half in the car. In a cloud of exhaust they started off. 'The key!' shouted St-Cyr. 'I've forgotten to leave it.'

Kohler swore and ground the car into reverse. The key was waved and then dropped. The ring it gave as it hit the paving stones stayed with St-Cyr through the all-but-empty streets as they plunged downhill, heading straight for the Kommandantur.

'Von Schaumburg wants a word,' growled the Bavarian, reaching for a fag and letting go of the wheel. 'The shit must have got up on the wrong side of the bed!'

They'd start at the top of the chain of command. It would be the Army first, then the Gestapo, and finally Pharand of the SN.

And in between them, Hermann would pay Glotz a little visit.

Brooding darkly by one of the windows in his office, Old Shatter Hand swung to fix his gaze upon them. 'You took no fingerprints. You asked no questions of the local residents. Why haven't you been able to identify the victim?'

Kohler drew himself up. 'We have two suspects, General.'

'Their names? Why weren't they in your report, Sergeant?' He'd get to the 'report' later.

Blithely Kohler trod thin ice. 'We feel discretion is best, General – to protect innocent lives and let us carry on the investigation without undue interference.'

Von Schaumburg tore the cigarette from its holder and crushed it into an ashtray. 'You call yourselves detectives, Kohler. I want their names. *Undue* interference, how dare you suggest . . .'

Kohler even managed a smile. 'General, the daily police reports, and those of this office, are circulated. We'd like to stake out the suspects' flat and see if anyone else is involved in the case.'

That was nice, thought St-Cyr, wondering how Hermann would handle Boemelburg.

Von Schaumburg fussed with the Iron Cross First-Class with Oak Leaves that was at his throat. 'All right, one more day of your discretion, Sergeant. Then some answers.'

'*Jawohl*, General.' Kohler crashed his heels together.

The Frenchman found the general looking at him. St-Cyr . . . not entirely reliable. Questions were being asked about his loyalty.

'Dismiss, the two of you. St-Cyr, you're to see that the diamonds are handed over to this office.'

There was a moment of silence, an impasse. Then the Frenchman said, 'Wouldn't it be best, General, if you told us what you know of the case?'

There was a brief smile – more like a grimace. 'Inspector, you of all people should understand that when a general of the Reich gives an order to dismiss, he means it.'

Boemelburg was worse. He kept them waiting for an hour, then standing in front of his desk as he slid two freshly signed telexes over to them.

'A transfer for you, Hermann. To Gestapo Centre Kiev, effective three days from now. You'll see that Gestapo Mueller has signed it.'

'But, Herr Sturmbannführer, we've two suspects . . .'

'Have you searched the woman's flat?'

'No, sir. Not yet.

'Then do so and don't tell Glotz about it.'

St-Cyr read his deportation order – forced labour in Silesian salt mines. Three days hence as well.

So much for past acquaintances.

'Now the diamonds, Louis. Let's have a look at them.'

When handed the pouch, Boemelburg hefted it as a good cop would. Then he found a sheet of white paper and poured the stones on to it.

The eyebrows went up; the lips went down at their corners. There was a nod, bags under the eyes – the frames of past cases clicking over. 'Russian, Louis?'

'Perhaps, Walter. It's hard to say. They'll have come from South African mines.'

'Who evaluated them?'

'A Jew, but we guaranteed his being left alone.'

Again there was that nod, the blunt head moving only slightly.

'We'd like to keep those for another day, Walter. It'll help when we confront the suspects.'

Boemelburg ran a stumpy forefinger through the stones. They were such pretty things. 'Blackmail?' he asked.

Was there sadness or resignation in the look he gave? 'Blackmail perhaps,' said St-Cyr. 'But until we confront the woman, we won't really know.'

'Herr Himmler is insisting that I send him daily reports. I'm sorry, gentlemen, but I have no other choice but to demand the names of your suspects.'

Kohler wrote them on the paper, dotting the i's of Gabrielle Arcuri's name so hard that the diamonds jumped.

'Be quiet about this, the two of you, and I'll see what I can do about those telexes.'

Pharand was feeling very left out of things. 'You've not been straight with me, Louis. You've betrayed the good name of the department. As of now, this moment, your rank is back to that of inspector with the consequent loss of pay.'

St-Cyr knew that it was useless to argue. Kohler grinned hugely.

Pharand began the onslaught again. 'Talbotte, Préfet of Paris, demands to know why you have not consulted him about a murder in his territory.'

Talbotte was a real bastard.

'Well?' demanded Pharand.

St-Cyr let him have it. 'We have hardly had a moment's sleep,

Major. We're already working round the clock. If we have to deal with the Préfet of Paris *and* that of Barbizon *and* the General Staff *and* the Gestapo in Berlin, we'll . . .'

'Berlin . . .? What is this, please?'

Insidious, territorial himself, Pharand gripped the edge of his desk.

'It's nothing, Major. You know how Berlin is,' offered Kohler. 'Herr Himmler is always suspicious of you French.'

'Herr Himmler . . .' Pharand dropped his gaze. 'You should have warned me, Louis. It was most inconsiderate and unwise of you to have neglected this.'

'We only just heard of it, Major. I was about to tell you.'

'And the suspects – have you suspects?'

St-Cyr glanced at Kohler before shaking his head. 'Not yet, but we've some pretty good leads.'

Pharand touched the pasty brow. Three fingers . . . always it was with three fingers. 'Then I must tell you, Louis, that I have better sources of information than yourself.'

Fortunately, perhaps, the Americans chose that precise moment to direct one of their daylight bombing runs over Paris, heading for the Reich. But as the sirens wailed, Pharand refused to move. 'Their names, Louis. I must have their names and the value of the diamonds.'

The anti-aircraft batteries across the river had begun to open up. A duty sergeant stuck his head into the office and shouted, 'Air-raid!'

'Piss off,' said Pharand. 'They're not leaving this office even if a stray bomb should fall on us!'

St-Cyr gave him the names and the value of the diamonds.

'Was it a crime of passion?' demanded the major.

Did he like to hear it? 'Yes . . . yes, I think so,' said St-Cyr, 'and with your permission, Major, I think I can prove it to you.'

'Within three days,' said Pharand – had the Germans actually hit one of those blasted planes? The scream of shattered engines roared overhead. He waited for the crump of the explosion and when it didn't come, he said, 'So, that's all for now, Louis. A full report this evening, eh?'

Records still didn't have the boy's name and Glotz proved very difficult when Kohler went to see him alone.

'I warned you, Hermann. We've managed a bit of film and we'll have more by tomorrow.'

'Philippe!'

'Papa!'

Kohler parked the car two streets from Gabrielle Arcuri's flat on the boulevard Émile Auger. Marianne and the boy had obviously been for a walk in the Bois de Boulogne.

'I'm sorry, Louis. I didn't mean this to happen.' He felt a fool.

'It doesn't matter, Hermann. Me, I've missed the boy and his mother.'

St-Cyr started across the road. Released, the boy ran to him and, in spite of knowing there could be no traffic, St-Cyr tore his gaze away to search the street.

Relief flooded through him. The boy leapt into his arms and he lifted him up.

Marianne looked well. The straw-coloured hair had been braided into a rope which fell from under the scarlet beret to hang over the right shoulder against the dark blue overcoat. The face and brow were strong and wide, the eyes clear blue with crinkles at the corners. There was the blush of youth and weather in her cheeks.

'Marianne, there's no need to say anything. Me, I understand.'

St-Cyr rubbed the boy's back and gave him a hug and a kiss but didn't set him down. Not yet.

The dark blue gloves and black leather boots were new, not so the scarf he'd given her with the beret.

'How have you been?' she asked, searching his eyes – feeling perhaps some twinges of remorse.

Was she having second thoughts?

'Me? Busy on a case as usual. I've hired Madame Courbet to look after the house. There'll always be a key under the mat. I suspect you'll want to get in from time to time.'

'Are you hurting?' she asked. There was such sensitivity in her eyes.

'But of course I'm hurting. To be cuckolded by a German officer . . .'

'Would it have been any better if he'd been French?'

'No . . . No, of course not.'

They walked along the street, each feeling lost with the other, Philippe playing with his water pistol and saying, 'Bang! Bang!' at his father.

The poor sap, thought Kohler. He's mush before the woman when he ought to have smacked her face at least a couple of times.

They reached the corner. Kohler lit a fag and leaned against the car. There was only one thing to do for Louis. Keep the poor bastard hopping until he forgot about the woman. And as for Glotz and his film . . . von Schaumburg would tear the roofs off Paris if he found out what was going on.

'You must take what you like from the house, Marianne. Please, I insist. The boy's things . . . It's not easy to find good warm clothing these days in the proper sizes.'

'Erich's very generous. There is no problem, Louis.'

'Is he also married?'

'Of course. Look, it doesn't matter, eh? I couldn't go on. I had to escape.'

'You should have told me how you felt.'

She found the will to smile – she had such a warm and generous smile but this one was all too brief. 'Would you have listened? Louis, you were never home. Nights I'd lie awake wanting you beside me. A woman can *want* a man, can't she?'

St-Cyr nodded. He shrugged. He said, 'So, it's okay now, eh? He's there beside you.'

Louis could see through anything. 'I know he'll leave me, but it doesn't matter.'

He set the boy down. She took Philippe by the hand. 'Isn't Papa coming with us to our new house?'

'Ah no, chéri. He has to go to work.'

'Always he's going to work. He never stays at home.'

'Take care of yourself, Marianne. Me, I really mean it.'

'And you,' she said, giving him a moment more. Poor Louis, he looked so lost in his shabby overcoat and rubbers. 'Find someone else. Quit that lousy job before you do.'

St-Cyr watched as they crossed the boulevard Henri Martin. When they reached the other side, the two of them turned to look back – Marianne still emanating that strength of character and determination he had so much admired.

'Don't forget the key will be under the mat,' he shouted and gave a last wave.

Kohler raised his eyebrows. 'Come on, Louis, let's have a look at the woman's flat.'

'Yes, let's attend to business. We both know those papers Boemelburg shoved at us are for real.'

'I can't see you working in a salt mine.'

'Kiev is full of partisans, Hermann. You'd be assassinated on the second day. Me, I'm positive of this.'

'Then tell me just who the hell wants us out of the way and has taken the steps to see to it?'

'You tell me. You know the Berlin Gestapo better than I.'

'Mueller wouldn't have signed those papers of his own accord.'

'Then Himmler must have ordered it.'

'Three days – why three, Louis?' The number three had come up again!

'Why?' shrugged St-Cyr. 'Because it's one more than von Schaumburg gave us.'

'Do you get the feeling everyone's after us?'

'God included,' said St-Cyr. 'Him most of all.'

The building at number 45, boulevard Émile Auger was like all the rest. Flat, square, unfeelingly modern, cold, and facing the street and the world as if through hooded eyes.

The black-out curtains were still closed in one of the second-floor apartments though it was nearly noon.

'You or me?' asked Kohler, looking up at the curtains.

'Me, I think, Hermann. Yes, let me handle it.'

In the late 1920s and 1930s many of Paris's upper middle class had moved out of the old and fashionable areas of the city. Like decadent nomads, they had brought all the trappings of their lives but relished plumbing that worked, heating systems that, for the times, were the best available, and electrical wiring that did not blow too many fuses.

Even as they went up the steps, St-Cyr had a pretty good idea of what the apartment would contain.

The concierge, a middle-aged woman, reflected her station in life. Several strands of agate beads complimented the soft yellow cardigan and patterned blouse. No fool, she saw copper right away and demanded to know what they thought they were doing.

'Merely a matter of discretion, madame,' said St-Cyr, taking off his hat. 'A few questions of Mademoiselle Arcuri.'

'She's not here. She didn't come back last night.'

'Her maid?' he asked, lifting his eyebrows.

'She neither. Such weeping . . . that girl . . .'

St-Cyr waited, but the woman knew she'd already said too much.

'We'd like to take a look through the flat, madame. It's a matter of some urgency.'

He unbuttoned his overcoat and slid a hand into his jacket pocket, removing a black leather notebook stuffed with slips of paper, small bills, his ID and badge. 'We have a search warrant, madame. Do I have to show it to you?'

The brown eyes were wary. 'A search warrant? In my building? What's she done?'

St-Cyr tucked the notebook away. 'Nothing that we know of, madame – please don't alarm yourself – but her life, and that of her maid, Mademoiselle Yvette Noel, may well be in danger.'

At the door to the flat, St-Cyr gave the woman yet another look of grave concern. 'You may leave us, madame. I'm sure you have other things you must do. We will touch nothing and take nothing, of this you have our word.'

Tartly she told them to remove their rubbers and shoes. 'Mademoiselle Arcuri is very fussy.'

'I'm sure she is,' said St-Cyr. 'The rubbers and shoes, Hermann. It will be just as if we were at home, madame.'

'You may leave them in the hall. No one will steal them. Not in my building.'

The toe of Kohler's left sock had been completely eaten away and the toe itself was badly in need of a wash. He tucked it under and smiled subserviently at the woman. Not a word. Louis continued to surprise him. That business with the notebook was new . . . he must remember it.

Like so many of the wealthy upper middle class, Gabrielle Arcuri's flat was cluttered with furnishings of one sort and another, all of which, under the subdued light of day, gave back just that: their sumptuous clutter.

Polychromed deer, frogs, camels and Coromandel screens

framed Louis XV chairs and Chinese coffee tables. The baroque Italian mirror above the mantelpiece was huge, heavy and ornately carved with gilded cherubs, grapes, drapes and other things. A bronze Buddha on the mantelpiece was reflected in the glass, as was the Belle Époque chandelier among whose many crystals hung clouds of amethyst and smoky quartz.

Here was a woman, then, who had a taste for expensive things.

Kohler ran a hand over the headless, limbless statue of a young man. Since everything else was gone, only the most important parts were left. The kid had lots of fruit. A nice one too. Uncircumcised. 'Our girl, Louis. Just what the hell is she doing singing in a place like that?'

'My thoughts exactly, Hermann. Shall I take the bedroom while you find that of the maid?'

'Let's do it together, eh? Don't spoil my fun.'

Gabrielle Arcuri's bedroom had been done in soft pastel shades of green, yellow, powder blue and white. It was tastefully and distinctly feminine – less of the clutter, more room to walk around. One could imagine her doing so. The carpet was very soft, of a dove grey with a faint wash of blue.

Flowered chintz covered the walls; brocade and lace, the modest pastel green four-poster that was heaped with cushions and pillows.

Tidy . . . that was a first impression. Two crystal vases held white roses, there was a painted Louis XVI settee near the windows to catch the sun; an unpainted, Louis XVI dressing table and blue-covered, painted stool against the far wall.

She'd have seen the bed's reflection as she took off her make-up or put it on.

St-Cyr wished Kohler had taken the hint. 'Your vibrations are disturbing me, Hermann. This is not entirely as I expected.'

'Oh, in what way?'

'The purse and the condoms, eh? Quite obviously Mademoiselle Arcuri kept this room entirely to herself.'

Trust Louis to notice it. 'So, were the condoms for real or not?'

St-Cyr moved towards the closets on either side of the dressing table. 'Perhaps, but then . . .'

He left the thought hanging.

'What is it, Louis? You look as if you've found a body.'

'The clothes, my friend. *Très chic*, of course, but mixed with them, rough trousers of tweed and corduroy, a worn leather jacket, three-quarter length and not unlike the boy's, riding breeches, even a crop.'

'A whip,' enthused Kohler, reaching in to get it. 'Brown leather across the buttocks, Louis. Can you imagine that woman flailing some poor guy to get it up?'

'Frankly, no.'

'You're not offended, are you?' Kohler pulled down a lower eyelid.

'A little, yes. Hermann, we're dealing with a very complex character. On the one hand a second-rate . . .'

'Downright seedy . . .'

'Nightclub and this,' said St-Cyr, with a lift of his bushy eyebrows. 'A woman . . .' He touched a silk chemise. 'Someone's daughter, Hermann. You must always remember that even with the worst of prostitutes there has been a mother.'

'A château . . .' went on Kohler, prying open a hat box and ignoring the lecture.

'A monogrammed silver cigarette case.'

'Russian initials, Louis, and Russian diamonds.'

'Perhaps, but then . . .'

Again he left it unsaid. There were several evening gowns – all neatly pressed, nothing rumpled. The everyday dresses would have come to mid-calf length. Wools, cottons, two of corduroy for rough wear. A pair of brown leather driving gloves, a pair of Swiss hiking boots.

The gloves had been stuffed into one of the boots. Bits of oak leaves clung to the mud that was lodged between the rubber treads.

'Fontainebleau Woods?' asked Kohler.

'Perhaps,' said St-Cyr, 'but if so, then . . .'

'I'll check the maid's closets. Maybe the shoes will be there.'

St-Cyr waited, and when the Bavarian had left the room, he closed the closet door and moved over to the bureau, a sumptuous piece of inlaid mahogany that had been painted a pistachio green.

A rebel? he asked, or one so positive about the décor, she could ruin a valuable antique and think nothing of it.

Underwear – slips, brassieres, chemises and camisoles – lace again, but sensible things as well.

He lifted a stack and felt beneath it. Nothing.

When he found the revolver he let out a stifled gasp not just because it wasn't expected but because the hiding place was so stupid and the gun far too big for a lady.

A mirage.

It was a French Army Lebel six-shooter, one of the original 1873 models. It even had its lanyard.

Using the stem of his pipe, St-Cyr carefully fished the weapon out and brought the muzzle up to his nose. The weapon hadn't been recently fired. In fact, he had the thought it hadn't been used in a very long time. Not since the last days of the Defeat.

Breaking the cylinder open, he saw that the gun was fully loaded. He flicked a glance towards the bedroom door, didn't hesitate. Stuffing the gun into the waistband of his trousers, he buttoned up the overcoat.

When he moved towards the bed, St-Cyr imagined Gabrielle Arcuri stretched out on it, lounging with a book perhaps. Silk pyjamas – a soft, coral pink. The smell of her perfume . . .

A tall and very beautiful woman in that sanctuary of sanctuaries, her bedroom. With a loaded revolver but a few steps away. Why the gun? he asked and answered, Why unless she'd been afraid for her life.

'Louis, have a look at these.'

Kohler thrust the snapshots at him. All were of the boy – two showed him sunbathing in the nude.

He had a dreamy look in his eyes, was smirking up at the camera. No attempt had been made to cover himself.

St-Cyr gruffly said, 'Ah!' and stuffed the photographs into a pocket. 'Now take a look at this, my friend.'

The portrait photograph, in its silver oval, was of a French officer – quite handsome, quite the gallant, about thirty-six or so years of age, with a distant look in his warm and sensitive eyes. A dream.

'There's a son, also, Hermann. A boy of about Philippe's age.'

'And a map,' breathed Kohler, sliding open one of the bedside table drawers. 'A kid's drawing of the château and its grounds, Louis. In crayon.'

At sounds from the hall – at an argument of some sort – St-

Cyr snatched the child's sketch from Kohler and tucked it away in a pocket.

'The living-room,' he hissed. 'We've company.' *Merde!* Could nothing be done in private? Just when he was getting a feel for the woman, an interruption . . .

'Your names?'

'Kohler. Gestapo Headquarters Paris, General.'

'St-Cyr, of the Sûreté.'

'Your search warrant?'

The black-gloved fingers were bared and then snapped.

'We have none,' said St-Cyr, watching him closely. Such a man . . .

'Then get out!'

It was the general from the balcony at the club. 'General, could I ask why you're here?'

The French! 'Don't be impertinent. Your superiors will hear of this.'

'They will only ask me the same question, as will the Sturm-bannführer Boemelburg.'

The man swore. 'Her maid's been found. I thought she'd like to know.'

'Where?' asked St-Cyr, holding his breath.

'Fontainebleau Woods. Now get out of here, the two of you, and find her killers.'

Kohler went down the stairs first, then St-Cyr, then the woman and lastly that piece of Prussian SS glass with its black-gloved hands and once handsome face that was now such a mass of scars.

As they passed the concierge's room, St-Cyr stopped suddenly. 'Is that the morning's mail, madame?' he asked, ignoring the general.

'But yes . . .' she began.

'Permit me, please, to examine those two little parcels.'

'I thought I said . . .'

'General, we're on a murder case – expressly on orders from Berlin,' said Kohler. 'When my partner sees something, it's usually of interest.'

'Very well, but I must warn you . . .'

St-Cyr broke open one of the parcels – it was no more than ten centimetres long by perhaps two in width and height.

The woman sucked in a breath and gripped her heart as the little black coffin was exposed.

'The Resistance,' breathed Kohler. 'Louis, what the hell's going on?'

'One might well wonder, Hermann. It appears the Resistance have chosen to make an example of Mademoiselle Arcuri.'

'And her maid,' breathed Kohler.

'Fontainebleau Woods.'

'The house first, Hermann, and then the woods. I must pick up a heavy sweater and my hiking boots.' And hide a certain weapon.

It was only after they'd got into the car that Kohler told him, 'Louis, it wasn't me who said Fontainebleau Woods just then.'

St-Cyr nodded but said nothing.

Madame Courbet had been in to tidy up. The geraniums even looked better. She had put the day's mail on the kitchen table. St-Cyr fished through it searching for the negative of him and Kohler on safari and when it wasn't there, he began to worry.

It was raining when they got to Fontainebleau Woods and that didn't help. The Gorge of the Archers was south of the road that ran from Fontainebleau town to Milly-la-Forêt on the western edge of the forest.

One went in by a bit of rough gravel, but only so far. From a small clearing, a footpath led up into the gorge.

The flics in blue from Barbizon and Fontainebleau were everywhere and viewed their intrusion with hostile eyes.

'A classic Resistance killing,' snapped Beauchamp, the Préfet of Barbizon. A ferret with nasty looks and a manner that silenced.

'One through the back of the head,' added Cartier, the Préfet of Fontainebleau, a big man who enjoyed his soup. A father of ten, and strict about it. 'So, we can wrap things up, eh? Now that you two have seen all there is to see.'

'A moment, please, Commissioner. Allow us the privilege of assisting you,' said St-Cyr, water pouring off the brim of his fedora. They'd both get pneumonia.

Yvette Noel's wrists had been tied tightly together behind her back. She'd been dragged from a car and hustled up the footpath into the gorge, then thrown to her knees.

There were powder burns on the back of her head. Blood had run from her nose and mouth but with the rain, most of this had been washed away.

St-Cyr crammed his hands into the pockets of his overcoat. She'd been a little thing and so afraid. After hitting the ground she had tried to crawl away and her assailant had grabbed her by the wrists, dragged her back to her knees, and forced her head forward. No time to say her prayers. No time for anything.

'Time of death?' he asked.

'Does it matter?' snorted the Préfet of Barbizon. He'd show the SN.

'Yes, as a matter of fact, it does.'

'Our coroner has the flu.'

'Then get someone else to have a look at her!'

The ferret hit his forehead with the heel of a hand and swore. 'Another doctor, he wants! Georges, did you hear that?'

'I will send Lauzon for Dr Dandelin. He'll do a job for us,' said Georges.

'That drunk?' snapped St-Cyr.

'Ah yes, that drunk. He's very good with corpses.'

Something passed between the two men. Both St-Cyr and Kohler had a good idea what it was.

'We will want some photographs,' said St-Cyr, 'even though the light is poor.'

'Photographs!' You'd think he'd asked for the moon.

The Préfet of Barbizon motioned officiously for one of his men to go and fetch Hermé Thibault on his bicycle, a two-hour jaunt!

'We're old friends,' said St-Cyr, not bothering to explain or raise objection to the delay.

Kohler began to walk slowly around the girl, eyes glued to the ground. Each circle was enlarged. 'You bastards,' he said at one point. 'Fucking slobs. Don't you know anything?'

'The Resistance . . .' began Cartier. It all seemed so evident.

St-Cyr looked up at him. 'The Resistance from where?'

'Melun. Those bastards have been stirring up the shit with the local farmers.'

Who supply the Reich and the black market in Paris, thought St-Cyr. 'This girl had nothing to do with them.'

'Oh, and how can you be so sure, my friend? She has no ID. The bastards emptied her pockets and took everything.'

'She's the one who killed the boy on the roadside near Barbizon.'

'Ah! Why didn't you say so?'

'You didn't ask.'

Someone used a bit of sense and stretched a piece of canvas between the trees to keep the rain off her.

She was, of course, soaked through. The brown beret had been flung off by the hand that had swept her hair forward and had forced her head down.

The pistol had been crammed against the base of her skull, the shot fired upwards into the brain. She would have been no trouble for a man.

The flat-soled pumps were of a dark blue leather, the argyle stockings of greys and blues to match both the plain blue skirt and the shoes. Had she been wearing them last night? he asked, but couldn't remember. It would come to him in time.

'I should have stopped you,' he said, having been given a moment's privacy. 'Did you know this might happen, Yvette? Is that why you were so upset, or was it simply that you'd committed murder and known the Church would condemn you for it?'

'She can't answer, Louis. Maybe the slug that killed her will.'

Kohler had come to have a look. When St-Cyr raised questioning eyebrows, the Bavarian said, 'Nothing, Louis. They've buggered it all up. No tracks but their own flat feet. Not a thing.'

'Why would the Resistance send this girl a black coffin *after* they'd executed her?'

It was a good question. 'Maybe the post got delayed.'

'Those little parcels were mailed this morning in Paris, Hermann.'

'Are you thinking what I'm thinking?'

'Yes, I'm afraid I am.'

'The pond gets deeper and deeper.'

'And at the bottom there is only a mirage.'

Dr Émile Dandelin squeezed the last bit of good out of a soggy fag before pinching it out and pocketing the butt. 'So, my friends, another crime of passion, eh?' Fontainebleau Woods was famous for them. The things one found . . . Twice now, three naked couples . . .

When he saw the ropes, he cocked a pale blue, wary eye at Kohler who blithely said, 'Looks like it, doc. That brandy I smell?'

'Armagnac, please. It helps to keep out the weather.' A Resistance killing . . . an execution in the grand manner.

Dandelin dropped his little black bag and crouched to thumb the girl's eyelids and flex her fingers. Cold . . . she was so cold. A pretty little thing. A virgin? he wondered.

'Eight hours into rigor,' said Kohler curtly.

The bushy, rain-plastered head was tossed. 'An expert, eh?' snorted Dandelin. 'Not even the decency to examine her pretty toes.'

'We know she's dead, doc. We only want to know when it happened.'

A hustler. A typical German. 'Since when was Fontainebleau Woods on the Sûreté's beat?' he asked of St-Cyr.

'Just tell us the time, Émile. Don't kibitz.'

'So, okay, nine, maybe ten hours.'

'That would put the time of death at between 5 and 6 a.m.,' said Cartier, the Préfet of Fontainebleau. 'A dawn killing. It's typical of them.'

'The dawn comes a little later, Commissioner,' commented St-Cyr drily. 'We're almost at the winter solstice.'

Ah, Mon Dieu, the Sûreté . . . such big words . . . 'the winter solstice', as if the killing had been some sacred rite.

'You want an autopsy done?' asked Dandelin.

Kohler roared, 'We already know what killed her, doc. There's no need to examine the contents of the chicken's stomach!'

'She's a girl, a person . . .' began St-Cyr, only to shut up, shrug briefly and give an apologetic smile.

Hermé Thibault arrived, all arms and legs and gun-shy. Real lightning today. Two of the flics were delegated to hold a tarpaulin over him and the box camera on its tripod. In spite of the protection, he fussed, dropped things, forgot to wind the film, and in the end St-Cyr cornered him. 'So, where is that negative, my friend?' he asked.

Thibault's eyes darted away. 'The Resistance . . .'

'What do you mean, the Resistance . . .?'

'They came. They smashed all our billboards – my backdrops – and cut off my wife's hair. She . . .'

'She *what*?' demanded St-Cyr. Hermann was watching them.

'They asked if we knew the names of any collaborators in important positions and she gave them that negative of you and him.'

'Thanks . . . thanks a lot, my friend!' swore St-Cyr. As if they didn't have enough trouble already!

To make it a full house, Talbotte, the Préfet of Paris, arrived in a fresh downpour. A man of around sixty, square of build and of medium height, he had Basque blood in him somewhere, the swift, hard eyes of a gangster and a voice that carried.

Everyone present knew why he had come. The Île-de-France* was his turf and the Sûreté had the rest of the country to forage.

Barging through the assembly, he strode up to the corpse, took one look around, then snorted, 'As they say at the track, St-Cyr, step into the shit and let us get on with the race.'

'We only wanted the time of death and a few photographs for Berlin,' offered Kohler, enjoying himself.

The Préfet scoffed. 'Since when would Berlin be interested in such a death?'

'That's what we'd like to answer,' offered St-Cyr evenly.

'You'd like to answer,' mimicked Talbotte, clucking his tongue. 'Well suck lemons, my old one. This little thing is ours.'

'Come on, Louis,' urged Kohler. 'We'll let the brass sort it out.'

'Me, I am the *brass*, my friend,' challenged Talbotte.

Then he asked the one question no one had asked. 'Who notified you of the killing?'

It was Beauchamp, the Préfet of Barbizon, who answered, 'A woman, Commissioner. By telephone, this morning at about eleven o'clock.'

'From where?' demanded Talbotte.

'From the Jardin des Lapins Petits, that little restaurant in the woods on the outskirts of Arbonne.'

'Half-way between Fontainebleau town and Milly-la-Forêt,'

* Paris and its environs.

said St-Cyr. 'Perhaps four kilometres to the north of us, Hermann. A little more by road.'

'How did she sound?' asked Talbotte. 'Distressed?' he all but shouted.

'Ah yes, Monsieur the Commissioner. Very distressed.'

'And her name?'

The Préfet of Barbizon was apologetic. 'She gave none – she refused to do so when asked.'

'Then go to that restaurant and find out, idiot! St-Cyr, leave it. I'm warning you. This little pigeon is ours.'

'Then put her to bed beside the other one in your morgue, Commissioner, and tag her toe with the name Yvette Noel.'

He and Kohler had reached the clearing before Talbotte caught up with them, and it was obvious from the delay that the Commissioner wanted a word in private.

'So, my friends, what's really going on, eh?'

You ingratiating bastard, thought St-Cyr. 'We only wish we knew, Commissioner. Berlin *are* very interested.'

Talbotte threw a level gaze at the two of them, relishing the moment. 'As are the General Oberg and his deputy at number 72, the avenue Foch.'

'The Sicherheitsdienst,' swore Kohler. The Secret Service of the SS.

'Everyone, it seems,' said St-Cyr, casting a woeful eye towards the heavens. Even God.

The Jardin des Lapins Petits looked out over a piece of woods whose naked branches were drenched by the downpour and the rising ground fog of evening.

'A typical December night in these parts,' said Kohler airily. 'Not a legal day for brandy. Therefore we are allowed the *vin ordinaire*, the red also, and a single cup of the Führer's ersatz best.'

The wine was sour.

'You're the people that made it possible,' countered St-Cyr tartly. His overcoat was strung across the backs of three chairs and still dripped quantities on the floor.

'Vienna was nice,' muttered Kohler, referring to the Anschluss, when he had been among the first into that city.

Cakes and ale and cream like he'd never seen before. 'So my little friend, what do we do? Go back to Paris to face the music?'

'Use your charm and find out if it really was our chanteuse who made that telephone call from here.'

'And you?' snorted Kholer. He was in rare form. Soaked through.

'Me, I will continue with a reading I should have completed some time ago. Namely . . .' He held up Gabrielle Arcuri's little notebook.

'Oh, that thing,' muttered Kohler. 'It'll tell you, Louis, the Gorge of the Archers was one of their rendezvous.'

'"12th July, 1942 – met at the Gorge of the Archers, in the turn-around." So, in the car,' said St-Cyr.

'Nice, eh? Laying that gorgeous stack of woman in a car.'

'Perhaps. But there is no time given, Hermann. Now if we flip forward, my friend, there is an entry for 22nd November – one of the girls might remember if they stopped here, eh? "Arrived at the Gorge of the Archers and took the footpath up into the woods. Waited from 2.30 p.m. until 3.30 p.m. Sat in the car and talked until 5.10 p.m., after which, drove back to Paris."'

St-Cyr lifted his bushy eyebrows. 'A talk, Hermann. About what? I wonder. Sex in the car, eh? Or a certain pouch of diamonds?'

'I'll go and forage the local pulchritude.'

'We're not staying here tonight. We've a trip that has to be taken, Hermann, so don't get any ideas.'

'Paris?' he asked, only to see St-Cyr shake his head.

'The Loire, my friend, guided hopefully by the sketch of a child.'

'You think she's next then?'

'Certainly. Why else the telephone call from here?'

Kohler shrugged. 'Maybe our girl got tired of her maid – did you ever think of that?'

'Or the Resistance did, Hermann, but me, I think she's on the run.'

More he wouldn't say but went back to his browsing. The gun in her bureau drawer: its hasty and careless hiding implied a sense of urgency and panic that had begun – and this was important – before they'd left for the club last night. So, Gabrielle Arcuri and her maid had known trouble was on its way. The

100

police, yes, because of the boy's murder, but trouble from another source as well.

But, and this was important also, they hadn't gone back to the apartment after the club had closed at dawn.

The maid had by then been dragged, screaming from a car, and executed in a most vile and brutal fashion.

A girl of . . . what? he asked. Sensitivity – ah, but of course, such eyes . . . such tragedy in them . . . Tears falling over the photograph of the boy she had killed.

A girl who had worn argyle stockings of grey and blue to match the plain blue skirt and shoes . . .

Brown . . . the girl had been wearing browns at the club. He was certain of it. She must have gone somewhere afterwards or changed at the club, but why? To look her best? To meet a lover? It didn't make any sense, but she had changed her clothes, had spruced herself up only to be dragged . . .

'13 July/42 – Fontainebleau Woods, the pond. Spent the afternoon sunbathing. Went swimming twice. Drank champagne. After the chase, there is resignation and acceptance.'

Puzzled by the last line, St-Cyr flipped back to the sequence that began with two days at the château on 18th June, and then went through a quick run of places: Marseilles on 27th June, Lyon on the 28th, Nevers on the 29th, Orléans on the 30th, Tours on 1st July, and finally Angers on the 2nd.

And then, a meeting in a very public place – the Galeries Lafayette at 4.17 p.m. on 7th July, in Paris.

Clearly the pursued had made a run for it after those two days at the château. Marseilles had been followed by a race down the Loire as if to escape the liaison perhaps or to . . . what? he asked himself.

To taunt the pursuer?

Why else the meeting in the Galeries Lafayette in full view of thousands unless the pursued had wanted witnesses to what was going on and had decided to prove a point? To say nothing of having avoided all the checkpoints and controls, the need for passes that the war's restrictions imposed.

But who was the pursued, who the pursuer, and who . . . ah, yes, the observer?

The writer of this little diary? The blackmailer – was that it?

'It was our girl, all right,' said Kohler gruffly. 'The manager remembers her, and not just from this morning, from before.'

'So?' asked St-Cyr, pocketing the notebook.

'So, he remembers she met a certain general here and that they had lunch at this very table.'

'That doesn't tell us much.'

'It wasn't meant to. He's gun-shy, Louis, and in bed with a snake.'

'Then we will leave him on ice, eh, and head south. Pouilly-sur-Loire, I think. The child's sketch shows five stone towers to the château and a maze in which there is, yet again, another small tower.'

'What about our reports?'

'They'll be a day late, I think, Hermann. Frankly, let's let them all trip over each other while we sort out the truth.'

'The Arcuri woman was in tears, Louis.'

'A mirage can have many faces, Hermann.'

'You talk as if you'd been in the Foreign Legion.'

'Was our general with Rommel, do you think?' asked St-Cyr suddenly.

It was a thought for which they had no answer. 'A library then,' swore Kohler. 'Louis, find me a municipal library – the bigger, the better.'

'Let's try the one in Fontainebleau. We can get a reasonable meal at the Auberge de la Reine de Soleil.'

At a quarter to six Kohler strode up the front steps to Fontainebleau's municipal library, appearing shortly afterwards with two heavily burdened, badly frightened clerks, one chief librarian – still complaining and demanding that it wasn't their fault – and several stacks of magazines.

'*Verboten!*' thundered Kohler. 'Confiscated. Be thankful we don't shut you down.'

The magazines were piled into the back seat. Kohler flung his cigarette away before slamming the car door and hitting the gas.

'We'll have dinner on the Loire,' he roared. 'That'll have to suit, Louis.'

Air . . . we need air.

As they headed out of town, St-Cyr reached into the back seat. It was heaped with copies of Hitler's picture magazine, *Signal*.

'Now we're going to get serious,' snorted Kohler.

Suddenly he stopped the car and said, 'Remove the black-out tape, my friend.'

The road leapt before them. Fortunately there were no other cars and, in all the 150 kilometres, but one motorized patrol of three Wehrmacht trucks that didn't bother to pursue them.

The Auberge of the Miller's Second Son was in a converted sixteenth-century grist mill on the outskirts of Pouilly-sur-Loire. One could hear the constant trickle of water over the wheel while gazing raptly at ancient beams, hanging copper pots and paniers, sheaves of drying herbs, and a roaring fire in a giant stone hearth.

'You're full of surprises, Louis,' said Kohler, beaming appreciatively.

Few patrons were about – some Wehrmacht officers who kept to themselves, a party of locals, who did the same.

Lanterns instead of candles or electric lights. Dumpling farm girls with rosy cheeks and roly-poly chests who waited on the tables and were given to giggling when tossed the proper eye.

'A family business,' said St-Cyr dreamily. 'The salt pork with lentils to your liking?'

'Too much,' sighed the Bavarian. 'That sausage and red cabbage . . .'

'*And* the pâté, the bread, the green salad, *and* the leek-and-potato soup. If one strained credulity, Hermann, it's almost as it was before the war.'

The *coq au vin* had been superb.

'You ever bring Marianne here?'

'Twice, yes. Our honeymoon – Pharand gave me three days off then – and once after the birth of our son.'

'Steiner's a louse, Louis. I'll fix it for you.'

'Don't do me any favours. She'll come back when it's over and me, I'll take her back.'

'You're not really worried about the Resistance getting your number, are you? That negative . . .'

The wine, a Pouilly-Fumé, was a truly remarkable vintage whose spicy flavour he had always found to his taste. A gunflint wine, though not of a gun or of flints, he had said to Marianne that first time.

'A wine so named, Hermann, because the Sauvignon grape is called *le fumé*. When ripe, it acquires a gunsmoke bloom.'

'End of travelogue. I asked about Thibault's negative and your number with the Resistance of Melun.'

'That we must wait and see, Hermann, but yes, I, Jean-Louis St-Cyr of the Sûreté, do take the threat most seriously.'

'How could they be so wrong?'

Was it a moment of truth between them? 'I like to keep out of things, Hermann. I stick to crime, not to beating up my brothers and sisters like a punk. I'm a detective and, God forbid, I shall always be one, eh? But,' he gave a shrug, 'the boys from Melun will not yet be aware of this.'

Louis had always been on the side of the French and in his heart of hearts Kohler respected him for this. 'Perhaps when we find Mademoiselle Arcuri, our chanteuse can straighten it all out.'

'Perhaps, but then . . .'

Mais alors . . . mais alors . . .! 'Drink up, Louis, and stop worrying. The great German Gestapo will look after you, eh? Now come on, let's hit the sack.'

'Your Chantilly cream with baked pears and chocolate sauce with almonds has not yet arrived.'

If one had the money and the right connections, one could have almost anything.

Kohler refilled their glasses. Was it to be a last supper for them? 'I still can't see you working in our Silesian salt mines though Herr Himmler was obviously very serious about it.'

'Nor I you in the Kiev headquarters of the Gestapo.'

The fire drew their gazes, the wine seeped out to their pores and when the pear-Chantilly came, they ate in silence, two men poised on the dilemma of their own private chunk of war.

St-Cyr tossed and turned half the night – wild dreams, wet dreams – at dawn, naked flesh beneath a hand, the warm blush of a girl's bare rump nestled softly against his aching groin. 'Marianne . . .'

The breast was plump, soft, full and round, the nipple warm and stiff . . .

'Marianne,' he cried out desperately only to awaken to the

mirage and lie there swallowing thickly and thinking about that girl he had rescued in the night, the kiss she'd given him, and the shoes she'd left him with.

Now why had she been out after curfew like that, and why had she had no room in her own pockets for her shoes?

He had the thought those shoes of hers would be a complication he could do without. Madame Courbet would be sure to notice them and think the worst – the whole street would hear of it. And Marianne . . .? What if Marianne should come home to pick up a few of her things as he'd suggested? Ah, Mon Dieu, she'd think the worst herself.

The dream had been so real. That young girl of the night had been naked and he had closed a hand about her breast. Marianne had been there too – but, and this was important, just at the moment of waking, it had been the girl and not the wife.

In punishment of what Marianne has done? he asked, but had no answer.

At least he hadn't dreamt of Gabrielle Arcuri, though this, he had to confess, he found somewhat a puzzle.

To see Gabrielle Arcuri naked would be to see Venus herself.

Another mirage. The torrid shores of the ancient Mediterranean must have been full of such things in Jason's day. Golden fleeces and rockbound, waiting sirens in flimsy costumes of cheesecloth and dreams.

'Hans Gerhardt Ackermann.' Kohler slung a magazine away. It sailed up into the morning air, giving wing to its pages, before descending in a flutter to hit the water and be swept away. 'Married. The father of two girls. Home town, Stralsund on the Baltic.'

The Bavarian sat on a drift log on the most distant of the mid-channel gravel bars that interfingered with the cold blue waters of the Loire, which here flowed downstream towards the hilltop town of Sancerre.

Beauty and the beast. The woods were bare of leaves and grey or spatulated – willow, plane and oak or beech – the bars wide and bare of cover or grey with last season's grass.

Goats cried in the distance. Hermann puffed on a cigar. He'd thumb the pages of an issue – there were stacks still waiting on either side of him. He'd curse and fling the magazine away or fold it over and tramp it underfoot.

'Ackermann, Louis. Attended the Ordensburg in Marienburg, in East Prussia. A real son-of-a-bitch for Teutonic order and all that bullshit. One of Himmler's élite. An original member of the SS-Verfügungstruppe, the forerunner of the Waffen-SS, our glorious military arm, the pulp crushers of Poland.'

He seized another magazine. 'SS-Obersturmführer – that's lieutenant to you – 1936, no less. *Gott in Himmel*, were those pricks at it that early?'

He peered at the fine print. 'Made a Sturmbannführer right in the heat of battle. A major, Louis. 11th September, 1939. "A specialist in flame throwers." Such pretty toys!'

The general who'd been on the balcony. The general who was Gabrielle Arcuri's friend, or so it would seem. Her lover?

Kohler stomped on that one. Several other issues followed, each taking to the air and to the water until St-Cyr was moved to say, 'You're quite a litter bug these days.'

'You'd be surprised what's in these things,' said Kohler darkly. 'Pure pornography, Louis. *Gott in Himmel*, are people still impressed with this stuff? Russia in flames. German tanks firing pointblank at some poor peasant's hovel. Look . . . Look at this one.'

He swung the magazine back. The Russian Front was unpleasant. The photograph showed several shabby prisoners in the act of being shot. The caption read, *Ukrainian terrorists are being seriously dealt with as is only right and proper.*

Four of the captives were children. A fifth was merely an old woman. Flames leapt from the burning boards behind them. All had worn thick felt boots even in the heat of summer, but these had been respectfully removed as if too precious to soil, and now stood in a row of their own.

'Are you acquiring a conscience, Hermann?'

'Certainly not! I'd have shot them too, Louis. My point is merely that people ceased to believe this shit years ago but Herr Dr Goebbels continues to crank it out in defiance of all logic.

'Ah! Hans Gerhardt Ackermann, the Hero of Rovno, no less. Shown atop one of his favourite chariots. A Mark Four with the 7.5 centimetre cannon. No flame throwers today. Come to think of it, Louis, no burns either.'

106

The magazine went underfoot. Another was seized. The farmers downstream would begin to wonder what was going on, especially since each issue bore the heavy stamp and kangaroo pouch of the Fontainebleau library.

The Hero of Rovno had also been the Hero of Berdichev and then the Knight of Krivoy Rog. One photograph revealed his tanks swimming the Dneiper under fire. Another showed Ackermann interrogating a young Slavic woman.

St-Cyr pitied the poor girl. Such defiance could only have brought a painful retribution.

He turned the page – was surprised to find a close-up of the girl's body. She'd been garrotted with wire but not before she'd been tortured. Her plump, bare peasant arms were a mass of bruises and cigarette burns. The homespun sweater and shirt had been torn from her, to hang about her trouser waist revealing the plain cotton halter shift and sagging breasts. A long welt marred the left underside of her jaw. There was nothing in her eyes but hatred and this had remained even after death.

'You thinking what I'm thinking?' asked Kohler.

'Our friend makes interesting reading, Hermann. Perhaps I ought to help you.'

'Get a proper fix on him first. Here, let me find you these . . .' The Bavarian lifted his shoe to retrieve the five or six issues he'd salvaged so far. 'Begin with the bottom one. It's nice, Louis. Really nice. One of Himmler's boys and we'd better not forget it.'

The photograph showed two smartly dressed, black-uniformed SS subalterns, complete with ceremonial swords. Both men were slim-waisted, tall, young, handsome, virile . . . black gloves, black ties, white shirts and death's-head insignia on their caps. The busy street behind them was probably Berlin's Kurfürstendamm. Girls shopping, a little stroll in the sun.

Ackermann was the one on the right. The peak of his cap shaded the eyes. The mouth was grim-set for such a lovely day. The ears stuck out a little. The face was a smooth, wide oval, the chin wide, clean-shaven and round, not belligerent in the slightest. The nose . . . Teutonic perhaps. He looked into the camera as if only slightly tolerant of the attention. His companion was openly smirking.

'Pretty,' mused St-Cyr. 'Handsome, yes. A lady's man.'

Kohler snapped the latest issue at him. 'Streets of Kiev. Interrogating prisoners again.'

The woman was on her knees. Her wrists had been tightly bound with wire behind her back. The long, blonde braids fell over pendulous breasts. The shoulders were rounded.

'Turn the page.'

She lay on her side gaping at the paving stones. 'Still no tank trouble,' said the Bavarian blithely.

They found the desired issue on the bottom of the left-hand stack. By then St-Cyr had been through half the right-hand stack in spite of Kohler's pleas to go slowly.

'"Hero's return",' mouthed the Bavarian, reading the headline and holding the issue from him while puffing on the cigar. 'General Hans Ackermann of the Waffen-SS.'

The cover showed the general on a stretcher, his face and hands swathed in bandages. An insert photograph showed the young subaltern from the Kurfürstendamm. Just a head and shoulders.

'Apparently someone with a Molotov cocktail chose to teach him the lesson the Finns first taught the Russians. Don't smoke in your sardine can,' roared Kohler. '"The sheet of flame erupted, turning the tank into a blazing inferno." Well, I'll be. Is that what it does? Knight's Cross with Oak Leaves and Laurels, Louis. Holder of a half-tonne of zinc. He's not likely to forget us, not this boy.'

'Nor we, him.' The eyes hadn't just been blue but of its hardest shade, the scar tissue on the left, puckered about the eye and glazed beneath it to the chin.

Even the nose hadn't been spared. St-Cyr recalled how the general had looked at them outside Gabrielle Arcuri's flat.

The nose had been half eaten away and the lips . . . twisted and thin on the left, merging into those of the subaltern on the right.

A man of two faces, depending on which he chose to let you see.

Kohler found the photo of the last partisan. She hadn't been garrotted. She'd simply been shot.

He found the first partisan, held her photo from him as a man would while mentally undressing a woman, even to pulling down a lower eyelid. 'A lot like a Resistance killing, eh, Louis?' he said. 'Yes, my friend, there's not a hell of a lot of difference.'

St-Cyr got to his feet. 'I think we've seen enough history, Hermann. Let's be on our way.'

'You want any of these?' asked the Bavarian with a grin.

The two men flung all of the remaining magazines into the river.

'We wouldn't want the Gestapo to find us with them,' whispered Kohler.

'No doubt the General Ackermann will have his own scrap-book, should we need to refer to them again.'

The beauty of the Loire was momentarily lost, but then, as the last of the magazines drifted downstream, the sun came out.

'Do you know,' said the Bavarian, 'I think God just smiled. Your God, Louis. The one you always keep referring to.'

They started back to the car.

'What would Ackermann be doing in Paris, Hermann?'

'On rest and recoup probably, or attached to the Sonderkommando-SS under the General Oberg, the Butcher of Poland, and the Sturmbannführer Helmut Knochen, his deputy.'

'Number 72, the avenue Foch, and the Secret Service of the SS. The Sicherheitsdienst.'

'Perhaps that's why the Resistance has taken such an interest in Gabrielle Arcuri and her maid.'

'Perhaps,' said St-Cyr, but didn't elaborate.

At noon they were no closer to finding the château but the day . . . ah, what could one say? Of course, the late spring, early summer and fall were always best. But the Loire . . . its many châteaux . . .

St-Cyr sighed contentedly. With the fire going well in the bowl of a favourite pipe and a good lunch beneath the belt, what more could one ask? Hermann had even mellowed and drove more as a tourist should.

Still, it would not hurt to go over things. Sometimes the German mind needed that. 'Five towers surround a courtyard,' he insisted, again consulting the child's sketch. 'There are two gates, as in a medieval stronghold. Outside the château are grounds, and a road, a grand entrance, runs through these, in part along a tunnel under the lime trees.'

They'd been asking along the way without success. Kohler had heard it all before.

Undaunted, St-Cyr continued with a toss of his hand and half an eye to the unfolding scenery. 'There is a wood, Hermann – me, I'm certain of this – and between it and the château, gardens of which the crowning glory is a maze, perhaps quite tall and of box or yew, well trimmed and quite complicated.'

Louis could still go on at length about it. The bugger was really enoying himself.

'In the centre of this maze stands a small, round tower of stone with embrasures. The boy is positive, so it has been a favourite of his tender years.'

Thinking again of his son, no doubt. 'Mere scribblings,' snorted Kohler. 'You should have been a schoolteacher, Louis. That paper's so well thumbed it has the look of a mother's love.'

'Fields lie below the woods, Hermann, and one can, I think, see the château's towers from the far bank of the river.'

The sketch could well have been done years ago and the kid now grown up.

They came to a bridge near St-Dyé, and crossed over to the left bank, pausing on a hilltop to scan the horizon and warm themselves in the welcome sun. The German presence, so apparent as one moved nearer to Paris, was almost totally absent in the countryside.

'Osier beds, Hermann. These lie on the flatlands by the river which suggests Touraine to me, as does the boy's mushroom logo with feet, hands and eyes but no ears.'

'You talk as if the kid were right between us.'

'It's surprising what the mind of a child can reveal.'

No hint of warning of Marianne's abdication? wondered Kohler but said only, 'You're the expert, my friend. I'm merely the chauffeur.'

'Osier beds for the baskets, Hermann. So, a working château, I think. Vines, yes. Caves for raising mushrooms and racking wine. Fishing on a Sunday afternoon if one is lucky – there are some punts drawn up among the reeds near the osier beds. No doubt there are ospreys on the river, and the boy is very fond of spying on them.'

He'd built such a mental picture of the place, Kohler hoped he wouldn't be disappointed.

'Vouvray, Hermann. Yes, I think we shall find our château near there. It is at once one of the most strikingly beautiful parts of the Loire Valley and yet one of the most poignantly haunting. Tufa cliffs lie to the north. Valleys funnel down to the Cisse and its confluence with the Loire.'

The last light of day gave them a view of the river flats and, in a distant backwater along the other shore, someone in a large felt hat poling a punt among the reeds.

There was a boy of six or seven years of age sitting in the bow; behind the two of them, on the hill beyond the woods, the rising slate-grey towers and grey-white stone of the château.

An osprey floated over everything just as the boy had sketched it.

'Me, I'm humbled, Hermann. There is the mother, there the son.'

'Do you think they've seen us?' The air seemed to shimmer.

St-Cyr shrugged. 'Would they realize who we were?'

'The woman might?'

'Dawn will see, Hermann. For now, let us leave them in peace, eh?'

There were tears in Louis's eyes. Mush! for Christ's sake!

'Philippe would have loved it here. Me, I never took the time I should have with the boy.'

'A life of crime, eh?' snorted Kohler. 'Listen, my friend, don't let sentiment interfere. That woman's in danger for her life and so are we. She may also be a killer for all we know.'

St-Cyr merely nodded. 'And now, a bottle of Vouvray, Hermann, creamed leeks and mushrooms, eh? And then . . .' He paused. 'The trout Vouvray for me, or the whiting.'

At dawn, fog rose off the river. Moisture dripped from the barren branches. Rooks cawed and, in the distance above the far bank, they drifted eerily through the gossamer.

'Louis, you'd better take this, just in case.'

Kohler dragged their weapons out from under the driver's seat and handed the Lebel to him in its shoulder holster. 'If you

111

continue to keep our guns lying around like that, Hermann, someone's bound to notice.'

The Bavarian grinned. 'The glorious Gestapo of the Third Reich bends the rules of the Armistice to save your bushy pink tail, my friend. Don't shoot anyone, eh?'

'Me, I'll try not to.'

'You still convinced this is the way to do things?'

'The river, the woods, grounds, maze and walls afford too obvious a hasty route of exit, Hermann. Gabrielle Arcuri will only pull the disappearing act on us if we both go in through the front entrance. So, we will do the unexpected, eh? You flush the bird and me, I will take it on the wing.'

Kohler held the flat-bottomed punt for him. St-Cyr sat between the oars. 'Once I've crossed the river, give me an hour or so, Hermann. Perhaps a little more. Distances are deceiving. That hill may also be steeper than I've anticipated.'

'You might get lost,' snorted the Bavarian, shoving him out. 'So long, chum.'

'Remember you're working alone. No hint of an accomplice, eh?'

Must he always go on about it? Kohler lifted a tired hand. 'Don't be a pain in the ass. I'm not stupid.'

'Just wanting to be sure.'

The sailor drifted out into the current and began to row in earnest. Water gurgled off the prow. There were several sand-and-gravel bars, a few low islands and one, a little downstream of these, that held a smattering of willows and the ruined walls of a Norman keep.

Kohler knew Louis would be enjoying himself like a kid on an adventure, but he also knew the Frenchman was absolutely right. They couldn't afford to lose Gabrielle Arcuri, not now.

The fog soon closed about the oarsman. The rooks departed, and the river returned to itself. In the hush, Kohler could hear the current as it trickled over the gravel. Hands in his overcoat pockets, he stood on the bank. Louis had said Norse raiders had come up the Loire in search of booty, and he could certainly imagine them doing so on a morning like this, but somewhere further back in time, Caesar had been here too.

The place was dotted with monasteries and steeped in money. Everyone knew the wealthy of France had bolted to their châteaux on the Loire or fled farther south to sit out the war in relative comfort. For the most part, they mingled freely with their conquerors, socializing and accepting them but with that aloofness so characteristic of the French élite.

He had it in mind what the château would hold. A matriarch – the grandmother – then the mother and father, perhaps a son bought free of the war or from some prisoner-of-war camp in the Reich – Maxim's and payment of 150,000 francs into the hands of the right waiter who would feed it to his contact and, *voilà*, some lucky bastard found himself standing outside the barbed wire with his bundle of rags under one arm.

Corruption was rife both in Paris and in the countryside. He had no illusions about it. Germans could be, and were being bought, all the time. He, himself, might well have kept the diamonds. Yes, he might have.

The son would, of course, be Gabrielle Arcuri's husband but the family'd prefer to keep him out of sight. Ah yes, but of course. No sense in rubbing salt into local wounds, eh?

These things were not too difficult to figure out, but why would she take up living in Paris, why consort with a German general – especially one whose features had been so buggered up?

And why be an accessory to a murder no one ought to have taken the slightest interest in?

Perhaps the boy, as yet unidentified, had been the younger son of the owners? Perhaps Gabrielle Arcuri had tried to look out for him?

Perhaps . . . perhaps, but then . . . *Mais alors*!

Damn! He'd begun to say it himself!

A lone duck broke through the fog out over the river only to veer sharply away and bank high as it spotted him. Kohler listened for the flat report of a shotgun but there was none. Hunting was forbidden, of course, as was the possession of guns of any kind.

Yet one could hide all sorts of stuff like that in a place like this and, if given the chance, no doubt lifting the roof off that château would yield all manner of secrets.

Even a few tidbits about that little maid of hers? he asked.

Lost in the fog, the towers of the château remained hidden from him and, as two more ducks came swiftly across the water, he had the thought Louis wasn't being as careful as he should have been.

If one could see the ducks take wing, so, too, could another.

St-Cyr stepped cautiously out of the punt. Mud welled up around his boots but the mat of dead and fallen reeds was thick enough to hold him. Those damned ducks! He'd almost been upon the boy when first the one had cruised out into the lead, only to see the punt and take off.

Then those two others. *Merde!* He'd been so close. The boy had been crouched among some reeds, spying on the ducks. For a second, the two of them had looked at each other. Like a wraith, the boy had disappeared, leaving only a memory of haunted dark brown eyes and a hank of straight brown hair over the brow.

The kid would sound a warning.

Fed up with himself, St-Cyr drew the punt up on the bank, then made his way through the reeds to where the boy had been hiding.

A blue woollen toque and a pair of knitted gloves were lying on the ground. He picked them up and followed the boy, hoping against hope that the early hour and the lost warm clothing – not so easily come by these days – might keep the boy silent for a while.

A trail led through the reeds to the first of three punts and he saw the one the boy and his mother had used the previous evening. The oars were still in it and not leaning against a tree as were the others.

The trail became a footpath, wide enough for two to walk side by side. Railings of peeled poles had been nailed to tree trunks where necessary. There were even log steps, though these were badly in need of replacement.

The woods opened into a clearing – stacks of firewood here – then the path wound upwards beside a small stream. There was a footbridge, none too sound by the look, more steps, a turning off to the right, a bend, a rise and . . . he caught his breath.

The boy was at the other side of a clearing, standing beside the ruins of some beehives.

Was that guilt in the look he gave, or fear? Even from a

114

distance of perhaps forty metres, the resemblances to Gabrielle Arcuri were noticeable but these were all in the finely boned face, the high and studious brow, the height and slimness, not in the colour of the eyes or that of the hair.

'A moment . . .' began St-Cyr, only to see the wraith disappear.

Twice more the boy hesitated, making certain he was being followed. In time they reached a high stone wall. Again the boy looked back. Gargoyles surmounted the wall – stone dogs begging on their hind legs, griffins with folded wings. The boy took no notice of them but twice again he waited to make certain the stranger was following.

Then he ducked away and St-Cyr was left alone, cursing his luck until, at last, he found the opening, a portal which led across a piece of lawn through statues and ornamental shrubs to an entrance of the maze.

Again the boy waited. He was at least seven years of age, so the photograph in Gabrielle Arcuri's flat had been taken some time ago.

The boy let him start out then left him to find his own way through the maze.

Now there was only the fog, the tall and enclosing walls of the passageways, the ever-present smell of cedar, the sound of distant geese, and from somewhere distant too, that of poultry, most expressively, the harshness of guinea fowl.

When he found the rabbit, grey, fat and with very soft and floppy ears, he knew he was lost. And so was the rabbit by the look, for it led him down this passageway and that, into one dead end after another.

Now he didn't know if he was going deeper into the maze or back towards the entrance. At last he came to a T-junction and the first of a long aisle which pointed straight towards the stone tower in the centre. It was still some distance from him.

St-Cyr thought the boy was up there watching him from the highest of the embrasures but when he reached the tower, it was empty.

And the spiral of stone steps that had, echoing, led up to a leaded skylight in the dome, now looked down to the floor below yet he was certain the boy hadn't left the tower.

What have we got ourselves into? he asked but had no

answer, only a sense of doubt he didn't like. Quite obviously the boy had been told to lead him astray and, quite obviously, whoever had told him to do so, hadn't wanted to be seen.

That could only mean there'd been someone else among the reeds.

4

Château Thériault, Clos de l'Oiseau de la Brume lay at the end of the gigantic plane trees whose greenish-grey and pistachio-brown spatulated branches reached eerily up into the fog.

As Kohler eased the Citroën down the lane, he looked off to the right and away from the river. Vines began on the lower slopes, the fog giving but glimpses. Perhaps forty hectares in all so far.

Some people had all the luck. This was money – very old money.

Moundlike shapes of box, yew and hawthorn stood sentinel nearest the arched stone entrance which was set in the base of one of the towers. Flanking stone walls held crenellated battlements. Where once there'd been a drawbridge, there was now a stone bridge.

There were no flags that he could see – a dovecot, yes, there was one of those. Towers upon towers but hidden by their shroud. The gate had three conical roofs, with slotted embrasures below them. Ivy climbed the walls.

Immediately inside the gate there was a house. Beyond the house, the central courtyard opened up in lawns and formal gardens, mothballed fountains and statues that were shrouded in the ever-present mist.

The place was huge, a bugger to heat. The five towers stood around, and between these there were defensive walls only at the opposing gates. Otherwise the château went from tower to tower. Cut stone, beautiful slate, copper eaves and lots of tall French windows – barns and stables to his left at the back, now the garages perhaps, so self-contained but all part of the enclosing pentagon.

Five greyhounds stood in a cluster. A tall woman in a dark blue overcoat with turned-up high collar held the leashes. The help had all gathered humbly about her for the morning's instructions. Well, what the hell . . .

Still some distance from them, Kohler got out of the car to wait. The dogs fidgeted. She spoke quietly to them. One by one the help ducked their heads, clutching their berets in respect – clogs on some, blue denim jackets, overalls and bulky turtleneck sweaters, the fog drifting. As each man paid his respects and received his orders, she seemed to exist only for him and he left without so much as a glance towards the visitor.

Kohler knew he wasn't just witnessing a daily ritual but the iron and benevolent rule such a place as this would demand.

She let the dogs go and he stood there not knowing whether to get back into the car as they came at him. Such graceful things . . .

'Sasha!' One word, that was all. The lead dog. Its name echoed from the towers as the dogs stopped.

Each one held its position, watching him, and he had the thought then that Sasha would have torn the heart out of any of them if they'd moved, and that the woman would have approved.

As she came across the courtyard, she gathered in the leashes and he saw that she wore black leather riding boots.

'To what do I owe this visit?' she asked.

Kohler took in the regal bearing, the dusky eyes, pale complexion, high forehead, thin, smooth, delicate, oval face – beauty, *Gott in Himmel*, this one had been a smashing thing. Now in her early sixties, she retained haunting traces of that beauty. Russian . . . was she of Russian descent? he wondered, thinking of the cigarette case.

She moved with grace and ease yet as if resigned to life. There was about her an aura of sadness that puzzled him. The shoulders were thin, the frame that of a willow wand, the open dark navy overcoat revealing several strands of amber beads and a needlepoint sweater of maroon and gold brocade. Very ornate, perhaps quite fashionable, and worth a small fortune. But . . . and of this he was certain . . . not exactly the sort of thing one would wear to get the work going on the farm.

118

'I believe I asked you a question, monsieur. To what do I owe this visit?'

Had she been expecting company of another sort? That why the dress-up?

Was that the trace of a Russian accent?

The hair was raven – long and flowing loosely over the thin shoulders. Not a touch of grey and brushed to beat the Jesus.

'Kohler, Countess. Gestapo, Paris Central. I've come in connection with a murder case. Actually,' he raised his eyebrows, 'it's two murder cases and likely to involve a third if we're not careful.'

At once the woman pulled rank and showed her irritability. 'I know nothing of such things.'

'But you might be able to help, Countess?'

The eyes were very striking.

'Must I? You people . . . I've the quotas to see to, Inspector – you are an inspector, aren't you, or do they give you ranks?'

'Inspector will do just fine.'

She began to unleash the dogs, restraining each until it shot away to zoom around the courtyard, ranging far and near. 'I only hope my grandson has had the good sense to lock up his rabbit. If he hasn't, it'll teach him a good lesson.'

One by one the dogs raced out through the far portal. Kohler and the woman began to walk that way.

'My husband was killed in the last war, Inspector, and now my only son in this one. What more can I say but that I think all wars are lousy.'

'Was your son the husband of Gabrielle Arcuri?'

The eyes found him again. 'I think you know this, Inspector, so why ask it? She's not here. Gabrielle and I . . .' The woman shrugged. 'We do not understand each other. We're both fighting our loss but in different ways.'

'We have reason to believe Mademoiselle Arcuri's in grave danger.'

'We?' asked the woman.

'Gestapo Central. The Sturmbannführer Boemelburg, my chief.'

'Then you do have ranks. What's yours – just so that I know with whom I'm dealing?'

'Captain, Countess – a Hauptsturmführer.'

119

'Captain . . . ah yes. My son had such a rank. It has a nice ring to it – conjuring images of dashing young men in uniform, isn't that so? Do you prefer war to fighting crime?'

Was she trying to provoke him to hide the fact she'd been expecting someone else, was still looking for that visitor? 'Crime doesn't stop just because there's a war, Countess.'

She gave him a brief smile as if to say, *Touché*. 'I would have thought in your case, Inspector, the two were one and the same. Tell me something, Herr Hauptsturmführer Kohler, do you enjoy interrogating the French? Which are more fun? The men or the women? The young or the old? The Resistance . . .? Oh, we've some of them about here, too, and that's why Gabrielle wouldn't dare to come here.'

Kohler drew out his cigarettes and offered them. Surprisingly, the countess accepted one, and when he thumbed the lighter for her, she held his hand and let him feel how cold and calm were her fingers.

The dark eyes looked questioningly at him. She tossed her head and drew in gratefully, filling her lungs then blowing smoke up into the fog. She'd fix him. They'd visit the pigs.

'Are you married, Captain?' she asked, indicating they were to leave the courtyard by the back gate.

'Very much so,' snorted Kohler. 'My Gerda keeps house in Wasserburg.'

'That's near Munich, on the River Inn?'

Was she toying with him? 'Yes, yes, it's on the Inn. Her father's farm. She's happier there. We've two boys in the Army, both in Russia, I suppose.'

'You don't keep in touch?' she asked, smiling knowingly. She had his measure now.

'The mails are not what they should be, Countess. I have to move about a good deal.'

Roasting the Gestapo – one ought to enjoy it! 'Such a lame answer, Captain? Ah, Mon Dieu, be honest, eh? It's a sort of holiday, an extended vacation? Yes, me I can imagine that is how it must be for you and lots of others. The clubs and cabarets, the girls, ah yes, and then touring about our beloved France in one of the Sûreté's cars. King of everything. One of the master race. Have you a mistress, or are Gestapo inspectors allowed such things?'

'We're kept rather busy,' said Kohler drily. 'Apart from the odd prostitute to calm the loins, Countess, they don't really give us much time off. Usually twice a month if we're lucky.'

It was on the tip of her tongue to ask if he preferred French whores to German ones. He'd like the young ones, that's for sure. Men like this always did. Most men too.

So, she would say nothing more of it. She would lead him on a little walk and stall for time. Perhaps the general would arrive and put a stop to him. Perhaps.

Beyond the walls, the grounds opened into a park-like setting whose focus was the maze. But they didn't head for it. Instead, they went off to the right along a road, the land dipping down to barren trees and scattered farmsteads, pig-pens, chickens, ducks, geese and guinea hens, a flock of goats.

Kohler was impressed. The sow was huge. They must have received special dispensation from the local Kommandant to raise as many pigs as they wished. The woman had friends in high places then. Normally only one pig was allowed. There'd been no sign of her having had to billet any officers either.

She put a boot right in the shit and he was forced to follow. As she closed the gate behind them, the sow snorted angrily and lifted its dripping snout from the slops.

The woman called out, 'Judith, be nice to our Gestapo visitor, eh, my sweet? He likes you. You can pat her, Inspector. Tickle her behind the ears.'

Crossing the pen, they ducked as they entered a thatch-roofed shed, only to find the young ones still crowded inside. Perhaps forty or fifty of them. 'Countess . . .'

'Yes?'

'Could we go somewhere else? A private talk . . .?' he asked.

Had he had enough already? 'Me, I thought being German, you'd like to see them.'

'So, okay, I like pigs. Now maybe you'll tell me what the game is?'

'Game? But what is this, Captain Kohler? Each morning I must make my rounds. If you want to ask questions, then ask them but don't take up my time.'

At least twenty piglets were at his shoes and trouser cuffs. There were no runny noses. Kohler stooped and gathered one under each arm.

Grinning, he said, 'They need to be castrated, Countess. At home we bite them off.'

'Here we are more civilized,' she retorted. 'So, what is it you want to ask?'

Kohler set the squealing piglets down. 'First, the identity of this boy.' He dragged out the photographs. Her breath steamed in the rank air. There was nothing quite like pig manure to clear the nostrils and the brain. All about them there was the squealing, butting, nudging turmoil.

The yearlings were kept in separate pens that gave on to the far yard. One boar had mounted a young sow. Grunts and squeals . . .

The woman's dark eyes flashed professionally over the copulation before focusing on the photograph. 'I don't know him. He's not from around here.'

Naked as the day he'd been born and such a pretty boy.

The Bavarian manoeuvred himself so that her back was to one of the pens and there was no easy escape.

'Take another look – this one, eh?' He handed her one of Thibault's shots of the body.

For just a split second there was hesitation – he'd swear to it – then she shook her head, ignored the rutting that went on and on behind her. 'I've never seen him. Perhaps the local Préfet of Police, Monsieur Hector Poulin, could help you, Inspector.'

Nothing in the eyes. How could a woman like this have become such a competent liar? 'What about your daughter-in-law's maid, Yvette Noel?'

'A silly girl. Me, I'm sorry to hear she was killed but . . . I did not know her well. Gabrielle seldom brought her here.'

Kohler drew himself up. Her forehead was at eye-level. The piglets kept at his ankles. Was it the salt they liked? 'And I didn't say she'd been murdered, Countess.'

'But you said . . .? Two murders? I have thought . . .'

The performance wasn't quite good enough. 'Why not level with me, Countess? It'll save us both time and it just might save your daughter-in-law's life.'

Merde! What was she to do? 'A coffee, I think, and a marc. Look, I'll tell you what I can but it isn't much.'

He took her by the arm, was surprised at how readily she accepted the gesture.

He hasn't seen the boy, she told herself. He doesn't know Gabrielle is here.

Kohler, his hat and coat hanging in a closet somewhere, stood waiting in what the countess had called her Green Room. Though it was huge, high-ceilinged and draughty, there was about the room a sense of intimacy. Curtains made of seventeenth-century French embroidery in creams, soft yellows, beiges and greens gave vegetable hangings that matched the coverings on the armchairs that had once belonged to the Duke of Tallyrand.

She'd said he could sit in them. She'd asked him to wait a few moments – now more than a half-hour. Three cigarettes! And why had she made him feel nervous?

A magnificent Bouelle armoire, in ornate gold and mirrored jet, matched the desk. An ivory humidor held pre-war cigars. It was all he could do to desist but he had the thought then that the woman would be watching for just such a thing.

The carpet, an Aubusson perhaps, was of flowers and vines. Bits of sculpture were everywhere, lending a slightly Roman touch.

From any of the windows he had a full view of the courtyard and he wondered if this had been intended. The Citroën looked decidedly out of place. The dogs still hadn't come back and he wondered then, as he had off and on since she'd released them, if she'd done so deliberately.

The innkeeper where they'd stayed last night could easily have given the château a ring. The dogs had probably treed poor Louis. The morning wasn't turning out as it should.

The Countess Jeanne-Marie (pronounced Jianne) Thériault was more than just a power to be reckoned with. She had them by the cold hard plums and she'd let him know it. Why else the cooler of her little salon? Why else the chance to go through her writing desk if he should choose – which he would, she'd assume.

Why else unless she'd known the desk had contained nothing incriminating?

Glancing towards the door she had left open, he had the thought then that perhaps she had been watching him all along.

These old places . . . peepholes where you least expected them. Arsenic in your soup, belladonna in the cakes. No love between brothers, sisters and heirs . . . Lots and lots of places to hide a fugitive.

He left the desk alone and walked on. The coffee and brandy were taking one hell of a time.

She chose her entrance with a timing that was impressive. He'd only just seen the general's staff car drive in under the stone arch, when there she was, standing in the doorway with a tray – huge and glittering – coffee-pot, cups and saucers, a bottle of Armagnac and crystal glasses . . .

'You must forgive my keeping you waiting, Captain Kohler. Business . . .' Again a shrug but now an apologetic smile, quite pretty too . . . 'When one lives alone, there is never enough time.'

Kohler took the tray from her and set it on the verd-antique coffee table whose top rested on four golden cherubs. How nice . . .

She'd given the hair more brushing but still wore it loose, had composed herself if ever one such as this needed to. The needlework turned out to be the ornate and beautifully worked front panel of her dress. The amber beads made sharp little noises as she indicated he was to sit. 'So, these murders, Captain. Tell me about them, please. Leave nothing out.'

The stall then, until the general arrived. The use of his rank instead of Inspector. A put-down, or to set the stage for a later confrontation with the higher rank of the general?

He had the idea there were carefully arranged rings of defence around the Château Thériault and that she had a network of informants only too loyal to her.

But he liked the way she poured their coffee. Absolute control – hesitation, glances, dropped dusky eyelids, slight touches of slender fingers. Was the woman flirting with him? *Gott in Himmel* . . .

'Please, I must insist, Captain Kohler. All the details.'

As she sat back in her armchair, she crossed her long legs and he liked that too. Still gunpowder in the old barrel, eh? A woman who had liked to have her lovers and probably still did.

He set his coffee aside and laid out all the photographs for her. 'That willow the boy's lying under must be down by the river, Countess. Whoever took the photographs knew him only too well. When we examined the body, he was fully clothed as you can see, but dressed as if from one of the seminaries. A boy of some means, I think, Countess. The clothes were good.'

'He had entered the priesthood – there's a Benedictine monastery not far from here. Brother . . . Brother Jérome had enrolled as a novice but if you ask me, Captain, he had no inclination whatsoever towards the priesthood.'

'Just a dodge then, from the military call-up?'

Was that genuine sadness in those dark and dusky eyes?

The nod was almost imperceptible. 'My son had no patience with him and refused to speak to him when he heard of it.'

Quite obviously the general had been told by someone to cool his heels.

'Was his wife's maid in love with the boy?'

'Yvette Noel was his sister, Captain Kohler. The family are not wealthy – they've been employees of the Domaine Thériault for some ninety-seven years, this coming spring. Riel Noel is my Chef de Culture, the keeper of our vines. His brother, Morgan, is our wine master and oenologist, so you can see, I hope, that the matter is of a delicate nature and that I had, of course, to search my heart before answering your questions.'

Gott in Himmel, she was fantastic! Louis should have been witness to this. 'I quite understand, Countess,' he said humbly.

Reaching for his coffee, he took a sip – glanced over the rogue's gallery of naked shots of the boy, the young David with his pecker asleep in the sunshine of the Loire or of Fontainebleau Woods.

'Jérome Noel . . .?' he asked, just to get it right.

'Alain Jérome Noel. The Alain was taken from my husband's name as a gesture of sympathy and honour.'

'How old was the boy?'

The sad eyes lifted, the fingers traced the line of her right thigh to which the material clung. 'Twenty-four. He looks much younger and that was a part of the trouble, I think. He *was* young for his age. And silly.'

'Like the maid?' he asked.

He had remembered. 'Yes . . . yes, like his sister, Yvette.'

Kohler affected the seriousness of a high-court judge. 'With all due respect, Countess, that's not the impression my partner got of your daughter-in-law's maid.'

'Your partner . . .?'

Gott in Himmel, she was good! Genuine surprise . . . questions in the look she still gave him. 'We always work in pairs – on criminal investigations. It's safer that way. My partner and I deal with common theft, bank robberies, arson and murder mostly.'

Again she said, 'Your partner . . .?'

'Jean-Louis St-Cyr of the Sûreté Nationale.'

Lost in thought, she said, 'The owner of the car.'

'I've only borrowed it for the duration. Actually, it isn't St-Cyr's. He had the use of it *and* a driver before the Armistice but manpower being scarce, we've had to dispense with the driver.'

'And where is this partner of yours now?'

Kohler found himself secretly relishing the moment. Had they really got the better of the woman? 'He's in Paris, on another case, Countess. The manpower thing.'

He gave a futile shrug; she, a pleasant little smile. 'Have you any suspects, Captain?'

Was she being coy? He found the use of his rank a pain in the ass. 'Two as a matter of fact, but I'd rather not say who they are at the moment.'

'Two but . . . ah, I see. Yvette's killer might possibly also have killed her brother. Is that what you mean?'

No mention of the Resistance. 'Something like that, yes. You see, Countess, it can't have been the sister, can it?'

Her coffee was cold and there was no place to dump it. 'Then who?' she asked but couldn't find the will to look at him – she knew she must! He had no proof! Just supposition. A shot in the dark. The police were all the same!

'Who indeed, Countess?' Nothing yet about the diamonds, nothing about monogrammed cigarette cases from Russia and bottles of perfume in beaded silk purses or condoms in their little silk sleeves.

'He was a silly boy, a foolish boy. So foolish. Gabrielle . . .'

'Gabrielle *what*, Countess?'

'Nothing. It . . . it doesn't matter now in any case. Nothing matters. It's finished – finished for the two of them, Inspector, and me, I have somehow to pick up the pieces for the family.'

'Is your daughter-in-law really in danger from the Resistance or was Yvette's murder merely made to look that way?'

'I . . . I don't know. I wish to God I did!'

Kohler poured the brandy and handed her a glass. Their fingers touched, again that same icy calm and yet those dark eyes . . . had they touches of violet in them?

'You must excuse me, Inspector. I've kept the General Hans Ackermann waiting far too long. I can spare you no more time this morning but if you wish, I will be only too glad to see you again.'

In hell. 'That's decent of you, Countess. Please give the general my regards. We're old friends.'

St-Cyr poled the punt through the last of the reeds then let it glide out into the backwater pond. The greystone mill and silent water wheel reeked of Balzac's novel, *The Lily of the Valley*. The tall, steeply pitched cedar roof had dormer windows in the loft, skylights and lots of moss.

Again he was surprised he and Kohler hadn't seen the mill from the other side of the river but the well-treed island had been behind the one with the ruins and almost a part of the far shore. Their attention had been distracted.

Giving the boat a final shove, he steered it up to the wharf and in beside the punt he was certain Gabrielle Arcuri had taken.

Had it not been for the boy's rabbit, the dogs would have torn him to pieces. The rabbit had drawn them off and he had retraced his steps through the maze and back to the river only to find one of the punts missing.

The island with the ruins had yielded nothing. Balzac's mill would be different.

Quietly he pulled the punt along the wharf and leaned out over the water to secure it. Then he climbed on to the wharf and made his way alongside the water wheel.

Ivy grew about the heavy wooden door. He took a moment – she'd know of his presence. She'd be listening for him.

Nudging the door open, he stepped inside the mill, stepped into the gloom. It was as if a hundred years ago. Dust lay everywhere. The husks of wheat littered everything but once a flour mill, always one. The smell of the grain never really disappeared. It reminded one of brewer's mash.

Sunlight streamed down the far stairwell, touching each heavy pine step and the honey-amber of its sturdy railing. The machinery, the leather belts, pulley wheels, shafts and giant grindstones, lay still and silent.

As he crossed the floor, St-Cyr eased the Lebel in its holster.

The stairwell angled up to the first floor before jogging abruptly to the second. 'Mademoiselle Arcuri, my name is Jean-Louis St-Cyr of the Sûreté Nationale. I have reason to believe your life is in great danger.'

It sounded so melodramatic. The mill gave back the censure of its stony silence.

One foot and then another. Step by step – more machinery on the first floor, more of it on the one above. Gearboxes and bearings, subsidiary pulleys, shafts and wheels, even a small woodworking shop, complete with lathes and shavings on the floor.

He raised his bushy eyebrows to the timbers above and knuckle-dusted the moustache. So, she would hide on him. Okay, mademoiselle.

Crossing the floor, he opened the hoist door to check the pond below. There was no sign of her leaving the place. Good!

A last set of stairs led up into the loft, into the stronger sunlight. He had started up them, was reaching for another grip of the railing and looking into the sun when she levelled both barrels of a shotgun at him and said, 'That's far enough.'

Ah, Mon Dieu, to be caught like this! Thank God Hermann wasn't around. 'Mademoiselle, please, there is no need for that.'

Still he couldn't get a good look at her – that blasted sun. She'd chosen her place well.

She pulled back the hammers of the fowling piece, first one and then the other. 'Remove the revolver, "Inspector", and leave it on the steps.'

This was a chanteuse, a mirage? A woman with the voice of an angel and a body fit only for the gods?

Gabrielle Arcuri motioned him to step away from the stairwell. 'Back,' she said but not in panic. 'Over there, by that window. Yes . . . yes, that one.'

She went down the steps to retrieve the revolver, had returned before he could move.

The gun she tucked into the waistband of the brown whipcord jodhpurs she wore.

There was an open hacking jacket, a knotted paisley silk scarf, soft yellow mohair pullover, no lipstick, no make-up of any kind but . . . and he was surprised at this . . . the thick, shoulder-length hair was not blonde as he'd thought at the club, but the soft shade of a fine brandy. Tied back in a pony tail with a bit of dark brown velvet ribbon.

The eyes were, of course, violet but such a shade . . . Ah, Mon Dieu . . . the face, bone structure, aquiline nose, lovely smooth brow and ears – even the lips – those of the son.

She said, 'So, okay, you've found me. Now what? I didn't kill her – I'd never have done that. Yvette was too close to me.'

'That's what they all say, mademoiselle, but me, I think it was the Resistance.'

'Those bastards? Pah! What do they know? Little black coffins in the mail? The trick of cowards, isn't that so?'

Perhaps five metres and some leather belting separated them, the belts angling upwards. He'd like to get that shotgun away from her.

'If you think to impress me with your hatred of the Resistance, mademoiselle, then forget it. I'm not one of the Gestapo's informers. I'm not a collaborator.'

The look he gave was one of flint. Steady . . . so steady. A dangerous thing to have said to the wrong person. So, he'd gambled, made up his mind about her quickly. This she liked. It pleased her immensely to be so flattered.

The brandy eyebrows arched. The lovely eyes seemed to grow as she studied him. One thing was certain. She wasn't as young as he'd thought, was perhaps in her late thirties or even her early forties.

But, a woman who took great care of herself. 'Did you meet my son?' she asked.

He nodded. 'A clever boy. He had me completely fooled.'

The smile she gave was instantaneous – a brief insight, one so soft and yet . . . ah, what could he say? Complex? Filled with sadness too?

'René,' she said. 'His name's René Yvon-Paul and he's a

Thériault through and through so, monsieur, what do we do? I didn't kill Yvette and I didn't kill Jérome either.'

'Did Yvette kill him?'

'Yvette? Are you crazy? Ah, Mon Dieu, you cops are all the same. Yvette, in the name of Jesus, why? She was his sister, idiot! She loved him and forgave him time and again. He drove her crazy.'

'Why not put the shotgun down? Those old hammers . . .' St-Cyr gave a shrug . . . 'Use the revolver if you like. It matches the one I found in your bureau.'

'*Merde*! Ah no. What right had you to . . .'

It was no use. In a way she was glad the hiding was over.

Thumbing the hammers into place, she leaned the shotgun against the wall by the stairs. 'There's a thermos of coffee, some bread and cheese in my rucksack. Look, I'll tell you what I can but it won't help much, and as for the Resistance being after me, all I can say is that it's crazy of them. I've done nothing to be ashamed of and neither had Yvette.'

It was on the tip of his tongue to say, And neither have I yet they're interested in me, but he let the matter go and picked up the rucksack. 'Then who killed her?' he asked.

She was either flustered by the question or a very good actress. 'I . . . I don't know. I wish I did, but I honestly don't.'

He took out the thermos and handed it to her. 'Then perhaps you'd tell me how it is that your purse was found at the scene of the boy's murder?'

'My purse . . . but . . .?'

He could see that the news was genuinely unexpected and distressing yet she knew exactly which purse he had meant. 'That purse . . . I hardly ever use it, Inspector. It's a prop – it goes with my outfit. I usually leave it in the dressing-room at the club.'

'Empty?'

'But of course,' she snorted. 'I don't exactly like getting up there in front of all those men. Their grins, the catcalls when some of them see me for the first time . . . Would you, Inspector, if you were me and married to a man you loved very much?'

'Then you were framed?' said St-Cyr, speaking his thoughts aloud. 'And my partner and I have been completely fooled.'

'Have you got a cigarette?' she asked, watching him so closely he dropped his eyes to pat his pockets and fish out a crumpled packet.

As he lit her cigarette, her eyes found his. Pools of violet innocence, a cross for any man to bear. He hoped Kohler would have better luck but somehow doubted it.

'Are you married, Inspector?' she asked.

'Yes, I'm married.'

'Happily?'

Was there laughter in her eyes, or the swiftness of cruelty? 'Exactly how much do you know about me, Mademoiselle Arcuri?'

She unscrewed the thermos and filled the cap, which she handed to him. 'Enough to know, Inspector, that your wife has run off.'

St-Cyr laid the cheese and bread on the knapsack and used his penknife to cut them. 'I should ask, how is it that you know this, Mademoiselle Arcuri, but,' he gave another shrug, 'me, I don't think you'd tell me the truth.'

'Try me.'

She had such a nice smile, warm and sensitive and very quick. But was it understanding? Ah, how could one hope for such a thing?

'The General Hans Ackermann?' he said.

'The Hero of Rovno and Berdichev, the Knight of Krivoy Rog. He telephoned us last night. We've been expecting you.'

'Is the general a friend?'

It was her turn to shrug but she did so with complete innocence. 'Of a sort, yes. One needs such friends these days, Inspector. Look, it's nothing sexual so don't get the wrong idea. My husband's dead – he was killed at Sedan in 1940 but me, I'm still married to him and intend to stay that way.'

The coffee was good, not ersatz, and laced with cognac. The cheese was a *chèvre crottin*, a small circle that had been dusted with dill and chives. Very dry and strong in flavour. Real goat's cheese, three, maybe four weeks in the ageing.

The bread was crusty and, with the cheese, a meal. If only there'd been some of the château's wine. He'd have liked to try it.

So she would stay married to a dead man? For love or money or some other reason? 'Mademoiselle . . .'

'Why not try calling me by my name? It's easier.'

'Gabrielle . . .'

'That's better. You've a son and I've one, Inspector, not much older than yours if what the general says is true.'

He passed her the coffee, turning the cap so that she might drink from the clean side. 'Lovers kiss and think nothing of it, Inspector, but I appreciate the gesture. A singer has to.'

'Mademoiselle . . . Look, I want to help.'

'Don't all cops?'

'Why not tell me exactly what happened? As you see it. Leave nothing out, no matter how insignificant it might seem.'

'Have you been an inspector long?'

'The past seventeen years.'

'And before that?'

'A cop on the beat – Montparnasse and Montmartre. Whores and their pimps, bank robbers and their banks.'

'A chief inspector. And the war?' she asked suddenly. 'The first one.' She had to find out everything she could about him.

'Signals Corps, as a sergeant. I was wounded twice. Once in the thigh, and once in the shoulder. My left side seems to be the vulnerable one.'

He could laugh at himself, a good sign. 'Then you'll understand how we feel about the Germans, Inspector. The sooner they're gone, the better.'

'Yet General Ackermann is a friend?'

'He's also a relative. A distant cousin of my mother-in-law.'

The bushy eyebrows lifted. The coffee was replenished. 'I didn't go to Fontainebleau with Yvette, Inspector. When she came back, she was in tears, tearing her hair, wanting to pray and yet so afraid of doing so. She knew the police would accuse her of the murder. She was convinced of this but . . . but when she found Jérome, he was already dead.'

St-Cyr asked the obvious. 'How did she know where to find him?'

Mademoiselle Arcuri looked away. 'She found the bicycle first, at the side of the road, and then the body. She tried to "wake him up". She turned his head so that he'd be comfortable – you can imagine what it must have been like for her. Panic, terror – her brother, for God's sake! She even placed his arms at

132

his sides – tried to tidy him. Look, I didn't kill him, Inspector. I swear I didn't and neither did she.'

There was the shrug of the unconvinced and then the woeful eyes of the same. 'If not you or she, then who?'

'One of the monks, I think.'

'One of the monks?'

Was it so incredible a thought? 'Jérome hated the seminary. He was always getting into trouble – that's why Yvette had to ask for time off and why I let her go home to look after things. If you ask me, Inspector, I think he spied on the other monks and when he threatened to expose them, one of them killed him.'

'In Fontainebleau Woods?'

'Yes. Isn't that a good place for murders? I'm always reading about them in the papers.'

Never mind the necessity for a car – they went on bicycles perhaps. Never mind that there were plenty of closer and far better places, or that there'd been a diary in her purse, a record of liaisons and little tête-à-têtes.

St-Cyr finished the coffee and wrapped up the last of the cheese. 'For now we will let it be, Mademoiselle Arcuri. Your revolver is safe from prying Gestapo eyes but I would like the return of mine. And if I were you, I'd put that shotgun safely away.'

'You're angry with me.'

Was that a pout? 'A little, yes. Me, I had thought we might be square with one another since neither of us particularly likes the Germans.'

'But your partner's a German?'

'War throws the strangest people together. Don't be fooled by him. He's far cleverer than he lets on. It's a way with him. Munich and then Berlin, now Paris Central. A damned good cop.'

And a warning? she wondered. 'I didn't kill Jérome, Inspector, and I wouldn't have killed Yvette. I chased after her, yes, but when I got there, she . . . she'd already been killed.'

No mention of the diary yet or of how she had known where to look. 'So now it's a time for some thought, eh? And a few tears. You can reach me at the Sûreté, number 11, the rue de Saussaies.'

Must he be so tough about it, so obviously disappointed in her? 'Look, if it means anything, Inspector, I hope your wife comes back.'

'So do I.'

Dwarfed by the courtyard and the enclosing walls of the château, Kohler stood waiting beside the car. He *would* leave the keys in the blasted ignition! A lousy habit the General Ackermann had been quick to take advantage of.

And waiting on generals – any of them – had always been a bind.

He glanced at his watch only to see that the time – now 11.18 a.m. – had advanced a mere three minutes since the last look.

Ackermann was letting him cool his heels. Perhaps he and the countess were having a good laugh about it. More likely the general had simply said, My dear, please allow me to deal with this.

Ah yes, you son-of-a-bitch!

Surprisingly there was no flagpole in the centre of the courtyard. If there had been, he'd have stood under it just for old times' sake. Parade grounds and all that garbage!

When Ackermann, less his greatcoat, gloves and cap, stormed out of the château, the bastard walked so swiftly he threw the fear of God into one, and wasn't it a marvel how generals could walk?

'Your marching orders have been moved up, Kohler. If I were you, I'd return to Paris and pack your bags.'

He'd been on the phone to Boemelburg and to Berlin. Kohler knew he ought to shut up but this Prussian flame thrower with the hard eyes, this hero of whatever, had got under his skin.

'General, neither you nor Herr Himmler will stop us from finding out who murdered that boy. I may be Gestapo, but long before that I was a cop. I always have been and I always will be.'

Slim, tall, straight at attention – a ramrod – Ackermann longed for his gloves. He'd have struck this bastard gumshoe across the face for such insolence! 'Pretty speeches will do you no good, Kohler. Your revised orders are being signed by the Führer himself.'

Oh-oh. 'Spare me the invincibility of our illustrious Führer, General. When von Schaumburg hears what I have to say, not even the Führer will put a stop to our investigation.'

Ackermann sized him up. 'How dare you . . .?'

The scars were twisted, the half-eaten nostril flared. There were furrows and gouges in the withered cheek.

'I *dare*, General, because that's my business. Now go and mesh heads with your lady friend but remember, please, she's a suspect and so are you.'

Ackermann swung. Kohler's hand flashed out to grab the withered wrist. 'You incompetent lout!' shrieked Ackermann. 'I'll see you're dealt with!'

The Bavarian released the wrist. 'I'm going, General, but I'll be back, and when the questions start coming, I'll expect your fullest co-operation or else.'

'Get out of here.'

Kohler nodded. 'As soon as you give me the keys.'

Ackermann sucked in a breath. 'Try looking in that drain. I'm sure you'll find the keys if you do.'

No one can turn on his heels quite like a Prussian. Kohler swore under his breath. The general reached the drive which ran in front of the main entrance. A servant, a butler – a broken-down retainer, God knows what the French called them – came out with his coat and things.

The countess came to say goodbye. As they shook hands, she glanced across the grounds towards him.

Then the general left sedately, the Daimler purring past the Citroën, and the lady started towards him.

'You mustn't mind the general, Captain Kohler. Our Hans is not himself these days.'

The keys were in the palm of her outstretched hand.

Lamely Kohler shrugged. 'I never did get on with generals, Countess. That one's only worse than most.'

'Louis, did the general do it?'

'I don't know, Hermann.'

'He's showing all the signs but making such a mess of it.'

'Murderers often do.'

'Not when you've had tanks and flame throwers at your

135

command. No, my friend, Ackermann is deliberately being stupid so as to take the heat off someone else.'

'The countess?'

'Perhaps.'

'Not our chanteuse, our mirage?'

Kohler finished his cigarette and flicked the butt out of the car window towards the Château Thériault that lay above the woods on the other side of the river. 'You've not fallen for the woman, have you, Louis?'

'Me, ah no, of course not. Traces of sympathy, yes, Hermann. I'd like to think her innocent. But no, such feelings won't interfere with the course of justice.'

'Let's go and have a word with the monks. It'll fill out the reports and give Pharand and Boemelburg something to chew on.'

'I wish I knew who wrote that little diary and who had the meetings. I'm not at all certain they are one and the same, Hermann. I didn't get a chance to ask Mademoiselle Arcuri, but she denied leaving her purse, so someone else must have planted it.'

'Or she's lying, Louis, and those violet bedroom eyes have got to your brains which have sunk to your balls.'

St-Cyr heaved a sigh. By all accounts, it had been quite a morning. 'In another time but not in another place, me, I would have to agree with you, Hermann, but are we seeing the truth or is she but the mirage she is forced to play out?'

Kohler switched on the ignition. As he eased the car on to the road, he said, 'When we get back to Paris, I'm going to have to settle things with von Schaumburg. It's our only chance.'

'You don't need to apologize, Hermann. I quite understand.'

'Good, because the fur is going to fly!'

The road to the Abbey of St Gregory the Great seemed to take for ever. It wound up into the tufa hills behind the terraced village of Vouvray, before angling off to the west. Each ridge led down into another valley. It was all the same. Second gear half the time. Goats, barren trees, distant watchful, isolated, cowled monks who exuded only suspicion as they worked the soil or tended their flocks.

Then an old stone bridge fit only for a cart and horse. Narrow – Jesus, it was pinched.

The arches beneath the bridge leapt from a ragged gorge.

Kohler drew the car to a stop. The engine ticked as he hunched over the steering wheel, looking across the bridge and up the winding Roman road to the abbey.

Beehives lay beneath the naked branches of an orchard. Rows and rows of vines reminded him of the military graves in Belgium.

'Louis, this place . . . It gives me the creeps. *Gott in Himmel*, were the monks afraid of something?'

'They built to last, Hermann, and in the twelfth century, they had plenty to fear.'

The place was stark – right on a hilltop. A massive turret of bleached stone, whose portals stared out and down at all visitors, was surmounted by a cake of low-roofed stone buildings and capped by a square bell tower that could only be described as brutal.

'Then those monks knew what they were doing,' said Kohler, easing his crotch. A pinched testicle again. Son-of-a-bitch! 'Ah, this underwear of mine, Louis! It's like a novice whore's first touch.'

The door burst open. He winced as he eased himself out of the car. 'That left ball of mine, it's never been right since the war. Swelled up ten times its proper size – did I ever tell you, Louis? An infection . . . a cold in the balls from all that mud.'

'A thousand times,' said St-Cyr.

'Like a Corsican lemon. Hard as a walnut,' went on Kohler. 'One squirt, Louis. God but it . . .'

The tall black wooden cross above the bell tower drew their attention. 'We're being watched,' said St-Cyr. 'The Benedictines' bush telegraph is at work.'

'Shall we leave the shooters?'

'It's not necessary. They'll expect them. Please remember my car keys, though.'

Kohler tugged at his trousers to ease the underwear down. 'Never mind the bullshit, Louis. I won't forget them again. You can bet your last sou on that.'

'Good!' St-Cyr looked up at the rustic signboard that stood beside the bridge. 'They raise mushrooms, make goats' cheese, sell the wine they produce and the honey. Perhaps we can stock up, eh?'

'Personally, I can't see us lugging a couple of sacks of clinking bottles down that road. Come on, let's get on with it. We're lucky it isn't raining, that's all I can say.'

The abbey was perhaps a kilometre from where they had been forced to leave the car. From time to time they paused to look back. Monks pruned the vines. The last of the harvest was in. Some tilled the soil, others tightened the wires along which the vines had been trained, or replaced the stout wooden posts. No idleness, of course. Five . . . perhaps six or even seven hours of manual labour a day. Cold bare hands, raw splits in the knuckles. Cold rooms. No heat but God's and vesper candles.

The road wound beneath the tower. As yet the gate was out of sight.

Then there was the Loire in the distance below them across innumerable rows of vines and shelving terraces.

'Château Thériault, Louis. Gabrielle Arcuri could have told you how close this place was to it.'

'It's not in her nature to have warned us, Hermann. After all, we're not exactly on the same side, eh?'

The low stone walls of the abbey's vineyards ran downhill towards those of the Domaine Thériault. Woods, stony patches of pasture, a stream, two apple orchards, a road . . . all these things they took in.

'Would she be a friend of the abbot, I wonder?' commented Kohler. 'If so, Louis, we'll never pull that woman in if we have to and neither will the Resistance.'

Everywhere they looked there were potential hiding places and routes of escape.

St-Cyr yanked on the heavy iron chain. A distant bell thudded in cloistered warrens. An eternity passed before the bolts clashed and at last the iron-studded door was eased open.

A silent rock of ages with bright, mischievous eyes, stooped shoulders and a toothless grin motioned them in as if in secret.

The House-guest Brother.

'It's a day for silence, messieurs. Our humble apologies but none are allowed to speak until after the service at midnight.'

His eyes lit up at the prospect of such a late service. Kohler simply lost patience. 'Gestapo, you ancient fart! Take us to the abbot and I'll show you the worth of your "vow" of silence! We're on a murder case.'

The mischievousness disappeared. Brother Andrew calmly studied this German as if such a thing had never been seen before. Without another word, he beckoned them to follow. He even left the door wide open. Perhaps it was too heavy.

An easy exit? wondered St-Cyr, glancing sternly at Kohler before saying, 'Hermann, I think you'd better leave this to me.'

'My patience is gone, Louis. Half those bastards in the fields are of military age, and most of that half are in their twenties.'

'Why else would France have lost the war? If not at the breast then at the prayers, eh? A nation of shits, Hermann. I don't like it any better than you.'

All this, of course, the monk overheard.

Columned cloisters led to others and others. Open portals let in all weathers and the wind up here sighed as their steps echoed.

They passed a scriptorium where monks diligently copied centuries-old writings or made fervent little notes to themselves on scraps of paper – odd bits of old envelopes, the backs of letters from home.

They crossed the main dining hall beneath arched beams and carved stones. The heavy, dark oak tables and their benches were the original ones. Kohler would swear to it.

Great black iron rings on heavy chains held candles that hung from the ceiling but how the hell could they possibly light the things? They were way up there among the gods.

Down a narrow passage, now thoroughly lost, they came to a black oak door upon which a fierce and much-bearded Adam held the gnarled club of a branch in one fist and a shield in the other. Some poor bugger's head was clutched by the hair. Now what the hell . . . had that been in the Good Book?

The corridor resounded to the banging the monk gave the door. A slot shot into place – black letters on white wood: BUSY.

Nothing else.

The monk indicated two narrow benches. You must wait, he motioned, touching his lips in the gesture of silence.

Kohler stepped past him and tried the door. 'It's bolted. He's busy,' whispered Brother Andrew. 'I must leave you now, messieurs. May God forgive me for speaking on this holy of holy days.'

His departing figure fluttered down the draughty passage. Sandals and bare feet . . . Jesus Christ! 'They've got us right where they want us, Louis. So, why the cold shoulder, eh?'

'Because of this, I think, Hermann. Did you not notice them?'

Kohler looked at the fist-sized boulder St-Cyr placed in his hand. 'Flint,' he heard himself saying. 'A brownish, off-white, cream-coloured flint.'

The Bavarian lifted questioning eyes to his partner.

St-Cyr fished out his pipe. Hermann needed a little time – one must not appear too intelligent.

He lit up, got the furnace going, then ran his eyes over the Adam and Eve. Such differences the progress of civilization had made in the perception of those two. They were very savage, very Germanic-looking. At war with the world.

'The boulder that killed the boy, Hermann. I should have seen it. It was stupid of me not to have.'

'A hunk of flint like this?' asked the Bavarian incredulously.

The Frenchman nodded. 'At the time, I thought nothing of it – river transport, glaciers – gravel from somewhere. It comes from many places when it's spread along a road. But I have to admit, Fontainebleau Woods is blessed with much dark brown and grey sandstone. That boulder came from here.'

The rheumy, sad dog's eyes lifted in their pouches. 'Louis, just what the hell have we got ourselves into this time?'

St-Cyr savoured the moment. Crime never ceased to fascinate him. 'We have a real murder on our hands, Hermann. What was once apparently so simple has now become a quite different matter.'

'Then you no longer think we had it pegged?'

'Far from it. No, my friend, we are almost certainly going to be forced to strip back the layers of the fungus, teasing out each slender thread until we have unravelled the whole thing.'

Louis loved nothing better than a good case but . . . 'I only hope von Schaumburg will listen.' Glotz . . . there was also the problem of Brother Glotz to contend with, and Boemelburg, of course.

'Von Schaumburg will listen, Hermann. It's the Resistance that bothers me.'

'They won't have sent you a little black coffin, Louis.'
'Me, I'm afraid that is just what they've done.'

'The flint is what gives our wine its noble flavour, messieurs,' said the Reverend Father, gazing sadly at the boulder the French detective had plunked down in the middle of his desk.

St-Cyr knew the business of the boulder was still very much a gamble but a little emphasis wouldn't hurt, and as for the vows of silence, the boulder had shattered them. 'It's what led us to your abbey, Reverend Father. That and my humble knowledge of the Vouvray, that greatest of the Loire wines, next to the Anjou of course.'

The Anjou . . . pah! 'Our silicious clay, Inspector – the *perruches* – produces a delicate wine, very light, you understand, but exceedingly noble, whereas the *aubuis*, our other clay, has much limestone in it. The fruity flavour of its grape is therefore very piquant and the wine a good keeper. We do not blend them. The one cancels the other, but I suppose you know all this?'

The abbot searched the faces of the two men. He must be careful. God grant him the grace and wisdom to deal with the matter. So much was at stake. The boulder had come from the *perruches* on the hillside below the abbey but had the one which had killed the boy also come from there?

'Brother Michael was the Novice Jérome's mentor. You will want to talk to him, Inspectors, and I must release him from his vow of silence.'

The heave of his robust shoulders was one of, You see what a man of the cloth has to do? 'Our Lady Scholastica, messieurs. The brothers are always having their little visitations. Ever since this past summer, in the heat of August. First one dreams of her and then another. All plead for a day's silence and me, I can see that it can do no harm to allow them a certain penance.'

You wise old owl, thought Kohler, snorting inwardly. Who was it they saw bathing in the river? The Arcuri woman or her maid? 'Our Lady Scholastica . . .' A hiked-up habit, eh? Come on now, Reverend Father.

The abbot's gaze was clear. 'We will find Brother Michael in the caves, messieurs. If you would be good enough to follow

141

me, I will, of course, have to take you there myself. No one else can release Brother Michael from his vow. He's very strict, that one. He refuses even to communicate by gestures or written words on such days. Me, I am concerned he might fall ill at such a time but . . . ah, God will never refuse grace. He had much patience with Brother Jérome, you understand. Infinite patience. They argued of course. What more can I say? The wine, you understand. The shipments to Paris and elsewhere. The Germans . . . Forgive me, Inspector Kohler. Once released, you see what the tongue does. Midnight is still a long way off.'

He lifted tired, brown, worried eyes from the boulder, then thought better of leaving the thing so openly on the desk.

Pocketing the boulder somewhere in the coarse black habit, he came round the desk, was all graciousness now. 'We will have a glass of our wine in the cellars, eh? In honour of your little visit, *and* perhaps if it is to your taste, a bottle or two to take away with you.'

One thing was certain, they'd never get to talk to Brother Michael alone.

A corridor led to stone steps and these, down to the start of a long tunnel which ran under the hill for some distance.

'Voilà, our caves, messieurs,' said the abbot. He was obviously pleased with the effect, though he must have shown the place thousands of times.

The 'caves' were huge and lit by infrequent electric lights. Rows and rows of barrels lay on their sides. Beyond the barrels there were other caves that held racks of bottles. Here and there in the feeble light silent monks patiently turned bottle after bottle.

'It's done each day,' confided St-Cyr.

They could hear the patient drip of water and against this, the shuffling sandals of the monks and the hush each bottle made as it was turned in the rack. It was like no other sound Kohler had heard.

Brother Michael was in the fermentation room, holding a glass of the white before a lighted candle, grim, taciturn, grizzled – well up in his sixties, a man of little patience when it came to the youth of today.

The black beret was clapped on the wide grey head. Hairs sprouted from beneath it. No monk's tonsure for this one. No

142

habit either. A man of less than medium height, he wore blue denim from head to ankle and sensible black boots.

The lips were turned down in grim contemplation of the wine. Sad grey eyes, bags under them, a full, hooked nose, so typically French, warts and moles and jowls . . . Kohler could just imagine him discussing the doubts of the flesh with that young boy. Had Brother Jérome's pecker been stiff? he wondered. Had the good Brother Michael not caught the younger man at a little self-gratification?

Ah now . . .

'Brother Michael, hear me,' said the abbot, making the sign of the Cross.

The eyes fled anxiously from the glass to take them in. 'Our Lady Scholastica frees you from your vow of silence, Brother,' went on the abbot.

Still there was no sound from the man. Hurt-filled eyes now flicked from one to the other of them. 'But I had a dream, Reverend Father . . .?'

'It's all right, Brother Michael. Our Lord will understand. Now don't take on. A glass of your wine for our guests and then a private word, I think. Yes, that would suit God's way and that of our Holy Rule.'

The wine was drawn from a barrel in yet another of the caverns. Brother Michael waited tensely for their reactions. St-Cyr wafted in the bouquet before letting the wine pass his lips.

It was a *moelleux*, of Sauterne sweetness and robust fruity flavour. Clean and crisp on the palate.

He nodded curtly. 'It's magnificent, Brother Michael. Me, I would like to purchase a dozen bottles if it were not for the rationing.'

Brother Michael heaved his shoulders. 'It's all sold in any case. Goering of the Luftwaffe sent his buyer. We will of course keep some for ourselves, but not much.'

'Brother Michael . . .' began St-Cyr.

'Please allow me,' interrupted the abbot. 'Brother Michael, these gentlemen have come to see you on a matter of great delicacy. It appears, Brother, that the rock which killed our beloved Brother Jérome came from our district. Perhaps from as much as seven . . . perhaps eight, or would it be twelve

143

kilometres over which the *perruches* would be found with its boulders?'

Brother Michael didn't bat an eye. 'Twenty-eight kilometres, Reverend Father. Much of the Domaine Thériault, our own, and downstream, I believe, as far as Rochercorbon there is such a silicious clay. Those boulders . . .' He clucked his tongue. 'They cause much trouble with the plough.'

St-Cyr again tried to step into things but the abbot smiled benignly. Apparently the vow of silence could only be broken one way. 'They wish to know your opinions of Brother Jérome, Brother Michael. Please, I know how distressing this must be for you, but,' the abbot clasped his hands in the sign of prayer, 'God's grace is infinitely understanding.'

The monk clucked his tongue and ground his false teeth. 'The boy had no sense of vocation, Reverend Father. Always going off to see his sister. Doubts . . . plagued by doubts. Paris . . . when we shipped wine to Paris, he hid in our truck, our beloved gasogene. Brother Emanuel discovered him. He was *not* at the appointed place on the return journey.'

A fussy man once unleashed. The abbot, far from discouraging him, said, 'And, Brother, what else? Theft, I believe.'

'Yes . . . Yes, God forbid – we have nothing of our own here, but some will covet little things, Reverend Father. You know I've urged the birch many times. A small gold figurine the Brother Lucien found in the fields. Seven centuries of mould and worth something, I am certain.'

He paused to blink and blow his nose. He was obviously greatly distressed. 'Brother Jérome sold the figurine in Paris, Reverend Father. He said he had to have money for prostitutes, Father. I have prayed for his soul ever since.'

'Did anyone visit him here?' attempted St-Cyr.

Kohler merely watched the proceedings, likening the pair of them to a couple of carnival shysters.

'Visit?' exclaimed Brother Michael, darting eyes at the abbot for reassurance. 'Yes . . . yes of course he had visitors. Always that sister of his, always the long walks and talks, the cajoling, the pleading. Always picnics by the river. Swimming . . .' He knew he'd said too much. God forgive him. 'Brother Jérome was unclean, messieurs. Soiled.'

'Now, Brother . . .' began the abbot.

'Our vows of chastity are sacred, Reverend Father.'

'You have no proof, Brother Michael. This business of prosti- tutes in Paris was never proven. There wasn't a shred of evidence. The boy was merely telling you to mind your own business. You must search your soul on this matter, Brother. I command that you do so.'

'He made allegations of an improper nature against Brother Sebastian, our beekeeper, Reverend Father. I didn't wish to trouble you with the matter until I had had the opportunity to investigate. He borrowed my bicycle far too many times,' went on the wine maker. 'I'd *like* to have it back. These old legs of mine . . .'

Again St-Cyr stepped in, this time with more success. 'The Préfet of Barbizon will see that it is returned to you, but tell me, Brother Michael, to ride so far . . .? Would someone not have given him a lift?'

'Plenty of times. The countess in her car. Others, too, per- haps.' He gave a shrug and turned away.

Was the interview to be concluded on such a note of innu- endo? 'A moment, Brother,' said St-Cyr desperately. 'The Gen- eral Hans Ackermann perhaps? He visits the château, I believe?'

'The general . . .?' Brother Michael flung a look at the abbot who calmly said:

'A distant cousin, I believe, Brother Michael.'

'Me, I don't know about such things. I only know Brother Jérome was absent far too many times.'

St-Cyr gave them another moment then gambled. 'Did he sign his will, Brother Michael?'

'His will? No . . . No, he . . .' Dear God forgive him. 'No, he . . . he refused. When . . . when I went to look for it in his box in the scriptorium, it . . . it was missing, Reverend Father. I would have told you but . . .'

'You *should* have told me, Brother Michael. I'll see you before chapel. In my office! Gentlemen, your interview is concluded. Follow the arrows and they will lead you out to our road. Good day.'

'What was that all about?' asked Kohler when they'd gone some distance.

St-Cyr tossed his hands in a gesture to the gods of gambling on a shoestring. 'As a Benedictine novice, Hermann, Brother

Jérome was required to renounce all worldly goods and give himself to Christ and his God.'

'So, what's the problem?'

'Ah, the problem, my friend. The problem . . . Before taking their final vows each novice signs over his worldly goods to the monastery. He makes out a will and it's as if he has already died.'

'But he couldn't have had anything in any case? His father's the Chef de Culture at the Domaine Thériault. The countess told me the family had worked for them for the past ninety-seven years. If that isn't indentured slavery, I don't know what is!'

'It's what the countess didn't tell you that puzzles me, Hermann. Why, for instance, should the Benedictines accept such an unworthy candidate – true, he was escaping his military service like so many others and true, money – a donation – may have changed hands, but still . . .? And why was he such a pretty boy, as is the son of Mademoiselle Arcuri? No, my friend, there's more to this than meets the eye. These old families . . .' St-Cyr clucked his tongue and shook his head. 'Sometimes life is so simple, Hermann, we don't see the obvious.'

'Perhaps it's time we paid our respects to the grieving family?'

'My thoughts exactly.'

Visitations were being held at both of Vouvray's funeral homes but it was to the larger of them that they went.

The countess was waiting for them and, as she got out of her car, St-Cyr nudged the Bavarian and said, 'She's decided to save us time, Hermann. Better this than a confrontation with the grief-stricken parents.'

He was impressed. When the chips were down the countess hadn't hesitated. That's what it took to run such a place. Decisions, decisions, always things to decide.

'Let the parents have their grief in private with their friends and relations. Jérome was fathered by my husband. Look, I don't know who told him of it but he had some crazy idea that it would entitle him to a share of the Domaine Thériault and the monks believed him.'

'But the Domaine belongs to your grandson on your death?' exclaimed St-Cyr.

'Yes, of course René Yvon-Paul inherits everything unless Gabrielle should marry before he comes of age.'

'How many people know of this?' demanded St-Cyr. No time for pleasantries or introductions. A stunning woman . . .

'Too many. Now, please, I've told you what I can. Leave them in peace, for God's sake. They've suffered enough. Both of their children . . . No bodies to bury as yet . . .'

She turned away so swiftly, on impulse St-Cyr reached out to comfort her.

A silk handkerchief was found in her purse. He helped her to her car. 'We'll be in touch, Countess. For now it goes without saying, no one is to leave the district and we'll pop into the préfecture to make them aware of it.'

This one was kinder than the Bavarian. Though sudden, her tears had convinced him that at least she was sincere.

'Give my regards to Mademoiselle Arcuri, Countess. I'm sure we'll all have much more to say when we meet again.'

She managed a weak and grateful smile. 'I knew you'd understand. Gabrielle was quite taken with you, Inspector. She liked your honesty. She said you were very considerate for one so diligent.'

5

It was well after curfew when Kohler let him out at the foot of the rue Laurence Savart but then drove up the street into the darkness anyway. St-Cyr cringed as the sound of the Citroën's muffler fled through the city, he following its location with uncanny accuracy.

Hermann shot across the boulevard de Belleville. When he reached the Place de la République, he swung the car in a screeching loop and pelted back up the hills going faster . . . faster . . . leaning on the horn as well. Ah, Mon Dieu, what was the matter?

The car shot into the street, the Bavarian braked hard. 'Get in, Louis.'

'Hermann . . .'

'Look, you son-of-a-bitch, I told you to get in and that's an order!'

When they reached the house, Kohler threw the car into neutral and yanked on the emergency brake. 'Now give me your torch. Mine fell on the road and broke.'

Leaving the car door open, he proceeded to sweep the front gate with the light, crouching to run his fingers lightly round the sill and then up over the latch. 'So far so good,' he breathed. 'I'd hate to be picking butcher's pieces of you off the walls.'

Gingerly Hermann opened the gate. All his training in demolitions came to the fore. Intuitively he knew where to look. 'Okay,' he snorted. 'Now for the walk, eh, Louis?'

There were no tripwires, no hidden grenades or mines. 'Clean,' he said with surprise. Perhaps they'd been cleverer than he'd thought? 'Now give me your key, Louis. Come on, don't waste my time.'

'It's under the mat. Hermann, Madame Courbet comes in each day. If there'd been any surprises, her youngest son would have been waiting to tell me.'

'Idiot! Boys can't always be trusted, Louis. You of all people ought to know that after this morning.'

Kohler found the key then felt around the door jamb before easing the door open a millimetre and shining the torch all round.

Satisfied, he nudged the door wide and shone the light into the vestibule – did the floor and walls, picked out a chair, a cabinet with its mirror and the coat pegs one by one.

He crouched to place three fingers lightly on the floor, then gingerly lifted a corner of the carpet. 'Your housekeeper ought to do under here,' he said. So far so good . . .

'Hermann, if the Resistance wanted to nail me, they'd have simply waited in the street.'

The Bavarian shone the light up into St-Cyr's face. 'Louis, why do you think I came back? Those bastards were waiting for you. I flushed them out and chased after them. They had a motorcycle. There were two of them.'

St-Cyr blinked painfully and shielded his eyes. A motorcycle . . .

'Let's have a look at your mail, eh?' said Kohler, swinging the beam of the torch over the cabinet.

A motorcycle . . . 'It'll be on the kitchen table. Madame Courbet will have put it there.'

She'd done more than this. Several of his books, including the Daudet he'd been reading, had been destroyed, their pages made into papier-mâché balls which were now being patiently dried for use in the stove. Two of the books had been from the central library . . . In the name of Jesus, why couldn't the woman have asked?

'We'd better get you some coal and a couple of sacks of kindling out of Gestapo stores,' snorted Kohler.

'You do and my neighbours will only hate me. Envy's a terrible thing, Hermann. Pity is much better.'

'Fuck your neighbours then.'

Among the dross there was a small brown package.

Kohler stopped the Frenchman's hand. 'I'll get the Unexploded Bomb boys to deal with it, Louis. Why take the chance?

Then we'll clean the rats' nest out. We can't have them interfering at a time like this.'

The Resistance . . . 'Hermann, leave it, will you? It's only a warning, eh? Me, I can take care of myself.'

'Since when? *Gott in Himmel*, it's not your ass I'm worried about! It's mine, you idiot! If something should happen to you, what the hell could I say to von Schaumburg? Oh sorry, General, but the man whose wife ran off with your nephew has just been blown to pieces?'

St-Cyr tore the wrapping paper off the thing and laid the little black coffin on the table between them. The Resistance had spelled his name correctly, even adding the Jean to the Louis.

Kohler gripped him by a shoulder and gave him a brotherly shake. 'Try to get some sleep, eh? I'll be in touch.'

They both stood there looking down at that thing. The beam of the torch fell on it as a stage light in some seedy nightclub, a last act, a fond fairwell. A chanteuse in an iridescent sheath of silk and pearls, a mirage, an angel with a voice . . .

'It doesn't make any sense, Hermann. It simply doesn't.'

'Does anything in war? If so, be sure to let me know.'

St-Cyr followed him out to the car, then stood at the kerbside long after he'd left. It had been such a worthwhile day, so good to be out of the city and in the country. A real challenge and now this, a complete misunderstanding, a piece of foolishness.

As he turned to go back into the house, the swish of slippers came to him in a rush and then a woman's silhouette and the hesitant, breathless and inquisitive tongue of Madame Courbet, still in her nightdress and cap.

Thank God it was dark! 'You had a visitor,' she said. 'Late this afternoon. He wouldn't take no for an answer when I told him you were away, and how was I to refuse? I had to get the key and let him into your house. A general . . . one so disfigured . . . Ah, Mon Dieu, those boys . . . the filthy urchins, my son Antoine excepted, all ran from him in fright but called him names.'

'A general?'

'Yes, Ackermann. A friend of yours. He noticed the shoes, Inspector, just as I did.'

The woman clutched the throat of her nightgown. When there wasn't any response, she continued. 'Such pretty shoes, Inspector. It's a shame one of the heels has been broken but my husband's brother, the one with the limp, he is very good at fixing such things. Me, I could arrange to have them repaired.'

The rumours must be flying. 'The girl was only someone I met in a street after curfew, madame. I don't even know her name.'

'Then you'll want to sell the shoes?' asked the woman quickly.

No . . . No, he wouldn't want to do that. 'They must be returned,' he said, digging an even deeper hole for himself. 'She was very young, a student, you understand, madame. You know how such girls are.'

Ah yes, she did – who didn't? A student. Pretty no doubt. Young and stupid and thinking only of a warm bed and a meal. Warm in that house? God forbid.

She rubbed her slippered toes together. So, the girl had come back with him and had left her shoes . . . They'd have spent the night together. It was just like a man! The wife not gone and he'd taken up with someone younger . . .

'Madame Courbet . . .'

'Yes?' she demanded haughtily.

'The postman . . . When did he leave that little parcel?'

The girl had sent him a little gift, stolen of course. 'This morning, Inspector.'

You don't need to get uptight! said St-Cyr inwardly, resigning himself to more difficulties. 'And the General Ackermann saw it?'

'But of course. He picked it up.'

St-Cyr thanked the woman and waited until she'd gone out through the gate before closing the door.

Then he stood facing the darkness of the door while listening to the silence of the house. It was mad – crazy. Mayhem . . . yes, yes, mayhem! Ah, what the hell was he going to do? Go into hiding? Hermann wouldn't let the matter lie. Hermann would have to do something about it.

Kohler breezed into the garage at Gestapo Headquarters, number 11 rue de Saussaies, to let the graveyard shift know they ought to take better care of the muffler. Then he went through to the duty sergeant to file a report on the incident.

151

'A Wehrmacht dispatch rider's bike, camouflaged and with the insignia of the Fifth Armoured Division. Bastard's probably in bed with the sister. He'll have paid her off by loaning the bike to her brother. A girl rode behind. There was just the two of them. Green as grass and nervous as hell. About twenty or twenty-two years of age – the girl, that is. Short hair, but wearing the usual beret, so the hair could have been longer.'

Porki Schultz lifted lead grey smouldering eyes from his typewriter. 'Any idea where to look?'

Schultz always liked the young ones. A real sadist. 'I'd be there now if I had. Tell countersubversion to keep an eye on St-Cyr's house. The bastards have put the number out on him.'

'St-Cyr?'

'That's just what I said, wasn't it?'

'Have you seen Glotz yet?'

There was a grin Kohler didn't like. 'I only just got in. How could I have?'

A man of forty-seven winters, one wife and eight children back home, Schultz loved exercising authority. 'A hot little number. You'd better go and see him. He was hanging around the front door not ten minutes ago.'

'He's probably snoring it off in the toilets then.'

'Not likely. Try the sound room. They've set up a projector and matched the film with the recording. Your partner's wife has an ass like a full moon, Hermann. Round and beautiful. You can see right up it.'

Son-of-a-bitch! 'I'm getting to like it here less and less.'

Schultz grinned. 'From what I hear, we won't have the pleasure of your company for long. Oh, hang on a minute. A note from our boss. The Sturmbannführer Boemelburg will see you at 8 a.m.'

'I've got to see von Schaumburg first.'

'Orders, my dear Hermann. Orders.'

'Fuck your orders. I've more important things to do.'

'We'll be sure to let him know.'

'You do that then!'

Kohler went down the marble steps to the basement. There was blood and hair on two of them; some poor bastard's front tooth on a third. A small pool of blood and vomit lay at the bottom.

Screams in the night, the sound of truncheons and then silence. Absolute silence.

As he passed one of the interrogation rooms he couldn't help but see through the open door. The girl was naked and hung by her wrists from a meat hook. There was blood all over her back and rump. Her face had been badly battered. Her breasts were bruised . . .

'*The names of your accomplices*?' shrieked the interrogator.

The girl found the will to mumble, 'Never!' and they laid right into her. While one grabbed her by the hair and savagely yanked her head back, the other one hit her across the breasts and stomach. You'd think they hated her. You'd think she'd done something to them personally.

'Dead,' shouted Kohler. 'She's dead. You've broken her neck, you stupid bastard. She'll not tell you anything.'

The eyes were wild. Sweat poured from the brow. 'Escapists . . . British pilots . . . there's a gang of them operating out of the Gare de l'Est. They send the bastards through from Brussels.'

'Maybe so, and maybe not, eh?' snapped Kohler. 'But that one's finished, so you'd better cut her down.'

He was glad Louis wasn't with him. Apart from the interrogator, who was Gestapo, the enforcers were French, real tough guys when it came to wires and ropes and kids.

Glotz was eating sausage and having a beer while watching a rerun of the latest film. He'd just got to the foreplay part. Marianne St-Cyr was still wearing most of her things – an open blouse, a slip whose shoulder strap had been brushed down over the smooth contours of her flesh, no skirt, meshed stockings that went up under the slip, a brassiere and underwear. She was leaning back against something, a table perhaps, a bureau – it was hard to tell. Her legs were spread for a better grip, the feet planted firmly. She had good pins.

Steiner was fully clothed as befitted a German officer, but he wasn't in uniform. His hands were on her breasts. The couple were kissing, teasing each other.

They weren't in the bedroom – so Glotz's boys must have set up more than one camera.

They were in the dining-room perhaps. It was still too hard to tell.

Glotz affected a bored air. 'The slip's crimson, the stockings are black, and the brassiere and briefs are white. It's a pity we couldn't get it in colour for you, Hermann, but we're trying.'

Kohler switched off the spool but not the lamp. Glotz dropped the sausage and spilled the beer as he leapt to prevent the film from burning. 'Idiot! What the hell do you think you're doing?'

The Bavarian's pistol was levelled at him. 'Merely borrowing the film, my friend, for a meeting with von Schaumburg.'

'You wouldn't . . .'

Glotz was aghast. The Wehrmacht would gladly turn back the Gestapo's clock. 'Oh, wouldn't I?' said Kohler.

'We've copies – two of them. Berlin will hear of this.'

The carp's eyes were popping. 'So will von Schaumburg.'

'A truce?' blurted Glotz. He didn't like the look in Hermann's eyes.

'A truce? Why? I don't owe you a thing.'

'Then perhaps you'd better see what else we have.'

Ah, *merde*! 'Weren't the two of them alone?'

The man from Special Unit X, the Watchers, knew he had the Bavarian by the short hairs but he wouldn't smile. He'd be serious about it. 'Why not wait and see? After all, Hermann, if you're going to blow the whistle on your friends and comrades in the Gestapo, you should know exactly what else we have. Old Shatter Hand will only ask. He'll want you to be thorough. There's no sense in your going off half-cocked, now is there?'

Three . . . had there been three of them in the flat, apart from St-Cyr's son and the nursemaid? A ménage-à-trois? Ah no . . .

Glotz waited. Somehow he had to find out what Kohler and St-Cyr had come up with on their unauthorized trip. Berlin was insisting they be kept informed. He needed details of the murders, details of Ackermann's position in things. 'The girl, Hermann . . . The wife of your partner . . . It's not on that spool of film.'

It was a lie, of course, which the Bavarian was only too quick to sense.

But was it really a lie? Kohler knew he couldn't take that chance. 'Okay, so let it roll. I'll watch.'

Glotz heaved a sigh. 'While I'm rewinding this, Hermann, you can fill me in on things. I gather Ackermann paid the Château Thériault a little visit only to find you there?'

'Why's Berlin so interested?'

'A hero, why else? One of the Waffen-SS's finest. Ackermann's been on to them about the murders. They want results, Hermann. They're insisting on it.'

'Yet they've issued St-Cyr and me with marching orders?'

'The General Ackermann was upset with your handling of the case. I gather you made an unauthorized search of the Arcuri woman's flat?'

'We didn't find a thing. I still say Berlin's too interested. What's Ackermann done that he shouldn't have?'

So it had got to that already? 'Why not wait to see the film?' Baiting Kohler – whetting his appetite – was enjoyable. 'She's really quite a handsome woman, this wife of your partner. St-Cyr will see these, Hermann. This I can guarantee you unless . . .'

Glotz would do it too. 'Gabrielle Arcuri's maid was murdered in Fontainebleau Woods by the Resistance. We've several new suspects in the murder of the boy.'

'The Countess Thériault?' asked Glotz, running the film through the rewind.

'Yes, her. She's only a distant cousin.'

'Once a cousin, always a cousin. Who else?'

'The boy's sister – Gabrielle's maid – and perhaps one of the monks at a local monastery.'

'But you said several *new* suspects?' demanded Glotz. 'The Arcuri woman?'

Kohler hated himself. 'Yes, her, of course, and someone else but I'm not saying who it is.'

'Oh? Then you'd better see this, and you'd better remember that St-Cyr will see it before he heads off to the salt mines. It's all up to you.'

'Ackermann . . . we're not sure of him. He's far too close to things.'

The sausage lay beside the beer. 'Ackermann's only trying to look out for the countess, Hermann. He has his cousin's best interests at heart.'

'And Berlin?' asked Kohler quietly. 'Whose interests has Herr Himmler at heart, other than his own and those of the Führer?'

'The Reich's of course. This you shouldn't have to question, but I'll be sure to let them know in my reports. Now put the peashooter away and stop eyeing my sausage and beer.'

The film began to turn. Glotz clapped on the earphones and fussed with the tape recorder before handing him a spare headset. 'How's that for volume? We wouldn't want to hurt your ears.'

The volume was just fine and the focus perfect. Kohler pried one of Glotz's earphones off. 'There was a diary. Louis still has it, but it clearly spells out the boy's meetings with someone over the past eight months and it gave as one of the locations, the place where the maid was murdered.'

'A diary and a pouch of diamonds,' said Glotz, sucking on a tooth. 'Who's the someone?'

It was Kohler's turn to grin and as he did so, he shook his head.

So be it then. Watch and learn, you bastard. Berlin would hear of everything!

Glotz cranked the volume up. From all around him Kohler could hear the harsh, quick breathing of Marianne St-Cyr. It was like thunder to him, like agony. Then she gave a soft murmur – a melting as her lips parted and the kiss drained the breath from her. Wet . . . Jesus, the woman must be wet. But where the hell were the two of them? The rumpled bed was empty, the lens of the camera focused on the sheets and pillows while the action went on somewhere else.

'A minor difficulty we've rectified,' said Glotz, though Kohler couldn't possibly have heard him.

Naked, the woman appeared, draped over the footboard of the bed. There was no mistaking who it was. The screen was full of her – lust and passion in the wide blue eyes, the blood pounding in her cheeks, her chest heaving as she sucked in another breath.

Steiner now stood behind her with his hands on her buttocks. Moulding them, caressing them.

It began. It was going to go on and on.

'The diary, Hermann. Who wrote it?'

Kohler whipped off the earphones. 'What? What was that?'

Steiner was now milking Marianne St-Cyr's splendidly ripe breasts. She was pushing herself up against him. Did she like it that way best? he wondered. More contact? Poor Louis . . .

'The diary, Hermann? Who wrote it?'

'We don't know.'

'Was the other party named?'

Kohler found he couldn't take his eyes from the screen. As Marianne St-Cyr turned, she raised her arms and wrapped them about the tall, blond Aryan's neck. God, she had a gorgeous ass.

'No . . . No, the other party wasn't named.'

'Any ideas?' asked the film director.

Kohler wet his throat. 'None . . . Not at the moment. A lover, that's all.' Damn Glotz anyway!

'Could the diary have been kept by a third party?'

The couple were now lying across the bed. Marianne St-Cyr's head was over the edge. Steiner was spreading her legs. He was kneeling between them. His cock was as stiff as a hammer handle.

'A third party?' shot Kohler, surprised not by the possibility, only that Glotz should have such an idea.

'The countess, for instance,' said Glotz, 'or the Arcuri woman?'

'We hadn't thought of that,' said Kohler, lying through his teeth but lamely.

'Blackmail?' demanded Glotz.

The diamonds . . . 'Perhaps. Who knows?'

Steiner had parted the lips. The bastard was blowing on the woman's clitoris. St-Cyr's wife was running her fingers through her hair like a crazy woman. She was pushing her mons up at him, was rocking her head from side to side and straining for it. 'Erich . . . Erich . . . Ah, Mon Dieu, Mon Dieu, I love it when you do that to me!'

Steiner turned the woman over on to her stomach and the fun really began.

Paris at 3 a.m. was like nothing on earth. One might as well have been in Fontainebleau Woods for all the noise there was.

The whisper of the bicycle's wheels was St-Cyr's only company. There were no patrols, though he wasn't particularly afraid of meeting them. There was simply no one but himself, no light but the occasional blue flame of a kerbside pot. Nothing from the stars. No lingering moon.

Not even the added hush of falling snow.

He passed the Opéra. To meet no one on the boulevard Haussmann was eerie. When he reached the Arc de Triomphe, the eternal flame gave ghostly shadows to the innermost recesses.

He took the avenue Victor Hugo – wondered whether the war would erase the writer's work from the face of the earth. All those stoves in Paris alone; women like Madame Courbet who'd never read a book in their lives and had no appreciation of such things.

When he came to the avenue Henri Martin, St-Cyr got off the bike. At first it was a little hard to pick out the individual apartment blocks. Number 33 was just like all the others and when he'd finally located it, he stood on the walkway looking up at its dark silhouette.

Marianne would be asleep in the Hauptmann Erich Steiner's arms. Was he to wake the concierge, to cause a fuss? Marianne would be so embarrassed, she'd start to cry. She'd never come back to him if he did such a thing. After all, she had her pride as well as he, and Philippe would be bound to awaken.

The Resistance . . . It wasn't likely they'd use explosives. Far better the bullet and the fast getaway, hence tonight's motorcycle.

Hermann was just being his thorough Bavarian self. Taking charge of things as if he always knew what was best. He would have asked countersubversion to watch the house. He'd have filed a report on the incident. So, was the trip across town all for nothing? Simply an exercise in futility, a need to get out of that house, to do something? Anything?

St-Cyr remained rooted to the walkway, willing himself to go through with things, yet arguing everything would be okay and she'd not be in any danger should she chance to come back to the house for some of her things.

Me, I'm a coward, he said, a fool who is still in love. Would they sleep in the nude? he wondered – they'd have plenty of heat, no shortage of coal. Perhaps they'd dined out this evening at Maxim's or at the Ritz? Places he could never have afforded.

Perhaps they'd gone to the theatre, she in a new red dress,

new red shoes, black lingerie – new everything. Steiner in uniform.

Perhaps, perhaps – ah, Mon Dieu, what was he to do? Intuitively he knew he mustn't intrude, that to disturb her would be the worst possible thing, that given time she'd decide to come back to him and that all would be forgiven. He'd have to make certain of that, couldn't hold it over her. Ah no, of course not. One had to be big-hearted about such things, one had to bury one's pain.

He blew on a fist and cursed himself for not having thought to bring his gloves and hat. He'd catch a cold. To hell with colds.

Still feeling very much the coward and the cuckold, he began to walk the bike away. The sprocket made its tiny clicking noise, magnified greatly by the silence as he crossed the avenue Henri Martin and went around the corner on to the boulevard Émile Auger to number 45, the flat of Gabrielle Arcuri.

It was strange that the two most important women in his life at the moment should live within a stone's throw of each other. Fate had a way of doing things like that. Fate and the war.

Once more he stood on the walk gazing up at the darkened silhouette but now questions of a different sort started coming at him. What was the relationship between the singer and the General Hans Ackermann? Who had written the diary? Who had had the meetings with the boy and why had they been so well documented if not for reasons of blackmail?

Why and where had the boy been killed? Why hadn't he, a chief – no, an inspector – of the Sûreté – damn Pharand anyway – questioned the type of stone in that boulder? Had it been because of Marianne, a subconscious worry that something was going on behind his back? Had he known it then?

At any rate, he'd been sloppy. Never mind Hermann's desire for haste and the seemingly inconsequential nature of the murder.

Ah, it was far from inconsequential now. Berlin, no less. Von Schaumburg – the whole of the Paris Gestapo probably *and*, not the least but still not well defined, the Sonderkommando-SS, the Sicherheitsdienst over on the avenue Foch.

The General Oberg's boys, the Sturmbannführer Helmut Knochen and the Secret Service of the SS.

Oberg and Ackermann had both been involved in the Polish campaign. Strings that could be pulled, hence Ackermann's freedom to move about whenever he pleased and his knowing he could call on the powers in Berlin any time he chose.

Berlin seemed such a long way from such a small murder. One monk perhaps, one hastily grabbed boulder and one dead nuisance – a mistake of course, or had it been?

But who had taken the boy's body to Fontainebleau Woods? Who had offered the use of their motor car, if such a request had been made? The countess would seem a logical choice, but Ackermann, what was his position in this, eh? And what of Gabrielle Arcuri?

But why choose Fontainebleau Woods? Why, indeed, except that several of the meetings had been there and the purse, with its contents, had been deliberately planted.

Had that really been the case? If so, then Yvette Noel had much to answer for and her prayers would have been filled with remorse.

But why in the name of Jesus had the girl changed her clothes? She must have known who her assailant was, yet have suspected nothing.

There were so many questions, so many answers to find. Hermann would have to buy them time, that was all there was to it. Somehow von Schaumburg must be convinced of the necessity of their staying to finish the case.

And that, of course, meant putting a stop to Marianne's little love affair. Or did it?

Once a month von Schaumburg and his aide inspected the eighty brothels the Germans kept busy in Paris. Some were exclusively for use of the upper ranks, others for the common soldier, the Luftwaffe, the Kreigsmarine and so forth.

Some were also reserved for the SS and it was to one of these that he invariably went first. At 8 a.m. The place was on a side street just off the Champs-Élysées.

No self-respecting whore in her right mind would be up at that hour, yet there they all were, herded in their nightdresses and pompom slippers. Coughing, swearing, taking quick drags on their fags, gesticulating rudely and cursing the German High Command.

A doctor moved among them selecting an overtired eye – or was it too deep a cough? – as a farmer would a diseased animal.

The whore was then forced to strip, to lie on the table, knees up, legs wide as the doctor probed for unwanted microbes and other things.

No one else but the madam bothered to look. The other girls simply turned away in a huff. 'Wider . . . Wider, please. Yes . . . yes, that is better,' said the doctor. In with the swab and up. Deeply. 'You've gonorrhoea. Those sores . . .'

'I've always had them.'

'Since birth?'

'Of course.'

'Then you ought to be blind!'

'None of my girls have the clap. You're crazy!' shouted the madam.

Oh-oh, here we go, said Kohler to himself. 'General, could I have a private word? A matter of great urgency.'

It was Kohler of the Gestapo come to sing for his breakfast. Old Shatter Hand fitted the monocle to his eye. 'Well, what is it?'

'About the murder of that boy, General. There've been some new developments.'

'Why aren't they in your report? Why wasn't it on my desk at 0700 hours yesterday morning as I requested?'

A raging argument was now in progress but von Schaumburg appeared stone deaf to it.

'General, we're being pulled off this thing to hide the identity of the real murderer. It's our belief the General Hans Ackermann of the Waffen-SS was involved.'

At last, Ackermann.

'In what way?' asked von Schaumburg cautiously.

Kohler knew it was now or never. Glotz had been specific – shut up or else – but they had no other choice. 'It's our feeling several homosexual liaisons took place,' said Kohler blithely.

'"Your feeling",' said von Schaumburg quietly.

'Boys with men, General.' The girls were beginning to take notice.

'Ackermann?'

161

God help them now. 'We need time, General, to sort out the truth. There were teeth marks on the boy's right thigh.'

'The marks of one of these,' snorted von Schaumburg, indicating the bevy of whores most of whom had now taken a decided interest in the proceedings.

'Or the marks of the boy's male lover, General.'

There'd been rumours out of Berlin, idle chitchat – gossip – far too great an interest in far too small a murder. Insistence from von Richthausen, the Kommandant of Barbizon, that the murder be looked into in detail. 'Not Ackermann. No . . . No, this I cannot believe. Besides, it is forbidden. You ought to know this, Sergeant.'

'Then why is Berlin trying to protect him by pulling St-Cyr and me off the case and sending us to the far ends of the earth?'

'Silesia is not so far and neither is Kiev.'

'General . . .'

'Yes, yes, I get your meaning, Sergeant, but I cannot believe what you say. Ackermann would have been discovered long before this. He'd have been shot or asked to take his own life.'

Kohler knew he was desperate. In spite of Glotz's warning, he had to say it. 'General, there's another thing. Your nephew, Steiner, is running around with my partner's wife. St-Cyr's in such a state he's useless as a detective – one of the best brains in the business! If you were to stop the love affair, I'm sure he'd settle down and we'd sort things out quickly.'

The whores had stopped breathing.

'The Ackermann business,' puzzled von Schaumburg as if he'd only just heard it. No one could forget how in the winter of 1938 the Secret Service of the SS had tried to tie the label of homosexuality to the Colonel General Werner von Fritch, the Commander-in-Chief of the Army, when the Führer had needed an excuse to get rid of that very able man for objecting to his ambitious plans for war. There'd been such a stink, the air had still not cleared. And now two gumshoe detectives were willing to suggest the SS had one of their own! *Gott in Himmel*, it was almost too good to be true. Himmler would have to hide his face in shame.

'The Ackermann business,' breathed Kohler, trying to gauge the trend of the general's thoughts and ignoring the hawk-eyed gazes of the prostitutes. 'His love affair with this boy.'

God help him if it were true and God help him if it weren't!

'My nephew wouldn't dare to touch the wife of another man,' said von Schaumburg gruffly.

You pious old bachelor! You hypocrite! thought Kohler before giving an inward sigh at the trouble he was creating for himself. 'He has, General. The woman and her son have moved in with him. Section Ten, the Watchers, have film of the couple engaged in sexual acts I'd rather not describe. They've threatened to show the film to my partner if I don't cough up every little detail so that they can forward it straight to Berlin before either you or the Sturmbannführer Boemelburg hear of it.'

'*Film? Copulation?* An invasion of Wehrmacht privacy by the Gestapo? *Gott in Himmel . . .*'

Von Schaumburg sized him up. Either way one looked at it, Kohler was a doomed man and so was his partner. Yet was there not a hint of truth in what he'd said about Ackermann?

It would be so nice to know.

'You have a week, Kohler. Absolute confidentiality. No written reports to anyone. Verbals only to me at 0600 hours, the Hotel Ritz, room 33. My adjutant, the Graf Waldersee, will let you in. Leave Boemelburg and Pharand out of it until we know the worst, then let me deal with it.'

'And St-Cyr's wife and son?'

'No child should be subjected to such a thing as parental infidelity. You leave that business to me.'

A homosexual SS war hero, a holder of the Iron Cross First-Class with Oak Leaves? Himmler would be in a panic, the Führer in an absolute state of collapse! The Gestapo and the SS would be out of France on the next train and the Army firmly back in the saddle!

Steiner . . . young Erich up to no good and disgracing his family, eh? Well, he'd soon see about that!

The schmuck who controlled the pink entry tickets at Paris Central Morgue was an ox-headed French son-of-a-bitch with a fluting voice, bad teeth and breath that would kill a snake at a hundred metres.

'Talbotte, the Préfet of Paris himself, has forbidden that you or St-Cyr be allowed to examine the post-mortems.'

'Post-mortems?' snorted Kohler, still standing before the bastard's desk. 'One died of a boulder between the eyes, and the other of a gunshot wound in the back of the head!'

'Ah! So you are the expert, eh? Well, my friend, there's nothing for you here and you cannot bribe me.'

'Thanks!' snorted Kohler, dragging out a roll of bills that would have choked a horse.

He peeled off 5000 francs. The schmuck's eyes flicked to the open door of the office. 'Another five but not a word, eh?'

'My lips are sealed,' swore Kohler.

'Good! And another five for the boys, eh? It's hard work pulling stiffs for you guys to run your eyes over. The men will only bitch to the wrong people.'

In the name of Jesus, the economy of Paris was going to hell! 'You bastards are learning,' grumbled the Bavarian.

The man grinned. 'We've good teachers, my friend.' He lifted his fat ass from behind the desk and waddled out into the corridor to seize the first man in white who came by and whisper sweet nothings in his ear.

One 500-franc note changed hands and then, 'Not a word, Arnold, if you value your job.'

Arnold took Kohler to get the corpses. Both the boy and his sister were wrapped in canvas and submerged in chipped ice.

They'd both been eviscerated and the incisions only crudely sewn. Pity the poor grieving family . . . Once murdered, one lost all privacy and became the property of the state until such time as the remains could be released.

Yvette Noel was on her back and bluer than her brother. Rigor made her breasts firm, the nipples stiff. She'd once had a reasonable figure – quite petite, Louis had said. But the gash up her abdomen simply turned one off.

'You want the reports?' grunted Arnold. Shrouds of ice fog hung about.

'Yeah, I want the reports and a bit of peace, eh? Go and get them but don't be too long.'

The man snickered. 'Enjoy yourself, Inspector. Don't ride the girl in my absence. That's naughty.'

Kohler flung a chunk of ice at him. He wished that Louis was here. Louis was better at this. He had the eye for detail and the ability to turn his stomach off.

164

They had a day perhaps to come up with something really good. Boemelburg wasn't going to like it when he heard about the meeting with von Schaumburg.

In desperation Kohler moved between the corpses. The girl's eyes were brown and staring straight up into the feeble light; the boy's were closed but yes, now that he forced himself to look closely at the two of them, though there were facial similarities, there were marked differences. A coarseness in the girl's bone structure – petite, yes, but of peasant stock. One hundred per cent, whereas the boy, Jérome, had the mark of the French aristocracy about him.

Then it was true. Jérome had been fathered by the countess's husband.

Kohler found the teeth marks and, once again, he had to admit they were those of a lover's nip.

So, too, the tiny nick under the right nipple, though that could have been caused by a fingernail. The pair of them must have been really going at it.

But had Ackermann been the man on his knees? *Gott in Himmel*, what a fool he'd been to suggest such a thing! His name would be mud around Gestapo HQ. He'd never live the betrayal down. Berlin would ship him off to Kiev and Louis would hit the salt mines no matter what happened. Or there'd be worse for both of them. Yeah, worse.

The girl had a scratch about six centimetres long on her left leg, just above the knee – those briars, that torn stocking? he wondered, remembering the roadside with surprising clarity for a person who'd not yet had his breakfast.

Kohler bent closer. The scratch was thin and flecked with dried blood to which clung tiny threads of silk. So, okay, the girl had climbed the hill up into the forest after finding the body of her brother. She'd torn her stockings on the briars but had she left the purse up there or had she gone to hunt for it?

The right knee was bruised, but that could have happened when she'd been murdered.

Her hair was dark brown like the brother's but coarser and thicker. She'd a centimetre-sized mole at the top of her left thigh, next the triangle between her legs. A thing for a young girl to worry about, a birthmark the brother didn't have. She'd clipped the hairs on it.

What else would Louis have looked for? He'd have talked to the corpse of course.

Her fingertips and nails showed seamstress signs: needle pricks, a roughness of the skin and rippling of the closely trimmed nails which had been freshly lacquered with polish. She'd got herself ready.

Was there perfume – the stuff Louis had called Mirage? Had she taken some from her mistress's dressing table at the club? Had she touched the backs of her ears, done the armpits and shoved a hand down under the briefs?

He had the idea that Yvette Noel wouldn't have drenched herself like so many Parisian women did but that she'd have touched herself all the same.

Yet who had she met? Who had killed her?

By a stroke of fate or luck the bullet hadn't scrambled her eyes. She seemed to be trying to tell him something.

'A virgin,' snorted the man in white. 'Her hymen was intact. Brandy – plum brandy – that's all she had in her stomach. Three shots of it at least and not long before she was killed.'

'You're full of news,' said Kohler. 'You ought to apply to the Sûreté. They could use a guy like you.'

'The boy had eaten his supper but it was a mishmash due to the length of time. Rye bread with caraway seeds, boiled swedes and boiled potatoes. A little red wine and some green onions. Goat's cheese in lumps, as were the potatoes and the swedes so perhaps he'd eaten in a hurry.'

Then he'd been killed long before he'd ever got to Fontainebleau and he'd been killed at the monastery or near it.

'Anything else?' asked Kohler, not bothering to glance at the autopsies.

'Anal fissures – they could have been because of diet. Everyone around here knows what swedes do to the guts. The appendicectomies are now so prevalent even the corpses of the tramps have had the job done.'

The lack of potatoes in Paris was a curse, the smell of farts in the Métro something terrible. All the potatoes were still being shipped to the Reich except for those on the black market. The swedes were to take their place and the swedes were what caused the trouble. Never mind the fact that the boy had also eaten potatoes! But still . . . A sodomite?

'Why the plum brandy in the girl's stomach?'

The man raised his eyebrows and affected the air of a detective. 'Why indeed? Perhaps she liked it, or perhaps the guy who killed her made her drink it first.'

While sitting in a car, dressed in blue with argyle socks. 'It seems an odd thing for them to have drunk,' offered Kohler. 'Why not armagnac or cognac – coming from where she did?'

'There were droplets on her sweater and on the collar of her blouse but not on the overcoat.'

'She wasn't wearing the coat, not when she was killed,' said Kohler swiftly. Then where the hell was the coat?

'On the ground, some distance from the body. At the turn-around. Talbotte, the Préfet, has said this, so the coat must have been thrown out of the car *after* the girl had been killed.'

The coat would have been yanked down behind her back to pin her arms before tying them.

Plum brandy . . . Slivovitz? Polish brandy? Had Ackermann acquired a taste for the stuff?

Did he drink to numb the pain? Vodka . . . why not vodka?

'You sure you don't want to read these?' asked the man.

'Not with a walking encyclopaedia to tell me what they say.'

The guy grinned. Without the blood-smeared lab coat and cap he might have been okay, a reasonable sort. This place must do things to them.

'Is there anything else you can tell me?' asked Kohler, hauling out the bankroll.

'The bodies are to be released this afternoon on orders straight from your friends on the avenue Foch.'

The General Oberg then and the Secret Service of the SS, the Sicherheitsdienst.

'Talbotte was here with one of their men. A general with scars no one should have. The two examined the corpses. Scar-face read the autopsies and asked for copies and photographs of the bodies.'

Just what Himmler would do with the photographs was anyone's guess. Perhaps he'd have them framed.

Kohler peeled off a 1000-franc note and handed it over. 'I'll see if I can fix you up with the Sûreté, eh? Your talents are only going to waste in a place like this.'

'The bullet was from a Luger or a Mauser – a 9 millimetre Parabellum.'

He added another 1000-franc note.

'Talbotte is convinced the gun was stolen by the Resistance from Melun and used by them against the girl. This he told the scar-faced one.'

'And the boy?' asked Kohler, peeling off yet another thousand.

The brown eyes of the attendant were those of stone. 'Killed by accidentally falling off his bicycle in Fontainebleau Woods.'

'Talbotte's a better cop than that.'

'Perhaps, but he's also smart enough to know when to mind his own business.'

In the grey light of the early morning the Club Mirage looked like a hole in the wall. Soot and pigeon droppings streaked the plate glass windows. The black-out curtains were shabby and faded. What paint there was suffered from some incurable disease and the light bulbs that had once flashed on and off to draw the moths in, had now all disappeared as if by an act of God.

When the courtyard door swung open at a touch, St-Cyr had the thought the Corsican brothers had fled. He leaned the bicycle against the only free space of wall, slipped off the trouser clips and fitted the sturdy pre-war kilogram of Sûreté brass through a ring in the wall and through the spokes of the back wheel.

Locking the courtyard door, he undid the buttons of his overcoat and jacket, then loosened the Lebel in its holster. All very meticulous, all a routine.

Satisfied, he started for the stage door. Hermann would, no doubt, be busy with von Schaumburg or be on his way to Kiev. Right now there was only time for questions. All other thoughts must be erased, though he'd have liked to say goodbye if it should come to that.

Goodbye to a German, a Nazi, but not a very good one, a member of their Gestapo . . . but then, Hermann was Hermann and in better times they might well have gone fishing together, so what was the sense of making excuses to himself? The war had tossed them together and that was all there was to it.

He was standing in the dimly lit corridor, had almost reached Gabrielle Arcuri's dressing-room, when one of the girls suddenly appeared in her housecoat. 'Who the hell are you?' she shrilled hoarsely. 'A copper?'

How easily one could tell if one had the experience.

'St-Cyr of the Sûreté.'

'Jesus, another one! Hey, Remi! *Remi*! I'm being robbed!. . . That'll bring him,' she said, the pale blue eyes grey with suspicion. 'If I'd said raped, he'd not have bothered. So, what's it this time, eh? Hey, you're the one with the partner. You're the guys they told us about. You're off the case, Inspector. We're not supposed to talk to you. St-Cyr . . . yes . . . yes, that was it, and Crowler or Cowler . . .'

'Kohler.'

'Yes . . . yes, that was it. Kohler. You'll get nothing from us. We run a respectable club.'

The Corsican 'brothers' squeezed into the corridor, each moving so swiftly they jostled one another and fought for space. Remi Rivard, the one with the face like a mountain, was the taller of the two. He lifted his wife out of the way with one hand. She didn't say a thing.

'A few questions,' offered St-Cyr.

The fists were doubled, the dark eyes leapt at him. 'Beat it, Inspector. Your fangs have been pulled. Talbotte himself has said he'll shut us down if we so much as fart your way.'

'Then it's what Talbotte didn't tell you that you'd better listen to, my friend. A pastis, I think, and a little chat before the fire.'

'Fire? What fire?' shrieked the Corsicans. They were both livid.

'Yes, fire. You've been targeted by the Resistance. Talbotte won't have told you this but I, Jean-Louis St-Cyr of the Sûreté, offer it on the platter of my friendship.'

'You're lying,' said the shorter of the two.

'Then warm your hands at the blaze knowing I could have stopped it.'

He was unlocking the bicycle when the three of them came into the courtyard to brave the day. The woman looked dusty.

Her slippers didn't match. The fake feather trim on the pink housecoat caught the ugly twisting of a frigid eddy.

She clutched the garment's throat and huddled between the giants.

'So, okay, smart-ass, you can come in but it had better be good,' rumbled Remi. The barrel of his chest was clothed in plaid and the leather jerkin was open. Did the two of them never change their clothes?

The woman went first, and disappeared up a thin flight of stairs through a door one would have thought to be that of a water closet.

The Corsicans led him down the linoleum path and into the bar whose perpetual light gave the half-glow of the desolate. The bottles looked like so many rows of coloured water.

Leon Rivard was the one with the face of ground meat, the shorter of the two, but not by much. It was he who poured the pastis – one glass – and set a small pitcher of water beside it on the zinc. 'So, my friend, this little business of the fire?'

St-Cyr knew he'd have to lie like Tarzan.

The water had a skin. He added some to the pastis anyway. He'd take his time.

The green became cloudy – Philippe had thought it magic. Philippe . . . He shut the boy out of his mind and took a sip. 'So, what Talbotte would not have told you is that this thing is very much a matter of the Resistance and that they've got your number.'

'We're waiting,' breathed the mountain.

The two of them were now behind the bar. 'Yvette Noel was executed for her part in things. Now it is your turn, and that of Mademoiselle Arcuri. They're serious. Talbotte hasn't been able to make contact with them, and neither have the Gestapo or the SD, but I have.'

'We're still waiting,' said Leon.

Would they now think to set their knives on the bar? So, okay, my friends, here goes. 'Last night my partner chased a couple on a borrowed Wehrmacht motorcycle. During the chase one of the saddlebags fell off and guess what?'

'You do the guessing,' grunted the mountain.

'Incendiaries,' said St-Cyr, reaching for his glass. 'Property of the Sicherheitsdienst over on the avenue Foch, though don't ask me how the Resistance got them. These incendiaries are of a new type – perhaps you've seen them, eh?' He gave the brothers a moment. 'They have excellent timers – delays of up to four hours. You know how those people in the SD are. Always playing games. Murders, countersubversion, actions against the Jews and political people, et cetera, et cetera. Well, along with the incendiaries was the address of your club.'

'We're still waiting,' offered Leon, but this time he reached for a bottle of marc and poured his brother and himself a shot.

St-Cyr raised his glass and said, '*Salut!*'

'We're still waiting,' said Remi.

No one could have guessed what the two of them were thinking. 'So, okay. It's what was in the other saddlebag, eh? Six more of those little beauties – six, my friends! Our contact tells us that the lover of one of the Resistance people loaned the couple that bike and that the Resistance plan to use you as an example to others. You won't know who carries those nasty little things into the club and you won't know when they'll be set to explode because, my friends, one of them has a boyfriend in the German Army and this kid has got his heart set on deserting rather than face the prospect of the Russian Front. Or perhaps it's merely for love, who knows, eh? Sex is a funny thing. People do the craziest things because of it, isn't that so?'

St-Cyr took a sip and held the pastis on the back of his tongue. They'd either buy the story or forget it, but they couldn't afford not to give it some consideration.

The brothers ignored their drinks. It could be true. It was far more likely the puddle of a departing goose.

Remi Rivard fingered the rim of his glass. They could leave it but what was this flic really playing at? Elements of truth mixed in with fiction? 'What do you want in exchange?'

A wise people, the Corsicans. 'Another pastis and a few answers. Talbotte can screw himself as far as we're concerned. We'll pick the boy and his girlfriend up and throw a wrench into their little plans but only if you co-operate. Otherwise,' he shrugged, 'we can always leave them for a few more days just to make sure we catch the lot of them.'

It was the shorter one, Leon, who made the decisions but there was no nod to his brother, nothing but the slightest movement of the eyes, or had it been the way he'd put his weight on the left foot?

St-Cyr dug deeply into a pocket and took out the pair of dice he'd had since joining the Sûreté. Much worn, the ivory dull and yellowed by innumerable nights spent tossing them while trying to squeeze answers, he held them a moment in his open palm then tossed them on the zinc.

'A pair of threes,' he said as if in wonder. 'Everything in life is such a gamble, eh? The Resistance gamble with their lives, you do it with money and perhaps your lives as well, eh? And I do it. Gabrielle Arcuri does and so did her maid, Yvette Noel. Fire's a gamble too, especially now with all those planes flying over and keeping the pumper trucks busy elsewhere.'

'Some guy telephoned Yvette after you and that partner of yours had left the club.'

'She smiled at me,' offered Remi. 'Yvette, she has said, "I have to go out. Tell Mademoiselle Arcuri it's all going to be fixed."'

'Pardon?' asked St-Cyr, grabbing the dice.

'Fixed – you know . . .' offered the mountain.

'Yes, of course I know what it means, but are you absolutely certain that's what she said?'

'Leon, this prick isn't worth talking to.'

'Now wait, my friends. We must be certain, eh? It's important.'

Remi gripped the edge of the bar as if he were about to lift it out of the way. 'Fixed, fixed, fixed! In the name of Jesus, what the hell else do you want me to say?'

It was Leon who urged caution. 'The guy picked her up in a car about half an hour later. By then Yvette had changed her clothes and got dolled up a bit. She was never much, that one. A little lipstick, a bit of perfume maybe, but . . . Ah, she didn't have the money to dress.'

'Are you sure it was a man who picked her up?'

The brothers shrugged. 'Would a woman have killed her?' asked Leon.

'That's not impossible but, yes, it's far more likely the murderer was a man,' offered St-Cyr.

'But not from the Resistance, eh?' said the face of ground

meat, watching him so closely one could see the ghost of a wily smile behind the suspicion in his eyes.

'The Resistance don't drive cars so easily,' countered St-Cyr. 'The SS do.'

Ah now, so a certain general was at the top of the list and all that shit about firebombs was just the puddling of a goose. But why had the flic let them know?

St-Cyr gathered in the dice – there was only one way to distract the brothers. He rolled a seven, then an eleven, then snake's-eyes and a pair of sixes.

'They do what I tell them to,' he said.

'Yvette was happy when she left here,' offered the mountain. 'If we'd known that was going to happen to her, we'd have separated his skull even if he was an SS general.'

'Perhaps you'd better explain the "general" part,' said St-Cyr. 'Just for the record.'

Remi, you idiot! thought Leon. Sometimes Remi got carried away, but did he have to fall into that old trap?

'What my brother means, Inspector, is that the General Ackermann often paid the club a visit. Like a lot of other high-ranking Nazis, he came to hear Gabrielle but that was as far as it went, of this I'm certain. Gabrielle . . . Ah! some women. You know it with them instinctively, isn't that so? They don't sleep around. They're chaste, even if their soldier husbands have been killed and it's now more than two years since they've had it.'

'So, why the condoms that were found in her purse?'

'Rubbers? Gabrielle?' The brothers were genuinely mystified.

'Why the working in a place like this?' asked St-Cyr, striking while he could. 'Excuse me, my friends, but with that voice and that body, Mademoiselle Arcuri could have done much better. Let's not kid ourselves, eh? The Lido, the Moulin Rouge, the Alhambra, the Shéhérazade, the Cirque Medrano . . .'

The two of them leaned over the bar. The mountain spoke through his teeth. 'The Lune Russe, the Deux Anes and the Noctambule, my fine Monsieur the Detective. Gabrielle is an artist, idiot! She writes a lot of her own material, as she did before the war. Is it that you know so little about her? The Lune Russe used to be her place. Night after night, but then she got married and had a son.'

'So, why did she come to work here?' The Lune Russe . . .
The Russian Moon . . .

'Because . . . because she did and that's all there is to it, isn't
that so, Leon? One day she walks in the front door and we see
the money she'd bring us. We're not stupid, eh? Cash . . . a
voice like that's worth millions. She wanted ten per cent and we
gave it to her.'

St-Cyr studied the dice. The Lune Russe, the Deux Anes and
the Noctambule were chanteuse clubs in the old tradition, very
genteel, very intimate and respectable but not much favoured
by the Germans.

The dice told him to leave it for a moment, to let their
suspicions lapse. He rolled a miserable three. 'Did the General
Ackermann ever take her out for dinner, that sort of thing, eh?'

'Sometimes. Maxim's a couple of times perhaps, the Ritz too
. . . So what? Wouldn't you have tried?'

'Not with my bankroll. Did he show up here last night?'

Leon Rivard reached for the dice and rolled a seven straight
off and then a pair of snake's eyes. 'That one came in later than
usual – about twelve, I think – and when he heard that Gabrielle
wasn't singing, he left.'

'What sort of car does Mademoiselle Arcuri drive?'

So it was on to cars, was it? All by himself the cop was using
his noodle. 'A Peugeot, two-door sedan. Dark blue.'

Remi tried the dice. St-Cyr let him have a go. The Peugeot
was a sensible car, so, too, the colour. Von Schaumburg, as the
Kommandant of Greater Paris, would have signed the permit
and issued the gasoline allowance. None of the chanteuse clubs
would have suited, had this been what she'd had in mind.

But she could have got the same from any of the more popular
places – entertaining the troops gave one special privileges. The
brothers had made a decent financial deal with her as well. So,
okay, she had the freedom to drive to the château or to
Fontainebleau Woods, and she had good enough reasons for
working in this dump. Perhaps fewer questions would be asked
as well.

'About what time did Mademoiselle Arcuri leave the club?'

'Soon after she discovered Yvette had gone to meet someone.
She changed out of her dress, wouldn't take the last three acts.
I gave her 10,000 francs against her wages – we'd often done it

174

before,' said Leon. 'Gabrielle's always been straight with us. This is the first time she hasn't sung all night.'

'There's always a first time but like I've said, the Resistance are now after her and you'd do well to tell me everything if you want her back.'

'Then get them for us!' breathed the mountain, still clutching the dice.

'Today. This morning, Very soon,' said St-Cyr. 'So, a pastis for your thoughts and for the road, my friends?'

No self-respecting cop would offer to pay for the drinks in circumstances such as this and he didn't offer. They'd only have been doubly suspicious if he had. 'The boy, Jérome – Yvette's young brother – did he ever come here to see her?'

The bottle stopped. The pastis dribbled down the glass. Leon Rivard finished pouring. 'We didn't know she had a brother.'

No, of course they didn't. *Merde*! They were so difficult!

St-Cyr reached for the water and added a drop just to let them know he liked his pastis almost neat at times like this. 'Me, I think he did and I think you should tell me about it while there's still time.'

'Was he murdered too?' asked Remi.

St-Cyr set his empty glass on the bar between them and picked up the dice. Without a word, he turned and walked away. He was unlocking the bicycle when the brothers stepped into the cold.

It was Leon who did the talking. 'Yvette had to find her brother a place to stay. Number 17 rue Daguerre, on the other side of the cemetery. Our Aunt Isabella . . . she's the concierge. Jérome . . . Jérome didn't stay there often. He'd come for a few days. Yvette would be upset, in tears – frantic – and then the brother would go away and she'd settle down again.'

'We advanced her money for him against Gabrielle's share,' said Remi.

'And Mademoiselle Arcuri, what was her part in all of this?' asked St-Cyr.

The two of them exchanged glances. Leon said, 'Gabrielle had no use for Yvette's brother and told the girl she was a fool to help him.'

She said the family ought to disown him, that to fail as a

priest was to bring disgrace down on the whole of Vouvray and its surroundings,' offered the mountain.

'But she didn't kill him, Inspector. Not Gabrielle, and she wouldn't have killed Yvette either, not even if to murder them had meant saving her son from losing his rightful inheritance.'

They were full of news but it was time to leave. 'Don't telephone your aunt to tell her I'm on my way. The Gestapo will only be listening in and we wouldn't want that.'

Leon had the darker eyes. 'They listen in all the time so what's the difference? They probably have a recording of the guy who telephoned Yvette.'

But they haven't told you about it, have they? It was in the gazes of the two of them.

It cut the timber out from under him. Glotz . . . had Glotz access to that recording? Had he told Hermann? Had Hermann kept that little gem to himself?

'Was it Ackermann?' he asked, clearly in their hands.

The brothers shrugged. 'How should we know?' said Leon.

'Because the accent wouldn't have been French.'

'Then, Monsieur the Inspector, you can rest easy, eh, because the guy who telephoned her was as French as the three of us.'

'That's not good enough and you know it. Was it the voice of money and fine breeding?'

The aristocracy – a château on the Loire perhaps? The husband of a certain chanteuse . . . One could read a flic so easily. 'We wouldn't know about such things, Inspector,' offered Leon. 'He was just French like the rest of us. Impatient to get on with life.'

'And a murder,' breathed St-Cyr. 'A murder, my friends. Please don't forget that you were among the last to speak with that poor unfortunate girl. Keep her death on your consciences while you warm your hands at the fire!'

The Corsicans' aunt Isabella had conveniently gone to see her sister in St Lazare and wouldn't be back until evening. The slug she'd left in charge didn't even know his own name and was hard of hearing.

With no food in his stomach since the previous night's supper, and three pastis sloshing around inside him, St-Cyr began to look for a café.

The brothers had given him much to think about and a new and pressing task but ah! that was the nature of a good murder case. Threads and threads and lots of little unexpected things, all of which had to be followed up. Now more than ever Hermann and he would have to compare notes. This new development, it had that feel about it, like the taste of a good ripe olive or that of a glass of the Vouvray *moelleux*!

Gabrielle Arcuri's husband. Dead, of course, but what if dead only in name?

The voice of money and breeding over the telephone. Had Jérome discovered her secret? And what of Yvette? 'Tell Mademoiselle Arcuri it's all going to be fixed.' Those words had that certain ring about them, didn't they?

And what of the countess and of Gabrielle herself? What of Ackermann, the distant cousin?

And the monks . . . the monks . . . the monks . . .

As he pedalled towards the Luxembourg Garden, St-Cyr passed along the rue Vivan. It took him several minutes to realize exactly where he was. Then he remembered the girl with the shoes. She'd lived at number 23, 'upstairs at the top'. She'd lived with her sister and brother-in-law. 'They've two kids,' she'd said.

Number 23 was just across the road and down it a little. Several cyclists passed – it was still early, perhaps not yet nine o'clock. There was a gap in the traffic and then the car of some German official and more cyclists.

The doorway to number 23 was inset a little. He remembered standing there, remembered how impulsively she'd thrown her arms about his neck.

That kiss . . . such innocence. So poignant a memory. The excitement darkness had brought – it had been very sexual, very instinctive, very close and feral . . . yes, feral. Like animals in the wild.

Ah, to be young again and in a free Paris, a free France. To live again!

But had he ever been young – really young at heart? Weren't some men meant to go through life like slightly used rubber tyres? The sort that are always second-hand and a little worn when you buy them, and therefore suspect?

Used tyres give comfortable rides, he reminded himself. He

must stink of pastis, but wasn't the fear of a puncture a part of the excitement, eh?

So, okay, he'd cross the street and introduce himself. He'd tell her he hadn't forgotten the shoes.

He'd do no such thing, and he knew it. Shyness perhaps, he admitted. Fear too. She'd been so young and eager.

There was a café on the corner, a place much frequented by the locals, a good sign. Chaining the bicycle to a lamppost, he straightened his tie and marched into the place. A good morning's work demanded a reasonable feed but . . . ah! damn it, had he remembered to bring his ration tickets?

Deep down in an inside pocket he found the cursed things Marianne had left out for him. They were now out of date! Would the colour have been changed?

The bar was crowded with workmen all standing shoulder to shoulder. The tables were filled. There was only one vacant chair. Green tickets were still being used, so that was okay in so far as the colour was concerned. The things one had to do these days! Ah Mon Dieu, it was a pain in the ass, this war.

He took off his hat, nodded to the proprietor and made his way among the tables.

A girl was sitting right at the back and at first this puzzled him because she'd have a good view of the door and the street, of the whole place, even of the telephone . . . but she'd have had no reason to watch such things, would she? A friend perhaps? The table was too well chosen just for that.

The pile of books spelled student; the swollen right jaw spelled tooth.

She sipped her ersatz coffee – no milk of course. She dunked the bread into it.

'Mademoiselle . . .' he began.

Watering suddenly, her brown eyes fled anxiously to the door, the street, and back up to him. 'This chair,' he said, 'would you mind if I . . .?'

'The chair . . .? Oh! Yes, yes, of course. I was just leaving.'

'But . . . but you've not finished?'

The bowl with its coffee shattered on the floor, the books spilled about as she made a grab for them and the beret. The proprietor called out, 'Liline, is anything the matter?'

'My tooth, Monsieur Henri. I'm sorry about the mess. I have

178

to rush. They're fixing it at the Dental School's clinic. Those guys, you know how they are. No freezing any more – straight in with the drill or the hammer and chisel. It'll take three of them to hold me down.'

She paid up and darted out the door. Twice she looked back, and then a third time from the street.

It's her, said St-Cyr to himself. The girl with the shoes. And she had known him but that was not possible . . .

The night came back . . . the feel of her in his arms. He ordered a coffee and some bread – there were no croissants to be had any more, not in the places of the common people. 'Some jam if you have it, please,' he said.

That night . . . that street . . . the girl and her boyfriend . . . the patrol . . .

Out after curfew . . . out last night on a borrowed motorcycle? Was it possible? Had they come to collect her shoes or to kill him?

At that hour, it could only have been the latter. But she was such a pretty thing – most girls of that age were. It's what attracted the bees, wasn't it?

The furrowed brow, the swollen jaw, the anxious eyes . . . these all came rushing back to him and then the chin with its touch of swelling, the turned-up nose, the kissing lips, good lips, wide and sensual, the long lashes, the fine brush of her brows . . . A girl not unlike Yvette Noel but a student.

And a member of some fledgeling Resistance cell? he asked. Was it possible?

It would explain the kiss, the eager thanks for his having saved her life, the panic . . .

The mess at his feet was cleaned up. Bread, margarine, a dab of blackcurrant jam – pre-war perhaps – and coffee were set before him. 'There's no milk,' said the proprietor with a shrug.

St-Cyr asked him how many tickets he needed.

'Two – one for the kitchen and one for the bread. And thirty-five francs.'

'That young girl, what was her last name?'

'Marleau. She comes in here sometimes.'

'She lives across the street at number 23, doesn't she, with her sister and brother-in-law? They've two kids?' asked St-Cyr.

179

The proprietor put his back to the crowd and his hands firmly on the table. 'So, what's she done, eh?' Was this guy a cop?

'Nothing,' said St-Cyr. 'I just happened to meet her one night, after curfew. A close thing for both of us, you understand. That's how I came to know her address.'

The man's face broke into a wide grin and then into laughter. 'Hey, you're the one who rescued her, eh? And the two of you sat here face to face and didn't know each other? Ah, Mon Dieu, that's life! Liline has told us all about it.'

St-Cyr gave him a moment before quietly saying, 'Look, is she involved in something? Her boyfriend ran off and left her to face the music.'

'He's one of those. He dodges the labour round-ups and makes trouble.'

St-Cyr reached for his bread. 'Has he the use of a motorcycle – you'd have heard it in the night perhaps?'

The proprietor had. It was written all over him, in the doubt, the anger at himself for having been such a fool as to have placed the girl's life in danger and that of everyone else, himself and his family included.

'It's okay, my friend. I only wanted to ask,' said St-Cyr, 'but now you must tell her something for me, eh?'

The man nodded grimly.

'Tell her that I'm on her side and that she must not let the others make a mistake about this. There'll come a time when they'll need me again and I'll be there.'

'Why not tell her yourself, at the dental clinic?'

St-Cyr shook his head. 'She'll have avoided it like the plague even though that tooth is killing her. Besides, I have another matter that is far too important to leave. Tell her also that I will have her shoes repaired and returned just as soon as I can. She's not to worry.'

The proprietor slid the thirty-five francs back across the tablecloth. 'Let me see if I can't find you a little something else.'

He hadn't even bothered to touch the tickets. All along he'd known they were out of date.

But how had the girl known who he was?

*

180

Boemelburg was waiting for him when Kohler tried to slip into number 11 rue de Saussaies by a back door. Osias Pharand had been livid and screaming that it was all a matter of honour! St-Cyr had betrayed his chief and so had a certain Bavarian.

As he entered the office, Boemelburg remained standing with his back to him, looking up at the Army ordnance map of the Loire he'd had fixed to the wallspace immediately behind his desk.

'Hermann, let me tell you something.' He took a pin and stabbed it into the location of the Château Thériault. So much for a certain countess, the distant cousin of the SS General Hans Ackermann. 'You will go to Kiev, my Bavarian friend, if I've anything to do with it. It's only a matter of time.'

The chief seized another pin and drove it into the location of the Monastery of Saint Gregory the Great. So much for monkish things!

Kohler still hadn't been told to sit down. 'How much time . . .?' he began, only to blurt, 'Herr Sturmbannführer, I can explain the von Schaumburg business. I . . .'

Still the chief didn't turn to face him. 'I think you'd *better* explain, Hermann. You took an oath of allegiance when you joined the Gestapo. To the Führer, to the Party and the State but most of all, Hermann, to us, your associates and superior officers. Herr Himmler, Hermann. We must all answer to him, even myself.'

So it was to be like that? Kohler began. Boemelburg moved aside to study the map of France. He stuck pins into Fontaine-bleau Woods – the location of the girl's body, then that of her brother. He stuck one into Paris and stood back a little to eyeball the distances someone would have had to drive. Not satisfied, he pulled a length of thin yellow ribbon from a pocket and measured them off before fixing the ribbon to the three centres of this stupid little affair.

'Ackermann, Hermann. Did you have to accuse him of being a homosexual?'

So much for wind in a guy's sails. 'It was just talk, Herr Sturmbannführer. I had to buy us time. Glotz . . .'

Boemelburg chose his moment swiftly and turned on him. 'Yes, Glotz, Hermann. The brother of the wife of one of Herr

Himmler's brothers. What about Glotz, Hermann? Glotz, you *dummkopf!*'

'He was going behind your back and reporting straight to Berlin. There's talk, Herr Sturmbannführer . . .'

God help him now!

'Talk of *what*,' seethed Boemelburg.

So Glotz was related to Himmler . . . 'That you're becoming forgetful – it's garbage, Herr Sturmbannführer. We in the ranks . . .'

'Hermann, skip the crap and tell me the truth.'

'That you're becoming forgetful and will have to be replaced.'

'By Glotz? *Gott in Himmel*, Hermann, if it were not so silly I'd be furious, but all the same, Gestapo Mueller will hear of this.'

'No doubt he has, Herr Sturmbannführer. He'd have ordered Glotz to investigate St-Cyr's wife.'

'Films,' muttered Boemelburg, running an irritated hand over the all-but-shaven dome of his blunt head. 'The woman should have known better. Von Schaumburg has demanded the films. In a hand-delivered note, Hermann. Stamped with the seal of the Kommandant of Greater Paris and written in such terse terms a child could read them.'

Again Boemelburg turned his back on him to study the maps. Glotz would have to be dealt with but first this business must be settled. 'So I'm forgetful, am I, Hermann?' He seized another pin and drove it into Barbizon, the start of this whole affair. He strung yellow ribbon from there to Paris, said, 'Kommandant to Kommandant, Hermann, and the Army out to sink the Gestapo in France! Did you and Louis not think the General von Richthausen had some axe to grind? The Hôtellerie du Bois Royal in Barbizon, Hermann? July 8th – was that not in your little diary, eh? Ackermann, Hermann. Ackermann and that boy feeding their faces while von Richthausen said hello.'

'Herr Sturmbannführer, your blood pressure . . .'

'Never mind my blood pressure, Hermann. You've opened the wasps' nest with that little tête-à-tête you had with von Schaumburg. *Accusations* of unnatural sexual practices among the heroes of the Waffen-SS! Oh, *Mein Gott*, how stupid can you get? Did it never cross your mind that Ackermann could have been up to something else? Information, Hermann. Information for the Sicherheitsdienst!'

He turned, but didn't pause. 'If Ackermann doesn't kill you and Louis, the Resistance will. *And* if not them, the salt mines and the partisans in Kiev. You've gained yourself one week. That is all! Now open that envelope and take a look at its contents. Worry about your own blood pressure. I want everything, Hermann. No more of your little secrets, no more things like a few uncut diamonds that have been conveniently put out for evaluation and not mentioned in your report! Your loyalty, Hermann. The oath you took.'

And the penalty for breaking it: that of desertion but not the firing squad as with the Army. No, the Gestapo reserved for themselves the choice of using the wire and slow strangulation or the axe. What they did to others, they did to those few among them who dared to betray the cause.

One never knew which method it would be until the very end, so there was always that little extra bit of suspense.

Kohler shook out the contents of the envelope but found he couldn't speak.

Boemelburg waited. There were forty-three copies of the photograph of Kohler and St-Cyr at the edge of a road in Fontainebleau Woods. The body of the boy, looking as if it had just been bagged, was between them, and the photographs had been gathered up from all over Paris. 'You fool, Hermann. What did you think you were playing at? A memento to send home to that forgotten wife of yours? Do you know what's happened? Can you even guess?'

'The Resistance have the negative,' he managed.

'They've more than that.'

'They've made copies and had them circulated,' he said, swallowing with difficulty.

'At least two or three hundred of them. Who knows? Some left in the Métro, some posted on our billboards, but . . . what am I thinking of? Please don't be shy. Turn one over and read what it says.'

In pen someone had printed the words, *Down with Gestapo killers like these*!

'They're blaming you and St-Cyr for the murder of that boy.'

'But . . .'

'No buts about it, Hermann. Of course the matter's got out of hand, but then, so, too, were your accusations.'

In the name of Jesus, what were they going to do?

'You're going to sit down, Hermann. You're going to take your time – pretend I'm the Reverend Father of that monastery – the Abbey of Saint Gregory the Great, wasn't it? *If* my memory serves me right. Everything about the man who took this photograph, Hermann, and then . . .' Boemelburg gave him a moment. 'And then, Hermann, everything about this pair of broken shoes St-Cyr's housekeeper found in his kitchen.'

Glotz . . . had Glotz interrogated the woman who lived across the street from Louis?

'We'll be using Louis as bait, Hermann. You're not to tell him, no matter how much you seem to have slipped from our ways. All Resistance must be crushed, even if it foolishly hovers in the small recesses of what you might think to call a brain.'

'Thériault,' shouted St-Cyr impatiently. 'A captain from the Vouvray area, age about thirty-six, killed in May 1940, during the breakthrough at Sedan, I think.'

'You think!' shrilled the walnut. 'And what am I to think, eh? Hundreds and hundreds of thousands of dead, my fine monsieur, and you, like millions of others, want me to pluck one certificate from among them? Well, look yourself, Inspector. See what it's like.'

Angrily the man tossed an arm to indicate the first of the dingy rooms in the cellars beneath what had once been the Ministry of Defence. Rows and rows of damp wooden filing cabinets held the legions of the dead back to the first of the Napoleonic wars. Apologetically St-Cyr said, 'Hey, my friend, I know it's not easy, eh? But surely the Ministry and the Germans wouldn't have left you in charge had they not thought you capable?'

Margarine was it? The walnut merely shrugged and went on with sorting the stacks of mail – all similar requests for the proof absolute! 'I didn't ask for this mess,' he said acidly. 'The records will be destroyed down here and everyone knows it but no one gives a damn. The Minister of Defence and his colleagues should have taken them to Vichy when they ran away.'

'A cigarette?' offered St-Cyr. 'Me, I know what you mean. It

184

was the same with the Sûreté. A few of us stayed while the others scooted, including my chief who is still the chief.'

It took two hours of patient encouragement and searching but in the end he had it.

Captain Charles Maurice Thériault, born 25 August 1902; killed in action, Sedan, 13 May 1940.

Several others from the Vouvray area had been killed. St-Cyr pulled out their certificates as well and went to work comparing them with the captain's. The stamps on Thériault's certificate looked genuine, so too, the signatures, but purchasing a fake death certificate, particularly in the confusion of the Defeat, would have been relatively easy especially if one had the money and the determination.

'That one died,' said the walnut, only too familiar with the possibility. He fingered the certificate as a bank teller would a questionable note. 'Three requests were made for proof of death. See?' He tapped the bottom left corner.

The number three had been scribbled on the certificate.

The man turned it over. 'One request by the Countess Thériault, in the fall of 1940 – October 2nd, to be precise – then one by the wife, Gabrielle, a week later – that one came here just like you. See, there's a star beside her name. That's the code I use. And then a final request by the abbot no less, of the Abbey of Saint Gregory the Great, on 23rd November 1940. He also paid us a visit.'

Would the countess or Gabrielle have asked if they'd known the certificate was a fake? Had they been so clever as to have done this to cover their tracks in anticipation of someone like himself checking into things, or had it been in case the abbot should ask?

'Is the paper the same for the other certificates?' He knew it was.

Again the walnut felt the certificate. He held it up closely against the desk lamp, scanned it carefully for the watermarks all such genuine certificates possessed.

He pushed his glasses up and peered at the stamps and then at the signatures. Like so many, the certificate had been filled out after the Defeat. Vichy had then sent it on to Paris for filing.

'Perhaps the captain's mother, or his wife, got to somebody at the Ministry of Defence in Vichy, Inspector. Perhaps they want him listed as dead – all three of these people,' he tapped the list, 'but me, I have no reason to question the validity of this certificate.'

Could Gabrielle Arcuri's husband have run from the battle as so many officers had?

It was the unpleasant thought that had led him here and he still wasn't satisfied. Far too often fake death certificates had been used to cover such things, but damn! He'd hoped for proof. It would have made things so much simpler.

Patiently the walnut crossed out the three and wrote a four, then turned the certificate over and added, *Inspector St-Cyr of the Sûreté, 8 December 1942.*

'What's he done if he isn't dead?'

St-Cyr took in the toothless grin. 'Murdered a young boy and his sister for having discovered his secret.'

But then why leave the purse at the scene of the first crime, why the diamonds, why the cigarette case, the condoms in their little silk sleeves, the perfume . . .

Why, indeed, unless it had been someone else who'd done the killing and had wanted to point the finger at Gabrielle Arcuri.

Then why execute the girl in that fashion, why try to pin her killing on the Resistance?

The two killings had all the appearances of having been done by different people but had that been the case and had the killings been done by men?

From what he'd seen of the countess, she could easily have done them both to protect her son and the Domaine Thériault.

But not Mademoiselle Arcuri, eh? he asked himself as he left the building and went to unlock the bicycle. What of her, my friend? Is it that, after one meeting in an abandoned grist mill, you feel so sympathetic towards the woman you can believe her claims of innocence for Yvette and herself yet discount the fact that she had every reason to protect her husband?

Even to her singing in a club like the Mirage, where the Germans wouldn't think to question her loyalties because she was so popular with their men.

She'd have despised her husband for having run away. She'd have had nothing more to do with him.

Then perhaps that was the reason she'd gone back to Paris, to the life she'd once led?

Chantal Grenier, the petite designer of the shop, Enchantment, composed herself before earnestly saying, 'The Lune Russe, Louis. Gabrielle Arcuri was the chanteuse there before the war and before her marriage. Night after night Muriel would go there to listen to her. Me, I thought my Muriel was going to leave me, that she'd a crush on someone new. I could not understand her doing such a thing to me. I wept, Louis. I thought of suicide but, ah no, it was only that voice. Muriel had become entranced by it. She was like the archaeologist with a new bone, gazing raptly, always raptly. She simply could not leave the Lune Russe alone. Such magnetism, isn't that so? Such intensity in that voice. It is very sexual, very erotic. Muriel could not be blamed, and for this, I have long since forgiven her.'

There was a smile, never too much, always just perfect. The bleached blonde hair was tossed the appropriate amount. Sentiment registered in the large brown eyes beneath their long dark lashes.

Muriel had gone off on one of her 'scrounges' for materials. There were only the two of them in the office. St-Cyr sat back in his chair. 'So, when Muriel learned that Mademoiselle Arcuri was singing in Paris again, she went to hear her?'

There was a frown, the brief look of one so lost by doubt one must surely die for love, but all this passed at the thought of a recent kiss. 'Yes, several times since almost a year now, since . . . since she has discovered Gabrielle was back. Muriel has named our latest perfume after the club.'

'You should have told me. It was very naughty of you not to have.'

'You stole a vial of our perfume, Monsieur Louis! You behaved as a common thief, a shoplifter! This I can never forgive, not in a man I have always thought of as having principles. It's no wonder your wife has left you for a German officer, even though he came into the shop not an hour ago to buy her a going-away present.'

The woman ducked her eyes and waited pensively.

Poor Louis . . . it had been very naughty of her to have told

187

him. 'This young officer was nearly in tears, Louis. Broken-hearted. Three days, that's all they have left together. Three! She'll be back and then, why then Gabrielle and you . . .'

She couldn't say it. St-Cyr raised his eyebrows. 'Will not go to bed together,' she admitted. 'Gabrielle would have been much better for you than your wife.'

So Hermann had been to von Schaumburg and the general had put a stop to things. He felt sad for Marianne's sake. It would have been much better if she'd left Steiner of her own accord.

But as for his going to bed with Mademoiselle Arcuri . . . 'Chantal, let us bury our hatchets, eh? For myself, I regret stealing your vial of perfume and will gladly pay for it.'

'For my part, I apologize too, but it would have been much better, Louis, if you had confided in me fully. That's what dear friends are for, isn't that so?'

It was, but were the tears that had formed in her eyes really genuine?

'Is Gabi in trouble, Louis?'

Gabi . . . 'Her life may well be in grave danger. Her maid was murdered.'

'In Fontainebleau Woods. The Resistance . . . an *execution*, Louis! An *execution!*'

The news had been in the papers. She'd have got it there. 'Chantal, please don't distress yourself. Murders like these happen all the time.'

'But not to people you've touched, Louis! She was such a pretty thing. Yvette Noel . . . Muriel gave her a vial of our Mirage for herself when she presented two of them to Mademoiselle Arcuri.'

'Backstage?'

'But of course. Between acts.'

'What was Mademoiselle Arcuri's reaction?'

'To Muriel's naming the perfume after her and the club? Very pleased, very excited – enchanted that someone from before the war could remember her like that. After all, she'd been away for several years. Six, I think, or was it seven? But this was last year, Louis, and can have no bearing on the case.'

So Yvette had had her own vial of perfume and could easily have put it in that purse. 'Did Gabi ever come into the shop?'

'But of course. Several times after the episode of the perfume. Lingerie, stockings . . . whatever she needed.' Gabi . . . oh dear, what had she done?

'But not the dress she wore at the club?'

Louis knew all about the dress but was pretending ignorance. Very well, my dear detective! 'No . . . No, she had that made elsewhere. She didn't agree with us. I tried to tell her the pearls would only detract from the effect she wanted so much to achieve, but she wouldn't listen. She can be very stubborn, very determined, Louis. This you must believe.'

'Did Mademoiselle Arcuri ever smoke cigarettes in your presence?'

'Ah yes, lots of times.'

'Did she have a monogrammed cigarette case?'

'With the initials NKM?' asked Chantal mischievously. Oh, it was all so exciting. Muriel and she would discuss it for days.

'NKM,' confessed St-Cyr. 'You knew of this?'

Bird-like, the designer flashed him a brief, shy smile. 'But of course. One notices such things, isn't that so? But me, I could never get up the courage to ask her what the initials stood for. A man, perhaps. A lover – discretion, Louis. Me, I had to use discretion.'

'And Muriel?'

'She is convinced Gabrielle bought it in a flea market.'

A flea market! 'Had she had it long, do you think?'

Again there was a brief smile, no longer shy. 'What you really want to ask, Louis, is could she have been given it by the people at the Lune Russe when Charles Maurice Thériault asked her to end a fine career and marry him.'

St-Cyr heaved a helpless sigh. Outwitting the 'girls' was almost impossible. Age had put the mustard of wisdom on them. 'Well, yes, that is what I would have liked to ask.'

'If you had trusted me completely, Louis, there'd have been no holding back but I shall tell you, my friend, that if Gabrielle had been given it as a going-away present, the initials would not have been NKM unless her real name was something else.'

'Something Russian?' asked St-Cyr, catching a fleeting glimpse of the mirage Gabrielle Arcuri had created and wondering about it. What had the woman been hiding then, what was she hiding now?

'My poor Louis, she's exactly what you need. A beautiful woman not all that much younger than yourself, eh? A woman of mystery, not a Bretonese plough horse, even if she is pretty. But sleep well, my dear. Have fabulously exciting dreams, not nightmares. Muriel is usually right about such things.'

A flea market.

'Natasha Kulakov Myshkin. It was our little secret.' As he fingered the cigarette case, the White Russian proprietor of the Lune Russe gazed into the distance of memory. A big, sad man with the nomad's yearning for home, he tugged at the iron-grey beard. 'In 1917 she fled the Revolution of the Bolsheviks and became separated from her family, all of whom were killed perhaps, who knows? At the age of fourteen she arrived in Paris but she didn't do what most penniless girls of that age are forced to do. Natasha was a chanteuse, Inspector. She'd always wanted to be one, right from the earliest days. A real artist. It took her time to achieve success. Ah yes, a thing like that often does. She changed her name to Gabrielle Arcuri. Me, I knew right away that she was Russian but I let her tell me in her own good time and I was happy to have her here for nearly five years.'

'But then she met Charles Maurice Thériault and he wanted her to quit.'

'That one insisted. Some men are like that, Inspector. They can't stand to see their wives a success – so popular in Gabrielle's case she could wring tears from the coldest of hearts but . . . but why is it you have not known of her? Surely . . .'

St-Cyr gave the shrug he reserved for fate and time and internal politics. 'Paris and its environs are the Préfet's beat; the Sûreté has the rest of the country. Me, I've usually been out there some place or in the sewers. You were saying . . .?'

'Thériault, yes. He was madly in love with her. Night after night he'd sit here listening to her. She hesitated, she wanted to keep on singing. Gabi's like that – a natural. She just has to sing. His family . . . Ah! what can one say, eh? Snobs, if you ask me. The mother didn't like it one bit. He took Gabi away to the country, took her from us – my God, the trouble I had explaining things to the patrons. From time to time she'd come back and if she could, she'd sing a little for old times' sake.

190

Never when he was around, of course. She was like a daughter, Inspector. A daughter.'

'But she always insisted on being called Gabrielle Arcuri?'

'Yes, of course. Arcuri was the name of a family that had helped her. The Natasha was from a time before, a time of great sadness.'

'Yet she kept the cigarette case, knowing it would identify her?'

'She told people she'd bought it in a flea market. Me, I didn't mind. It was a part of her, Inspector, our little secret. Natasha Kulakov Myshkin came from a very wealthy family. They had a dacha in the Urals and a fine big house in Leningrad. Her father had been a doctor in the court of the Romanovs.'

'And you gave her the cigarette case?'

'But of course. A parting gift as I've said.'

'Would she have told her husband her real name?'

'Perhaps, but me, I don't think so. You see, Inspector, with that ear of hers, Gabrielle had picked up a pretty good accent. She'd have told her husband her parents were dead. The Arcuri name is what's on her papers. You won't tell the Germans, will you? She'll not have done anything, not that one. A heart of gold and kindness itself. A real diamond in the rough, but not so rough at all. Ah no. Please tell her that we wish her well and miss her. The Club Mirage is no place for her.'

And the husband? asked St-Cyr of himself. Could the husband or the mother-in-law have now wanted to get rid of her?

The cutting room of the Salon Chez Nadeau was as busy as ever. No sign of Julian Nadeau but his assistant, Sylviane Valcourt, waited impatiently for him to speak.

St-Cyr stood to one side of the cluttered windows looking down at the rue de la Paix. There were lots of pedestrians, lots of German officers and their French girlfriends, cyclists and velo-taxis. Good places to hide, good places from which to watch.

When he found the man, apparently window shopping and using the glass as a mirror, he passed on until he had the other one. Both of them were in their forties, dressed as if notaries or accountants – so nothing shabby about them. Good papers, no doubt, and good on their feet and on their bicycles. Ex-Army? he wondered. They had that look about them. Had it not been for his dodging the Gestapo earlier, he'd have spotted them.

He picked their bikes out, noting that each was chained to something. Were they armed and out to kill him? Had it gone that far? Surely they'd have had opportunity enough this morning. The bikes would be left as a diversion. They'd vanish into the crowd on foot.

Sylviane began to fret. 'Julian is out to lunch, Monsieur Louis. Me, I have to go myself. Is everything all right?'

She'd been fifteen years of age when he'd plucked her from the streets, not much older than Gabrielle Arcuri had been when she'd first come to Paris.

Again the girl asked if everything was all right. The incessant sound of scissors and sewing machines formed a background to their voices.

Still St-Cyr didn't turn from the window. 'Yes . . . yes. For the moment. Sylviane, I have only one question for you, but it's very important. Did Mademoiselle Arcuri's maid, Yvette Noel, call to ask you to make her mistress another purse?'

Snatching up a pair of scissors and a remnant, the girl moved to the window and began to study the street with the eye of an expert. 'Is someone after you?' she asked anxiously.

'Sylviane, please answer my question – there are two of them. The one looking at the ladies' hats, the other pretending to tie a shoe.'

'Me, I have already spotted them. Yes, the girl called and asked me to make another. She said the original had been stolen.'

'Not lost?'

'No, stolen, Monsieur Louis. Of this I am positive.'

'Was she in great distress?'

The girl continued to watch the men. 'In tears. Yes, she was in tears. It . . . it was not two days before she . . . she was murdered.'

'Who took the purse over to her?'

'Myself. Julian . . . You know how he is, Monsieur Louis. She was special, this Gabrielle. He . . . he had his eye on her, I think. Ever since the dress, you understand, the fittings. Julian, he is like the miser who always has a little something under the floorboards. Another prospect. A war widow. What could be better?'

Was Sylviane secretly in love with her boss? Was that why she was so upset? 'A murderess, if he's not careful, Sylviane. Please tell him it's hands off until the case is settled, unless he wants to deal with me.'

'You're angry with us?' she said, still looking down at the street. She had cut the remnant to pieces, was clutching the scissors.

'You should have told me about that second purse,' said St-Cyr quietly. The girl was pale . . .

'You did not ask, eh? How was Julian to know you suspected this . . . this chanteuse of . . . of murder? Of which murder?' she asked sharply.

Ah Mon Dieu, what was the matter with her? 'The girl's brother, or the two of them. Me, I'm not sure of anything yet. When you delivered the purse how did you find Yvette?'

The two men hadn't moved. 'Agitated. She didn't say much, only thanked me for having brought it over so quickly. If you ask me, Monsieur Louis, I think her mistress didn't know of the loss and the girl was trying to cover up.'

'What did you make of the Corsicans?'

It would start to rain soon – a freezing rain – but would that help him to get away? Would it? Ah Mon Dieu . . . 'Rapists with their eyes. Like most men, they undressed me with their filthy minds. In a second!'

Her chest heaved defiantly at the thought, moving him to kindness. In profile she was very pretty, very engaging but upset – yes, definitely upset and trying desperately to keep control. A puzzle to be sure. 'Don't be so hard on us men, my dear Sylviane. Life's small pleasures, eh? You're a very attractive young woman. Those two out there would be certain to look your way.'

The one with the troublesome shoe had moved along to the café. 'Are they Gestapo?' she asked, hoping that he'd say it was so.

Shoelace had now found his paper and was fighting December's curse to read the want ads. 'I lost them long ago, Sylviane. No, these two are something different.'

How wary he was. 'The Resistance?' she asked, turning to let him see the tears that had flooded into her eyes.

'Yes . . . Yes, I believe it is them, Sylviane, but it is all a terrible mistake.'

'Then you've seen the photographs – they're everywhere, Monsieur Louis. Me, I have tried so hard to gather them up.'

The girl had eighteen of them in her tiny office which was just off the cutting room. Choking back the tears beneath a fatherly hand, she had broken down completely at the prospect of the Resistance executing him.

How well she had tried to hide it. Ah, Mon Dieu, the Nile, the Amazon . . .

In black and white, Kohler and he stood on opposite sides of the boy's body.

'You are being *blamed* for his murder, Monsieur Louis! Blamed!' she blurted, banging the table with a fist.

St-Cyr tried to comfort her by a gentle massage of the shoulders. The seamstresses – older, married women – glanced fiercely their way. A plate glass divider. No privacy at all, well, so be it. 'I see that I have my friends,' he said gently. 'That is so good at a time like this, Sylviane. Me, I will never forget it.'

'Julian's being a pig! He refused to see you. He . . . he has said I was to send you away, that he wanted nothing more to do with you.'

'He's forgiven. It's only understandable he be cautious for . . . for all of your sakes.' The coward!

The girl flung herself into his arms and hugged him tightly. 'Me, I will slash their tyres, Monsieur Louis!'

'No . . . No, you will do no such thing. You will toss me out on to that street and scream at me never to come back, eh? Then you will throw that fistful of photographs at me.'

It was so brave of him, so considerate. Ah, Mon Dieu . . . to think of such a thing at a time like this!

Short and just as petite as Chantal Grenier, Sylviane Valcourt stood on tiptoe and pressed her fine young body against him. All of it. A kiss of such passion, he had to think of that other young girl, that student . . . Liline . . . the girl with the shoes and the swollen jaw.

A time for love, and a time for death. Danger! Always danger! Was it this that attracted the young girls to him?

194

Or the lack of suitable young men? The war and the forced labour had taken so many.

She brushed an uncertain hand over his face, let her fingers linger on his moustache – still kept herself pressed against him. The smile she gave was brave. 'So, my Monsieur Louis, the great detective, me I will do exactly as you have asked but please do not take what I am about to say down there as the truth, eh?'

At his nod, they parted but still she lingered. Not looking at him now, shy – was she being shy? – she fingered the table top, hesitated a moment, then said, a whisper, 'I've learned to cook. I'm a good housekeeper, Monsieur Louis. Me, I could still work here but I . . . I could be so useful.'

St-Cyr chucked her under the chin and kissed her on the cheek. 'Come and help me now, eh? Come on, let's give them something to remember.'

The Galeries Lafayette was crowded but safe. Its magnificent cupola of wrought iron and glass rose through the layer cake of columned floors to tower above them.

Department stores were such suitable places for meetings. Jérome Noel had even used this one. July 7th to be precise. At 4.17 p.m., on the main floor. In full view of every passer-by.

Hermann was late and he wasn't himself.

'Louis, I've got an idea we should get out of town for a few days. Question the monks – give them a thorough going-over. Pry away at the countess's armour. Try the Arcuri woman again. Her ice is bound to break for you. She'll be sure to climb into the sack.'

'Three days?'

'Yes, three should do it. Von Schaumburg and Boemelburg have okayed a week. The first is insisting; the second agreeing because Berlin has reluctantly said he must. If we wrap it up in fine style we might just get off with a lecture.'

'And Ackermann? What does he have to say about things?' Was Hermann looking slightly green or was it simply the lighting?

Kohler took an agitated drag at his cigarette. 'Oberg, over on the avenue Foch, wants to see us.'

195

The Butcher of Poland, the head of the Secret Service of the SS in France and Ackermann's new boss.

'We're in the shit, Louis. I'm sorry. The best thing we can do is to take a little trip. Boemelburg isn't exactly in total agreement. He wants the diamonds in his safe. You've still got them, haven't you? You've not lost them? You can't have done that!'

He was positively shaking.

'Pharand?' asked St-Cyr.

'I wouldn't want to see him if I were you. The diamonds, Louis? Don't keep me in suspense.'

Sometimes prying things out of Hermann was difficult. Clearly Boemelburg didn't want them leaving town. 'And Ackermann?' he demanded again. One had to be tough.

'The bastard's challenged me to a duel. It's strictly against the law – German law, Louis. Gestapo law and SS law. Pistols at thirty paces. A match pair. God knows where he got them.'

A duel . . . 'Perhaps the countess loaned them to him.'

'Agreed?' asked Kohler of the trip. Boemelburg could stick the diamonds. 'I've been by your place to pick up your things. I even spoke to your housekeeper. Everything's okay. The geraniums . . .'

'The diamonds are still in the inside pocket of my jacket, so stop worrying so much.'

'It's you who ought to be worried,' breathed Kohler, pinching out the fag.

'Yes . . . yes, I know. Perhaps I should ask the Reverend Father to let me join the monks. But three days, Hermann? Is it that you've bartered for the release of my wife?'

Had word already got round? *Gott in Himmel* . . . 'Steiner's being sent to where his cock will be of only one use to him if he can get it out in the cold.'

The Russian Front at Stalingrad. 'Then let us go to Vouvray. Marianne can choose what is best for her and hopefully she'll be there when we return.'

Did Louis have to be so naïve? With luck von Schaumburg would have got the films out of Brother Glotz's hands by then and had the blasted things destroyed!

With luck Boemelburg and his boys would have pulled in the girl with the broken shoes and found out who all her friends were.

196

Perhaps no one would decide to take a shot or two at them. Perhaps the Resistance from Melun would leave them alone until the case was settled and they could clean those bastards out in style, *sans* Louis of course.

Maybe Ackermann would forget about his duel. Maybe . . . maybe . . .

'It's all right, Hermann. You watch my back and me, I'll be sure to watch yours, eh?'

'Then rest a little easier, my French Frog friend. I went past Gestapo HQ on the fly and swiped us two Schmeissers and seven hundred rounds apiece for good measure.'

There were a dozen stick grenades lying loosely on the floor of the car.

St-Cyr planted his feet among them and hung on as they lost their Gestapo tails.

6

The morning was crisp and clear, the wind in off the Atlantic and up the valley of the Loire to threaten an early blizzard. The sound of church bells was resonant.

Kohler and St-Cyr stood in the midst of Vouvray's largest cemetery. A crowd had gathered in the distance round the entrance to the church – the curious, the uninvited. Murder always brought them. There'd be whispers, questions – rumours of incest perhaps.

The church's slate-roofed bell tower and spire rose to a substantial cross which had defied all weathers and all wars since the mid-sixteenth century. The horse-drawn hearses were parked well to the far side; the only cars – that of the countess and that of the local German Kommandant – were to the other.

St-Cyr brought his gaze back to the pair of open graves at their feet. One thing was certain. They buried deeply in these parts.

So, too, was another. 'The *perruches*, Hermann. That silicious clay with its flint boulders. They don't just grow grapes in it.'

Kohler stubbed out his cigarette and thought about flicking the butt into one of the graves. Decently he pocketed it. 'Why the two graves, Louis?'

'My thought precisely, Hermann. You're improving. Why isn't Brother Jérome being buried at the monastery?'

'Any ideas?'

'Several. The countess may well have intervened on the family's behalf; the abbot might not have wanted to go against her wishes but then . . . and I stress this . . . perhaps, in his wisdom, he saw advantage in not claiming Brother Jérome's body. But then again, Hermann, has a feud developed between

198

the parish priest and the abbot? Ah now, that is a distinct possibility. Perhaps the priest has insisted on a double-barrelled burial and the countess has sided with him. One thing is certain. Authority has been challenged and custom breached.'

'You going inside?'

St-Cyr tapped out his pipe against a tombstone. 'Cover the curious and the whole of this place. Have a look for Charles Maurice Thériault just in case he's had a twinge of conscience and come to pay his last respects. Me, I will step inside as you have suggested, to study the mourners as they view the bodies.'

'Enjoy yourself. I'm taking a Schmeisser with me.'

'No one's going to shoot up a funeral. Not in France. Even the Resistance will show some respect.'

'Ask Yvette that when you blow her a kiss, or are you planning to lean over the girl and bring her back to life?'

Funerals brought out the worst in Hermann. 'I'm not sure the caskets will be open, but in the countryside it's usually the case, no matter what the damage.'

Louis could always be counted on to add that pleasant touch. Kohler grinned hugely. 'I ought to let you have the last word, my fine Frog friend, but I simply have to say, Don't do anything in there I wouldn't do.'

'For a man who has been challenged to a duel, you're extremely light-hearted?'

'Ackermann didn't come, chum!'

It was on the tip of St-Cyr's tongue to say, Let's wait and see, eh, but he left it.

One had to do things like that with Hermann. Having the last word was important to him.

The church was packed. The bells continued – did they ring them twice as long if there were two burials? Everyone but the priest, his two assistants and the altar boys was at their rosaries or sitting stiffly. All in black. Not a suit or a dress of brown. He'd stick out like a sore thumb but . . . ah, Mon Dieu, it couldn't be helped. Funerals were so useful. They brought so many together in one place.

The abbot, for instance, and Brother Michael, the monastery's wine maker and mentor of Brother Jérome.

Only one other monk was present – all three of them sat at the very front, next the aisle, but on the right side.

The third monk was the farthest from the aisle, a younger man with tears in his eyes, by the look. Much weeping. Yes . . . yes, it was so. Could it be that Brother Michael was gripping him firmly by the hand in hopes of calming him?

Was that third monk Brother Sebastian, the beekeeper Jérome had made unjust accusations against?

The monk was of about forty-five or fifty years of age – very strongly built. The neck and head were those of a wrestler, the shoulders also.

But why the tears if he'd been wrongly accused? Why indeed?

The countess, Gabrielle Arcuri and her son, René Yvon-Paul, sat in the second row across the aisle and behind the immediate family of the deceased.

The caskets were open. Lilies . . . White lilies . . . Where had they got them at this time of year and in a country at war?

From the south, from Provence perhaps? A greenhouse . . .

The lilies were of silk and he knew then that the countess had seen to everything but that she hadn't asked her distant cousin from Germany to help.

Grateful for the advantage standing gave him, St-Cyr was still perturbed that he couldn't see as well as he'd have liked.

It was going to be a long funeral.

A columned balcony ran along both sides of the church and led to the bell tower and the ringer of the bells. The stained-glass windows were magnificent, so, too, the frescoes in the vaulted ceiling. The community had much to thank the Family Thériault for. The silver service, the candlesticks, the richly embroidered altar cloth and cushions no doubt, the seats of course, the newish roof – perhaps two hundred years old – the robes the priestly folk wore, even the ring the people kissed and the illuminated Bible.

There was only one way to get a brown suit and tweed overcoat out of this.

St-Cyr squeezed along the wall, nodded apologies to four of the pallbearers who'd all been through this sort of thing thousands of times and, in spite of their objections, went up the stairs to the balcony.

It was such a view. Perfect! Magnificent! The smell of incense was all around him. They were burning lavender to which a trace of cinnamon had been added.

Keeping to the outside of the balcony, he moved towards the altar until he came at last to stand in the shadow of one of the columns.

Gabrielle Arcuri and the countess both wore veils. Completely dressed in black, the mirage looked very estranged, very sad and poignant – a war widow, so many things. But Russian? he asked. Did Natasha Kulakov Myshkin look Russian?

Did the countess even know her son's wife had been the daughter of a very wealthy family who'd found favour at the court of the Romanovs? Would she have believed it if she'd been told?

Somehow he didn't think the countess would know. Gabrielle Arcuri would have kept that little slice of her past entirely to herself just as the owner of the Lune Russe had said.

So, perhaps a small stint as a streetwalker after all? Just to pay the necessary bills and get established.

She was holding her son's hand. The boy looked afraid – terrified that something would happen – but then, don't all boys of that age worry at funerals?

The caskets were near. Though in death and wax, yet the resemblances between Jérome Noel and René Yvon-Paul were striking.

Not so Yvette who, beneath the wax, the face powder, rouge and lipstick, had the coarseness of both her mother and father.

Madame Noel, a plumpish woman in her early fifties, was weeping buckets but did she weep not only for her lost children but also because she'd been the one to tell Jérome who his real father had been? At fifty some women do get twinges of conscience about such things, especially if a son is about to give himself to God and so must have the truth.

The face of the father, a man in his early sixties, was impassive; that of the abbot the same. Grim, taciturn and unforgiving. Angry too.

If only Yvette could tell him what had really happened. If only the girl would sit up suddenly and shout it out.

Her hands were clasped. Three lilies and her rosary had been placed in them. Even from a distance of perhaps twenty-five metres, St-Cyr could tell the funeral parlour had·worked miracles and touched her up like a chef with a fallen cake. There was no sign of the bullet that had killed her. The eyes were closed and she slept. The wedding dress was white and of lace, her mother's perhaps? Ah no, the grandmother's. The end of the family. No need to save such things any more.

Gone . . . gone to ashes and to dust.

With Jérome they'd not been so successful or perhaps they hadn't cared so much. One could still detect the place where the boulder had struck him.

Although there were other possibilities – Charles Maurice Thériault in particular – St-Cyr felt certain that somewhere below him was the murderer of Jérome Noel.

But not that of his sister? he asked. Was her killer absent?

Kohler cursed their luck as the Daimler turned into the grave-yard and drove slowly to the church. Ackermann had brought his driver and adjutant with him, and one other man – his second perhaps. Heaps of cut flowers: three white wicker baskets for a couple of kids he didn't even know – or did he? – and three large wreaths. A classic National Socialist barf? Flowers and concern for those you'd bumped off?

All were SS and in uniform. The son-of-a-bitch had duel written all over him and so did the other two. Now what the hell was he going to do? Leave Louis to it and scram?

Ackermann took one frozen look his way before marching swiftly to the door and whipping off his cap.

In under the left arm with it. *Ja . . . Ja*, that is correct, Herr General!

The adjutant yanked the church door open and snapped to attention. Stiff as a pecker at dawn and beautifully done.

The other one took a little longer to survey him. No smiles, just an emptiness that was unsettling.

They followed the general into the church. The flowers and the wreaths were stuffed in after them by willing assistants and no doubt passed from hand to hand and up to the front to announce their late arrival.

So good of Ackermann. Some guys had what it took.

'Ah, Mon Dieu, Brigitte, that's the one I saw Jérome with. Me, I am certain of it,' whispered the shopgirl nearest him.

'Are you sure?' whispered her friend. Both of the girls were in their mid-teens and had obviously got time off from work.

Brown Eyes said, 'Positive! Jérome got into his car – me, I recognize it – but they were alone, Brigitte. At dusk.'

'When?' Kohler heard himself ask like a voice from another planet.

'When?' blurted Brown Eyes, glancing apprehensively up at him. Ah no, a cop!

Kohler nodded. The girl flicked her eyes at her friend and then back again. 'Last summer – in June . . . the middle of June. Yes . . . yes, I am certain. They . . . they drove down to the river.'

Oh, did they now? 'At dusk?'

'Yes . . . Yes, it was at dusk.'

'And you followed them? You were on your bicycle?'

The brown eyes fled to the church. She'd just known today would be a disaster. First her period and now . . . now this. 'Are you from the police?' she asked, summoning a courage beyond her years.

'I'm from Marseilles. I came up because I'm a distant relative of the Noels. We heard about things and wanted to see if there was anything we could do.'

The girl tossed her wavy hair and stared straight ahead. From Marseilles, eh? More like Munich! 'Me, I did not have my bicycle with me, monsieur. I did not follow them to the river.'

Oh yeah? Kohler gripped the two of them firmly by the arm and hustled them out of the crowd. When they reached the open graves, he let go of them. 'Now start talking. I'm from the Gestapo. Everything your little hearts can cough up unless you want to find yourselves in one of these.'

They both began to cry. At fifteen or sixteen years of age what else would one have done? 'Look, I've been a lousy father but I need to know a few things, eh? A life may well be in danger. Real danger. Another murder perhaps.'

Brown Eyes broke. 'Yvette . . . Yvette, she met me on the road just above the river and she stopped me. I was only going to watch. I wasn't going to say anything!'

'Yes, yes. Now calm down and let me have the rest of it.'

'She . . . she has said I was to mind my own business, that I was *trespassing* on the Domaine Thériault. Me who has always gone there to swim! And now she's dead! *Murdered!*'

Kohler held the girl by the shoulders and tried to comfort her. He knew he was all clumsiness at this sort of thing.

'What else did she say? Hey, come on now. I'm not going to hurt you. Me, I was just kidding about the graves.'

The kid sniffed in. 'That . . . that the general, he was a very powerful man and that he'd . . . he'd send me to Germany as forced labour if I didn't do as she said. Me, I was to keep my mouth shut and I have, monsieur. I have! Until this day.'

There was more blubbering, more shaking, the face buried in the hands and the forehead pressed against him with the other girl looking on like death.

Kohler dragged out his handkerchief. 'Blow,' he said gruffly. 'It's clean, even if it is German. Dry your eyes.'

The girl did as she was told. 'Thanks . . . thanks. That is very kind of you, monsieur.' Kind of the Gestapo!

'So, okay, now listen, eh? Can you remember anything else about that evening?'

The girl sucked in a ragged breath and shook her head.

'Think hard.'

'No, nothing, monsieur. I swear it. I . . .'

'Well?'

'Me, I have passed one of the brothers on the way home. He . . . he was heading for the river and in a great hurry. He didn't look up at me.'

A coldness came to Kohler. 'Which of the brothers?'

'Michael . . . the one who makes the wine.'

So Brother Michael had gone after Jérome as had Yvette. 'Were they lovers?' he asked. God help him. 'The general and Jérome?'

The girls stiffened in alarm. Lovers . . .? Jérome who had such a slender body? Jérome who swam in the nude and brushed the water from his body while standing in the shallows.

Neither of them could take their eyes from the graves. Lovers . . . Jérome who would lie naked on the sand . . .

The one called Brigitte hastily crossed herself and whispered, 'Perhaps.'

Brown Eyes emptily said, 'It can't be so.'

*

204

Ackermann's entry into the church fulfilled a detective's dream. Miraculously three places were made for him and his associates at the front, next to the aisle, the abbot and the brothers shifting over.

In one glance from the balcony St-Cyr could sweep the lot of them into focus, both the dead and the living. Ah, Mon Dieu, to have the camera rolling at such a moment. It was almost too good to be true.

But why had Ackermann done it? To allay suspicion? To cover up? Or out of courtesy to a distant cousin?

His presence could only tar the countess with the label of a collaborator. Had that been what he'd had in mind? It was a thought St-Cyr was certain he shared with the countess.

The eulogy droned up to him. Two young people taken in the flower of life. A brother and his sister, et cetera, et cetera.

St-Cyr shut the priest out and concentrated on the mourners. The abbot was nervous – understandably so. To sit next to the SS, to have had to move aside for them, could not have been easy. But had Ackermann wanted to warn him? Was that it?

Brother Michael was telling his rosary. The beads trickled through the workworn fingers. The sad grey eyes, now granite hard, searched the new flowers and the wreaths for answers as he grimly moved his lips.

The beekeeper's head was bowed – real grief there, was that it? Had the beekeeper made advances to Brother Jérome and been rejected? Had he then killed Jérome in a fit of rejection and somehow moved the body to Fontainebleau Woods? And the bicycle . . . one mustn't forget Brother Michael's bicycle. And one mustn't forget that the abbey possessed a gasogene and made regular deliveries to Paris. Ah yes.

But, had Ackermann and Jérome been lovers? To be a homosexual in the SS was to ask for death yet the general looked as cold as steel. Was it Poland all over again and 50 millimetre cannon at a stone's throw or the flame throwers?

Ackermann's gaze never wavered. Not a muscle moved. Perhaps he was used to ceremonies. Perhaps he was here simply to make an arrest for the Sicherheitsdienst and to fight a duel.

The scar tissue glistened.

13 July/42 – Fontainebleau Woods, the pond. Spent the afternoon

sunbathing. Went swimming twice. Drank champagne. After the chase,
there is resignation and acceptance.

22 November/42 – Arrived at the Gorge of the Archers and took the
footpath up into the woods. Waited from 2.30 p.m. until 3.30 p.m. Sat
in the car and talked until 5.10 p.m., after which, drove back to Paris.

Sat in the car and talked . . . Whose car? Mademoiselle Arcuri's?

Waited from 2.30 p.m. until 3.30 p.m. . . . . Had the person being
met – Ackermann, presumably – not shown up? Had Jérome
then gone back to the car and talked with its driver for nearly
two hours?

Had that driver been Gabrielle Arcuri or the countess? Had
the diary even been written by Yvette?

Or had the driver been Ackermann and they'd simply waited
an hour before settling down to business?

They had braided the girl's hair and had pinned the braids
across the top of her brow. It was very French, very of the
countryside.

7 November/42 – The Ritz again. From 9.00 p.m. until after curfew.
Was driven back to the flat on the rue Daguerre. The Corsicans' aunt.

Yvette could not possibly have followed her brother to all of
those places. Only one conclusion could be drawn. He'd told
her of them and she'd written them down. *If* she'd written the
diary at all.

Or had he told them to Mademoiselle Arcuri, who had then
recorded them?

After the chase, there is resignation and acceptance . . .

A boulder and a bullet – two vastly different killings, both
linked by more than blood.

A virgin . . . Three stiff shots of plum brandy in her stomach
when she died. 'Tell Mademoiselle Arcuri it's all going to be
fixed.'

Ackermann had developed a nervous twitch in the left side of
his face. From time to time he touched the cheek and cursed
whoever had been responsible for the burns.

He'd kill Hermann. He wouldn't miss. They'd use the gardens
inside the walls of the château and the general would choose
the time.

Did you fall in love with that boy? asked St-Cyr. Did you
caress his young body to forget the pain of your disfigurement?
Was it you who bit his thigh or one of the countess's dogs?

206

Ah yes, one of the greyhounds could well have done such a thing in play. Jérome would have known them well.

A key . . . there had to be a key. Something they'd overlooked. The Russian angle, was it really deep enough to drive Ackermann to look into Gabrielle Arcuri's past? After all, he was working with the Sicherheitsdienst. Oberg could have assigned him her file. Jérome could simply have been the inside source. Hence, *After the chase, there is resignation and acceptance*, but why tell Yvette of it, why tell one who was obviously so loyal to her mistress?

Or had she been? What of the condoms in their little silk sleeves? What of the cigarette case, the purse itself, and the diamonds?

Had the 'theft' of the purse simply been a lie, tearful though it was? Had its contents been planted by Yvette to hide the truth of the killing and throw suspicion on to her mistress?

Were the condoms there to signify Natasha Kulakov Myshkin's brief past as a young girl of the streets or were they but the precaution of a married woman in a time of war?

A woman whose husband wasn't dead.

And the diamonds, Mademoiselle Arcuri? he asked, studying the veiled mirage with an intensity that frightened him. Death . . . death was down there in more than two places. He saw her naked, shorn of her hair and lying beside the river, saw the blood draining from the gash in her throat. The Resistance.

The diamonds . . . were they to pay someone for their silence, Mademoiselle Arcuri? Jérome perhaps, or were they the result of his blackmailing the SS General Hans Gerhardt Ackermann?

Would Ackermann have even stood for such a thing, no matter how much he'd been in love with the boy? No, of course not. He'd have killed Jérome if someone else hadn't done it first, and then he'd have killed Yvette. He'd kill the chanteuse too. He'd try to put the blame on the Resistance and he'd put a stop to everything. He'd even come to witness the burials.

René Yvon-Paul hesitantly took his mother's hand in his. She squeezed the boy's fingers. It could mean nothing more than the touching bond between a mother and her son.

Or it could be that the boy knew full well she was desperately afraid and badly in need of reassurance.

207

At a word from the priest, the mourners rose and began to file past the caskets.

Kohler opened the door of the shed behind the church to find two men sitting on the floor, leaning back against a wall and having a bite to eat. As gravediggers went, they were a pair of princes. The ox-eyed one with the walrus moustache and the little black bow tie was bursting the buttons of his vest and the seams of the stovepipe suit he wore; the weasel, a tough, belligerent little bastard, looked as if he was waiting to rob the dead. All nose, thin, tight lips, a parsimonious moustache and eyes that were as hard and dark as anthracite.

Being their guest, Kohler magnanimously offered cigarettes and intro's but declined to share their much-swigged bottle of wine, even if it was from Vouvray. 'It's too hard on my stomach,' he quipped. 'Gives me gas – any wine, you understand. German, French, Italian, it's all the same. Pickle juice.'

They nodded with disinterest and kept their thoughts to themselves. Gas, eh? Bavarian farts! Too much good French cabbage and black market olive oil in the diet!

The whores, thought the weasel. Little French girls under the age of sixteen. Dolls in their underwear. They're what's given Big-foot the wind. Wine . . . since when did wine bother anybody?

The weasel dragged out his handkerchief and in the process scattered the more than two precious handfuls of funeral-parlour oats he'd stolen from the horses. In dismay he searched the floor for mice to gobble it up.

'Hang on a minute,' said Kohler blithely. 'I think I've got just the thing.'

He went out to the hearses, not to get one of the nags, though he would have liked to do so, but to strip the feedbags from two of them and fill the weasel's pockets again.

'So, my friends, a few questions, eh? While the dead give up the last of their prayers.'

The weasel had by then, on the insistence of his partner, swept up the offending oats and hidden them away. He now filled a small sack, taking equal amounts from both feedbags. 'Questions . . .? Is it that you are from the police, monsieur?'

'The Gestapo,' said Kohler quietly, as the grains fell from that thieving hand.

'Gestapo?' asked the walrus, swallowing tightly. 'But I thought you said you were from Paris, from one of the newspapers? *Le Matin* . . .?'

'Gestapo,' said Kohler. 'It's a murder case, isn't it?'

'But . . . but the SS, they are inside the church?' bleated the walrus.

'Oh them,' said Kohler. 'They're just friends of the family.'

'Friends . . . but that is not possible, monsieur. Riel Noel knows no one in the SS.'

The man was a real klutz.

'The countess does,' spat the weasel acidly. 'She's asked that cousin of hers for help. That's why he's here. To teach the Reverend Father some manners.'

'Over the land claim,' offered the walrus apologetically. They'd best keep talking a little. This one had to stoop to avoid banging his head on the roof. He'd not stay long.

'The land claim?' asked Kohler.

The walrus went on. 'Yes. The upper vineyard of the Domaine Thériault has always been a private passion of the Reverend Father. The deeds, they are not entirely correct, you understand. Written by monks who knew nothing of surveying, and by magistrates in Paris or Rome who liked to write in Latin but had never visited this area. The matter has been in and out of the courts for centuries.'

'That's why the abbot accepted Jérome Noel into the order – to gain favour with the countess,' said the weasel.

'It didn't work,' added the walrus. 'Now our parish priest, the Father Eugene, has the body and the abbot and the countess continue their fight. It's always the same with these powerful people. One gains a little by trickery, then the other gains something back. They go at it like cats in the night, monsieur. Most of the action is in the howling.'

Kohler knew he'd have to remember that one.

The weasel grinned. The Gestapo was loosening up. Good . . . good . . . that was very good. Big-foot liked these little stories . . . 'Our parish priest was chosen by the countess from among the fifteen candidates she and the abbot interviewed. Even Rome will fart for a countess.'

'Any ideas who killed the brother and sister?'

The weasel shrugged. 'The Préfet thinks it is the work of a sadist, monsieur, but then he is only the Préfet of Vouvray and the murders, they were not committed in his district. Talbotte, the Préfet of Greater Paris, has telephoned to give him the facts, you understand. The girl Yvette was raped in the you-know-where, but they're not saying. They're hushing it all up to preserve the sanctity of our minds.'

'The brother, God forbid,' offered the walrus, trying to help but not quite making it.

'The brother, eh?' snorted Kohler. 'Flying up her backside after death! You two are under arrest for withholding information.'

'Under arrest . . .? But . . . Ah no, monsieur,' struggled the walrus, 'you would not do that to us.'

Kohler yanked out his pistol. 'I would and have. Stick up your hands. We'll use the two graves you've already dug. They can dump the coffins in on top of you.'

Both armpits of the walrus's jacket had split long ago. The poor bastard wet himself. In the name of Jesus, was his bladder that weak?

'The countess's car was seen leaving the area late on the night before Jérome's body was found,' blurted the man.

Now that was better. 'Up by the monastery?' demanded Kohler, cocking the pistol.

Dear Jesus, he means it! 'There was a bicycle tied to the back of the car,' managed the weasel, his eyes never leaving the muzzle of the gun. Gaston would be the first to get it.

'Who was driving?'

The walrus coughed up. 'The countess, who else? Me, I did not see so clearly, monsieur. Please, you must believe this. The rabbits are best in among the rocks, isn't that so? Me, I was out . . .'

'Trapping?'

Ah Mon Dieu! why had he said it? Now the forced labour for hunting and taking the spoils of the victors! 'A few rabbits,' he grimaced and tried to gesture with his arms up like that. 'Only a few, monsieur.'

'Three?' demanded Kohler not letting up on the heat.

210

'Four?. . . Six? *Gott in Himmel*, six furry little bundles or was it . . .?'

Ten years – he'd get at least ten years! The walrus's eyes melted. Thank God there was no more in his bladder. 'Eight, monsieur. I . . . I have the ferret and the nets. My wife, she makes the pâté for the butcher. I could let you have two pots . . .?' It was a hope, a gamble, a possibility . . .

'Six,' said Kohler. 'I'll want the address later. You two keep co-operating and I'll be sure to tell her what happened to you. Did anyone else see the car?'

The two of them glanced apprehensively at each other. Again the walrus had the tongue. 'No . . . No, there was no one else.'

Kohler stepped forward and came to crouch between the man's outspread boots. The stench of urine was overpowering yet he reached out to straighten the man's tie. 'We like to have our people looking their best,' he said softly. The gun tapped the walrus under the chin. 'You're lying,' said Kohler. 'It's a shame you're so big in the belly. It'll make the coffin on top of you tilt.'

God forgive him, he'd have to tell the truth! 'The . . . the abbot or . . . or one of the brothers, monsieur. He . . . he was standing on the road, watching as the car drove away.'

Oh, was he now? The tears were very real. 'And was Yvette at home having her backside reamed or in Paris?'

The walrus winced. The weasel came to the rescue. 'Yvette was at home visiting her parents.'

So he'd found his voice again, had he? 'And did she know how to drive a car?' asked Kohler.

The weasel didn't like the look in the Gestapo's eyes. 'Madame Thériault has taught her this some years ago. When . . . when Yvette was eighteen, I think.'

'Gabrielle . . .' offered the walrus. 'In the name of Jesus, monsieur, could we not lower our arms?'

'Jesus isn't with us, so I can't ask him,' said Kohler. The ox-eyes swam as they fled. 'No . . . no, please, I insist,' breathed Kohler. 'You must look at me. It's one of our very first rules when dealing with shits like you two. Hey, tell me, my friend, are the bowels okay – the back ones? You're not about to empty them or choke on them?'

The man nodded quickly. To be humiliated like this . . . 'I

was in the last war, monsieur, at Verdun. Ever since, my system it has not functioned so well in times of crisis.'

'An old soldier, eh? Hey, listen, I know all about it. So, okay, I'll let up a little if you'll tell me – was Gabrielle Arcuri also at home, visiting the countess and her son?'

'The son is dead, monsieur. Monsieur Charles, he was killed at Sedan during the invasion.'

Kohler let that one pass. 'Gabrielle's son, René Yvon-Paul.'

'Oh, him. Yes . . . yes, me, I suppose she did come to see the boy. She often does.'

'But you don't know for sure she was here?'

'No . . . no, I cannot say that.'

Kohler stood up. The weasel, like all of his kind, had let the walrus blurt it out and take the rap.

He waved the gun at the man to indicate that the arms must remain aloft. 'Was the General Ackermann at the château?'

Anthracite eyes stared defiantly back at him. 'The general, monsieur? No . . . No, I do not think he was here, but I cannot say for sure.'

Had the man any reason to lie? Plenty, if the matter had anything to do with the SS. 'Look, I'll give you to the count of three, then I'll have your friend drag you out of here.'

'That is the truth, monsieur. Gaston and I both live in the lower part of town. It is not far from the main road, you understand, but far enough and very far from the Château Thériault, so we don't exactly see all that's going on, and since we dig graves, our presence is not all that welcome among the citizens of this stinking place, and those miserly bastards don't often pass the time of day with us.'

Okay, fair enough for now, said Kohler to himself. So, Yvette and the countess were around but there are doubtfuls with Ackermann and Mademoiselle Arcuri.

The Corsicans could be asked for confirmation – if Ackermann and his duel could be avoided! Glotz might somehow be convinced to cough up what he knew of the general.

He reminded himself that Glotz was the brother of the wife of one of Himmler's brothers and that he was none too pleased at the moment.

The weasel's eyes still hadn't moved. The thin lips parted as a mind reader's might.

'The Countess Thériault would not have killed Jérome with a rock, monsieur. A gun such as the one you're holding perhaps, if her cousin could be convinced to loan it to her, of course, but not a rock.'

'Unless she'd wanted it to look like Jérome had accidentally fallen off that bike,' said Kohler, giving his thoughts aloud. 'Could one of the monks have done it?'

The weasel began hesitantly to lower his arms. 'Perhaps . . . Yes . . . yes, that is entirely possible.'

'Which one?' snapped Kohler.

The arms shot back up. The weasel glanced at his buddy and nodded. The walrus took the oyster. 'Both Brother Michael and Brother Sebastian, they have been seen often with Brother Jérome, the one always arguing like the sister, always giving the lecture, you understand, the other talking quietly but earnestly. Very earnestly.'

'Down by the river,' said the weasel with venom. 'Bathing, monsieur. The Brother Sebastian and the Brother Jérome.'

'And afterwards?' asked Kohler blandly.

'Afterwards, the long walk back up to the monastery after dusk.'

St-Cyr watched the mourners intently. The countess laid a rosary over Jérome's hands. Was she forgiving the boy his transgressions against the Domaine Thériault? Was it merely an act of kindness, or acknowledgement of his real father?

The gesture didn't go unnoticed by the abbot and everyone else. Just what the devil was going on?

The rosary didn't look expensive. Rather commonplace perhaps. An odd thing then for the countess to have done.

She moved on to Yvette's casket and, lifting the veil, bent over the girl. A last kiss on the brow, the lingering touch of a hand on a shoulder. The abbot was still watching her.

She passed on to comfort the parents. Riel Noel had shunned his 'son' but had dwelt long with Yvette. He'd all but shunned his wife as well, failing even to comfort her at a time like this. Could one never forgive?

The countess took them each by the hand and wrapped her

arms about them to share their grief and tell them she was with them no matter what.

It was the act of one who had the interests of all her people at heart, but the abbot viewed it distastefully as one would a good performance.

Mademoiselle Arcuri and her son stood beside Jérome's casket, the boy under the comforting hands of his mother. They both crossed themselves. They lingered. The chanteuse couldn't seem to take her eyes off the rosary the countess had placed in the casket.

René Yvon-Paul glanced uncertainly up at his mother. Maman . . . St-Cyr could hear him whisper. Maman, what is the matter?

The abbot watched her like a hawk. Storm clouds brewing? The mirage glanced quickly at him, at the rosary and back again, all through the darkness of her veil.

René Yvon-Paul led his mother to Yvette's casket. No kissing, no touching. Mademoiselle Arcuri just looked stoically down at the girl for the longest time then suddenly back to Jérome, to the abbot and along the waiting line to Ackermann. Hatred . . . was there hatred in her heart or fear?

The general didn't move a muscle. She turned suddenly away and, with her son at her heels, went quickly down the aisle and out into the fresh air.

Ah now, what was this? Had she signed her own death certificate with that look? Would Ackermann have to kill her?

The abbot had taken in the exchange of glances but had his mood lightened with it?

Ah no, not at all. If anything the storm clouds had got worse.

The Mayor of Vouvray, the Préfet of Police . . . several other dignitaries paid their last respects before Ackermann had his chance. He and his two cohorts gave one look, perfectly timed, and then the Nazi salute over each of the caskets. The crashing of their jackboots startled everyone and offended the parish priest.

The abbot's turn came at last. What secrets were there in his soul? Guiding his little flock couldn't be easy. Brother against brother at times, and always the 'visitations', the dreams. Naked bathers in the river and spies in the bushes.

The time he spent over Brother Jérome was longer than that

taken by Mademoiselle Arcuri but his gaze, like hers, was not focused on the boy's face but on the hands.

It was as if the abbot struggled with himself, the titans of Good and Evil waging war.

But he left it in the end – set temptation aside and left the second rosary there, even though Jérome's own beads were draped about the boy's hands.

Brother Sebastian, the beekeeper, broke down and went all to pieces, so much so that it took the combined efforts of the abbot and Brother Michael to remove him.

Yvette got no attention from them at all, but then, in the midst of everything, the abbot rushed back to quickly kiss the girl's hands and give her his final blessing.

St-Cyr knew what he had to do, and when the line was thin and the church all but empty, he waited tensely.

A last mourner departed. The priest gave the couple his blessing. A final few droplets of Holy Water, a final kiss . . .

The undertaker and his assistants moved in. The bells began to toll . . . No time now to question the ringer of them. Ah damn, these stairs, he said to himself.

And rushing through the church, said, 'A moment, my friends. St-Cyr of the Sûreté.' He flashed his badge and while they were busy with it, he dipped a hand into Jérome's casket and lifted the countess's beads.

'So young,' he said. 'Such a tragedy, isn't that so? Me, I just wanted to pay my last respects.'

Like crows, they waited anxiously to remove the carrion. But they didn't believe one damn word of what he'd said.

Except for that bit about the Sûreté.

The smell of wet clay, the damp, boxwood odour every old graveyard seemed to have, came to St-Cyr. The wounds in the earth had been closed. A last pat of the shovel had been given some fifteen minutes ago, a heaping of silk lilies to be plucked away by the wind or some thieving hand. The SS wreaths and bouquets had already begun to feel the cold.

Alain Jérome Noel and Yvette Marie Noel lay side by side. The mourners had all gone. Like scattered cattle about a saltlick they've amply tasted, the onlookers were straggling away in search of grass. There'd be much to talk of, much to whisper. Rumour would chase rumour until the clods of time had covered everything and only vague memories remained.

But what had actually happened?

'Hermann, I'm afraid.'

'Me, too,' said the Bavarian, concentrating on the clay, the precious *perruches* of Vouvray that was spread over such a wide area an abbot could bring the matter to their attention. 'I never did like the sight of fresh graves, Louis. I've seen too many of them.'

'You still think Ackermann means to kill you?'

'The duel? Yes . . . yes, I think he means it.'

'You're a good shot.'

'With a flintlock pistol?'

'They'll be newer guns than that. Cap-and-ball, and beautifully tooled. They have a little soft leather pad you wad down on the charge before you ram the ball home.'

'I wish you wouldn't, Louis. If I kill him I'll be dead anyway.'

'Then perhaps I'd better stall him, eh?'

Stall? 'It . . . it would help a little, yes?'

'And Mademoiselle Arcuri, my friend? What of our chanteuse, our Russian, our mirage?'

'I think we'd better get to her before someone else does.'

'Then I must crash the party and you must find the maze and its tower. Enter by the exit, Hermann, and please, be on your guard at all times.'

'Like ice. Let's meet at the river later in the afternoon.'

'The bathing place?'

'Yes . . . yes, that'll do fine. We'll bare our souls there just as others have bared their . . . well, you know what I mean.'

Even at a time like this Hermann could try to make light of things. 'Dusk comes early, my friend. Let's say 4 p.m. give or take fifteen minutes, to be on the safe side.'

'Any contingencies?'

Good . . . that was good. 'Yes. If for some reason I don't happen to make it, take one of the punts and make your way down to the mill. I'll try to join you there after dark but please, if I call out, don't answer at first just in case I've been followed.'

'By then the protocols will be over and Ackermann and his seconds will be out for blood.'

'But whose, Hermann? That is the question.'

Kohler drove him to the gates of the Domaine Thériault. He'd have to hide the car somewhere.

'The walk will give me time to think, Hermann. The countess won't short-change the mourners. Tradition must be maintained. It's my belief the countess is a stickler for it.'

'Among other things?'

'Yes, among other things.'

'Then, it's good luck, my friend.' Hermann stretched out a hand.

'And you also, my old one. We'll talk things over later.'

'Let's hope we have the chance.'

'Let us hope Charles Maurice Thériault is not involved in the local Resistance.'

'The head of it perhaps.'

'Perhaps.'

'I'll be watching your back, Louis.'

'As I'll be watching yours.'

The Grand Salon of the Thériaults was magnificent. Done over in the 1780s by Italian artisans, its pale blue marble floor and walls gave base and background to tall, gilded Corinthian columns, draped gold damask, exquisite tapestries, pieces of sculpture, paintings, four magnificent gilt-and-crystal chandeliers and mirrors . . . such mirrors as St-Cyr hadn't seen outside Versailles. They curved in fluted gold leaf and gilded carvings. Grapes, vines, leaves and birds that reached to the ceiling high above where ornate neoclassical mouldings enclosed superb frescoes. Such thunder! – Christ the Fisherman dividing the loaves and the fishes (had He merely asked some of the fishermen to share their lunches with the others?). Mary and her child in the centre . . .

Mirrors curved in the tall French doors that led, on either side of the fireplace at the far end of the hall, to the main dining-room. They were in wall niches at regular intervals around the inner part of the hall.

The Salon Thériault was at once a place to show off the family's wealth and to entertain royalty. A place for the grand *bals masqués* of bygone days, a place for funeral receptions.

As he moved into the room and tried to lose himself in the crowd, St-Cyr picked out Riel Noel and his brother. Their wives were mute and standing a little to one side. He found the Mayor of Vouvray, the Préfet, the local Kommandant, the parish priest who floated easily among his flock only to leave by a side door. Another of the mirrors . . . It must really have been something to have been at one of those balls. Little liaisons in back rooms or on some darkened staircase no one else would ever find.

Other landowners, other growers – everyone who was anyone in Vouvray had come yet the salon could have held twice as many with room to spare. Coffee, tea and wine were being served by waiters in black with befitting dignity and solemnity. Small sweet cakes, poppyseed biscuits with goose liver pâté, cheeses – there were several of these – little bits of refreshment but not too much. Ah no, it wasn't a time for such a thing. Death must be fed small crumbs just as war must lend a hand to fasting.

'A glass of your *demi-sec*, if you please, and one of your small cakes.'

The waiter, short, rotund and in his late fifties, couldn't help but blurt, 'You are not one of the mourners, monsieur.'

'A friend, that is all. Please go about your business and do not announce my arrival to the countess.'

The crowd closed about the man. There was no question but that he'd gone to find the countess. Damn!

St-Cyr swallowed the cake – honey and crushed almonds. He made for the Reverend Father and the two brothers. He'd pounce while time allowed.

The three men were in a cluster of their own, well positioned at the other side of the hall in front of one of the mirrors. Gilt, gold vines and black habits. Thoughts of Christ and thoughts of murder. Stir the hornets' nest, ah yes. Antagonize the suspect into reacting because all reactions, even the most seemingly insignificant, could prove useful.

'My friends, a fine funeral.' St-Cyr lifted his glass in a toast. The wolfish grin would displease, as it had. 'Reverend Father, a few questions . . .'

The abbot glowered darkly. 'Brother Sebastian is forbidden to speak.' How could the Sûreté question people at a time like this?

So it was of Brother Sebastian that the questions were to have been asked. As before, as now, eh, Reverend Father?

St-Cyr was disappointed in the abbot's lack of finesse and put it down to strain. 'Another of your vows of silence, Reverend Father?'

The man was insufferable! May God have mercy on him! 'You may ask of either myself or Brother Michael, Inspector, but not of Brother Sebastian.'

Whose grief was still all too evident.

'Then perhaps, my friend, you would be kind enough to tell me if Brother Sebastian has lost anything?' The *demi-sec* was excellent – neat on the tongue, clean and not too sweet.

The abbot raised a hand to silence Brother Michael. 'We cannot lose what we do not possess, Inspector. Material things are beyond our simple hopes and desires.'

But not the lands Thériault, eh? Their uppermost vineyard? St-Cyr left it unsaid for now and turned his gaze to Brother Sebastian whose head was unfortunately bowed.

The bald crown with its fringe of brown hair had been weathered to the parchment of old vellum, yet the man was still comparatively young. A beekeeper.

'A strand of simple beads, Brother Sebastian. Not ruby, not even agate or ebony – those of a simple monk. Remember, please, Brother, that though you have had the vow of silence imposed on you, God will curse you if the truth is not told with your eyes or a nod. These beads,' demanded St-Cyr. 'Look at them! Are they not your own?'

A hand brushed his. 'They are *not*, Inspector. It is the rosary that I, as the Countess Thériault, gave to Brother Jérome when he first entered the monastery. I was merely returning it when I placed it in his casket and I think it despicable of you to have taken it!'

Had they been alone, she would have struck him. As it was, St-Cyr ignored the woman and held the rosary under the bowed head of the beekeeper. 'Are these not your own, Brother?' he demanded.

'Inspector, please, I must insist.'

'As I must, Countess, if we are to prevent another murder. Look at them, Brother Sebastian. Look, damn you!'

The beekeeper lifted his head as if prepared to meet his God.

Pain, sorrow – grief and anguish – all were in those storm-grey eyes but was there also rebellion, jealousy and murder? 'Brother Sebastian, if this is your rosary, nod your head.'

The monk tore his gaze away and threw himself into the enfolding arms of Brother Michael. 'There, there, Georges, it's all right. Everyone knows that as Brother Jérome's tutor in the arts of beekeeping you were very close to the boy.'

Those who couldn't have failed to notice what had gone on watched as Brother Michael led the beekeeper from the hall, but the two left by the mirrored door the parish priest had used and that was a most curious thing.

'Well, are you satisfied?' demanded the countess. 'Have you no sense of decency? I thought I told you . . .'

The veil had been lifted. Anger – rage perhaps – lay just beneath the thin veneer of iron-willed control.

The dark eyes softened, pleading for understanding. 'This is no place for you to question my people, and they are mine, Inspector, all of them.'

'It is the very place, Countess.'

'May God forgive you then,' said the Reverend Father angrily.

'Inspector, please, I beg you. They're good people. Let them have their grief in peace. Afterwards, if you insist, I will ask those who are most concerned to remain. Reverend Father, would you be so kind . . .?'

Arm in arm they walked away, the crowd parting before them and then closing ranks in solidarity.

St-Cyr headed for the far end of the room where space had been reserved before the fireplace. Six Louis XIV chairs, in white enamel and royal blue, patterned damask, had been carefully arranged in a semicircle on a carpet that was centuries old.

The middle armchair faced the length of the hall and had a footstool placed in front of it. The abbot? he wondered, taking a sip of forgotten wine. Was this to be the salve of recognition after the wounds of the church service?

Six chairs . . .

His arm was yanked. The wine sloshed – a waste, such a waste! 'I demand to know why you're here?'

Calmly St-Cyr found his handkerchief and began to dry his fingers. 'General, I am conducting an investigation into the murders of Jérome Noel and his sister Yvette.'

'Where's Kohler? I demand to see him.'

The one half of Ackermann's face was more livid than the other, but one should not dwell on such terrible things. Yet still, St-Cyr could not resist antagonizing the man and gave that nonchalant shrug he reserved for infuriating obnoxious Nazis. 'That I do not know, General. We often work alone before comparing notes. That is the way these things are usually done.'

Ackermann snapped his fingers and the two men who'd been with him at the funeral service came instantly forward – young, tall, blond Aryans with perfect blue eyes and clean-shaven cheeks that looked burnished by the lotion. Immaculate in their black uniforms.

Killers if given the chance.

'Find him. Search the grounds and when you have him, take him to the stables and then come and get me.'

'Pistols at dawn is it?' taunted St-Cyr.

'Pistols at dawn, Inspector. Now if I were you, I'd leave here while you can.'

St-Cyr ruefully studied his glass. The Domaine Thériault's *demi-sec* had been superb. Not too dry, and not too sweet.

Ackermann could barely control his temper. 'But you are not me, General, and I have my duties to perform so please don't get in the way.'

'French pig, I could have you shot for that!'

'Perhaps but then you are in no position to do so if you wish to clear your name, isn't that so?'

Ackermann's right hand swung back. St-Cyr waited. They were alone – isolated from the crowd who had kept their distance for all too obvious reasons.

'You are the prime suspect in the murder of Yvette Marie Noel, General. If I were you, I'd desist entirely from this nonsense of duels. Let the investigation proceed to its conclusion. If you've nothing to hide, you have no fears. Then and only then should you settle whatever differences you may have with Hermann.'

'Kohler . . . you mean Kohler. The Resistance killed the girl, you fool. I've the written reports of the préfets of Paris, Fontainebleau and Barbizon as well as those of your superiors, Pharand and Boemelburg.'

'But not that of the General von Schaumburg,' said St-Cyr quietly.

The hard blue eyes raked him savagely. Again the hand started its swing only to remember place and protocol. 'One voice is nothing among so many,' snorted Ackermann.

'Then you will have no objections, General, to answering truthfully. Did you kill Yvette Marie Noel?'

That face became a mask of control.

'I did not kill that girl. I had no reason to. I didn't even know her. I'd only seen her once with Gabrielle.'

Ackermann touched the scar tissue to calm the twitch. St-Cyr gave him a moment. Exhaling sadly, he said, 'And me, I believe you did, General, and what is more important, I can prove it.'

Again there was that contemptuous snort, a lifting of the right hand.

'You're bluffing. I wasn't anywhere near Fontainebleau on the night she was killed.'

'Yet you answer so readily, General? Is it that Yvette in her last moments failed to tell you of the little diary she kept? That girl meticulously recorded everything, General. Places, times – your name is repeatedly mentioned in connection with that of her brother.'

'I don't believe you. You're lying. Produce the diary. Let's see it then.'

His voice hadn't climbed. He'd been exceptionally cool, the face a mask to thoughts. Had he known that bit about his being mentioned had been a lie? Had Jérome told him what was in the diary? Ah now, had he? What if he had? Mon Dieu, this thing . . . Another thread . . .

'I demand to see it,' snapped Ackermann angrily.

A reaction at last! St-Cyr gave that infuriating shrug again. 'Because of the . . . ah, how should I say it, General? The delicacy of the matter, it is being kept securely in the General von Schaumburg's private safe. Together with our signed reports, of course.'

The snort of contempt was even harsher than the last one. 'If you're so certain, then why are you here?'

The lie had really worried the general. 'Because of Jérome. To complete the case we must find his killer.'

One could read nothing in the Frenchman's gaze. 'And have you?'

St-Cyr turned away to sweep his eyes over the assembled chairs. 'One for the abbot, one for the parish priest, two for the parents Noel, one for the countess, and one for René Yvon-Paul who must, of course, take his father's place as the future head of the Domaine Thériault. Six chairs, General. Six.'

'I asked you a question.'

Pale and badly shaken by the sight of them, Mademoiselle Arcuri had started towards them and then had thought better of it.

'Six chairs, General. A most interesting observation and the very key I've been looking for.'

As St-Cyr and the general stood there, the six filed out of the side door and began to make their way towards the chairs.

'I demand an answer,' seethed Ackermann.

'Then I will give it to you, General. Yes . . . yes, I believe I have now found the killer of Jérome Noel.'

'The countess? *Gott in Himmel*, you're an even bigger fool than I thought!'

Like the lady she was, the head of the Domaine Thériault indicated the abbot was to sit in the chair with the footstool while the parish priest sat on his left and she herself on his right.

The Noels waited until René Yvon-Paul had taken his place next to the countess, then they, too, sat down.

Coffee was served, a glass of wine . . .

It was all so beautifully clear. The countess, by arranging the chairs at the head of the room, had simply ensured everyone would see that the abbot, the priest, the Family Thériault and the Noel family had agreed the matter of the land claim had been settled once and for all.

The price had been paid and the sum accepted because that was the way things were really done in the countryside. The law and justice came second because there was a greater law and that was the one they had to live by.

'General, you must excuse me. My glass needs refilling. Please do not leave the premises until your name has been cleared.'

*

'You took the heat off me. Why did you do a thing like that?'

Without the veil, the mirage was still a mystery. 'Because, Mademoiselle Arcuri, you and I have much to say to one another and the sooner we do so, the better.'

She refilled his glass without spilling a drop. 'He'll try to kill you and your friend.'

'Perhaps, but then . . .'

'He'll try to make your death look as if the Resistance had done it.'

The violet eyes were anxious. A tough woman, just like the countess, but tough in her own way. Not on the run, not yet but in fear of her life, that was all too clear. 'Will you answer my questions freely?'

His tone of voice, it had been . . . Ah, what could she say? That of a man who could be moved to compassion? Or that of subterfuge? 'Yes . . . yes, I'll answer if I can, but not here.'

'Then please find us a place where we won't be disturbed.'

'Let me ask René to take you to my room. As soon as I can, I'll join you there.'

'René is needed here to fill your late husband's shoes.'

Damn him! 'Then give me a moment to speak to Jeanne.'

Any excuse. Was it to be like that? 'The countess won't miss you, Mademoiselle Arcuri, so please, which door must we use?'

He was sharp – but she'd felt this since that first sight of him at the club. 'The main one but wait until I've left. I don't want the general seeing us together.'

'He already has.'

She found a clean glass and filled it. 'Then follow me, Inspector. This place is like a warren. Secret doors and secret passageways. I wouldn't want you to get lost.'

Corridors and corridors, room and rooms. They walked and walked, neither of them saying a thing, and when they entered yet another wing there was at last a distinct change in the décor.

'The servants' quarters,' he said.

'Paris is where I live. Remember?'

The room was plain – excruciatingly so when one thought of the flat she had in Paris. The single iron bed with its high, curved iron tube and straight rod ends had been painted white so long ago that the ivoried, flaking paint lent a flea-market desperation to the thing.

224

The quilted coverlet was a homespun green with pink and cream-coloured roses. Two hooked rugs half hid the bare wooden floor. There was a bureau, a mirror, none too big at that and mounted at an awkwardly low angle for a woman as tall as she . . . an armoire, a chair, a chamber pot beneath the bed . . .

Few pictures were on the walls – country scenes that had been cut from magazines and then pasted into rescued frames. A cross.

An antique chiffon dress, a gorgeous thing whose gladiolus print fairly leapt from the off-cream fabric, hung from a hanger to one of the armoire's hinges.

St-Cyr was at once puzzled and deeply troubled by the sight of the dress. Was it to be something to wear at the club or in a casket? It had that look about it. The bed, the room . . . Had she chosen the room to spite the countess? Perhaps.

She found the will to laugh at him and to smile with her lovely eyes as she unpinned her hat and veil and tossed them on the bed, but had she misinterpreted his concern?

'So, Inspector, you find me at home in the Château Thériault. No secrets any more.'

'Madame, I . . .'

'Charles is very dead, Inspector. He isn't here. We're not hiding him. That's all a crazy notion.'

'I didn't ask if you were.'

Her gestures were quick. 'Not yet, but me, I know you'll get around to it, eh? It's not possible to discuss things without considering him.'

She began to unhook the back of her dress. 'I hate black. I always have, ever since I was a little girl and they made me watch my grandmother's funeral. The Russian Orthodox Church, Inspector. Black is very black there, and most of the priests have black beards or ones that are fiercely grey with black hairs in them.

'Could you . . .? Would you . . .?' she asked. 'This blasted hook . . . Jeanne insisted I wear the dress. It's one of hers. How any woman could possess two mourning dresses is beyond me. You'd think she would have given it away years ago but not her. Ah no, not that one, my fine Inspector. A miser, a real miser.'

The hook was bent. The touch of her – the crescent of black

mesh, of very fine lace across the back, the feel of her skin was like satin and warm, so warm . . . Ah, Mon Dieu, was she taking him back through the years to the streets? Would that be her method of attack?

'When my family and I became separated during the flight from the Revolution, I saw black funerals night after night and sometimes now, I see them at the oddest times.'

She was waiting for him to undo the buttons. 'My funeral,' she said. 'Jérome's – Yvette's, of course. Those two are still so fresh in the mind, isn't that so, Inspector?'

'Mademoiselle Arcuri . . .' Her hair was so soft . . .

'Gabrielle . . . I thought we'd agreed to that at the mill.'

Still her back was to him. 'Gabrielle, then.' He hesitated. At last he began to undo the buttons.

'Jean-Louis St-Cyr. It has a nice ring to it. Like Natasha Kulakov Myshkin, Inspector, but once a cop, always a cop, eh? And once a girl of the streets, always one. Me, I think I liked you better at the mill. Then there was a confrontation, and once that was over, a sense of kindness, a genuine concern. You're a man of the world. You know all about life, all about young girls who have nothing and must somehow eat. Girls who are caught, trapped . . .'

The last button was just above the slender waist and when it was undone, she slid her hands deftly under the shoulders and stepped out of the thing.

'Mademoiselle Arcuri . . .'

'Gabrielle, remember?'

'Yes . . . yes . . . Ah, Mon Dieu, madame.'

'It's not as if I was naked, Inspector. This slip is decent enough and if not it . . .' She dragged the thing off. '. . . then what is underneath.'

St-Cyr watched as she crumpled the slip into a ball and threw it at the bed. 'A warm shirt, I think, and a sensible skirt – I mustn't taunt my mother-in-law too much by wearing trousers on a day like this even though she often wears them herself. Relax, Jean-Louis St-Cyr, I'm not about to seduce you.'

'Mademoiselle Arcuri, a few questions . . . Please, we must . . .'

'There you go again,' she said, tossing a hand as she went over to the armoire to open one of its doors. 'Mademoiselle this and Mademoiselle that. My God, it's freezing in this lousy place! Always freezing or boiling or damp. God, it's damp when the rains come in the spring and in November. Water pissing on that roof, pissing, always pissing.'

A soft yellow hunting shirt, forest-green pullover and flecked beige skirt came out of the armoire, she handing them to him and then pausing to run her fingers through her hair before shaking it out. 'Funerals, ugh! Why can't we just be allowed to go to sleep in peace? They're so undignified. No privacy whatsoever. One can't even be allowed to remember what a person once looked like.'

The shirt went on but she wouldn't button it just yet. Ah no, she'd let him have an eyeful of her breasts. She would grab the skirt and purposely bend forward as she stepped into it, then think better of the brassiere. 'I hate these things,' she said. 'Would you mind?'

'What?' he managed.

Petrified now, the poor man. 'Holding the shirt again.'

'Mademoiselle Arcuri . . .' Ah, Mon Dieu, such magnificence! So round and firm and gently uptilted, the nipples rosy . . . the scent of perfume in his nostrils. No thoughts of Marianne . . . no thoughts . . . A mirage . . . a mirage . . . 'Please cover yourself,' he winced. The bed . . . He felt hot, confused . . . What was she really up to? Death . . . was she defying death by forcing him into a corner?

'I thought you were a man who understood the streets, a hunter of animals,' she said. He looked so ill at ease it was almost comic. Perhaps after all his wife had had good reasons to leave him? 'You poor, poor man. They're good breasts, aren't they? Nice to look at, but I won't let you touch them,' she said harshly.

A girl of the streets.

'The past must always be forgiven, madame. Circumstance is the measure of us all.'

And one must not be bitter, eh? She let go of her breasts and began to tuck the shirt into the skirt and to button up. 'How did you find out?'

'I went to the Lune Russe and had a talk with its proprietor. He didn't say you'd once worked the streets. He said you would never have done such a thing.'

227

'All Russian men are the same. Full of sentiment in a world that has no place for it.'

Dressed, she brushed out her hair and tied it with a red velvet ribbon. 'You haven't got a cigarette, have you?' she asked.

At the sight of the cigarette case she was momentarily lost in thought. 'Victor's a good man, Inspector. The Lune Russe treated me like a real chanteuse, but since I've gone back to Paris to live I've not had the courage to face him.'

'No artist would, but why work at the Club Mirage? Oh, for sure, you had a deal with the Corsicans. Ten per cent of the take and you knew with that voice of yours, you'd soon pack the place. That was very shrewd of you, and me, I admire such a quality in a woman.'

St-Cyr took two cigarettes from the case and lit them. 'But there was something else,' he said, placing a cigarette between her lips. 'Another reason, isn't that so?'

Was she a suspect after all? she wondered, indicating that they should sit at either end of the bed. His eyes were watering.

'Madame, the Kommandant of Greater Paris okayed the necessary permit for your car and gave you an excellent gasolene allocation, am I not correct?'

The mirage tilted back her beautiful head and blew smoke towards the ceiling. 'It's no more than I'd have got had I worked at any of the other clubs.'

'Ah yes, but could it be they had singers in plenty?' He coughed.

'Not of my class. Believe me, Inspector, I know where I stand in things. One has to.'

'Spoken like a true artist, not the star performer of a third-rate club. No, madame, it's my belief you chose the Mirage after very careful consideration. As its only star you could pull in the troops, making quite a name for yourself and stifling any questions the German security forces might have asked about you.'

She tapped ash carefully into a palm and leaned back to gaze steadily at him. This one was good, so very good. 'I didn't kill Yvette and I didn't kill Jérome.'

'Jérome I have settled. It's Yvette's killer I need to pin down.'

St-Cyr took a drag of his cigarette and let the smoke rise before his eyes, fighting down the need to choke. 'Jérome was blackmailing you, Mademoiselle Arcuri. He knew your husband was alive and in hiding here. Under the decree of this past spring, by aiding an escaped prisoner of war you, your son and the countess were liable to be sent to Germany, the two of you women into forced labour and an almost certain death, the boy to a reform school and probably death as well. The General Hans Ackermann was after you. He'd read the Sicherheitsdienst file on the wife of his cousin's son. The countess had said a few things perhaps, let a hint or two drop, or simply shown she didn't really care for you the way a mother-in-law should. Jérome threatened to sell you out to Ackermann, and you gave him these.'

He found the diamonds in a pocket and pitched the little velvet pouch on to the bedspread between them.

Deliberately it landed next to the cigarette case but she gave no sign of recognition until he took her hand in his and guided it to the pouch. 'Open it,' he said.

'I . . . I don't need to. My father asked me to carry those when we escaped from Leningrad. The children were often the last to be searched. I could run faster than my brothers and sisters. I . . . I ran. God forgive me, but I ran.'

St-Cyr drew in a breath and held it for the longest time. With a sigh he said, 'And you've kept them ever since in spite of your needing money when you first arrived in Paris.'

'Was it such a crime? I loved my father and my family. I hoped we'd see each other again – we'd need the money the diamonds would bring. I didn't hear the shots. I swear I didn't. Jérome was horrible. Poor Yvette, she knew he was being used by Hans. She tried to intervene.'

'Many times, I think. That is why she kept the diary.'

'A diary? Me, I don't know about such a thing. I never saw it.'

Ah, Mon Dieu, must she be so difficult? 'But you remembered the exact spot where she'd be in Fontainebleau Woods?'

The woman flicked ash on to the floor, forgetting completely about being tidy. 'All right, I knew of it. Jérome boasted to her of his liaisons with Hans, and Yvette wrote them down.'

St-Cyr searched his pockets for the diary until he had the thing. For a moment he looked at it, then this, too, he tossed on to the bed between them. 'Just before she left the club Yvette changed her clothes, then went to tell one of the Corsicans – Remi, I think it was – that . . .'

'There's no thinking about it, Inspector. You're certain it was Remi, so why try to hide such a little thing?'

'Yes. Yes, of course. Forgive me. Old habits . . . it's the cop in me, eh? She said . . .'

'I know what she said, Inspector. "Tell Mademoiselle Arcuri that it's all going to be fixed."'

'The voice on the telephone. It was not that of the General Hans Ackermann, madame, but that of your husband.'

The violet eyes were limpid pools that brimmed. 'Madame, please listen very carefully. I am not, I repeat not against the Resistance and its objectives but my partner, Hermann, you understand, is of the Gestapo no matter what he would sometimes like me to believe. If your husband is alive and you are hiding him, then now is the time to tell me.'

'And the SS General Hans Gerhardt Ackermann?' she asked harshly. Ah damn, what was she going to do?

'The general is of the enemy of course,' said St-Cyr, feeling a sense of loss he had trouble explaining.

As he watched, she brushed away the few tears and stubbed out the cigarette on the iron standard of the bed.

'All right, you win, Inspector. You'd better come and see for yourself.'

She stretched out a hand and stood there waiting as he snatched up the cigarette case and the diary.

Their fingers touched. She was so close – a stunning woman, a chanteuse in great trouble, a mirage even yet.

The pouch of diamonds was pressed into his hand. The smile she managed was soft and introspective but the moment passed so suddenly as she shrugged and said, 'I'll be glad when this is over even though I'll be dead.'

7

The sun was almost gone, and back here, wandering in the maze, a quiet had come that was now broken only by the distant sounds of geese and guinea fowl.

Kohler didn't like it one bit. The cedars were too tall, too thick and pungent. Underfoot, the grass had been crushed by footsteps other than his own.

Again he listened intently. Louis had said there must be a secret door in the tower at the centre of the maze. Mademoiselle Arcuri's husband could then come and go as he pleased from the river and the mill. But of that tower there'd been no sight for some time. Continually he lost his sense of direction and was forced to double back. Ah *merde*! What the fuck was he to do?

In desperation, he lit a cigarette and left it on the ground. From the next aisle he could barely see it through the fronds. One step . . . two . . . he drew his pistol . . .

The toe of a jackboot gleamed. A fly alighted then thought better of it. Ackermann had sent his buddies. Christ!

He turned and ran – went along another and then another aisle, hit a dead end. Shit!

'Klaus, the bastard's over here!'

But where?

Kohler yanked off his shoes and socks, and leaving them, backed away. The aisle was long and at its far end there were openings both to the right and left.

'Helmut, I'm over here,' shouted the one called Klaus – close, too close! 'Let's make the bastard sweat.'

'Calls himself an SS man,' came the answer.

'Gone too French. Been saying nasty things about our general.'

'There's no cooked spinach in the SS!' shouted the one called Helmut as he began to run. Kohler saw him and turned – Jesus, was that the other one too?

He tore his way through the cedars and sprinted up the aisle, hit a turning and went left, then right – right!

The banter ceased. His heart hammered. 'Louis . . . Louis,' he began, but knew he mustn't shout.

Moisture clung to the ancient stones of one of the château's towers. As St-Cyr and Mademoiselle Arcuri climbed to meet her husband, their steps rang hollowly. These old châteaux . . . Ah, Mon Dieu, the labour of their restoration. It must go on and on for centuries.

Embrasures gave increasing views of the grounds. At a point five storeys up, he could not help but see that Hermann was in trouble.

The maze with its little tower was directly below them. 'Hermann, can you hear me?' he shouted.

Bewildered, Kohler threw up a hand before bolting round a corner and out of sight. 'Go left, idiot!'

The Bavarian reappeared, doubling back. 'Now left again.'

'Klaus, he's getting away!'

'Work to the left as he's been told, Helmut!'

The two men were now so close to Hermann, it was only a matter of seconds until they caught him.

Gabrielle Arcuri put her hands on the Sûreté's shoulders and stood on tiptoe to look out over him. 'Right – your friend must first take the right aisle, Inspector, but not go into the tower. He'd never find its secret door. Then he must run to the left and back into the cedars.'

As Ackermann's men bolted into the central clearing around the little tower, Hermann did as he was told. Harried, winded – terrified and in a sweat.

'Now another right,' she said, gripping the shoulders.

St-Cyr yelled it, and then . . . ah, Mon Dieu . . . 'Hermann, duck!'

Kohler threw himself down. Shots ripped over him. He

returned fire, just to let the bastards know he was carrying. He didn't want to hit them. Not the SS, not his buddies, his confrères. They'd garrotte him, that's what they'd do.

As he got up to run, Mademoiselle Arcuri said breathlessly, 'Now a right, and another and another. He must not go left no matter how much he desires it.' One could feel the tension in her.

Kohler started to make his way towards the front entrance along an aisle that seemed to lead him there, but the left . . . the left . . . this place. Should he not go left?

St-Cyr shouted the orders and the Bavarian went right at the next doorway but Ackermann's men were swift. Firing as they ran, they came to the doorway and turned to the right. Ah damn!

'Now a left, Jean-Louis. A left!'

St-Cyr yelled as never before. Still clinging to him, she said, 'Now round the maze and into the woods. He must lead them away. He must give us time.'

Ah, what was this?

Kohler found his legs but so did the other two. No thoughts of shooting him now, only those of stopping him.

Zigzagging among the topiary in his bare feet, he headed for the stone wall at the back. Too many cigarettes . . . too many late nights . . . Ah, *Gott in Himmel*, was he to die like this?

The gargoyles frowned from atop the stone wall. Tearing his fingers on the rough stonework, tripping, falling flat and losing his gun, his precious gun, he dragged himself up and pitched through the opening.

The other two followed, and the grounds soon fell to silence while the woods gave up an occasional yell.

Satisfied, the chanteuse breathed in deeply, and when St-Cyr turned to face her, there was still the ghost of a momentary excitement in her eyes.

'So, we make a kind of team, eh, Inspector? You and me, we fit pretty good after all.'

He hated to spoil things. 'Madame . . .'

The excitement disappeared. 'Yes . . . Yes, I know, Inspector. I'm a married woman. Me, I have not forgotten that you wish to meet my husband.'

The wind sighed through the embrasures. As before, the

central stairwell was surrounded by a landing off which four gaps gave out to embrasures. Heavily studded doors with ancient locks led to rooms. It was the sort of place they used to put erring daughters or sons who'd lose their heads.

When they reached the top floor, she watched him as his eyes settled on each of the doors.

Again he heard the sighing of the wind. To have no heat, to always be cold . . . Surely the husband . . .

Stepping away from her, he went to look out over the maze to the woods beyond. Hopefully Hermann would lose them. They'd have to meet at the mill after dark. 'Mademoiselle Arcuri . . .'

Would he arrest her after all? 'There you go again, Inspector. Mademoiselle this, and Mademoiselle that.'

'Your husband, madame?'

'Which room do you think he's in?' she asked. 'Let's see how sharp you are, Jean-Louis St-Cyr of the Sûreté Nationale.'

How bitter she was about it. 'The key . . . we'll need the key,' he said.

'The key,' she echoed. 'Me, I am sorry, Monsieur the Inspector, but I've forgotten to bring it.'

Deliberately she'd made him feel stupid. 'He's not a prisoner, is he?'

'Yes . . . Yes, in a manner of speaking he is.'

The forest-green sweater, the bright red ribbon in her hair, the skirt and shoes made her appear innocent – the adventuress, perhaps, but a murderess . . .? Ah, Mon Dieu, it was so hard to tell.

She knew he still had his doubts about her. It was to be of no use then, that bit of fun, that chance to forget things for a moment as his partner had escaped from the maze. Now this. A final confrontation. A time of decision for him, a last sad song for her.

'The key's hanging up there,' she confessed, and reaching beyond him into shadow, took the thing down. 'It opens all of them, but he's in the room directly across from us.'

As he took the ancient key from her, St-Cyr said humbly, 'What happened to him?'

'Just open the door, will you? We really don't have all that much time.'

She was angry with him – disheartened, perhaps, but definitely disappointed.

The lock was stiff, the door even stiffer and heavy . . . so heavy. 'Our ancestors . . .' he began, heaving on the thing.

The room was empty except for a plain oak casket that lay in the centre of the floor where it could catch a bit of sun from the only window. She remained on the landing, framed by the ancient doorway, caught as it were by what he'd found.

'When . . . When did he die?' Damn, he felt a fool! That voice on the telephone to Yvette. He'd been so sure . . .

'In August, the twenty-third to be precise. Two days before his thirty-eighth birthday. We hid him, yes – since the defeat of 1940 – but he didn't run away from the fighting, if that's what you're thinking. Two of his men stole a staff car and drove him half-way across France to be with his mother because, Inspector, when a man is in great pain all he can do is cry out for his mother.'

Not his wife, not his lover. 'Madame, please forgive me.'

'Jérome found out. Hans Ackermann suspected – they leave no stones unturned, the SS and their Gestapo.'

'Yet you helped my partner just now?'

'Only because I had to. If Hans should find this, he'll do exactly as you've said. Jeanne will be sent into forced labour and René Yvon-Paul to a reformatory. Me, I don't care much about this place. Perhaps Hans secretly has it in mind to confiscate it. I wouldn't really know. But I could not stand to see my son sent away.'

'Did you murder Yvette? Please, I must have the truth.'

'Would you send me to the guillotine if I told you that I had?'

Dear God, must she make it so hard for him? 'Yes . . . yes, though I would hate myself ever afterwards, I would have to do so.'

'Even in a time of war? Yvette couldn't be allowed to live, Inspector. You do understand? She knew far too much. Hans . . . Hans was getting too close. I couldn't sleep. I couldn't think straight. The Resistance . . . those little black coffins, I . . .'

At last she stepped into the room. The slender fingers sought the casket, she crouching to give it a last goodbye. 'Jeanne bought this in le Mans, well out of the district. We squirrelled it away after dark. No questions. Only the doctor knew about

Charles and he'd been sworn to silence – she's very good at things like that. Have you noticed?'

St-Cyr said nothing – so it was to be the silent treatment after all. 'It doesn't matter, does it, Inspector, if a Frenchman is alive or dead, so long as you've hidden him and the German authorities want him?'

'Mademoiselle Arcuri . . .'

'There you go again. It's Gabrielle. Not Natasha, never Natasha. Not any more.'

'We have no time. They've caught my partner.'

The stables were not far but when they got there, Hermann had already been tied by the wrists to the stall boards on either side of the central corridor. His feet were bleeding. One trouser leg was torn. There was a cut above the right eye. He'd lost his hat and had for company two of the Château Thériault's more curious brood mares and one of Ackermann's men.

'Louis, it was a good try. Have you got a cigarette? This miserable bastard . . .'

'No cigarettes are allowed,' said the man in French, waving his Luger their way. The thing was mounted with a drum clip of thirty-two rounds. The look was anything but friendly. 'Your revolver, Inspector. Please take it out and toss it over there.'

If only Mademoiselle Arcuri was not so close to him. 'Do it!' said the man.

Gingerly he fished the Lebel out of its holster.

'Louis, they won't harm you – not . . . not until it's over for me.'

There was a training whip, one of those long, rawhide things, leaning against a stall. The Arcuri woman took a step towards it . . .

'Please don't,' said St-Cyr, not looking at her. 'He would only kill you, madame.'

The Lebel landed in the manure pile. Ah damn! 'So, my friend,' he said with a shrug, 'what now, eh? No more reports, no more worries . . .'

'We wait for the general. That's what we do.'

This one was not so tall as Hermann, but tough. Big in the shoulders, stiff and strong in the neck. About twenty-eight years of age. In all that chasing around he hadn't lost his cap. The uniform was immaculate.

'Your name?' asked St-Cyr pleasantly. Perhaps five metres separated them. 'You will allow us a cigarette, eh? For Mademoiselle Arcuri if not for myself?'

'Klaus Jensen, from Hamburg. Sure, smoke if it helps, but not him.' The Frenchman was up to something. 'No tricks, eh? Just a cigarette. She can light it for you.'

As Mademoiselle Arcuri slid a hand into his jacket pocket to find the case, they exchanged glances. 'Have you a match, my friend?' asked St-Cyr. 'I seem to have run out.'

Jensen set his lighter on the floor and nudged it towards the woman. A real looker, a general's woman but then . . .

The smile she gave was brief and grateful as she crouched to pick the thing up and flicked it into flame. Kerosene . . . was there any kerosene for the lanterns? she wondered.

St-Cyr accepted the light, holding her hand to steady the flame. Again they exchanged glances. Perhaps no more than five minutes had passed. 'You didn't kill Yvette,' he said quietly. 'Forgive me if I gave you the impression that I thought you had.'

'But . . .?'

'Ah no, not here. Please.' He shook his head.

'But I *did* kill her. Me, I did it.'

'No, madame, that is not possible, eh? But let us leave it for now.'

'What was that you two said?' demanded Jensen, waving the pistol. He'd shoot the Frenchman then the woman if he had to.

St-Cyr filled his lungs. When the choking fit had passed, he said, 'Merely that your French is excellent. Where did you learn it?'

'At the Sorbonne, from '36 to '39. Among other things, that is!' He grinned.

Other things like organizing the Fifth Column and recruiting French students into the Nazi cause.

'Me, I would have thought you one of us, isn't that so, Hermann? A real Frenchman of the upper crust.'

Just what the hell was Louis on about now? 'Yes . . . yes, he speaks Frog like a well-heeled native, Louis. So what?'

'So nothing, my friend. I just thought it curious.'

*

237

The mourners had departed. The waiters had disappeared. The abbot still sat at the far end of the salon with the countess on his right. The parish priest had taken his leave, discreetly perhaps, as had the parents Noel in whose places a stern-faced Brother Michael sat beside Brother Sebastian. Lost in prayers that one, and mumbling them over and over again without the help of his rosary. Ah yes.

René Yvon-Paul came towards his mother and when they met, she brushed a hand fondly over the boy's hair, then stooped to kiss his cheek.

The boy gave her a doubtful look but sat between her and the countess in whose dark eyes one could detect nothing but a cold watchfulness.

Ackermann told his man to wait just inside the main entrance to the salon and to let no one enter or leave. 'We shall give him his moment, and then we shall deal with the two of them.'

So much for the pleasantries.

'Countess, Reverend Father, a glass of wine, I think, to slake the thirst, said St-Cyr.

She looked to Ackermann and back to him. 'Yes . . . Yes, of course. Hans, would it be all right?'

'A little of your *demi-sec* for me,' enthused St-Cyr. 'The small taste I had was superb.'

'René, would you . . .,' began the countess. Ackermann nodded curtly.

As the boy left by a side door, St-Cyr stuffed his hands into the bulging pockets of his jacket. 'May I, General?' He indicated the pipe. 'An old favourite Hermann has been good enough to supply with fuel.'

'Did he steal the tobacco or break someone's hand in the process of persuasion?' asked Ackermann.

Hermann must have quite a reputation at number 72 the avenue Foch. 'He bought it, I think, General. Hermann's a man of mystery, though, and one can't always tell what he'll do even in the tightest of situations.'

'If that was meant to worry me, forget it. He'll be dead before nightfall.'

Ackermann crossed his legs. 'So, a little tête-à-tête, Gabrielle? But you've changed your things? Now that was wise. Good travelling clothes are what will suit this whole business best.'

Fortunately the wine arrived.

St-Cyr waited patiently for the boy to serve them. 'It's a pleasure to see things done so properly, René. Not a drop wasted, eh? And the order of the serving absolutely perfect.'

He took a sip, held the wine a moment on the tongue, then moved it around his mouth. 'Magnificent!' he said. 'Countess, I commend your efforts. So, my friends, let us begin, I think, with the murder of Yvette to which Mademoiselle Arcuri has already confessed.'

'But you . . .' began the chanteuse. The others were startled.

Smiling good-naturedly, St-Cyr lifted his glass in a toast to her. 'Please allow me to proceed.'

'Just don't take too long,' snorted Ackermann.

'General, I will be as brief as possible. Countess, could I have the use of that splendid Russian table you have over there? Such inlays of semiprecious stones – the pink of rhodonite, the green of malachite and blue of lapis lazuli. For one who appreciates beauty and rarity, it's a wonder you don't value your daughter-in-law more. Brothers, would you mind . . .?' He indicated the table.

Together, the three of them moved the table closer to hand, but left it to one side of the gathering. 'I prefer to stand and to walk about,' said St-Cyr apologetically. 'René, would you be so kind as to find my pipe a suitable ashtray?'

That, too, was done and while the moment availed itself, the countess said quietly, 'If she killed the girl, Inspector, why haven't you arrested Gabrielle?'

Could one remain so calm in the face of death? 'Because, my dear Countess, there are confessions and confessions. Some are of the heart and worth everything to those who are students of it, isn't that so, Reverend Father?'

There wasn't even a nod from that grim-faced pillar of salt. 'Others are for the judges, juries and the lawyers,' went on St-Cyr, 'as the Brother Michael knows only too well.'

'Then why did she confess?' asked the countess sharply.

'Why indeed, one might ask except, my friends, for the fact that these are not normal times, eh, General? The German presence implies new rules and orders under which we all must live.'

If Ackermann thought anything of that he gave no indication

beyond the smoothing of the fingers of his left hand over the palm of the right hand. St-Cyr reached for his glass and brought the wine under his nose, holding the pipe well to the side. 'Ambrosia. A perfume, too, of the gods. So, it is my belief, Mademoiselle Arcuri, that by confessing, you are trying to protect the countess.'

'She hates me,' snorted the countess.

'I do not! I have never *hated* you, Jeanne. I simply don't like the way you feel I'm not good enough for you and your son.'

'The son, ah yes,' said Ackermann with a smile. It was all working out perfectly. The Sûreté was leading them down the garden path.

'A small matter to which we will come,' countered St-Cyr. It had been a good exchange, an opening volley which the abbot and Brother Michael had watched with fascination while Brother Sebastian had studied, and still did, his neglected wine.

'So, a confession to protect the countess and save René Yvon-Paul perhaps.' St-Cyr tossed a nonchalant hand. 'Let us pass on quickly. Mademoiselle Arcuri believed, and still believes, her life in great danger. Next to Yvette, she is the only one who really knows the substance behind the killing of Jérome. She is afraid, Countess, that she will be murdered.'

'That is simply not true. Who would do such a thing?' asked the woman. An excellent performance for one who knew only too well who'd do it.

The abbot's look was one of incredulity. 'Murder? Another murder? Perhaps you'd get on with simply telling us who killed the girl and the boy, Inspector. We have our prayers . . .'

The old fox knew damned well whom he'd meant! 'The Angelus, ah yes. Forgive me, Reverend Father. I know how demanding a task such as yours must be but you do see, don't you, that the web of Jérome and Yvette has been spun to include others, eh? All those who might know even a hint of why those two tragedies have happened stand in jeopardy of losing their lives.'

They'd think about that. The countess and the abbot exchanged hurried glances, she shaking her head ever so slightly even though she must have known the gesture would be noticed by others.

240

Mademoiselle Arcuri sat very quietly with her hands folded in her lap and her son, equally subdued, sat beside her.

Ackermann was waiting. So be it then. Ah yes. 'No, Mademoiselle Arcuri did not kill Yvette. But could it have been the Resistance? Black coffins were received in the mail by them both but only after Yvette had already been killed. General, you were there at the flat when I opened them.'

'I believe you also received one.'

Could nothing unsettle the man? 'Yes, a sad mistake, General, but a horse of a different colour, I think. It is possible, I suppose, that the Resistance should wish to make an example of Mademoiselle Arcuri and her maid. After all, she is extremely popular with the Wehrmacht's troops and makes lots of money.

'But it is also far too convenient. On the night Yvette died, she received a telephone call and left a message which said, "Tell Mademoiselle Arcuri it's all going to be fixed."

'What, you might well ask, Reverend Father, and you also, Brother Michael, but not, I think, Brother Sebastian.' Ah no, not him . . .

' "It's all going to be fixed," my friends. She changed her clothes – wished to look her best at short notice for a meeting with the Resistance? How could that be? She knew with whom she was going to meet. She'd settle things.

'Once in the car, she was taken to Fontainebleau Woods. Her wrists were tied behind her back. She was pushed – shoved up the trail – brutally hustled into the forest and thrown to her knees. Weeping, my friends. Begging for her life and for forgiveness.

'Ah yes, Reverend Father. Forgiveness. You see, she'd done a very brave but foolish thing. Yvette had kept a diary of her brother's travels over the past several months – since early in April, I believe, the fifth to be precise – and that diary, my friends, had fallen into the hands of the Sûreté and, what was more important, those of the Gestapo.'

St-Cyr paused to take a sip of wine. It was not a time, however, to give them opportunity to think, nor was it a time for him to worry too much about their individual reactions, but simply to put the run on them.

'Word gets round in those circles, isn't that right? Word got to Berlin. Himmler and the Führer became genuinely concerned.

241

The wires started buzzing. Hermann, my partner, received marching orders for Gestapo Kiev; I was to be sent to Silesia.'

'Where you'll go in any case,' said Ackermann quietly. He'd had about enough of this. Gabrielle was looking at him. So many questions in her eyes, so many doubts and worries.

St-Cyr saw that his pipe had gone out. He'd relight it and talk at the same time . . . 'Perhaps I will go to Silesia, General. But it is to the diary we must turn, is it not?'

He waved the match out and puffed in. 'You see, General, it really does detail liaison after liaison. It even details a chase from Marseilles to Angers.'

Nothing could be read in Ackermann's look. 'I was using the boy to find the truth about Gabrielle's husband.'

Merely performing his duties, was that it? St-Cyr gestured expansively with the pipe. 'Of course you were, General.'

'I really don't see what this all has to do with us,' complained the abbot.

'Everything, Reverend Father. A little patience, eh? That is all I ask. So, General, you were investigating the whereabouts of Captain Charles Maurice Thériault. And perhaps, my friend, that is why Yvette's entry for 13th July read, "After the chase there is resignation and acceptance."'

'The boy agreed, finally, to assist me.'

St-Cyr tossed the hand of dismissal. 'Then Hermann's accusation is incorrect, General, and you may well shoot him in this duel you insist is so necessary.'

'That is correct, although I would have said, I *will* shoot him.'

'Ah yes, were it not for two things, General. First, the murder of Brother Jérome – the catalyst, I think – and second, the weapon that was used and the manner of his killing.'

'I had nothing to do with it.'

'Of course not. A rock? A flint boulder from the *perruches*, eh, Reverend Father? A crime of passion, my friends. A sudden impulse after a violent argument in which voices that should have been discreet were raised in anger and, in the case of one of them, jealousy, such jealousy.

'A crime of passion,' said St-Cyr, letting his voice climb sharply to startle them all. 'Not a simple matter of the Resistance having shoved the muzzle of a 9 millimetre pistol against the back of some young girl's head, eh?'

His voice fell to quietude. 'No, my friends, it was much more than this. Berlin would not have taken so much notice and you, Brother Sebastian, would not have lost your rosary.'

As he drained his glass, he watched them all. St-Cyr refilled the glass and offered the bottle.

There were no takers. The countess began to say something . . . 'Countess, a moment, please. You have said that this strand of beads was not the Brother Sebastian's and that it was the one you gave Jérome when he first entered the monastery. Yet Jérome had his rosary wrapped around his hands?'

'That was the one he had as a child. I also gave that to him.'

What a marvellous woman! She should have been born two hundred years ago. 'Forgive me, Countess, if I say that you are like the lawyer whose client is guilty. You have an answer for everything but if I have to, I will have that casket dug up and the rosary examined. All the brothers have similar ones, is that not so, Reverend Father?'

He yanked the thing out of a pocket and thrust it at the abbot. The answer he would leave to the gods. 'This one was accidentally left with the body of Jérome Noel on the road that lies below the monastery. When you found the boy dead and realized what had happened, Countess, you kept it until the funeral. A crime of passion, Brother Sebastian, for which God will be your judge but for which I charge you with the murder of Alain Jérome Noel.'

St-Cyr moved swiftly to stand over the monk whose head was still bowed. What prayers were going on in that mind, what guilt, what shame . . .

The voice was tortured. 'He wouldn't listen. I tried to tell him . . .' began the monk.

'It's all right, Brother. Me, I am certain there were reasons enough. Keeping bees must be a solitary vocation and God's love is, after all is said and done, a little distant for most of us.

'Reverend Father, would you and Brother Michael be so kind as to take Brother Sebastian home? My partner and I will call in later. A signed statement, that is all. The Préfet can then . . .'

'Your partner will be dead,' said Ackermann.

Stung by the interruption, St-Cyr turned on him. 'General, you are so sure of yourself. Is it that generals, having all the power, never question their own judgement?'

243

'Not when they hold the cards.'

'Even though I might try to make a deal with you to let the matter lie?'

How harsh and unexpected of him. The abbot, of course, and the monks. That's why he'd sent them away. 'It's an offer you would never make, Inspector. In any case, I'm not interested.'

The abbot and the two brothers had reached the main entrance to the salon. Ackermann had to give the okay for them to leave and he did so with an uncaring wave of dismissal.

St-Cyr struck. 'Countess, would you like to fill in the details or shall I?'

Was there sadness in the look she gave him? He felt it everywhere, from all angles of the room.

'You seem to know everything, Inspector. Am I to be charged as an accessory?'

St-Cyr feigned surprise. 'To Jérome's murder? You knew who had killed the boy and you hid this from the authorities, that is correct. But you also used that little piece of information to blackmail the abbot into giving up his land claim.'

'That is nonsense and you cannot prove it.'

'But I can, Countess. On the night of Jérome's murder, Yvette went to meet her brother and found him dead. She then ran to you for help and we know the rest except that Brother Michael was a witness to your removing the body, so when you placed the rosary in the casket you accomplished two things.

'You let the abbot know that you knew who had killed the boy, and you told him by that action that you would say nothing so long as the land claim was settled.

'You then,' he indicated the seating arrangement, 'showed the town and the district that there would be no more talk of this claim or of disharmony.'

'I have my duties. I have my husband's lands to protect and the interests of my grandson.'

'But not those of your daughter-in-law.'

Mademoiselle Arcuri and the countess exchanged glances. Ackermann was carefully watching the proceedings. Good!

'Let us now go back to the night of Jérome's killing. When you and a distraught Yvette moved the body to a roadside in Fontainebleau Woods, you took a terrible chance. There was every possibility you'd be stopped by a German patrol or at one of their controls. You would have to use your cousin as an excuse. After all he was a general, a hero, one of the SS. Am I right? A visit to Paris – urgent business perhaps – a body in the boot of the car, a bicycle tied on to the back – that would have to be the girl's. You'd have to tell them she was pregnant perhaps – reason away the tears.

'You were stopped, Countess. Not once but several times, if my guess is right. But one can't say anything to German patrols but that word of it gets around – slowly sometimes. It reached the avenue Foch, didn't it, General? After all, you were heading the investigation into the whereabouts of Charles Maurice Thériault.'

'The boy had served his usefulness.'

'So you kept an eye on things and said nothing. But then . . . ah then, General, the fur began to fly in Berlin. A purse was found. Condoms in little silk sleeves, perfume, a cigarette case, a small pouch of uncut diamonds. A diary no less. All left as if dropped in haste by the killer. All pointing the finger if it should be pointed at . . .'

'Please, that is enough,' said the countess anxiously. 'I did not attempt to pin the murder of Jérome on Gabrielle. You must believe me, Gabi. As God is my witness, I swear it was a foolish accident – an impulse. Yvette was beside herself with grief. She kept on saying he was just asleep. She tried to make him comfortable. I . . .'

'You went through his pockets like a killer, Countess, and you found the purse,' said St-Cyr.

'Yes . . . Yes, I found it. Jérome had decided to leave the monastery for good. That's why he was dressed the way he was. That's why Yvette had come home – to stop him. I . . . I thought it would help to remove his identification. I took the purse up into the woods and threw it as far away as I could.'

'In the dark and in among the trees, which you would surely have known were there,' said St-Cyr drily.

'Yes . . . Yes, I knew it had hit a tree and fallen somewhere near.'

'Yet you did not try to find it – even though you knew it might incriminate Mademoiselle Arcuri?'

Damn him! 'I couldn't wait that long! There was so little time.

A patrol . . . When would one come by? I'd torn my stockings, scratched myself . . .'

'Countess, please allow me to correct you. It was not yourself who took that purse up into the woods, but Yvette Noel.'

The woman bowed her head and ran a worried hand over her brow. 'May God forgive me, yes.'

'You knew the police would find it.'

'I didn't. I swear I didn't! I was far too anxious about the patrols. I didn't want them searching the car and finding anything incriminating. Yvette . . . I sent the girl up into the woods – yes, I forced her to do it! I waited in the car with the engine running. The girl said she'd thrown it away.'

He'd have to let it go like that but it saddened him to think ill of her. All of Jérome's ID would have been burned in the girl's absence, including his last will and testament, the countess leaning out of the car window to do so while anxiously listening for the patrol.

Even greatness had its weakness. Especially greatness.

'Then you are forgiven and I must ask you why you drove all the way to Fontainebleau Woods to dispose of the body?'

Must he continue with it, dragging each detail out of her? 'Because Yvette had to return to Paris if I was to hush up what had happened – one look at her and everyone would have known. I was afraid of the Nazis – yes, you, Hans. I knew you'd see in Jérome's murder the final straw and come looking for Charles even though he was dead.'

'Dead?' exclaimed Ackermann with genuine disbelief.

'Yes, *dead*, my cousin. I'm sorry to have to disappoint you but Charles died last August. We dared not bury him so I kept him here in the château. Jérome . . . Jérome thought my son was still alive. He was blackmailing Gabrielle.'

'The condoms and the cigarette case were to signify my past,' said Mademoiselle Arcuri sadly. 'The diamonds I'd given him . . . even you must know, Hans, that by the decree of June 1940, all valuables above a sum of 100,000 francs were to have been reported to the authorities in writing. By not declaring them I had committed an indictable offence and would be deported to Germany, to a concentration camp. Full responsibility for hiding Charles would then have rested with Jeanne, and Jérome . . . Jérome would be left to claim the Château Thériault and all of its lands. No doubt you made that little deal with him, fool that he was.'

A perfect candidate for a monastery, thought St-Cyr. 'So, my friends, we come full circle to an Yvette who knew too much and who set out to "fix" things.'

'I am not a homosexual,' said Ackermann evenly. 'The very thought of such a thing is abhorrent to me.'

'Then why the crime of passion, General, in the death of Jérome? If the boy hadn't taken another lover, Brother Sebastian would not have flown into such a rage and killed him.'

'The brother merely misinterpreted my meetings with Jérome.'

'Perhaps, but had he not seen a little more than that – down by the river perhaps, or when the two of you sat in your car on the road beneath the monastery? Jérome, I think, would also have talked – he'd have told Brother Sebastian in no uncertain terms that the affair was finished and why it was finished.

'You were lovers, General. Yvette knew only too well what was going on, so, too, the abbot and Brother Michael, and I think also Mademoiselle Arcuri and the countess. But they were afraid of you. Isn't that right? After all, you had the upper hand, the last laugh, the use of the boy's body and what he knew about the Family Thériault and the whereabouts of Charles Maurice.'

'You can prove none of this. My name's not mentioned in the diary.'

Did she cry that out to you before you shot her? Did she say it after you had thrown her to her knees? You killed her, General. You murdered that poor girl.'

Ackermann drew his pistol. 'There is little you can do about it, Inspector. The diary, please, and the other things you have in those pockets of yours. "Von Schaumburg's private safe . . ." Did you really expect me to believe that?

'Countess? Gabrielle? René Yvon-Paul?' He pointed the gun their way. 'A short walk. Some exercise and a little relaxation after all that grief. Please don't think I'll hesitate to use this. If I don't kill you, my men will.'

'A last clue, General, for which I must say I'm grateful,' said St-Cyr. 'Had you been so certain of your innocence in Paris and Berlin circles, you would have come with far more men.'

'Even though there was only yourself and Kohler to deal with? Don't make me laugh, Inspector.'

'But you did not know that, General. You thought Mademoiselle Arcuri's husband was alive. And surely the countess and she could be counted on to cause trouble, eh? Oh, by the way, my friend. I take it that you sent Mademoiselle Arcuri and her maid those little black coffins and that you like plum brandy?'

The Frenchman would keep on trying to antagonize until a bullet shut him up. It was a pity the Resistance hadn't got to him.

'The brandy?' asked St-Cyr.

'A taste I acquired during the Polish Campaign. The girl drank it like water. I told her it would help to calm her nerves.'

'She spilled a little,' said St-Cyr with a far-off look. 'Did you shriek at her to be more careful, General? Presumably her hands had not been tied at that time and you were being friendly.'

'She deserved to die. All vermin deserve to die.'

Kohler knew his only hope lay in antagonizing the man. He had to get him close enough to kick but so far, the bastard had refused to budge.

'Jensen . . . That's Norwegian?' he asked, pleasantly enough.

'Pure Teuton. Now be quiet.'

'Are you bent like your boss? He's a faggot, friend Klaus. A queer and an SS general. A war hero. *Gott in Himmel*, no wonder the Reichsführer-SS Himmler was pissing his britches!'

Jensen smirked. He'd let the remark pass. Time enough to deal with it later through the proper channels. Of course there was no substance to it, and the Bavarian would get what he deserved.

He took out a small square of white felt and began to polish the blueing on the barrel of his Luger.

Kohler snorted. 'Keep it nice and tidy, eh? Hey, tell me something, does it shoot better if there's no dust on it? That thing's from the war that was supposed to end all wars. They're inclined to jam, my friend. Even the tiniest grain of sand and, *Gott in Himmel*, nothing up the spout.'

Jensen pointed the gun at the Bavarian's forehead. 'Be quiet.'

'Hey, I've finally got it!' shouted Kohler, grinning hugely and startling the horses. 'You two are as bent as your boss. It's a ménage-à-trois. No wonder there are only three of you. *Three* SS queers! Do you . . . well, you know . . . Do it in the you-know-where?'

The man lunged for the whip. The rawhide snapped back. Kohler had a sharp spasm of panic but he wouldn't beg, he wouldn't . . .

There was a crack! No pain yet, only shock as the shirt Gerda had sent him four weeks ago split apart at the right shoulder and opened to the belt.

Blood erupted all along the fissure. As the pain rushed in, he bit his lower lip and clamped his eyes shut. *'In the ass, you faggot!'* he shrieked. Ah, Jesus . . . Jesus, the thing was on fire.

The rawhide came back and tore his left cheek open. Beads of fear broke out on his brow.

Jensen caught a breath. 'I thought I told you to be quiet?'

'Do faggots often like to whip people?' shouted Kohler angrily.

The man leaned the whip against a stall and went to calm the horses. 'The General Ackermann is a hero. He's no more bent than you or I. The girl was pregnant and had accused the general of being the father. He had to deal with the matter. She was French and a whore, so it didn't matter, did it? Besides, she'd threatened him.'

'With marriage? You've got to be kidding. Are Oberg's boys over on the avenue Foch so goddamned dumb they can't read? The autopsy on the girl showed she was a virgin, you idiot!'

'A virgin . . . but . . . but that is not possible?'

Kohler laid it on thickly even though his cheek was on fire and the blood ran freely down over his chin. 'Hey, listen, my friend. These days, every girl in gay Paris lifts her skirt and drops her drawers, eh? But that one . . . Ah! It was for real. I saw the body. Prayers with her brother – that novice monk, that friend of the general's, the one who was buried. Yeah, that's the one. But never the real thing. They've the proof and it can't be denied. Von Schaumburg even had a look.'

Jensen threw a doubting glance towards the stable door. Kohler struck. 'What did he get you to tell her on the telephone, eh? That you were a French friend of the general's and that he'd asked you to intercede? A little meeting, eh? Everything would be fine. No problems, no more worries? Just a quiet little talk in the car? In Fontainebleau Woods, my friend. Did the two of you hold the girl while Ackermann tied her wrists?'

'We weren't there. He . . . he took her himself.'

' "He *took* her." You make it sound like a battery of Russian field guns. *Mein Gott*, for heroes we've got piss! Her brother was the General Ackermann's lover, you idiot!'

'Silence!' shrieked Jensen. 'No more talking.'

'Then get my handkerchief . . . in my pocket. At least have the sense to try to stop the bleeding, otherwise there'll be no duel.'

As the last of their steps rang hollowly in the tower, St-Cyr unlocked the door and pushed it open.

The casket was clear enough. Ackermann and the man called Helmut Bocke herded them into the room. The countess was pale and badly shaken. Mademoiselle Arcuri threw a glance at the window, at freedom and the sky. Her son was very afraid, yet was there not something else?

'Open it,' said Ackermann. 'It won't hurt the boy to see what death does.'

'I have no screwdriver,' said St-Cyr.

'Hans . . .' began the countess.

'*General*, my dear cousin. It's time you started addressing me by rank.'

'Is this really necessary? At least let René . . .'

'The boy stays.'

'Then let him face the wall. He mustn't be made to look. It isn't fair. Not at his age. Please, I beg you.'

'Bocke, use your pocket-knife. Give it to St-Cyr.'

'*Jawohl*, Herr General.'

The knife, an SS version of the Swiss Army's constant companion, was produced and laid at one end of the casket. The man then stepped back a pace.

St-Cyr glanced apologetically at the countess and at Mademoiselle Arcuri whose gaze he could not read except that something really was wrong and the boy knew of it. Had she lied to him? Had he been such a fool as not to have seen it?

She was standing well to one side of her son. About as far from the boy as she could get.

'René, please do as your grandmother has asked, eh?' said St-Cyr.

'I give the orders,' said Ackermann, motioning with his pistol. 'The boy looks at the corpse, just as all of us will.'

St-Cyr heaved a sigh. 'As you wish, General. I'm sorry, Countess, but . . .'

'Get on with it!' said Ackermann, raising his voice.

St-Cyr felt the tension in the room, the terror that was suppressed but lay not just in himself and the others, but in the general.

'Is it that you are fascinated by death, my friend?' he asked.

'Only that I must have the proof.'

The screws were tight and took considerable effort. It was Mademoiselle Arcuri who said, 'René, come here. Let me hold you by the hand.'

The boy did as he was told. That was good, so good. She'd remained standing as close to the door as possible.

'Hans, please, I beg you,' began the countess. 'It isn't necessary. I swear to you Charles is dead.'

Ackermann said nothing. As the last screw came gradually out of the wood, he watched it intently.

Bocke, standing a little to one side and behind St-Cyr, kept his eyes on all of them.

Jeanne Thériault took a step. 'Countess, please,' warned Ackermann, not looking up at her. 'Stay where you are.'

She had to try. 'Hans, you're a soldier. You've seen war at its worst. Charles was as good as dead when we got him. He'd received a piece of shrapnel in the head. No doctor could have operated. He was in a coma, mumbling in his sleep and crying out for me.'

Ackermann looked up at her. 'That has no bearing on this. None whatsoever.'

'But it has!' she implored. 'When he had recovered sufficiently to walk about a little, he wasn't the same. He said so little, it was as if he hardly knew us. Distant . . . he was so distant not just from me, but from Gabrielle. He began to wander. I'd find him in the maze, in the tower here, in the cellars . . . René and I had to watch him constantly. One day in summer we . . . we found him down by the river, hiding from you and hiding from us.'

St-Cyr paused. Was she trying to distract Ackermann? He'd have to say something. 'René, he was so good that first day I met him, Countess. I knew he must have had some practice when he led me completely astray.'

'He's a good boy and knows what has to be done. He's . . . he's exactly like the son I lost.'

Ah, Mon Dieu, of course she wanted to encourage the boy, but did she want sympathy as well? If so, it was of no use but . . .

Under cover of the exchange, Mademoiselle Arcuri had moved the boy to her left and now her hand rested lightly on his shoulder. She'd push the son away and scream as the lid was removed. She'd take the first shot, would sacrifice herself.

René would make a run for it.

As the last screw came out, St-Cyr put it in his pocket with the others. 'René, there will be nothing much left of your father. Just the hair, the teeth, the skin perhaps but dried and old, withered as if by the sun. The uniform, it will be stain . . .'

'Stop it! Stop it!' shrieked the countess.

Ackermann lunged and flipped the lid off. 'Bags . . . Bags of stone!' he swore. He lashed out at the countess and she fell back against the wall and to the floor.

'He's dead! I swear he's dead!' she cried.

'The boy! Get him, Bocke, or pay the price!'

'*Jawohl*, General.'

St-Cyr moved to help the countess to her feet. Blood trickled from a split in her lip. The dark eyes were filled with hatred as she looked past him to the general. 'You call yourself a man, my cousin, but you are nothing,' she spat. '*Nothing*! Compared to my son.'

'Where is he?' demanded Ackermann, jamming the muzzle of his pistol against the back of Mademoiselle Arcuri's neck and forcing her to bow her head. He had her by the wrist. He was hurting her . . .

Jeanne Thériault looked at her daughter-in-law. Was it to be the last time they'd see each other alive? Suddenly there was so much to say and no time in which to say it. 'I don't know what's happened to him, Hans. I really thought his body was here.'

*

Out of the corner of the only eye that wasn't swollen shut, Kohler caught a glimpse of the boy. The little nipper was down at the far end of the stables, over by the far wall. One minute he was there, the next he wasn't. He was making his way stealthily along the wall by climbing from stall to stall.

He had a kitchen knife clenched in his teeth, was scared stiff and yet determined.

'Water,' muttered Kohler. 'In the name of Jesus, give me something to drink.' Every effort to get away had failed.

Jensen wrenched open the door to the nearest stall and took the mare's trough from it. 'Water, eh? Then water you shall have!'

Sputtering, Kohler gasped then bellowed, 'Bastard! I'll see you in hell for this.'

'You'll see nothing if you don't shut up,' shouted Jensen, reaching for the whip. 'I've had enough from you.'

'Some duel I'm going to fight, eh? Blind in one eye and cut to ribbons. Weak from loss of blood – ' He kicked out fiercely and lost his balance, giving a scream of anguish as his wrist was wrenched.

A breathless Bocke appeared on the run. 'Klaus . . . Klaus, the boy has escaped. Help me to find him.'

Jensen looked to Kohler and then back to Helmut. 'Help me to tie his feet, otherwise I can't leave him.'

One of the mares whinnied and began to stamp excitedly about her stall, tugging on the halter rope. Again Jensen went over to the door and yanked it open. Straw on the floor, dung, oats . . . nothing out of the ordinary. Nothing. The boy? he wondered.

They tied Kohler's ankles together and ran the rope up behind him, bending his head back so far that if he moved, he'd break his neck.

'Rest easy,' snorted Bocke. 'We'll be back.'

The one good but bloodshot eye closed in pain rather than look at them.

The boy . . . where was the boy? These guys, they knew every angle. They'd let the boy show himself and then they'd come back and take him. The kid didn't have a chance.

*

Ackermann twisted Mademoiselle Arcuri's arm behind her back and forced her to her knees. 'One false move and she dies, St-Cyr,' he shouted.

The countess wiped the blood from her lip with the back of a hand. She was over by the window, caught in the fading light and contemplating a foolish, foolish thing.

The casket was between him and Ackermann. No chance there . . . Not yet. 'General, I am only too aware that you will kill Mademoiselle Arcuri. Me, I am at your service. Lock the two of them in the tower here and take the key, eh? Then you and I can settle this business with Hermann.'

He gave the countess a glance of warning which she failed to notice. The woman was going to rush Ackermann in a vain attempt to give them a chance.

'Countess, *please*,' said St-Cyr. 'Both the general and I know he'd only kill you.'

The wind came to feel its way through the embrasures, echoing softly in the tower. No one moved. Perhaps half a second passed, perhaps a little more. Ackermann still stood behind Mademoiselle Arcuri with the gun pressed firmly to the back of her neck and her left arm wrenched painfully upwards.

'I won't tell you anything!' she shrieked. 'There is no body. You'll never find it. We hid no one, Hans. No one! Charles died at Sedan. You have no proof we hid him. Nothing but a coffin full of rocks.'

Kohler . . . was the boy trying to get to Kohler? St-Cyr was watching for a chance. The countess . . .

Ackermann released the arm and seized Gabrielle by the hair. He'd make her scream. He'd tear it out by the roots. 'Talk,' he said quietly.

She winced in pain and gasped. 'With no body there is no proof. René . . . Ah, my hair . . . my hair.'

Her scalp was on fire. The skin was ripping . . .

'Hans, stop it, please! You're not a total coward. Let me talk to Gabi. She'll understand.'

The countess moved away from the window. Swiftly Ackermann lifted the pistol and shattered the glass behind her, filling the tower with the sound of the shot.

Again none of them moved. Gabrielle Arcuri's face was a

mask of pain. Her eyes were filled with tears which streamed down her cheeks.

'Please,' said St-Cyr. 'I beg you, General. Be decent.'

'Gabi, tell him where you hid the body. You can't hope to save the château for René. He's finished. Even without the proof, Hans will see that the boy is . . .' She couldn't say it and turned quickly from them to stare out through the shattered glass at the growing dusk.

Those who had been at the reception would now begin to leave the farmhouse of Riel and Sophie Noel. Some would walk slowly homewards along the roads, or make their way back to the château. Others like Morgan Noel would wander up to the caves to stand alone among the rows of bottles or by the fermentation vats asking God why it had had to happen. They'd all be very afraid. They'd try to stay clear of things and she must find it in her heart to understand their fears and to forgive them.

'Go and show him where the body is hidden, Gabrielle. Lock me in here with the inspector.'

Ackermann gave her a minute. The pistol never wavered as he again took aim.

'General, you are not so foolish as to kill her in plain view of witnesses. Berlin must have its answers, isn't that so? The General von Schaumburg will not let this matter lie.'

'Von Schaumburg can be dealt with.'

'But not the Oberkommando der Wehrmacht, General. Not the High Command with whom he is in constant communication. No, my friend, if you are to get out of this unscathed, you will need great tact and you will most definitely need to produce the body of Charles Maurice Thériault. Your word is no longer trustworthy, General. The General von Schaumburg will take things to the truth. Please make no mistake, he's out for blood.'

'Jeanne stays. You,' he pointed the Luger at St-Cyr, 'and Gabrielle come with me.'

Kohler eased his aching wrist. The boy had cut him free but there was no time.

'The revolver,' he gasped. 'Quickly!'

'The loft, monsieur. We must climb up there.'

The ladder was a thousand kilometres away and it went straight up to Heaven.

Jensen had appeared in the doorway. No sign of the other one yet. He'd be covering one of the exits.

This was it. Death at what? Twenty paces . . .? Ten . . .? Five . . .? Had the kid got to the revolver? The pile of manure was to the right and about three metres behind.

Kohler managed a shrug and a sheepish grin though his face hurt like hell. 'So, a last cigarette, eh?' he said.

'Don't touch that weapon, René! Come here,' shrilled Jensen. 'Hey, Klaus, I've got them.'

Kohler leapt sideways, lunging for the whip as two shots rang out and the boy . . . the boy . . .

He seized the thing and brought the rawhide down. A last desperate gamble as the kid tumbled over the manure and ran for a pitchfork and Jensen . . . Jensen . . .

The whip had torn an ear right off him. *Gott in Himmel* – SS and blood pouring all over the place! Startled eyes, shock, the gun coming up again. 'Klaus . . . Klaus . . .' the man muttered in bewilderment.

Kohler flung the whip at him and charged. He threw himself at Jensen, caught him by the arms – tried . . . God he tried to hold the pistol away. The gun went off – all thirty of the remaining rounds were sprayed about the place as the two of them rolled over and over on the floor and Jensen's finger was repeatedly jammed against the trigger.

One of the mares fell dead. Another was wounded and began to cry out in terror and kick her stall boards.

A lantern shattered. Blood . . . there was blood everywhere. A pail came into view. One eye . . . only one. His wrist . . . damn his wrist.

Kohler lay on his back and used both hands to force the pistol away. The kid flashed into and out of view, a blur. Jensen shrieked at him to stay put.

No hope . . . too powerful . . . thought Kohler desperately. Not as young as I used to be . . .

Jensen's eyes shot wide. His mouth gaped. He stiffened in shock, tried to release his grip, tried to turn . . .

Blood rushed into his eyes and trickled from a corner of his mouth, dribbling on the uniform as he stiffened yet again, then fell headlong at Kohler who pushed him aside. The boy . . . the pitchfork . . . *Gott in Himmel*, a seven-year-old boy, or was he eight or nine?

'Klaus,' gasped Kohler. 'The other one.'

The boy couldn't seem to move. He'd lost all colour. A German . . . a member of their dreaded SS. He'd *killed* him! He, René Yvon-Paul Thériault, had *murdered* him.

The wounded mare flung herself against the side of the stall and broke three boards. The sounds she gave were agony.

'Son, help me up,' wheezed Kohler. Where the hell was Bocke? Still waiting for them to make a run for it?

He tried to swallow. His chest ached. Had one lung collapsed? His heart pounded unmercifully. The kid had driven the pitchfork right into the small of Jensen's back. He must have taken a run at it. The mare . . . would the thing not be quiet for one moment? Jesus, the racket was terrible.

'Oh God, we're for it, kid. There's no way a thing like this can be hidden. Get me the revolver. No, not the Luger. Louis's gun. I'll kill the other one if I can and I'll say I did this. You hear me, eh? I killed him, not you. You're to make a run for it. Go and hide in the mill. The *mill*, René. Understand?'

The boy handed him the revolver. Kohler's aching fingers found a corner of torn shirt but it was impossible for him to clean the weapon.

Breaking the cylinder open, he held the gun out to René. 'Is the barrel free?'

The kid nodded. 'So okay, eh? You to the mill, and me to find the other one.'

This Gestapo inspector was almost dead himself and looking very grey. 'If we go up through the loft, monsieur, there is a small door which leads . . .'

'Never mind the loft. You beat it, eh? You've done your bit. I hope you live to see your grandchildren.'

'Will you shoot Christabelle? Please, monsieur. She is in great pain and must have broken something too.'

'Yeah, I'll shoot her, but only after you . . .' Kohler indicated the ladder at the far end of the stables. As he watched the boy hurry away, he thought of his own boyhood, of a stable not nearly so fine, of a desire even at that tender age to become a famous detective.

Such are the dreams of youth.

The boy disappeared into the darkness but then a feeble shaft of light, up high, picked him out as he waved.

Bocke . . . where the hell was Bocke?

Almost at a run, they were now passing through the château's Chinese Room, making for the cellar steps to what Mademoiselle Arcuri had called the Grotto. The chanteuse was in the lead, then himself and Ackermann – all three of them crowded too closely together. No chance to dart aside and slip away. No chance to turn and put a stop to the general.

St-Cyr caught only fragmentary glimpses of the room whose windows opened on to the central courtyard. A superb screen of painted silk . . . blue porcelain jars hundreds and hundreds of years old. A tiny white jade figurine – some sort of deity perhaps. A life-sized porcelain warrior dressed in full regalia, an embroidered silk robe . . . the Thériaults had bought history and had banked wisely. But of course, the war . . . The Germans would take all of it.

A gilded bamboo birdcage, in the design of a pagoda, was piled like a cake in tiers but held Italian faience birds of the finest porcelain.

A dagger encrusted with verdigris lay open on a small table of black lacquerwork and gilt. Could he chance it?

Ackermann jammed the gun into his back, propelling him into the next room as the woman said, 'We must go this way now. There are some stairs at the back,' and the sound of her voice, the tension and the fear in it lingered with St-Cyr.

They entered the Hall of Armour and he knew right then and there that she'd come this way on purpose. The Thériaults had a superb collection, much of which stood menacingly about the hall. Full suits of armour, the dull gun-metal blue fast fading with the last of the light. Swords upraised to deal Death's blow, pikes at rest. Which would it be? A mace? he wondered. Could he grab one?

As they threaded their way quickly among the armour, she suddenly shouted, 'Go left, Inspector!' and bolted to the right.

St-Cyr dodged under a mailed fist, twisted sideways near a

pike and heard the first of two shots as he ran full tilt into a breastplate and knocked it over.

Stumbling, he tripped and fell flat. Ackermann . . . where was Ackermann? Ah, Mon Dieu . . .

The ringing sound of the armour gradually lessened.

There were cabinets and cabinets – muskets, swords, dirks and pistols – how had the countess managed to keep them? No powder and ball, perhaps.

Ackermann's matched set of duelling pistols lay open on top of one of them – could he reach it? Could he chance it?

High on the wall behind it were the flags and colours of the regiments the Thériaults had led. Their shields, their heraldry . . . the Siege of Orléans, the Battle of Waterloo . . .

No sign of Ackermann and none whatsoever of the chanteuse. A quick glimpse of the maze over his shoulder, ever darkening but offering hope perhaps.

Stealthily he began to crawl out from behind the small cannon he had used as cover. Nothing now showed on the floor but those suits of armour. Gods in their times, they stood about, mementoes of bygone days, no words of comfort.

A step – was that a jackboot on the hardwood parquet?

'Inspector . . .?'

Ackermann had her by the hair again. In desperation St-Cyr closed a hand over one of the small cannon-balls that were piled in the iron basket beside the cannon.

There'd been two shots – presumably the Luger had been fully loaded. One shot up in the tower then and two here, so there should be at least four left and perhaps a fifth, if Ackermann had done as many did and left one in the chamber before inserting the clip.

Five shots.

He wound up and bowled the little cannon-ball across the floor, flinging himself aside at the same time and skidding to a stop behind one of the suits of armour.

'Come out at once,' commanded Ackermann. St-Cyr had spread his legs and was now standing directly behind the armour.

A battle-axe hung from a length of chain that was wrapped about a mailed wrist.

The battle-axe moved! He fired again, a screened shot that

deflected off a sword, splintered a pike shaft and ricocheted around the room.

St-Cyr yanked the battle-axe free and threw it. Ackermann fired. The woman shrieked at him to save himself.

They made for the door at a run and St-Cyr headed after them. The Luger swung his way. The hammer came back. She fought with Ackermann. She tried to get the gun, tried to . . .

St-Cyr tore him from her and knocked the gun to the floor. He went in with his fists, hammering. A left to the chin, a right to the shoulder. One, two; one, two. Now step away, feint to the left and in with a left. Yes . . . yes that's it! 'A bloodied nose, eh, General? Well, there's more of it, my friend. There's more.' He feinted left and left again, dodged and weaved, stepped in suddenly, then back and around, cornering, working, now a jab, now a withdrawal.

They closed and the general went down in a welter of blows they hadn't taught him at that fancy SS academy. St-Cyr fell on him like a stone and pressed both knees into his back. He gave a savage grunt as he whipped the handcuffs from a pocket and clapped them on the bastard. 'Done! Ah-ha, my fine, it's done!'

'Hermann . . .? Hermann, what has happened?' St-Cyr raised the lantern. He'd found Kohler outside the back door of the stables, a wreck and badly in need of medical attention.

'Louis . . .? Louis, where's Ackermann?'

'Locked up in one of the towers, with bracelets.'

Kohler wanted to say, Good work! Instead he had to say, 'We're not going to get out of this, Louis. Jensen tried to kill me. His gun . . . You know how it was. The thing went off and hit Bocke twice in the guts. A stroke of luck perhaps, but not for us.'

'I'll get a couple of blankets and cover them. We'll think about it, eh?' He'd never seen Hermann quite like this.

The Bavarian tore his one-eyed gaze from Bocke's body. 'I've already thought about it, Louis. I had no other choice but to kill Jensen with a pitchfork. It was either him or me.'

A pitchfork! 'Yes . . . yes, I quite understand. Shall I call Pharand or will you call Boemelburg?'

Kohler held his throbbing cheek. 'I think you'd better call

Boemelburg for me. Just tell him to come down here, Louis. Don't try to bugger about, eh? Words won't be of any use so leave them to me. Let's let him see this for himself.'

'And the General Oberg, over on the avenue Foch, Hermann? What about him?' The employer of the dead.

'Von Schaumburg, I think. Let the Kommandant of Greater Paris call him personally. Tell them all to come. We'll make a party of it and go out in style.'

'Then we'd better include the préfets of Paris, Barbizon and Fontainebleau.'

'Yes . . . yes, all of them, Louis. Now get me to a doctor, will you? I think I'm going to pass out.'

The flame of a single candle lit the room. Ackermann sat on the only seat, a wooden stool from medieval times. The casket still lay open with its burlap sacks of rocks. A black-out curtain had been placed over the window and stuffed into the hole in the glass to stop the draughts.

It was the loneliest of vigils and the night was long. 'You have the choice of honour, General,' said St-Cyr quietly.

'Do you think I don't know that?' snapped Ackermann.

'Burial with full military honours, General. A family name that is unbesmirched. No reflections on your wife and daughters. A hero of the Reich until the end of time.'

'You and Kohler will die with me. This place will be sacked and burned to the ground. The countess and the others will be shot.'

'A common grave, is that it, eh?'

'Yes, that's it. I've won, St-Cyr. There's no possible way you and that Bavarian traitor can get out of it.'

'Hermann is a man whose loyalties have been placed in confusion by events over which he had little control.'

'It'll do him no good to say those two tried to arrest me.'

'Then I will leave you with this, General. Until the dawn, eh? Let us hope the others arrive at first light. Me, I am anxious for it all to end.'

He placed a single 9 millimetre cartridge next to the candle, then laid the general's empty Luger beside it. 'My apologies if I do not take the handcuffs off you, General. I will check in from time to time. Should you feel the call of nature, please do not worry. I will be armed, of course, and always there will be someone else both to lock me in here with you and to let me out when I knock.'

Ackermann smirked at him. The Frenchman nodded adieu, then went over to the door and rapped soundly on it.

The key turned, the door came open only with difficulty, and he stepped out into the hall.

It was Mademoiselle Arcuri, not the servant who had accompanied him. She locked the door again and left the key in the lock. 'How's Hermann?' he asked. There was a torch in her hand.

They'd speak in whispers, their voices hushed. 'Fine. There's always the danger of tetanus, but Dr Cartier has used much antispetic and has sewn up the cheek. Me, I have given your friend lots of brandy. He's now asleep.'

'And René and the countess?' he asked.

He was such a sensitive man, this Jean-Louis St-Cyr. No cop she'd ever met had been quite like this. 'René is fast asleep – exhausted, poor thing. He . . . he has told me the truth of what happened.'

She looked steadily at him, didn't shy away from it. 'Hermann had to kill Jensen, Mademoiselle Arcuri. There was absolutely no other alternative.'

'Yes . . . yes, I understand but will your friend really do this for my son?'

He must be kind. There was so little hope. 'He will, but you must pack some things for the boy and see that someone is ready to hide him at a moment's notice. The Germans, madame . . . Two of their SS are dead. Even if they had killed each other, someone else must pay the price. This we cannot avoid. I wish with all my heart it were different but . . .'

She stopped him with a look. 'And Jeanne?' she asked.

'Yes . . . Yes, the countess as well.'

Doubt showed. 'Would it do any good for her to speak to Hans?' A last attempt.

'No . . . No, I have already tried. I'm sorry. It . . . it was of no use.'

'She won't try to sleep. She can't. She paces up and down

and goes from room to room chasing memories and having a last look.'

'That is as it should be, madame, and I am sorry I cannot offer more.'

'Will they really send you to the salt mines?'

'Silesia? Ah no, no, they will have a little something else in mind.' The firing squad.

Again doubt showed in the look she gave him. There was hesitation too, but this was quickly followed by resolve. 'Then it doesn't matter, does it, if your wife should come back to you?'

'Marianne . . .? Ah, I don't know what she'll decide to do. I haven't really had a chance to think about it lately. She'll either be there waiting at the house or she won't. My son Philippe as well, of course, but the Germans won't let me see them. Of this I'm certain, so in a way it really doesn't matter what she does since I won't know of it in any case.'

They both fell silent. Mademoiselle Arcuri hunched her shoulders against the cold and gripped the torch more firmly as its beam passed over the floor at their feet.

'Madame, I . . .' He felt so useless at things like this.

She looked up suddenly. 'Please, there is no need to say anything, Inspector.'

'Until the morning then? Try to get a little sleep, eh? You'll need your strength. You'll have to be stronger than you've ever been.'

Just before dawn an icy mizzle drifted over the Vouvray area. One could taste the smell of wet, decaying leaves, of vines and ripe, fermenting grapes, of woodsmoke, fresh dung and distant coal-fired furnaces.

Thick and blanketing everything, it made greyer still the grey of the château's walls as the light began to grow.

St-Cyr waited. The fog was a nuisance. Would it slow Boemelburg and the others? Was it only a local phenomenon?

Boemelburg's Daimler purred from under the entrance arch, its headlamps unblinkered. A great, shining Mercedes followed – von Schaumburg was taking second place, or was that the General Oberg's car from the avenue Foch?

'They've all come,' said Ackermann with a contemptuous snort. 'So, a little something for them to witness.'

A third car entered – another German staff car – then a fourth, a black Citroën, the car of Osias Pharand.

The Préfet of Paris followed in the Peugeot the Germans had allowed him. Three men tumbled from it, and even at a distance, St-Cyr recognized the préfets of Barbizon and Fontainebleau.

Ackermann took off his cap and placed it carefully to one side on the walk. 'There are some letters I would like delivered. One is to my Führer, explaining everything. One is to my superiors, and one to my wife and family. Please see that the General von Schaumburg receives them.'

Not the General Oberg. At the very end, Ackermann couldn't find it in his heart to trust the SS. 'I will, of course,' said St-Cyr. 'Is there anything else, General?'

A look, a last word, a prayer . . . They were standing right in the middle of the château's inner courtyard, right next to the central fountain whose stone greyhounds viciously leapt at a cornered stag.

'No. No, there is nothing. You may go.' The fountain had been turned off and the pond drained for the winter.

The countess had come out of the front door to stand on the steps beside Mademoiselle Arcuri and her son; so, too, the parents of Jérome and Yvette Noel.

Hermann, walking as quickly as he could, had reached the first of the staff cars and had given the Nazi salute. St-Cyr turned his back on Ackermann – he'd have to take that chance. He began to walk diagonally across the grounds towards the cars and Osias Pharand.

The fog was everywhere. Ackermann would wait until he'd reached Pharand and had turned to watch him just like the rest of them.

'Louis . . .?'

'A moment, Chief. A general must do his duty.'

Ackermann looked so very alone out there, standing rigidly to attention in his black uniform and giving the Nazi salute like that.

St-Cyr began to count silently. The muzzle of the Luger went into Ackermann's mouth. No one moved. There was a hush broken only by the whirring flight of a small covey of pigeons.

The shot, when it came, tore the roof off Ackermann's head and echoed from the surrounding walls.

It was Hermann who led them to the stables and who said in all seriousness, 'They tried to arrest him, Herr Sturmbannführer, and he killed them.'

'With a pitchfork?' asked Boemelburg blandly.

'With a pitchfork, Herr Sturmbannführer, and a pistol.'

Boemelburg studied this man who was an outright liar and a thief at times but a damned good cop.

Kohler took a chance and turned aside. 'Offer the Generals von Schaumburg and Oberg a deal, Herr Sturmbannführer,' he said quietly.

'A deal . . .?'

'It's in the interests of all of us.'

'Yours in particular, Hermann?'

'No, Herr Sturmbannführer. The honour of the Reich.'

Boemelburg nudged the corpse of Jensen with a toe. The prongs of the pitchfork would have made a mess of the kidneys. 'Proceed,' he said, indicating they should go outside.

'The price of that honour has been paid and guilt fully admitted, Herr Sturmbannführer. Tell them the whole matter should now be forgotten. Berlin will want the trowel of racial purity to smooth everything over and hide the defective mortar.'

In other words, shut up about it. 'Neither you nor I can tell generals anything, Hermann. What's in it for von Schaumburg?'

'Peace, I think, with Berlin first but also with yourself and the General Oberg. Let's face it, Herr Sturmbannführer, all three of you must know you have to coexist somehow. No more taps on the General von Schaumburg's line. No more watching his men – especially those like his nephew of which nothing whatsoever will be said. It's really a very small price to pay.'

'Steiner . . . Yes, yes, I can see that might help. There is one small matter for your tender ears, Hermann. Glotz was in charge of the investigation into that Resistance business with St-Cyr. He caught the lot of them and they're in the Cherche-Midi but will soon be transferred to Dachau and Mauthaussen. St-Cyr's pair of broken shoes proved useful. Louis will, of course, be upset.'

'Is that all he'll be?' asked Kohler warily.

Boemelburg didn't flinch from it. 'Glotz, being under Herr

Himmler's patronage, was a little over-zealous, Hermann. They had uncovered a tripwire attached to the front gate but had failed to remove it or to defuse the bomb.'

Kohler swallowed hard and blinked his one good eye. 'Louis's wife and kid?' he asked. In the name of Jesus, would this madness never end?

The Head of the Gestapo in France nodded. 'Only pieces of them, Hermann. The house is a mess.'

Outrage came from deep inside him. 'Did Ackermann and his boys wire it?' demanded Kohler, looking off towards the body which still lay out there in its no man's land. 'That bastard would have said nothing of it to Louis in hopes the poor schmuck would go home and blow himself to pieces.'

'Let's just say Glotz has been sent to Kiev, Hermann, filling the place you were to have taken.'

Then Glotz had left the bomb to pay them back. 'I'll try to tell Louis when we pick up the monk's confession. I'll leave it for now,' said Kohler.

Boemelburg studied him. 'Just don't become too friendly with your partner, Hermann. Louis is far too loyal a Frenchman. The girl with the shoes . . . Apparently Louis came face to face with her in a café. He told the proprietor that whole business with the Resistance was a terrible mistake.'

'I'll watch him. I won't let him get in the way and I won't let him get into any more trouble.'

'That's good, Hermann. I knew I could count on you but there is, of course, always a place for you in Kiev. Please see that you deliver the diamonds to my office when you file your report. They will, of course, have to be confiscated.'

'And the countess?' asked Kohler.

'Perhaps she would be able to offer coffee and the services of a small burial detail, all of whom will be sworn to silence. It's a pity the horses were killed. They both looked like decent animals.' Horses . . . 'Oh, by the way, that reminds me, Hermann. Osias Pharand has a small job he'd like you and Louis to handle. A carnival operator in the Parc des Buttes-Chaumont, one of those guys who runs a carousel. Some bastard tied him to one of his painted horses or something and slit his throat from ear to ear. They found him in the morning. An old woman noticed that the thing was still going round and round when it should have been mothballed for the winter. She wanted to give her grandson a ride and was quite pissed off when they wouldn't let her. It'll keep Louis busy and give him a rest from all this.'

'But . . . but that's a matter for the Préfet of Paris and his boys?'

'You leave Talbotte to me. Scrape the surface, Hermann. Find out what's underneath.'

'Full reports?'

'Yes, yes, full reports. The son-of-a-bitch had a girlfriend.'

The bell that summoned the monks from their toil rang hollowly in the ice-bound air but struck a note of urgency. Kohler looked up the hill towards the monastery whose stone walls seemed to drift eerily out of the fog like the prow of a derelict ship. 'It makes you wonder, doesn't it, eh, Louis? A place like that. No gloves – no woollies either. Must be a bugger at night without a woman to cuddle up to.'

'God wraps His cloak about them, Hermann. He is their Great Protector.'

'How's the tobacco supply?'

A note of warning, that? 'Fine . . . Yes, fine, Hermann. I've hardly had a chance to use it.'

'Not thinking of home are you, Louis? That wife of yours, eh? Gabi's sure some chick. I couldn't help noticing how she tossed you little looks of gratitude.'

'She's a chanteuse and a lady, Hermann, and me, I suppose when all is said and done, I'm a dry old stick who hungers for his slippers by the fire.'

'There's no coal in Paris, unless you've . . .'

'Hermann, what is it? What has happened? Ever since you and Boemelburg had your little chat, it's you who have been giving me the funny looks.'

'Nothing. I just wondered. Gabi would suit you, Louis. You couldn't do better – you know that, don't you? You both work nights – no sweat about that. You could sleep in the odd morning and . . . well, you know. A fag?' offered Kohler lamely. Things simply weren't going well.

They trudged onward, steadily climbing the road, as the bell continued its lament.

Louis stooped to pick up a pebble of flint. Still had his mind on the case probably – a rehash of things. He hefted the stone and cleansed off its surface.

'A small souvenir, eh, Hermann? A good murder case. A close thing, eh, my friend? Glotz giving you all that trouble. Me running into a girl whose shoe was broken . . .'

'Look, let's just find out what the hell that bell's for.'

Had something also happened to Marianne and Philippe? 'It's not for the Angelus, Hermann. It has the ring of something else and, unless I am mistaken, that is the Brother Michael coming to meet us.'

They both waited as the monk strode towards them in his cassock and sandals.

Bare feet no less! *Gott in Himmel*, hard as nails . . . 'Brother,' began Kohler by way of greeting.

There were no tears in the wine maker's eyes, only a savage, unrepentant discipline. 'Please follow me, Inspectors. The Reverend Father has commanded that I be the one to lead you.'

Were there onions or leeks on his breath? wondered St-Cyr. All things came to him in a rush then. The set of the monk's shoulders, the strength of his stride – the utter defiance of Nature in the splayed footpads, bare ankles and clenched fists. No boots today.

The way the rocks, some broken by the frost, crowded both sides of the road yet thinned rapidly upslope in the pastures. The way the sheep cried out as if lost and in despair. Lonely . . . did the place have to engender such a desperate feeling of loneliness, of memory? Marianne . . .

The slope increased substantially once they'd left the road and taken a path into the hills. 'The breeding hives,' grunted the monk without stopping or turning. 'We are going up to the hives where the queen bees are bred in isolation. Brother Sebastian was a lay brother, an amateur scientist, a naturalist.'

'We're only after his statement,' said Kohler who was second in line.

'That you shall have,' spat the monk fiercely. 'God is Grace and God is all-forgiving but will God provide us with another beekeeper as wise and experienced as the Brother Sebastian?'

It was as though the monk were blaming them. The hives stood about on an upper slope like miniature alpine huts in the fog. There were no trees from which the good brother could have hung himself, so that was ruled out. St-Cyr hunted the shrouded terrain until he found the sandals and the cassock well to their left. The sandals lay on top of the cassock which had been carefully folded. 'Brother Michael,' he hazarded, glancing quickly at Hermann, 'what has happened here?'

'Not another murder, I hope,' breathed Kohler exasperatedly. 'My chief won't stand for it. He'll clear the area and turn it back to desert.'

'Look for yourselves,' said the wine maker, anxiously crossing himself before dragging out his rosary and beginning to mumble prayers.

'Louis . . .? Shall you or I go over the ground?' asked Kohler.

'I think we walk carefully, Hermann, me treading in your footsteps until we can both have a look at him.'

The path became a goat run. The hives were perched on protected ledges and on flat slabs of rock that had been laid solidly atop small platforms of boulders.

There was blood beneath the fast-dwindling rime of ice on the boulder that was clenched in Brother Sebastian's right hand, bringing reminders of the death of Jérome Noel.

The monk had hit himself so hard in the face that he had broken his nose and most of the front teeth. He was doubled up as if in pain. The face also bore the mask of agony.

A small pewter cup lay on top of one of the two hives between which the Brother Sebastian had crawled while still clutching that boulder as if he couldn't give it up.

St-Cyr looked at the boulder, at the body again, and then at Hermann. 'First the poison and then the rock.'

'But why take off his clothes, Louis?'

'Why indeed?' said St-Cyr sadly. 'Unless he had been disowned.'

He reached for the cup and, swirling the dregs, gingerly brought it to his nose. '*Conium maculatum Lumbelliferae*, Hermann. Commonly called Mother Die or Poison Hemlock. Death is from paralysis and asphyxia due principally to the alkaloid coniine which attacks the central nervous system. The mousy odour is particularly strong, suggesting perhaps that the draught was made from the fresh grinding of dried seeds, which are the plant's most toxic part. The question is, did the abbot grind the seeds or did the Brother Sebastian?'

They both turned to look at Brother Michael who had found reason to study the soles of his sandals.

Back came the words, 'A lay brother turned amateur scientist, a naturalist.' Had they been given on purpose?

'Let's leave it,' said Kohler.

'Yes . . . yes, I think that would be best, eh, Brother Michael? Death by his own hand.'

'May God forgive him.'

'And be your Judge, I think, Brother. Please make sure he is buried in your hallowed ground.'

'Yes . . . yes. To this the Reverend Father has agreed.'

'Inspector, I must speak with you.'

St-Cyr absently tossed the stick he'd been fiddling with into the river. She'd found him at last, sitting with his back against the wall of the mill, staring into the past.

'It's not a good time for you to be alone, Inspector. You need friends. Me, I know that I should not intrude, but I would like you to consider me as a friend.'

Still he continued to look at the river. He wouldn't turn – he reminded her so of René when he was like this, hurting inside and tearing himself apart over something.

'I hardly knew my son, madame. Night after night I was away. Bank robbers, car thieves – murders . . . ah, murder, it became my specialty. Me, Jean-Louis St-Cyr, became "Monsieur the Detective", to the boys on my street. "The famous detective." So stupid a man, he could not see what was happening to his wife and son, that day by day they were growing more distant from him.'

'Don't blame yourself. It's this lousy war, the Nazis . . . ah, Mon Dieu, it's everything these days. Everything.'

She sat down beside him. 'Was she pretty?' she asked.

St-Cyr nodded. 'I think I still loved her. I know I once did.'

'And she you, also. Otherwise she wouldn't have come home.'

Must he carry that thought with him always? Wasn't it a time to be honest, eh? 'She had no other place to go, since Quimper, the home of her parents, is in the Forbidden Zone near the coast.'

Gabrielle tossed her hands as if in a shrug. 'It's the war, just like I told you then. War throws us together or tears us apart. Me, I only know I'm glad I found you here, that it's indicative you should have chosen this very place from among all the places you could have. Charles loved the river. We used to sit here so quietly, not saying a thing to each other, simply basking in the gentleness of its quietude and communicating in silence. We understood each other, Jean-Louis St-Cyr. It's so rare to find that in two people, isn't that so?'

'The Germans buried what was left of them, madame. I must visit their graves as soon as I get back.'

It would do no good, of course. A simple gesture, that was all. What was done, was done.

He'd not listen but she'd try. 'The front of your house is a wreck. You'll have to stay in a hotel. Your friend has suggested we be practical, as your wages will not be stepped back up to those of a chief inspector until the end of the month.'

'Hermann ought to keep that Bavarian nose of his out of my business.'

'Ah, it was only a suggestion. Please don't take such offence. For myself, I would appreciate a little sharing of the rent, for you . . .' the hands were quite still, 'I offer a roof and the use of my kitchen but only until such time as you're better fixed, of course.'

'Will you be going back to the Club Mirage?'

Had she made a mistake about him? 'Me? Certainly! It's too good a deal to let go.'

He still hadn't looked at her. Was he afraid to? 'That makes you sound like a collaborator?' he said.

'Or an entrepreneur with brains, eh? But it's good cover, and the times . . . ah, what should I say? They will only become more difficult as the war with Russia turns against the Nazis, so me, I think I must begin to help the Resistance.'

She'd let it fall like a bomb. She'd meant it too. He could tell by the stillness of her, the watchfulness, that she was constantly reassessing him. She'd deliberately laid her life in his hands. To say such a thing . . . Thank God they were alone.

St-Cyr found the pebble of flint in his pocket and, taking it out, ran a worried thumb over it. 'The Resistance, eh? Hermann is a good friend, madame. When this war is over I shall hate to see him go.'

Was it a warning then? 'If you were careful . . .' she began.

'Oh, I'm careful, but with Hermann, he is like something out of a magician's box. He has never lost someone he has set out to tail. Never! That one has glue in his blood when it comes to tailing someone.'

'Then the Resistance is a bad idea and I must forget about it but only if you agree to stay with me.'

It took him a moment to realize what she'd done. 'You're blackmailing me. If I don't take you up on your offer I might find myself inadvertently helping the Gestapo arrest you.'

'Or something like that.' He still hadn't looked at her. She'd slide an arm through his. They'd sit a while in silence and listen to the river. He'd have to think it over.

'Let's help the Resistance and say to hell with it,' said St-Cyr. 'It's time I took a more active part in things.'

There was sunlight on the far shore but then the shadows crept over it, silencing her answer and bringing their chill.